In the Comfort of Shadows

Laurel Bragstad

Orange Hat Publishing
www.orangehatpublishing.com - Waukesha, WI

Published by Orange Hat Publishing 2013

ISBN 978-1-937165-63-5

Printed in the United States of America

www.orangehatpublishing.com

This book is dedicated to my sisters and brothers, and to the years of love and laughter we were so lucky to share with Mom and Dad.

ONE

Ann's dream wasn't exactly a nightmare—simply a man and a woman walking away from a little girl who cried and begged to go with them. When she was a little girl, Ann's parents told her not to be afraid; it was only a bad dream. But they were wrong. They didn't know dreams could be memories—or that this dream was a memory with baggage. And ever since her dad's funeral, the old dream came to Ann more often than the night.

Ann flipped her pillow over and tried to get comfortable. Her thoughts drifted to a hot, humid August day in 1953, when it seemed half the city of Milwaukee was in the park that overlooked Lake Michigan. People in shorts or sundresses, funny hats, and bathing suits—people of all sizes and shapes sitting around drinking beer and soda, swatting flies, and hoping to catch a cool breeze. Ann could still hear the cicadas buzzing in the trees. She could still feel the cold rag against her bloody knee.

"We'll be right back," her parents called as they followed aunties, uncles, and cousins down to the lake. Seven-year-old Annie was left at the picnic table with fat Aunt Inga, who began her scolding as soon as the others were out of earshot.

"Hurts, huh?" Inga said. "Serves you right for climbing on the monkey bars when you were told not to. Just because you're adopted don't mean you can do as you please, you know. You should show some gratitude. Be thankful you don't live up north with that crazy miser anymore." She shook a finger at Annie. "And if you don't behave yourself, your mommy and daddy will send you right back."

With tears running down her cheeks, Annie lifted the rag off her knee and watched a trail of red run down her leg.

She understood what Inga meant about not climbing on the monkey bars. But Inga used words Annie didn't know. Adopted. Gratitude. Crazy miser. And the part about her parents sending her back scared her. *Back where?*

Sweat glistened on Inga's fuzzy upper lip while she bounced her baby mercilessly on her thick thigh and rocked the whole picnic table.

"My little Randy's going to learn to behave." She cooed in the baby's face. "You poor thing. Your mommy and daddy didn't want you either, did they? But we adopted you. Yes, we did. Yes, we did! And you're going to be a good boy, aren't you?"

That's when little Randy threw up on Inga's lap.

Later, as everyone packed up to go home, Annie wrapped one of her braids around a finger and asked her daddy what adopted meant. Her daddy knew everything, and he always made her feel better. Karl got down on one knee and spoke calmly. "It's a bad word, Annie. Aunt Inga shouldn't say it, and I never want to hear you say it again."

Little Annie had waited in the car as her daddy told her to, repeating the word "adopted" under her breath and watching Karl and Inga yell at each other—she flailing her flabby arms and he jabbing a finger in her face. Inga wasn't attractive compared to her tall, handsome brother Karl. She was wide and loud and rude. She stuck her nose in where it didn't belong and she often lied. But on that hot, humid day by the lake Inga had told the truth, forbidden word and all. And ever since that day, Ann had tried to explain to her parents why she couldn't help asking about her adoption any more than she could ignore the scar on her knee. All she wanted was answers; all they wanted was for her to quit asking questions.

She took a deep breath and rolled onto her side, her mind drifting between facts and feelings. Ann was five years old and her sister Elise only three when they met their new daddy and mommy, Karl and Ruth Olson. Not long after the adoption,

Ruth gave birth to a daughter and a few years later, a son. The four kids grew close and Ann truly loved her family—except for the whispering she heard behind closed doors, or when Aunt Inga and Granny Elizabeth talked about "when those pitiful little things lived up north." Ann wasn't sure how old she was when she realized that she and her sister were those pitiful little things.

She yawned, grateful for her sabbatical that was beginning tomorrow. The dean had liked her proposal regarding the influence of family stories on family relationships and awarded Ann one semester to research her topic. Of course, she had an obligation to complete the research and she would—right after she met Emmett Pederson, the old miser she believed to be her real father. December probably wasn't the best time for driving to north-central Wisconsin to find him. Still, it was odd how she was told about the sabbatical shortly after her dad died and the old dreams returned. She needed to go up north.

It seemed only a moment later when Ann woke up. The alley light shone through her lacy curtains, projecting rosette patterns on the opposite wall. Her clock radio said 4:32—way too early to get up. When a shadow moved near the dresser, Ann froze as her eyes focused on the figure coming toward her.

It was Karl, her dad. He wore his favorite plaid flannel shirt and corduroy pants. His gentle blue eyes looked calm and bright, and he was smiling. He didn't look at her or move his lips as he glided past the bed, but she heard his voice clearly. "It's okay, honey girl. You're doing fine." Then he sort of disappeared into the wall.

Ann threw the covers back and dashed around the corner to the bathroom. Sitting on the edge of the tub, she held on to the towel bar and shut her eyes tight, repeating, "It's not real. It's not real."

Gradually the fear left her. She told herself the experience was normal. *People conjure up images of recently deceased loved ones all the time. It's a psychosis of some kind, but it's normal.* She turned on the light and splashed water on her face, second-guessing herself. "He was here," Ann insisted to the mirror. "No illusion. I saw him."

She didn't know what he meant by "doing fine" or what was "okay," and since she didn't want to go back to bed either, she put her robe on and went down to the kitchen. As she dropped measures of ground coffee in the basket of the stovetop percolator her dad had given her, she remembered his dislike of modern drip coffeemakers. He said they didn't really perk the coffee but only ran the water over the grounds. There were other things he didn't like. He vehemently objected to her divorce, the first in the family. He didn't like it that Ann didn't go to church like everyone else, and he said her old house was too big and too much work for a woman alone. She had to admit he was right about the house.

She adjusted the flame under the coffeepot. Ann didn't deny that her dad was a good man, a good husband and father. A hundred people at his funeral said so. Everyone liked him. And when the minister talked about how Karl worked hard, respected authority, and told the truth, family and friends wiped their eyes in agreement. But Ann remembered staring dry-eyed at her dad's coffin, wondering about answers soon to be buried with him. After all, he didn't need Aunt Inga spilling the beans to know that two of his children were adopted. But what had prompted him to show Ann and Elise their birth certificates when they were thirteen and eleven? Why had it taken him so long to tell them they were born in Newland, Wisconsin, to Anna Miller, who was from Austria? Why had it taken so long for anyone to tell Ann that her full name was Anna? Anna Helena, not just Ann Helen.

"She went back there," Karl had said so simply that day. "She died there." When Ann boldly asked about the "father unknown" on the documents, Karl gave her a simple and final response. "That's all it says, Annie. Some things you'll have to be satisfied with not knowing." Karl should have known Ann was never satisfied with not knowing.

Elise had cried her eyes out on birth certificate day. As far as she was concerned, Karl and Ruth were her only parents, no matter what it said on some fancy piece of paper. She hated seeing her name as "Elise Marguerite" on her birth certificate instead of Elise Margaret as she'd been told. But Ann was intrigued; her new middle name sounded exotic, and she welcomed the idea of having four parents. After all, how many kids have four parents? She immediately devised a way to keep them separate. Karl and Ruth, the parents she knew, would be called Dad and Mom. She'd reserve the titles of Mother and Father for the parents she started her life with, the parents who lived only in her mind.

During those teen years, Ann often tried to talk to Elise about their birth certificates, or BCs as Ann called them just for fun. But Elise wouldn't listen. She didn't appreciate Ann's other definitions for BC either: Blatantly Clear, Blind Conception, Bold Catastrophe, Brazen Crime, Biological Clue. Of course, when Ann learned a few curse words from a kid at school, she kept Bastard Children to herself because she really didn't want Elise to cry. But on her low days, when Ann couldn't get adoption out of her head and went to her sister for comfort, BC Day invariably came up and the arguing began. Ann would insist on knowing how they came to be adopted, why their mother died in another country, and how a father could be unknown—and Elise wouldn't talk to her for days.

Ann opened the cupboard and reached for the mug from her dad. "Easy Does It" the bold lettering proclaimed. Ann couldn't imagine where he'd found a mug with his favorite phrase or whether he'd given it to her as encouragement or a warning, but one thing for sure was that she thought of him daily.

Her dad's death now left only Emmett and two other cousins up north who might know something about her adoption. Asking her mom was out of the question since dementia claimed more and more of Ruth's mind these days. But years ago it wasn't memory loss that kept Ruth from answering Ann's questions. Years ago, Ruth simply did what Karl wanted her to do.

"Go ask your dad," Ruth would say, and Ann did as she was told. Karl either avoided Ann's questions or told her not to hurt Ruth's feelings with adoption talk. Ann tried to obey, but when Karl started telling dinner-table stories about his boyhood summers up north on his cousins' farm near a small town called Newland, she paid careful attention.

Karl said his aunt and uncle were poor and their two sons, Emmett and Clayton, ran barefoot all summer in order to save their shoes for winter. He described their hurricane lamps, the outhouse, how he swung out on the rope swing over the creek, how he learned to milk a cow and get eggs out from under chickens without getting pecked. But the most unbelievable parts of his story came when he told his city-bred kids that his cousins' family never had a phone, a refrigerator, or indoor plumbing. He said the two brothers never traveled except for their time in the Army, and they'd never married. Karl talked of Emmett, four years his senior, as one might describe an admired big brother. He said Emmett was smart and could have been anything if he wasn't a farmer.

Ann remembered the letters her dad used to get from Emmett too—long, beautifully handwritten fountain pen descriptions of his garden and detailed accounts of life on the farm. Sometimes Karl let Ann enclose a short note or a picture with his reply, and Emmett always wrote a very kind thank-you letter back to her. But when Ann was in high school, Emmett's letters stopped, and Ann never knew why.

Two other things happened around the same time. Ann learned from a girlfriend's unfortunate experience that it was possible to have a baby without a husband, and she found an old black-and-white photo in her Granny Elizabeth's album.

From her girlfriend's undoing, Ann learned the phrase "born out of wedlock" and since Ruth wouldn't explain, Ann went to her girlfriend's older sister for all the horrible details about unknown fathers. But even with questions about procreation cleared up the photo was still a mystery. It was easy to recognize Karl, dressed in his Army uniform and sitting on the sunny side of an outdoor table. But the two other people were partly hidden in the shadow of a tree. From writing on the back, Ann knew the man in the shadow was Emmett, but the third person was not identified. Even with a magnifying glass, all Ann could make out was shoulder-length curly hair and a spotted dress, yet she felt sure this was a picture of her mother, and of course the mother of Elise, the only one in the family with natural curls. Ann also felt sure Emmett was her father unknown. It had to be Emmett, the smart and articulate letter writer, not Clayton, the other brother who'd hanged himself.

The coffeepot boiled over and brought Ann back to the present. She wiped up the mess, filled her mug, and took it to her desk where she clicked open a family tree diagram on her laptop that showed the names of her dad's cousins whom she'd never met. Emmett Pederson's name was highlighted in pink. Weeks ago, she wrote Emmett a letter to say she was coming to see him. He never replied.

Another cousin, Betty Johnson, highlighted in yellow, sent a Christmas card to Ann's parents every year, along with a cheery invitation to visit her and her husband on their farm near Newland. When Ann called to tell Betty she was coming up north, Betty immediately offered a guest room. Ann didn't tell Betty the real reason for her trip, but she did tell her kids and her brother and sisters.

Her son Mark said if he were adopted he'd do the same thing; her daughter Lisa said the parent search was a fitting resolution to start the year 2000. Ann's sister Karen and brother Neal said they understood her quest for the truth. They all told her they loved her and wished her well—all except Elise.

"Honestly, Annie, going up north to see him is the dumbest idea ever!" Elise's voice almost vibrated through the phone. "It's been fifty years! Let it go! God! You're upsetting everyone!"

Their adoption had always been a tender spot for Elise, and her reaction wasn't a surprise. But Ann didn't want another argument. Besides, she was going up north no matter what Elise said. She had to.

"Actually, forty-eight years," Ann said calmly. "And I'm not upsetting everyone. Karen and Neal are fine with it. They know I'm doing this for you and me."

"Leave me out of it! You know how I feel. You're not being fair to Mom either. She might be a little confused lately, but she's still got feelings."

"I didn't tell Mom."

"Huh. At least you got that part right."

"Why can't you at least wish me luck?"

"Because you're digging up family dirt," Elise told her smugly.

"Family dirt? What are you talking about? This is about our history. Our first parents. Where's the family dirt?"

"Well, it must be there, otherwise why did Dad always say to keep the past in the past?"

Ann's patience began to waiver. "I don't need you reciting Dad's rules."

"His rules kept us safe, kept us together, kept us—"

Ann lost it. "His rules kept us in the dark! We aren't children anymore. Do what you're told and don't ask questions doesn't work for me anymore. Think about it. You opened a resale shop even though Dad said it was a bad idea, and you're doing great. Neal took a year off in the middle of college against Dad's advice and still graduated with honors. And you know what

Dad thought of my divorce. The only one who did what Dad wanted was Karen when she married Steve after he got her pregnant." Ann paused and took a deep breath. "Dad's gone," she said quietly. "I have to do this before Emmett's gone too. He's my last chance."

"And he's older than Dad, right? What makes you think he'll see you, let alone have his wits about him?"

"That's a chance I'm willing to take."

"Ha! Right," Elise scoffed. "Do what you want like always. You're the big sister, the independent one. Stubborn and disrespectful and selfish is more like it."

The criticism hit Ann hard. She closed her eyes, hoping Elise would apologize. But she didn't. "I told you many times, Elise," Ann continued, "I need to know who my parents are. I want to know where I come from. I want to see my biological father's face. Why is that so strange?"

"Because you heard Dad tell about his run-down farm and the way he lives like a hermit. He's crazy."

"I have a feeling he isn't," Ann said quietly.

"You're going on a feeling? Is that like a wing and a prayer?"

"No. I'm going on what makes sense. Our mother was from Austria and Dad said Emmett was there during the war. We already know we lived up on Emmett's farm until Mom and Dad adopted us. Isn't that a bit odd? Don't you ever wonder about all that?"

"Yes. I wonder. I wonder why Dad and his so-called favorite cousin quit writing. I also wonder why Emmett never married our mother, and why his name isn't on our birth certificates."

Ann couldn't believe what she was hearing. "So, you think Emmett's our father too."

"Everyone knows about that rundown farm," Elise snickered. "I bet Mom and Dad rescued us from neglect—or worse."

"No one ever said that."

"Of course not! How can you be so naive? No one in the family would ever admit it!"

Ann tried again. "All I want to know is how we came to be adopted. We don't have adoption papers. I searched every county court in the state. We don't even have any pictures of us when we were infants or toddlers, only the ones that were taken after our adoption. Maybe Emmett can tell me what we were like as little kids. Aren't you even curious?"

"What's the big deal?" Elise reasoned. "Kids are pretty much the same."

"Come on, Elise, even kids from the same parents aren't the same."

"Ha! I guess we're proof of that! And you're going up to some godforsaken farm to ask some crazy, old, Norwegian, bachelor farmer what you looked like as a small child. Don't tell me that makes sense. Besides, Newland's four hours away, and it's winter, and you hate driving on the highway."

"I know how far away Newland is, and I'll be back before winter really hits. Besides, highway driving isn't as bad as driving in downtown Milwaukee."

"You never go downtown."

"Neither do you."

Elise gave a cynical chuckle. "Yeah, right, whatever. You better hope your old car makes it."

When Elise paused, Ann asked what she'd never asked her sister before. "You're afraid of what I might find out, aren't you?"

"I can do without the old rumors." Before Ann could respond, Elise grumbled, "Do what you want" and hung up.

Days later Elise left a message on Ann's answering machine. "It's not the same for me, Annie. I don't remember and I don't want to know. Just drive carefully and be home for Christmas, okay? We need to be there for Mom." Her voice cracked. "It's the first Christmas without Dad. I love you, Annie."

Ann wanted to take Elise's message as an okay to go ahead with her plans; it was too frayed around the edges to be a blessing. So Ann, the independent one, was on her own again.

Before putting her laptop back in its case, Ann took out the letter she kept there. After her dad died, she'd found it among his seed envelopes in the garden shed. No one else wanted the seeds, so no one else knew about the letter. Now she unfolded the brittle paper and read Emmett's beautiful script for the hundredth time.

> *October 14, 1961*
> *Newland, Wisc*
> *Dear Karl,*
> *Hope this finds everyone hale and hearty! Clayton and I are getting ready for winter. Yesterday I dug the last potatoes out. Overall yield of Pontiacs and Russets was decent despite the dry summer. I hope we have enough hay even though we're down to eight beef cattle.*
> *We don't look forward to our ancient adversary, winter, being upon us. Of course, we have reasonable defenses against the cold, but when allied with deadly wind, we can only retreat with more blankets and soup. Winter's punishment after summer's labor seems unfair to say the least.*
> *I see by the picture you sent that Annie and Elise have blossomed into fine young ladies. I should like to see them again some day. You may remember the studio portrait of Anna that I am enclosing. I hope you give it to the girls.*
> *Not much else to report. Remember, Anna's things will be here whenever you want them.*
> *Drop a line when you can.*
> *Most sincerely, your cousin,*
> *Emmett*

The writing didn't match her dad's description of Emmett as a poor, uneducated farmer in overalls. Why her dad had hidden this letter prompted more questions, especially about the studio portrait, or "Anna's things," or "see them again." Ann tucked the letter in a pocket of her laptop case with the photo from Granny Elizabeth's album and went upstairs to get dressed. She wanted to be in Newland before dark and in time for the welcome dinner Betty was planning.

Hoping to make a good impression on her dad's cousins, Ann fussed more than usual with makeup and her short, thick hair. She'd stopped coloring it a few years ago when she realized it had gone white early as her Granny Elizabeth's had done. Once when Ann wondered if Emmett had white hair too, Elise had laughed. Don't old people usually have white hair? Elise's other joke about how Ann's brown eyes stuck out in a family of blue ones was less funny since it was a fact only Ann and Elise seemed to notice.

Ann stood back from the mirror and imagined a friendly old man with white hair and brown eyes. She practiced a cordial smile, but fear of the unknown was definitely staring back at her.

TWO

By nine o'clock, Ann was on I-94 just east of Madison, watching for I-39 north. She'd lived in Wisconsin all her life but had never driven this far from Milwaukee alone. Now with only her car radio to keep her company, the gray sky and endless highway felt almost hypnotizing.

As Ann concentrated on the road, her mind went back to summers long ago when her parents loaded the station wagon for the family's annual camping trip—"the poor man's vacation" as her dad liked to say. There were no seat belts or air-conditioning in cars back then, no infant seat law, no I-94 or waysides. Ann always had to sit in back between Elise and Karen because they argued, while little brother Neal sat in front between their parents. Whenever Karl or Ruth lit a cigarette, they opened a window, which turned the backseat into a wind tunnel. But with Karl's singing and Ruth's bag of treats, the miles flew by, and poor man's vacation or not, they seemed to have fun wherever they wound up.

When she saw the billboard for a cancer center, Ann's thoughts drifted to sadder days. Karl was diagnosed with esophageal cancer at age seventy-seven. Everyone in the family felt as if they'd been cut off at the knees. Everyone except Karl. He remained stalwart and positive through the radiation treatments even as he lost his ability to speak and swallowing became impossible. Ever hopeful, he resigned himself to a feeding tube, and Ruth became his devoted nurse, diligently adhering to every detail in the doctor's orders.

Months of worry dragged on as the family's hopes and prayers for Karl's speedy recovery seemed to go unanswered. Ann knew some of her prayers had also been selfish. She wanted her dad to tell her everything about the adoption before it was too late, but she postponed her questions out of respect and love for him and because Karl was never alone. Months later, with treatments over and Karl's voice back, Ann got her chance.

Her sister Karen wanted to take Ruth shopping, but Ruth wouldn't leave Karl home alone because she feared he'd exhaust himself with the yard work he insisted on doing. So Ann offered to help her dad in the yard, secretly hoping she'd find a way to ask him a few questions. When it started to drizzle, Karl used his rake to get to his feet.

"Looks like we're done for today, Annie. Some things we can't control."

Ann took his comment as the perfect cue.

"There are lots of things we can't control, Dad," she said as she pulled the cart and followed him to the shed. "Why do you think I ask about the adoption? I mean Elise and I were just little kids. We don't know anything about how it all happened."

By the look on her dad's face, she realized she'd blurted out too much at once.

Karl yanked the cart away from her and headed for the shed. "Mom and I worked hard to provide a good home," he said sternly. "A lot of kids out there are far less fortunate."

"You and mom are wonderful parents," Ann assured him gently. "And, believe me, I know how lucky I am. But why is talking about our adoption always off-limits?" When he didn't answer, she tried again. "Can you at least tell me why our mother left Austria?"

"Lots of people came to the States after the war. You know that."

"But a young woman on a ship all alone? And coming to Newland, Wisconsin?"

Ann didn't say she had done the math years ago. Counting backwards from her birthday resulted in her mother being already pregnant when she left Austria.

Karl hung up his trowel, avoiding Ann's eyes.

"Did she know someone there?" She didn't say what she believed—that her mother did know someone in Newland. She knew Emmett. In the biblical way, she knew Emmett.

Karl threw his gloves in the cart. "Enough, Annie. Leave it be," he said on his way to the house.

It took Ann another few months to get the courage to write her dad a letter, asking him to please answer her questions. Karl never did. Then one evening, when everyone was gathered at her parents' house for dinner, Ruth took Ann aside.

"Promise me you won't ask Dad any more questions," she said tearfully. "He's got enough going on right now. The doctor said he's got congestive heart failure, and I don't want him getting upset."

Of course, Ann promised and continually hoped for the day Karl would be willing to talk. Instead, the cancer came back, and this time he was hospitalized. The family could do nothing but watch as chemotherapy and morphine weakened him further. Often in the midst of a visit with someone, Karl drifted off, mumbling about writing letters, or his grandmother Nana, or strawberries, or other nonsense. They all prepared for the worst.

Ann swallowed back tears now, thinking of the day she went to the hospital after work and found her dad alone and awake. His thick, white hair had just begun to fall out. She sat on the bed and Karl reached for her hand.

"I met your mother—Anna—at a USO show," he said weakly. "When I was in the Army."

Karl never talked about his military service except to say, "War is an awful thing" or "We had to do what we were told."

But that day in the hospital Ann sat perfectly still, absorbing her dad's every word.

"It was a long time ago, honey. Emmett wrote me a postcard.

He said I should come to Austria when I had leave so I could meet this wonderful girl he knew. We all went to the USO show together."

"Are you saying Emmett knew my mother in Austria?"

Karl nodded. "He still lives on his farm up in Newland. You and Elise were born up there."

"I know, Dad."

"My grandmother and Emmett took care of you after your mother died."

Ann felt his grip on her hand tighten. "What was our mother—what was Anna like?"

"She was quiet and pretty. Died too young."

"How?"

Karl barely got the word "leukemia" out before the drugs took over and he fell asleep.

The next day, with his family around the bed, Karl asked them to recite Psalm 23 for him. Tearfully, they did. He told them he tried his best to be a good father. He made them promise to take care of their mom and take care of each other. They promised, and he died the next day, March 14, 1999, nine months ago.

Ann loved her dad for telling her the USO story, even though it was too short and too incomplete. If he'd have had one more year, one more month, he might have explained how she and Elise had gotten from a farm in Newland to new parents in Milwaukee. But he didn't, and now Ann's hopes centered around Emmett's elderly memory and his willingness to tell her what happened after that USO dance.

Miles of memories later Ann came to her exit. The state highway cut through one small town after another, some with only a few old buildings and no signs of life, others with small business districts sparkling with quaint Christmas decorations. Ann noticed traffic moving more slowly, and instead of sedans and the increasingly popular SUVs in the city, people in these smaller towns seemed to prefer pickups of all sizes. Many pulled trailers—horse trailers, box trailers, or flatbed trailers carrying everything from Christmas trees to farm machinery to snowmobiles or wrecked cars.

Ann checked Betty's hand-drawn map again—a tangle of lines and letters. One road was marked H. Or was it M? And was the other line MM or had Betty crossed something out? As Ann looked for a place to pull over and check her state map, she passed a sign for "Newland 38" and forged ahead.

When her odometer registered thirty-eight miles, a single, rusty sign appeared. "Newland, Unincorporated, Pop. 1826." Soon Ann found herself on a narrow and somewhat busy Main Street where storefronts such as Newland Antique Boutique, Newland Seed-N-Feed, and Dessert a' la Newland told her she was in the right place. When she saw the parking lot for Townline Foods, she turned in. Better to call Betty and clarify her directions than get lost.

The black horse hitched to a black boxy carriage was hard to ignore. Shields on its bridle all but covered the horse's eyes, and its head drooped under the weighty collar around its skinny neck. Ann parked a few spaces away and punched Betty's number in to her cell phone.

"Where are you now, Annie?" Betty asked excitedly.

"I'm in town—at Townline Foods with a horse and buggy."

Betty chuckled. "Oh, that's the Amish. You'll see quite a few of them up here."

Ann heard a man in the background yell, "Where is she?" Ann held the phone away from her ear as Betty shouted her reply. "Townline Foods!"

"Tell her to stay on Main," the man said.

"I know, I know!" Betty told him. "Let me talk! I'm sorry, Annie. Are you there?"

Ann hurried to open her state map on the passenger seat.

"Yes, I am," she said calmly.

"Okay, here's what you do." Betty spoke slowly and deliberately. "Turn right when you leave the parking lot and follow Main to county road G at the end of town. All the county roads have letters, but don't ask me why. Anyway, you want to turn left when you see a sign for H and MM. You know, double M? They run together for a few miles. Follow along until you get to single M. Turn right and we're just a couple miles down. Okay?"

"I think so," Ann said, tracing the fine black lines on her map. "Are there any landmarks near your place, Betty? A restaurant or a billboard? Anything?"

Betty chuckled again. "No, dear, there's no restaurant nearby. You could watch for our cows. They're in the cornfield along the driveway."

"Cows?"

"Holsteins. You know, the black-and-white ones? Oh, and we have a long gravel driveway. Our house is set back a ways. It needs paint, but it's mostly yellow with a big porch. Watch for our mailbox. It says Johnson right on it. You really can't miss it."

"Okay. I'll, uh, watch for the cows and your mailbox."

As Ann snapped her phone shut, a bearded man in a wide-brimmed hat hurried from the grocery store with a bag. He unhitched the horse, took his seat in the carriage, and snapped the reins. Ann cautiously followed the carriage to the edge of the parking lot, where a huge pickup stopped to let the horse step out onto Main Street—not that the poor creature had any choice but to blindly join the motorized traffic.

The driver of the waiting pickup next motioned for Ann to go ahead of him. She waved her thanks and followed the horse and carriage toward a crossword puzzle of country roads.

THREE

Before Ann saw Betty's house, she saw the cows. There were dozens of them standing and chewing, lying down and chewing, looking at the horizon and chewing. None of them looked particularly interested in her arrival.

As she drove up the long gravel driveway, a big brown dog came out from somewhere and ran alongside her car, barking. Two pickups were parked near a porch, where a woman waved from an open door. A lean man in a worn-out jacket took the dog's collar and directed Ann to park next to one of the trucks. When she got out of her car, he released the dog, and it ran to Ann and sniffed her feet.

"Don't worry," the man said. "Mitch is all bark."

Ann guessed the lanky man was over six feet tall. His well-worn ball cap and gray hair framed a rugged, leathery face. He took off his right glove and slapped his hand against his pants before extending it to her.

"Hi there, Annie. Forgive the barn clothes. I'm Betty's husband, Frank."

Ann took his hand. "Hi, Frank. Nice to meet you finally."

"Same here." He gestured toward a man behind him. "That's Gordy."

"Hi, Gordy," Ann said. "Nice to meet you."

Gordy was shorter than Ann's five feet six and didn't look very friendly. His knit hat covered his eyebrows, and he held his right hand behind him. When he shot Ann a quick frown, his narrow eyes and droopy mouth reminded her of a villainous movie character—the tricky one with a predictable bad temper and ulterior motives. This was the cousin Granny Elizabeth had always called Gordy-with-the-withered-hand, as if his name was all those words strung together.

"Can I get your luggage?" Frank offered.

"Yes, thank you. I have a suitcase and a laptop case in the trunk."

The heavyset woman in the doorway urged Ann inside to a narrow hallway lined with hooks for jackets and coats.

"So good to finally see you, Annie!" she said as she gave Ann a bear hug. "I'm your dad's cousin Betty of course." Her deep blue eyes sparkled and her frizzy gray hair matched her sweater. "Welcome to our humble home. Please come in! Come in!"

Ann slipped out of her loafers and gave her jacket to a waiting Frank. "Thank you," she said again. "My goodness, something sure smells wonderful."

"Yeah, Betty's always cookin' somethin'," Frank replied.

Ann wasn't hungry, since she'd eaten a sandwich on her drive, thinking Betty's invitation for dinner meant supper instead of lunch. But it would be impolite to refuse.

"Looks like you inherited the family badge," Betty said, leading Ann to the kitchen.

"Pardon?"

"Your white hair! Looks good on you too. Nana and my mother got it, but it skipped me. Emmett and Karl got it but not Clayton. Isn't it strange how those things work?"

Ann felt uneasy. Was Betty hinting at her resemblance to Emmett or just making an innocent remark about family traits? Ann took in the homey kitchen and tried to relax. Magnets held pictures and reminders on the refrigerator, medication bottles lined the windowsill above the sink, African violets and geraniums flourished on a table near a window, and pots and pans hung on the wall next to the stove.

When a large pot rattled on the stovetop, Betty talked over her shoulder as she rushed to it. "Hope you don't mind if we eat right away, Annie. I can hardly hold these guys off anymore. I asked Emmett to come, but I guess you'll meet him sooner or later."

"Later would be better," Frank said.

"Fra-ank," Betty sang. "Please." Motioning to the table, she added, "Sit down, everyone."

Betty's table was carefully set with four soup bowls on plates, water glasses, coffee cups, and paper napkins with a holly design. Two thick hot pads waited in the center along with jars of jam and honey, a saucer of butter, a little porcelain cow with toothpicks sticking out of its back, and a mug full of spoons. When Frank offered Ann a chair near a window, Betty corrected him.

"No, no, no, not by the window! It's too cold. Gordy, you sit by the window. Annie will sit next to me on the other side."

When Gordy walked around the table, Ann caught a glimpse of the way his right wrist bent inward, the curled and useless fingers almost touching his forearm. Unlike Frank, who left his boots in the hall, Gordy had kept his boots on and tracked dirt across Betty's otherwise-spotless floor. Without his jacket, he appeared rather gaunt. But he hadn't removed his hat, and no one had asked him to. He sat down quickly and positioned his misshapen hand in his lap.

Betty brought a pyramid of corn bread to the table and then set a large red enameled pot on the waiting hot pads. Ann could tell the smell of chili a mile away. She hated chili.

"Hope you like chili, Annie. I guess I should have asked."

"I'm sure it's wonderful, Betty," Ann purred.

Frank reached for Ann's bowl, but Betty playfully slapped his hand with a ladle. "I'll do the serving if you don't mind. God knows where those hands have been."

"God knows they been in the barn as usual," Frank said with a wink in Ann's direction.

Betty filled all their bowls to the rim and made sure Ann had the first serving of corn bread. "So tell us about the rest of the family in Milwaukee."

Ann had told Betty about her family when they talked on the phone, but Ann wanted them to trust her, and small talk was one way of getting there.

"My daughter and her husband have two boys and a baby girl on the way," she said pleasantly. "My son doesn't have any children. He's getting married in June."

Betty reached for the butter. "There's nothing like grandkids! And a wedding! How exciting!"

Ann's first bite of chili was very spicy in an odd sort of way. She took a long drink of water.

"I was named after your Granny Elizabeth," Betty continued. "She was Aunt Lizzie to us, so everyone called me Betty to avoid confusion." She put her knife down. "Do you know how everyone in the family is related?"

Ann wasn't surprised by the question. Other people often made the same silly assumption—that being adopted meant she had no clue about the family she'd grown up with.

"Yes, I made a family tree," Ann began.

Betty wiped her hands on her napkin and counted on her fingers, making no apology for interrupting.

"First, our grandparents Krist and Ingeborg Pederson came here from Norway. We always called them Pa and Nana. They had four children—Albert, Elizabeth, Edna, and Carrie. Albert married Lena Torkelson, and they had Emmett and Clayton." She turned to Ann. "Do you know about Clayton?"

"About his suicide?"

"Yes," Betty answered in a whisper. "So sad."

Frank started to say something, but Betty was off again.

"Of course, you know your Grandmother Elizabeth married Olaf Olson, and they had Inga and your dad, Karl. Edna was my mother. She married Emil Johnson and had me and my brother, Mel." She lowered her voice. "He was killed in

Korea." Ann expressed her condolences and Betty continued. "Carrie married Stewart Halvorson, and they had Gordy here. Poor Carrie died so young," Betty said toward Gordy, who was hanging over his bowl and shoving corn bread in his mouth as if he hadn't eaten for days.

"Hard to believe Clayton, Karl, and Inga are gone," Frank said. "Course Betty and me are seventy-four already."

"Yes, but Emmett's the oldest," Betty said. "He's eighty-four. And Gordy's the youngest of us cousins. Forty-nine, right Gordy?" When Gordy didn't answer, Betty glanced at Ann's chili bowl, which was still nearly full. "Is the chili okay, dear?"

"Oh, yes. It's fine. I'm a slow eater."

"I think I overdid the chili powder this time. I won't feel bad if you don't eat it all. Do you like venison?"

With the odd taste identified, Ann took another drink of water, then smiled and said, "Never tried it before."

"Frank got a nice buck this year. It's a nice change from beef all the time."

Great, Ann thought. *I don't eat beef either.*

Frank and Gordy had second helpings of chili, apparently not bothered by the chili powder or the taste of venison. After the men scraped their bowls clean, Betty removed the chili pot from the table and replaced it with a huge pie that oozed red syrup from the top crust. Frank eagerly held out a dessert plate as Betty explained how she froze rhubarb from her garden every year.

Frank passed the first piece of pie to Ann. "Betty's famous rhubarb-raisin," he boasted. "Betcha never tasted nothin' like it." When Ann took the plate, he added, "We're pretty simple people, Annie. You might get tired of us, but you'll never go hungry."

As Ann picked delicately at her pie, Gordy gobbled his down silently, then went to the hallway for his jacket and left.

"You'll get used to Gordy," Betty told Ann. "He doesn't say much."

"Don't work much either," Frank grumbled.

After Betty cleared the table, they moved to the living room, where Frank took his place in a recliner and pushed it back as far as it would go. Betty asked Ann to join her on the plaid couch.

"We keep saying we're going to get new furniture," she said apologetically, running a finger over a small tear in one of the cushions. "Everything is so expensive."

Frank took the toothpick out of his mouth. "Betty said you're working on something, Annie. What's it called again?"

"A sabbatical," Ann answered. "It's a research project about how family stories influence family relationships. I thought stories of our family would be a good place to start."

"Oh," Frank replied with a slight nod.

"She came up to see Emmett, Frankie," Betty explained. She turned to Ann. "He knows a lot about the old days even though he's a bit—what's the word?"

Frank's expression changed at the mention of Emmett's name. "Ornery. Ornery's the word," he scoffed. "And crotchety, crazy—and a real scrooge. Too cheap to even have a phone for cryin' out loud. Takes after his pa, who was so cheap they barely got electricity in the house back in the 50s. And Emmett shoulda put proper plumbin' in the house when the leathers in his ol' hand pump rotted through. But no! He made Clayton haul water from the creek! Damn fool. Ha! I'm waitin' to see his ol' outhouse collapse with him in it!"

"Frank!" Betty scolded. "Annie's going to think you're the crazy one." She glanced at Ann and said more softly, "Emmett is not crazy, dear. And he hauled water too."

"I'm not the only one who thinks he's crazy," Frank retorted. "And you know it."

It was hard for Ann to listen to Frank's complaints about Emmett. Then again, in all fairness to Frank, she hadn't met

Emmett yet. Maybe he was crazy.

"I remember Dad saying Aunt Lena and Uncle Albert never had much," Ann said, hoping to change the subject. "But he loved summers at their farm when he and Emmett were kids."

Frank took a deep breath and spoke more calmly now. "Kids don't know what poverty is unless they're actually starvin' out in the cold. Albert wasn't much of a provider. Sure, he planted corn and hay, even kept a few cows for milk and beef. But he was never one to give enough attention to farm or family. You gotta pay attention to livin' things."

"Lena kept chickens and a garden," Betty told Ann. "She sold vegetables to make a little money, but they always struggled in winter. Aunt Lena did her best, poor thing. She lost two babies between Emmett and Clayton and one after Clayton."

"Your Uncle Albert worked her to death," Frank declared.

"He was a difficult man," Betty admitted. "Thank goodness for Pa and Nana."

"What do you mean?" Ann asked.

"Their place was right next to Albert and Lena's," Frank said. "Ol' Pa was always over to Albert's doin' most of the work."

"Then Pa died right after Lena," Betty added. "I remember because the war had just ended and everyone was so glad, but then we had to have two funerals. That's when Nana sold her place and moved over to Uncle Albert's to mind the house for him and the boys. Of course, they were grown men by that time, and Nana was getting up in years too." She stopped and sighed. "Emmett and Clayton built Nana a little log cabin so she could have some privacy. At least she wasn't alone."

"Yeah," Frank told Betty. "But as soon as Nana came over, Albert took off for a loggin' camp up in Minnesota somewhere and left all of 'em to fend for themselves."

"Uncle Albert came home now and then, Frankie."

"Clayton told me his father came home just to throw his

weight around. Just to let 'em know all they were doin' wrong."

Frank turned his head toward the window, took a deep breath, and let out a long sigh. Ann noticed the look of concern on Betty's face as she watched him. When the furnace wheezed in the basement and broke Frank's trance, Ann tried to sound enthusiastic.

"I'm looking forward to meeting Emmett," she said.

"Don't get your hopes up," Frank cautioned. "Emmett ain't exactly the hospitable type."

"Emmett took Clayton's suicide real hard," Betty said in a hushed tone.

"Do you know why he took his life?" Ann asked.

"He thought he had cancer 'cause he got the shakes," Frank told her. "Truth is, he got the shakes from drinkin' out the demons."

"Demons?"

"Korea," Frank said sadly. "Clayton was never the same after Korea."

Ann shook her head sympathetically. "And neither brother ever married, right?"

"Clayton got close once," Frank said. "Course drinkin' and bein' dirt poor don't help. And I bet Emmett's strange ways scared girls right off." He gave a sarcastic chuckle.

"Strange ways?" Ann asked.

"My mother said he was shy," Betty said gently. "And Uncle Albert pulled him out of school to work on the farm. Course he always got books from the library and ran off somewhere to read anyway—which infuriated Uncle Albert."

"Because he was always readin' junk about the government, or the military, or religion, or somethin'," Frank snickered. "And poetry. What does a farmer need with poetry?"

"You can't blame Emmett for wanting to learn," Betty told him.

"If you ask me, he's got a lot to learn." Frank brought the

recliner upright. "Here's a story for ya, Annie. Emmett didn't even come to his own brother's burial, so the VFW gave Clayton's veteran flag to me. When I took it to Emmett, the damn fool threw it in the burn barrel with the garbage! He not only desecrated the flag, he insulted his brother and every other veteran to boot!"

"He was upset, Frankie," Betty said. "Please. It's over. And Emmett is family."

"Your family, not mine." Frank caught Betty's glare. "Yeah, yeah, okay. Sorry, Annie."

After a few silent moments, Ann said, "By the way, Frank, pardon my city-girl question, but why are your cows in the cornfield when the corn is all picked?"

He sighed. "They graze on what the harvester missed. Saves on feed and the fresh air's good for 'em."

"Frankie takes good care of his cows," Betty said approvingly. "Want some more pie, Annie? Or some tea?"

"Tea sounds good."

Frank stood and stretched. "I could go for more pie."

Ann followed Frank back to the table while Betty rushed to fill the teapot.

"Gordy left already, Frankie?" Betty asked, glancing out the window.

"If you don't see his truck, he's gone."

"I don't mean to pry," Ann said. "But do you know what happened to Gordy's wrist?"

Betty nodded. "It grew like that from the beginning. Mother used to say it was like a clubfoot only it was his hand."

"Must be hard for him."

"He's able to help out at Emmett's a bit. Course he mostly wears pullover shirts and those pull-on boots. I don't know how he manages to zip his pants though."

"Sometimes he don't," Frank said over a forkful of pie. "And you need to realize he hardly takes proper care of himself,

Bett, let alone a crotchety old man."

"By the way," Betty told him. "Elaine from social services called again. She wanted to know when we're taking him to the Manor House."

"I thought you talked to him about that."

"I did," Betty assured him. "I mentioned it when I took him some stew. But you know he doesn't listen to me."

"Who?" Ann asked. "What's the Manor House?"

"It's a senior home in town where Emmett spends the winter," Betty said. "He's usually there by Thanksgiving, but for some reason he's putting up a fuss this year."

Frank snickered. "Yeah, I told him he's gonna wind up like ol' Eddie Spence, but he just told me to mind my own business."

"Eddie Spence was Emmett's neighbor," Betty explained. "He froze to death last year. He lived all alone too."

"Froze to death?" Ann asked, astonished.

"Stiffer 'n a board when they found him," Frank said. "Another bullheaded old fool."

Betty put her fork down and touched Ann's arm. "How about I show you your room?"

Ann got her suitcase and laptop case from the hallway and followed Betty to a room at the top of the stairs.

"This used to be our girls' room," Betty said, trying to catch her breath. "Now it's for grandkids and company. We use the bathroom up here, but you can have the downstairs bathroom all to yourself. I made room in the closet there, and the top drawer of this dresser is empty if you need it."

"Thank you. I'm sure I'll be quite comfortable."

Dolls, stuffed animals, toy cars, puzzles, crayons, and other playthings were arranged neatly on low shelves under the windows. Through one window, Ann spotted the light fixture on the barn's peak, glowing Amber now as the winter sky darkened.

"Feel free to use the phone on the nightstand," Betty added. "Do you have one of those little personal phones?"

"A cell phone? Yes, my kids insisted I get one for the trip. I'm still getting used to it."

"Those things don't work unless you're close to town, but we have unlimited long distance, so you help yourself. And if you hear a little noise in the ceiling fan at night, don't be scared. It's just our mice in the attic. But, don't worry, they can't get through." Betty paused and lowered her voice. "By the way, I do hope you forgive Frankie. He gets upset about Emmett and Gordy sometimes. Or sometimes he just has a bad day. That seems to be happening more and more lately."

"It's okay. I understand." Ann knew she didn't understand much yet, but Emmett may have declined Betty's invitation because of Frank, whose anger obviously ran deep where Emmett was concerned.

"And Emmett's not really crazy," Betty said. "He's got his own ways. But I don't believe he's crazy." She went to the door. "Well, you settle in, and I'll see you back downstairs."

While she unpacked, Ann glanced out the window in time to see Frank walk across the driveway with his dog following. A moment later, an old blue truck pulled up and Gordy got out. The two men exchanged a few words before Frank threw his hands in the air and went to the barn. Gordy threw a cigarette butt on the driveway and followed him. From what she'd witnessed so far, Ann wondered if Gordy suffered from mental illness as well as a physical handicap. She finished unpacking and went back down to the kitchen with old photos she'd brought to show Betty.

"Oh, how wonderful!" Betty said when she saw Ann's pictures. "Let me get ours."

Betty made three trips to the living room to retrieve albums and shoeboxes full of photos. Over tea, she paged through them, recounting reunions and Christmases, pointing out faces of relatives long gone. Finally, she slid the last shoebox across the table to Ann. "These are Emmett's. I meant to put them in an album for him, but I never got around to it."

Among the old black-and-white photos of cows, a creek, tractors, and trucks were pictures of Emmett and Clayton as youngsters. More recent photos showed Gordy as a little boy, not yet self-conscious enough to hide his right arm.

"Look," Betty said. "Here's one of Nana getting water from the pump. She was such a fussy housekeeper. We always had to take our shoes off when we came inside." She picked out another photo and read the handwriting on the back. "Two musketeers. Emmett and Karl. July 1927." She passed the photo to Ann and laughed. "Look at your dad in the knickers! You should take it and show your family."

While Betty mused over photos of Nana as a young woman, Ann noticed a bunch of smaller black-and-whites edged in the same ivy-like design as her dad's Army pictures. But unlike her dad's shots of guys in fatigues, laughing and goofing around, Emmett's pictures showed bombed-out streets and tired-looking huddles of people in tattered clothing. The last photo showed Emmett and another man, both equipped with rifles and backpacks. Ann read the writing on the back aloud.

"'EP and FN. September 1943'. EP must be Emmett Pederson. But who's FN?"

Betty raised her chin to position her bifocals. "Looks like Fred Noble. They were in the Army together. He's at the Manor House now too."

Ann stared at the picture. She hadn't considered anyone other than Emmett as her biological father. Fred was taller than Emmett and reasonably good-looking, but Ann didn't like the boastful look on his face. The next photo showed Emmett sitting in a patch of daisies, smiling serenely, his uniform crisp and clean, boots reflecting the sun. Again, Ann read the writing on the back. "'EP at A's September 1945.'"

"Maybe A stands for a town over there," Betty said.

Maybe A stands for a person, Ann thought. *Maybe A stands for Anna.*

Frank went upstairs around nine, and shortly after Betty and Ann headed up to bed as well. When Ann turned off the nightstand lamp, the guest room took on a soft glow from the light mounted on the barn's peak. She got under the covers and listened a moment. No traffic, no sirens, no dogs barking. No city noise. No noise of any kind except for rhythmic snoring coming from down the hall and a tiny scratching noise from the motionless ceiling fan. Betty's mice.

Frank's words echoed in her head—bullheaded, crotchety, ornery, damn fool, strange ways. Maybe Emmett would be angry at being found out after all these years. Then again, maybe he would be happy to see her again. After all, that's what he said in the letter Ann had in her laptop case. She decided to hope for that.

FOUR

Ann woke to the smell of coffee and sausage. She dressed quickly in jeans and a sweater before going downstairs to the bathroom, where she washed up and applied her usual light makeup. As she approached the kitchen a few minutes later, she found Betty coming up the basement steps with a basket of laundry.

"My, you look like a real country girl, Annie!" Betty blew out a puff of air as she slid the basket across the kitchen floor to a corner and paused to catch her breath. "Help yourself to coffee over there by the stove," she said, wagging a finger. "Cups are in the cupboard right above. But it's so early. Did you sleep okay? I hope I didn't wake you with all my clattering down here."

"No, not at all. I'm usually up pretty early."

"We don't have a choice around here. If we don't get up early, nothing gets done."

"I hope you let me help you while I'm here," Ann said, as she helped herself to coffee and sat down.

"No, no, no," Betty said kindly. "You do your project and don't worry about us." She brought bowls of scrambled eggs and sausage to the table as Frank and Gordy came inside and took chairs opposite Ann.

"Mornin' there, Annie," Frank said. "Sleep okay?"

"Better than I have in a long time." She smiled at Frank and let her smile drift over to Gordy. He ignored her.

"Yep, good clean country air does that," Frank declared.

"What do you want to do today, Annie?" Betty asked.

"I'd like to go meet Emmett."

Frank helped himself to eggs and sausage. "Good luck."

Betty turned to Gordy. "I hope you're making sure he's got enough wood." When Gordy ignored her, Betty leaned across the table. "You agreed, Gordy. I expect you to honor your word."

Gordy shoved the last of his eggs and sausage in his mouth and, as before, left without so much as a nod of thanks.

"What's gotten into him?" Betty asked Frank.

"No manners that I can see," Frank replied.

Betty shook salt over her eggs. "Why can't he at least be civil? He expects me to do his laundry, and he sure eats good whenever he's here. I don't think chopping wood for Emmett is too much to ask."

Frank sighed. "Okay, I'll talk to him again."

Ann sensed Frank's impatience—perhaps with Betty as much as with Gordy.

"If you don't mind me asking," Ann said, "how does Gordy manage to chop wood with only one good arm?"

"You'd be surprised what he can do," Frank said. "Gordy's not too bright, but he's strong and he can do plenty when he wants to." He cocked his head in Betty's direction. "And you'd think he was my cousin instead of Betty's from the way she complains about him."

"You complain about him too, Frankie," Betty replied.

They ate in silence until Frank pushed his plate aside and went to the hallway for his jacket and boots. "Where's my thermos?"

"You said it leaks," Betty said.

"Yeah, well, it's better 'n nothin'."

Betty got up and filled his thermos, wrapped it in a towel, and brought it to Frank. She said something under her breath before he went outside.

"It's getting harder and harder to live with both of them," Betty said when she closed the door.

From the window near the table, Ann saw Frank approach

Gordy, who was standing in the driveway smoking a cigarette. Gordy pointed to the house, talking and frowning. Frank pointed to Gordy, and then Gordy flipped his cigarette away and headed toward the barn.

"Where does Gordy live?" Ann asked.

"He's got a trailer home on the north end of town," Betty replied, taking dishes to the sink. "He's on disability, and he mostly works for us. I know I shouldn't be hard on him. Aunt Carrie died when he was only ten, and he didn't get along with his stepmother. The worst part is, he never finished school, and he doesn't really have any friends." She lifted the lid off a pot on the stove and gave the contents a stir. "I made some bean soup, but it's not quite done. Could you wait a bit so you can take some for Emmett? I'll pack up some cookies for him too."

"I'm sure he'll appreciate that," Ann said, even though she didn't have a clue what Emmett appreciated.

"Food is all he accepts from me," Betty said. "He gets meals on wheels and Gordy takes him to the café in town sometimes. Gordy's supposed to be taking out Emmett's garbage, so let me know if he did, okay?"

Ann washed dishes while Betty sketched out a map to Emmett's.

"It's easy to find," she said as she labeled lines on the paper. "Oak Road is where you turn right and stay straight until you come to the bridge. Be careful because there's only room for one car to cross at a time. Once you're over the bridge, watch for his mailbox. The house is set back a ways. In the summer, it's completely hidden by trees. Don't be surprised if he's suspicious at first. He doesn't like strangers."

"Well, I'm definitely a stranger."

"Want me to go with you?" Betty asked.

"No," Ann said confidently. "I'm sure I can find it."

"Don't mention the Manor House," Betty advised. "It would be better if Frank handled that."

It was almost ten o'clock when Ann turned off asphalt and onto the gravel of Oak Road. After about a mile, the old bridge came into view. It reminded Ann of a live trap her dad used one summer to try to catch whatever was eating his tomatoes. She slowed to a near stop and let her car ease forward onto the bridge's riveted steel surface. As the crisscross of rusty beams enfolded her, she peered down at a narrow stream of water hardly worth the imposing structure stretched across it. The bridge seemed to end in a thick stand of pines, but when Ann reached the other side, she found bridge and road joined at an odd angle, requiring a sharp turn. She wondered how many drivers crossed the bridge too fast and careened off into the trees.

The road led her to a rural mailbox on top of a fence post. "PEDERSON" stood out in white block letters. The house was indeed set back from the road—one hundred feet at least, Ann guessed. And even without summer's foliage, the bushes and trees were thick enough to hide a good view of the house until she turned in the driveway. She followed the curve of gravel around Emmett's old house to a wide circle in the rear. There, she maneuvered a slow turnabout and surveyed the scene around her.

A few smudges of faded red paint suggested one dilapidated building might be the barn, even though it resembled an oversized shed with a lean-to on each end. A small camper trailer was parked next to the barn, and Emmett's now-fallow acres stretched beyond. As she completed the turn, she saw the outline of a small log cabin, Nana's cabin, and then a narrow structure with a single door, no doubt the outhouse, slanted toward a very old truck with very flat tires. Next to the truck stood a large, rusty, metal barrel—perhaps the burn barrel Frank talked about. An ancient hand water pump waited on its own little platform near the house.

Ann parked and squinted as she looked over Emmett's

house with its weathered wood siding in dire need of repair and paint. She'd told her dad she remembered the farm in hopes of getting him to talk about Emmett, but the familiarity she felt now was disarming. She had been only five years old when she was taken away from this place, yet her brain told her it had a memory of it. She pictured a tire swing hanging from the big tree in front of Nana's cabin and a little barefoot girl balancing inside the tire on her tummy, twirling around lazily, poking a stick at bugs crawling in the dirt beneath her. *Did it really happen?*

She turned off the ignition and got out of the car, her eyes following a dry vine up to a broken second-story window. Smoke curled out of holes in the brick chimney. *He must be home.*

Ann's stomach rumbled a warning as she went up the four steps to the covered porch. An old wringer washer full of firewood stood next to a big plastic bag with garbage spilling out of shredded holes. Windows were missing from the storm door. She hesitated a moment, listening for a sign of life, but all she heard was a chickadee chirping its "dee-dee-dee" from somewhere. Ann reached through the storm door, rapped three times on the inside door, and stood back. She listened a moment and was about to knock again when the knob turned.

Once the door slowly opened, Ann found herself facing a hunched-over, wizened old man in a fake fur hat, a torn canvas jacket, and dirty gloves. His cheeks were sunk in for lack of teeth, and under hooded lids, his icy blue eyes were both rheumy and swollen. He cocked his head awkwardly to get a better look at her.

"Emmett?" Ann asked, half hoping he would say no.

Trembling, he said softly, "Anna. Anna."

Ann tried to smile. "Hi Emmett, I'm Ann. I'm Karl and Ruth Olson's daughter."

Emmett stared at her as if he couldn't believe his eyes. "Well, I declare. I declare," he said softly.

Ann was momentarily moved to stoop and hug him just

for being alive. But she didn't. His eyes were definitely infected. "I'm happy to meet you," she said as sincerely as she could. "I would have called, but I know you don't have a phone."

Emmett suddenly frowned. "You with the services?" he asked sharply.

"No, no, I'm not. I'm Ann. I came for a visit." She held up the bag from Betty. "Look, Betty sent soup and cookies for you."

He looked at the bag and considered her reply. After a long moment, he retreated. "Yes. Well then you should come in out of the cold."

Ann concentrated on holding her smile as she stepped into Emmett's kitchen and closed the door behind her.

FIVE

The first thing Ann noticed was the bare light bulb and pull chain hanging from the kitchen ceiling, surrounded by veils of cobwebs. The inside of the house smelled of smoke, reminding her of vacation campfires her dad used to make. Emmett shuffled along a path worn through the old linoleum and Ann followed, taking notice of the only appliance in the room—an ancient wood burning cookstove littered with paper plates, plastic forks, a plastic jug of water, a jar of instant coffee, two cans of peaches, and a jar of peanut butter. "Good Luck Standard" stood out in raised letters on the oven door. *Appropriate name*, Ann thought, *given the meager food supplies and the broken stovepipe leaning against the wall.*

In the living room, Emmett stopped and squinted at an old mercury thermometer on the wall. Ann wondered about his eyesight.

"Supposed to be a mild winter," he announced.

Ann checked the thermometer's reading as she passed. *Forty-five degrees? Inside?* She certainly didn't need a thermometer to tell her the house was too cold for habitation.

"Well, I'm glad to hear that," she said politely.

Emmett lowered himself into the rocker next to a huge black, cast-iron barrel stove. Ann's eyes followed the stovepipe up to the ceiling and a nest of cobwebs. She glanced around the room, trying not to look as dumbstruck as she felt.

A dark brown curtain was strung on a twine behind his rocker, hiding part of the room. A crooked metal TV tray held binoculars, nail clippers, a box of toothpicks, and candy bar wrappers. Stacks of newspapers blocked the front door—protection from a draft or visitors? A portable television with its rabbit ear antenna perched on top of a short bookcase. Books on the shelf below with the names Dickens, Emerson, Thoreau, and Plato caught her eye. And again, one bare light bulb and pull chain hung from the ceiling.

Emmett pointed to the old chrome dining set shoved tight against a door with a glass knob. "Might as well sit a spell," he said.

Mice had torn through a package of bread on the table and left droppings all over it. If she hadn't had mice in her basement years ago she may not have recognized the little black specks for what they were. Ann sat down and reluctantly put the soup and cookies on the table. It was hard to ignore the cold, damp air inside the house. It was even harder for Ann to look at the little man who sat across from her. His neck was dirty and one of his leather boots was wide open at the sole. Neither boot had laces. Her dad hadn't lied about Emmett's poverty and if she hadn't seen it with her own eyes, she would still be thinking that family stories about Emmett's living conditions had been grossly exaggerated.

Ann raised the collar on her wool jacket and pulled her knit hat over her ears. "I hope you don't mind me coming to see you."

"Not at all," he assured her. He pulled one grimy glove off and rubbed his eyes with his dirty hand. "I watched for you every day since I got your letter."

Watched for me? Ann thought. *Am I the reason he wouldn't go to the Manor House? And no wonder his eyes are infected.* "I wondered if you would remember me," she said pleasantly.

"The last time I saw you, you were only this high," Emmett said, stretching out one shaky arm. He worked his glove back on. "That was years ago, of course, but I do remember you."

Despite not having any teeth, he spoke clearly and didn't drop endings off words like Frank. But he hadn't looked at her since they sat down. Was he shy or nervous about seeing her? Suddenly Ann felt a twinge of anger. She wanted to fire questions at him. *Why didn't you marry my mother? Why did you give us away? Why don't you live like a normal human being?* She took a deep breath and told herself to calm down. So far everything about Emmett was simply depressing, but she needed patience, not anger or judgment.

"Now, you're a college professor, if memory serves," Emmett said.

"Yes, I am."

"I admire proper schooling. I didn't get much."

Compliment him, Ann thought. *Make him feel good.* "But you have quite an impressive collection of books here."

"It's not a collection," he corrected her. "I read them. Some people think poor farmers like me are stupid. But a person can self-educate as well as self-medicate."

Ann felt relieved at his little joke. Maybe he wasn't as cantankerous as Frank made him out to be.

"Betty thought you'd come for lunch yesterday," she said. "We missed you."

"I don't drive much anymore."

Ann wondered when he had last driven the old truck that waited outside on flat tires.

Now Emmett looked at her. "Would you like some coffee?"

Ann started to get up. "If you tell me where your coffeemaker is, I'd be happy to make it."

"No need. All I have to do is put some water and coffee in a cup and put it up here on the stove." Emmett patted the cast-iron hulk beside him. "After a while, it heats up just fine."

He's got to be kidding! Ann thought. "What about your kitchen stove?" she asked.

"I haven't used it for years. It takes too much wood. Peanut butter is my mainstay. Otherwise I get dinners three times a week from the services."

"Only three times?"

"It's enough."

Ann wondered whether Emmett even felt the cold. *Do people realize when they're freezing to death?* "Would you like me to go outside and get some wood for the fire?" she asked hopefully.

"No need." He reached inside a box on the other side of his rocker and pulled out a short piece of wood as lean as Ann's forearm. "My father used to get this stove red-hot, and sometimes we had chimney fires. I'm afraid of chimney fires, so I'm careful."

Slowly, he leaned over and lifted the latch of the old stove's door and dropped the stick into its cavity. Ann didn't see any flames, but a puff of smoke rose to the ceiling.

"How do you keep the fire going through the night?" she asked.

"I sleep right over there in my recliner," he said, motioning to the curtain behind him. "If I feel cold, I get up and put some wood on. When it's real cold, I stand between the wall and the stove for a while until I warm up."

Ann couldn't believe what she was hearing. *When it's real cold? Wasn't forty-five degrees inside the house considered real cold?* Betty and Frank would have to be told, but for now Ann wanted to keep Emmett talking. She rubbed her gloved hands together to warm them.

"Say, Emmett, I'm hoping you might help me. I'm working on a little project."

"A sabbatical is what you said in your letter."

"That's right," she said, glad he remembered. "I'm doing research about family stories. Dad said he spent summers up here when he was a kid, so I thought you might have some good stories to share."

Emmett pursed his lips. "What did Karl tell you?"

"He said you had a lot of fun swinging out on a rope and dropping into the creek."

Emmett's face softened. "It runs along the back field," he said. "When we were youngsters, that creek was quite substantial, more like a narrow river during the spring thaw. But then they dammed it some miles up." He shook his head. "Never made sense to me."

"Dad told me you were in the Army together too," she added, hoping to guide him to what she wanted to hear about.

"At the same time but not together. Karl was in Italy. My outfit moved between France and Austria mostly."

"I wish I knew about what that was like," Ann hinted. "You know, Austria and everything."

He studied her a moment. "Karl died from cancer of the esophagus, didn't he?"

"Yes, he did."

Emmett shook his head. "Cancer's a terrible thing."

"I know. But look at you. You seem to be quite well."

"Well like they say, I'm still kickin' but not raisin' much dust."

As they both chuckled over his little joke, Emmett's attention was drawn to the window. Ann looked over her shoulder in time to see a car coming up the driveway.

"Looks like you have more company," she said.

Emmett frowned and remained seated. Ann heard a car door slam and started to get up in anticipation of going to the kitchen door when the visitor knocked, but Emmett raised his hand and motioned for her to stay in place. After a couple of sharp knocks, the kitchen door opened.

"Yoo-hoo!" a too-sweet voice sang out. "Emm-mett? You okay? It's me-ee, Iree-ene."

Emmett didn't answer, and from where he was sitting, he couldn't see who'd come in his house. But Ann had a clear view of a stout woman in a pink puffy jacket carrying a Styrofoam carton. When she got to the living room, she stopped and scrutinized Ann. Her overpowering perfume filled the room.

"Well, hello," she said to Ann. "I'm Irene Jessop from the

Ladies Aid at Grace Lutheran. I don't believe we've met. Are you family?"

"I'm Ann. I'm, um, a cousin."

"You don't say? I wondered who belonged to that strange looking car. Where are you from?"

"Milwaukee."

"My goodness, that's quite a drive! How nice you came to visit! We make regular visits to our shut-ins, you know, following the Lord's teachings." Irene closed her eyes and aimed her face at the ceiling. "'For I was hungry and you gave me food, I was thirsty and you gave me drink, I was sick and you visited me.'" She looked back at Ann. "Matthew twenty-five, verse thirty-five."

"I'm sure you're right," Ann replied.

Irene turned her attention to Emmett and raised her voice. "Roast beef today, Emmett. With mashed potatoes and beef gravy and creamed corn. I cut the meat up myself. Gladys made chocolate cake too. You like chocolate better than angel food, don't cha, Emmett?"

Emmett, still frowning, stared out the window, his jaw tightly clenched.

"I keep telling him to come for our senior suppers," Irene told Ann. "We make good nutritional meals every Wednesday. It's free, of course, and we'd be happy to pick him up. Every month we take up a collection for our shut-ins."

Emmett's fist struck the arm of the rocker. "Don't talk like I'm not here!" he yelled. "I'm not deaf or feeble-minded, and I am not your shut-in!"

"Well now, Emmett," Irene said as if addressing a child. "It wouldn't hurt for you to come to church."

"Church is for people who don't know better!" he blared.

Ann stiffened, but now was not the time to ask Emmett what he meant. Irene, on the other hand, wasn't fazed. She must have heard it all before.

"There, there, there Emmett" Irene said. "No need for insults. Scripture says . . ."

Now Ann felt ready to take charge. She stood up, took the Styrofoam box from Irene, and nudged her toward the kitchen, trying to sound friendly. "You know what, Irene? This sure smells good. We'll heat it up later. Be sure to thank the other ladies too."

"It's our Christian duty," Irene replied. "Now take the cake out before you reheat everything. Course I don't know how you're going to do that. The poor man doesn't even have a microwave."

"I got him one for Christmas," Ann whispered.

"My goodness! Gladys will be so surprised!"

With a grateful sigh, Ann closed the kitchen door after Irene and went back to the living room, where she found Emmett grumbling.

"Insufferable woman! No humility. Downright insufferable!"

Ann put the Styrofoam dinner box on the table. "She thinks she's helping, Emmett," she told him gently.

"I don't need some high-and-mighty coming around with handouts and scripture!"

He seemed to be shaking all over. Ann tried not to picture him freezing to death. He already looked half-starved. She decided to try the strategy she used whenever her mom was being disagreeable: Don't argue or ask questions. Simply agree, change the subject and keep it short and sweet, but take control.

"You're absolutely right about Irene. But let's forget her." She pointed to her watch. "It's lunchtime, and she reminded me how hungry I am. Aren't you hungry?"

He stared out the window.

Ann waited a moment and then lowered her voice. "I don't mean any disrespect, but I'm sure you realize you can't survive on peanut butter and peaches."

"I eat enough," he replied defiantly, eyes straight ahead.

Thinking fast, Ann said, "I'm sure you're right. But I have to tell you something. Dad made me promise to take you for a nice lunch if I ever got up this way. So, how about it? May I please take you for lunch?" She watched him blink a few times and slowly lower his head. "I'd like to keep that promise to my dad, and I saw a nice restaurant when I drove through town yesterday. I bet they have some good hot soup."

Emmett fingered a loose button on his jacket. "Melody's Café."

"Yes, that's right! Melody's. Do you need a different jacket for outside?" She hoped he had something cleaner than the jacket he was wearing.

"No."

Ann tried not to sound disappointed. "Okay, I'm ready too."

Emmett slowly rose to his feet, steadied himself, and shuffled his way across the kitchen linoleum again. Ann followed closely with arms outstretched as if she were guarding a wobbly toddler.

"Do you have your house keys, Emmett?"

"No need," he said calmly.

"Don't we have to lock your door?"

"No need," he repeated calmly.

Ann shrugged and closed the door behind them, then held her breath as Emmett grabbed the rickety porch railing and took one very slow, cautious step at a time. At the bottom of the steps, she came alongside him and matched his snail's pace across the gravel to her car.

"What kind of car is that?" he asked.

"A Saab."

"They're foreign made. It looks like a Hudson. They were good cars."

"Yes, sir. My grandfather had a Hudson."

"He was my Uncle Olaf."

Ann smiled and opened the passenger door for him. "Right again."

Emmett held on to the doorframe and lowered himself into the seat, groaning all the way down. Ann closed the door after him then went around to the driver's side, feeling suddenly anxious about his frailty.

I must be out of my mind! Ann thought. *What if he has a heart attack when I'm driving? I can't bring him back here. But what am I going to do with him after lunch? I'll have to call Frank and Betty to pick him up and take him to the Manor House.* She turned the key, switched the heat to full blast, and adjusted her seat belt. Emmett looked like a crumpled heap of ragged clothes and smelled like the smoky haze in the house. He seemed to be breathing rather heavily, and she didn't think he could even see over the dashboard.

"Can I help you with your seat belt, Emmett?"

"No. I never cared for those things."

Since the seatbelt would probably cut across his throat anyway, Ann didn't argue. She proceeded to the end of his driveway, where Emmett held up a hand to stop her.

"Take a right here," he said.

"Don't we go left to get to town?"

Emmett nodded and pointed to the right. "We could, but this way's a prettier drive."

"Is it a shortcut?"

"Nope. Just a prettier drive."

SIX

A bell jingled when Ann opened the door to Melody's Café. She took in the welcome heat and the smell of cinnamon as she followed Emmett across the room to a corner table. Despite his shabby appearance and trailing scent of wood smoke, Ann had the feeling diners were watching her rather than him.

"This looks like a nice place," she said cheerily as she took her jacket off and sat across from him. "Would you like to take your jacket and hat off?"

Emmett didn't look up. "No, thanks."

He worked his soiled gloves off and put them on the table. He hadn't said a word during the drive to town and now seemed lost in the task of unwrapping his silverware with his filthy hands.

Ann scanned the room. Men in plaid shirts and ball caps filled most of the booths; a few older couples occupied the center tables. Two men in matching sweaters shared the booth directly across the room. The younger man was picking his teeth with a toothpick. The one with a white beard and mustache wore a black cowboy hat. When their eyes met, he gave her a slow nod. Ann never knew what to do with flirtatious glances and now quickly averted her gaze to her place mat. A minute later, a rather wide waitress walked up and blocked the whole dining room from view.

"Hi, I'm Lenore," the woman said as she gave Ann a menu. "I never seen you in here before. You the new social worker?"

Ann glanced quickly at Emmett, hoping Lenore's question wouldn't raise suspicions in him. But his eyes were fixed on the menu Lenore had placed before him. "No, I'm not."

When Ann pretended to be interested in her menu, Lenore turned her attention to Emmett.

"Nice to see you back at your table, Emmett," she chimed. "Today we got chili and chicken dumpling for our soups, and the special is meatloaf with mashed potatoes, cream gravy, and green beans." Lenore readied her pen and pad. "Something to drink?" she asked Ann.

"Hot tea, please. And I'll just have the chicken dumpling soup."

"Soup's free with the special," Lenore advised.

Still staring at his menu, Emmett piped up, "That sounds pretty good."

"Got it," Lenore said. "One special with soup and one soup. And I won't forget your coffee, Emmett."

Ann wasn't sure what Emmett had actually ordered, but she had a feeling he'd eat whatever he was given. It didn't take long for Lenore to return with a tray. "Here you go. Soup, coffee, and tea." She efficiently arranged mugs, bowls, and a small teapot on the table and promised to be right back.

Ann poured hot water over her tea bag and watched Emmett's shaky hand move his coffee mug closer to him. "Would you like sugar or cream for your coffee?"

"I always take a little sugar."

When he had trouble opening the sugar packet, Ann asked if she could help, and he thanked her politely, but when his food came, he ate without talking. Ann tried not to watch him slurp his soup and use his dirty thumb to push one mouthful after another onto his fork. Gravy dripped onto the front of his jacket, and he seemed to be swallowing everything whole. But despite the urgency with which Emmett ate, his table manners were almost delicate when he finished. He carefully placed his cutlery across his plate without clinking metal against china, set the coffee mug down precisely where it had been, and tucked his folded napkin neatly under his place mat. So far, Emmett Pederson seemed to be a man of contrasts.

Ann sipped her tea, wondering how she'd sneak away to call

Frank and Betty to come pick Emmett up and take him to the Manor House. Then she noticed the bearded man heading right for her. He was tall and carried a brown leather jacket. His walk was confident, even though his gait was rather lopsided, as if his hips weren't quite aligned. And unlike the wannabe cowboys she'd seen in Milwaukee, this man with the dark eyes looked as if he belonged in his creased jeans and pointy boots. When she heard his deep voice, Ann snapped out of her stare.

"Hi, there, Emmett," the man said. "How you doin' today?"

Emmett angled his head to see who was towering over him. "Can't complain."

"Remember me comin' out to your place with Frank? We talked about your truck. Hope we still have a deal."

Ann was glad the man didn't shout at Emmett like the church lady and Lenore had, but when Emmett didn't respond, the man turned to Ann. Red lettering spelled out Maplewood Motors and JOHN on the left side of his dark blue pullover. A few white curls stuck out from beneath his hat. His beard and mustache were also snow white, neatly sculpted around his mouth and along his cheek, and trimmed cleanly just below his jaw, a perfect outline for his handsome face.

He extended his hand to Ann and smiled. "John Bennett. You must be new around here."

Ann put her hand in his. "People seem to notice that."

He chuckled. "We got a small town neighborhood watch. You related to this old geezer, Miss, ah?"

Ann slipped out of John's grip and flashed a look at Emmett who seemed to have missed the old geezer comment. "Yes, I am."

John winked at her. "Lucky Emmett."

"Nice to meet you, but we need to be going," she said, looking for the waitress.

Emmett pointed to an empty chair and said, "Might as well set a spell, John."

"Thanks, don't mind if I do," John replied, flashing Ann another wink. He draped his jacket over the back of the chair and sat down. "So, whad'ya say, ol' boy? I still need a good used pickup on the lot. What's yours again? '80? '81?"

"She runs good," Emmett said.

"Yes, sir, I believe it. I know you always take good care of your vehicles. How many miles again?"

"Sixty thousand."

"How much ya need for it?"

While Ann wondered what Emmett's old truck could possibly be worth and whether she should intervene somehow, Emmett answered firmly.

"I was offered nine hundred."

John scratched his chin. "Hmm. Needs tires, ya know. How's the engine?"

Ann's eyes went from one man to the other—John, robust, neat, and confident; Emmett, bent over, dirty, and toothless. She decided to sit back and listen. If Emmett showed any sign of anger, she'd have to step in, but to do what, she wasn't sure.

He looked John in the eye. "I give you my word the engine's in good shape."

"I take your word," John said. "But snow's on the way. Wind and driftin' too. May be time to trade your truck for cash so you can move to town again before you get stuck out at your place."

Emmett thought a moment before asking, "You got a plow?"

His question reminded Ann of the annoying way her mom shifted from one topic to another without warning.

John didn't seem to mind. "Yep. On my tractor," he said.

"What kind?"

"Kubota."

"Mm-mm. Japanese. We had a Massey-Ferguson."

"They're reliable," John said agreeably.

"And if memory serves, you've got horses."

"That I do."

Emmett nodded thoughtfully. "We kept a few cows for milk and meat. One dropped a calf during that ice storm in March of '76. Ears froze clean off."

Ann winced, but John answered knowingly. "Yep, that happens."

Lenore returned and gathered the dirty dishes. "We got peach pie today," she said. "Got room for peach pie, Emmett? John?"

"You betcha," John said. He turned to Ann. "How 'bout you?"

"Ah, sure. Why not?" she replied, feeling quite out of control.

Lenore marked her pad and headed back to the kitchen.

John folded his arms on the table and leaned toward Ann. "See, Emmett usually spends winter in town with his buddies." He raised his voice slightly. "Where he gets three square meals a day and a warm bed. And Frank and Emmett and me made a little deal."

Emmett frowned. *Please don't make him mad,* Ann wanted to say.

"Right, Emmett?" John asked. "You said I could buy your truck before Frank takes you to the Manor House."

Emmett frowned. "Frank Johnson doesn't tell me what to do!"

"No one's tellin' you what to do," John said calmly. "No, sir. But Frank's a good man and they're family. They care about you. 'Sides, you promised me the truck."

Ann felt her throat tighten. "I don't think we need to settle this today," she told John quietly.

Lenore brought pie and coffee and after she left, John took a forkful of pie and spoke to Emmett again as if Ann hadn't said anything.

"Let's make this man to man, Em. You already had

pneumonia once this year. You also know you'll freeze your nuts off if you stay in your house over winter. So if, *if* you go over to the Manor House today, I'll give you five hundred on your truck right now. Cash. And another four hundred tomorrow. You have my word."

Ann watched Emmett's shaky hand press his fork into his pie. *Obviously,* she thought, *this John guy knows Emmett well enough to address him so directly. That's fine as long as he doesn't make him angry.*

John took another quick bite of pie, put his fork down, and took out his wallet. "Look, here's your first five hundred." He counted out five one-hundred-dollar bills and slid them over to Emmett. "I'll come by the Manor House tomorrow and give you the rest. Deal?"

Emmett's swollen eyes widened at the money. "I accept your offer," he declared with authority.

John held his hand out to Emmett and they shook.

"Deal," John said with a grin. "You're a wise man. And I think you got the best of me on this one."

Without taking his eyes off the money, Emmett worked a thin wallet out of his jacket pocket. "It's a good truck," he insisted.

Ann stared dumbfounded at the money as John got up from the table. "Be right back," he told her.

Sipping her tea, she watched John cross the dining room, trying to sort out the last several minutes. *Why would he give Emmett nine hundred dollars for a beat-up old truck with flat tires? What's in it for him? Not to mention having the cash on hand and knowing Emmett was related to Frank and Betty. Frank and Betty. I have to call them.*

"The last offer I got on my truck was seven hundred," Emmett told her as he put the money in his wallet, returned the wallet to his pocket, and patted the flap of his pocket shut. He flashed Ann a sly smile. "I'm usually at the Manor House by now anyway."

Ann grinned at Emmett's satisfaction. Maybe he wasn't

feeble-minded, but sitting in an ice-cold house didn't exactly demonstrate common sense either. And at eighty-four he could become feeble-minded any moment. No matter, he needed decent food to eat and a warm place to stay. Maybe John had helped after all.

Returning to the table, John picked up his jacket. "Ready to go?"

"Wait," Ann said. "I didn't pay."

"Took care of it," he told her.

"He needs his things and . . ."

"We're fine. Trust me."

John helped Emmett to his feet and talked to him about the weather all the way to the door while Ann trailed behind, adjusting her knit hat, and fumbling to find her cell phone in her jacket pocket. Outside, she noticed John take Emmett's arm protectively. "Careful. A little ice here," he said.

I should be helping Emmett, Ann told herself. *I should be the one holding his arm.*

John turned to Ann. "So, what are you drivin'?"

Ann pointed to her car.

"The Saab? You don't like American cars?"

"It's a divorce leftover," she said without thinking.

John gave a slight chuckle. "Huh. What a deal." He helped Emmett get in the front seat, closed the door, and walked around Ann's car. "Don't mean to be nosy, but what year's this thing?"

Ann flashed back to her divorce settlement twelve years earlier. Her ex had kept the newer Saab for himself, leaving her with the older one. At least it was paid for.

"I don't know—1984 maybe?"

"No kiddin'. You mean you got fifteen years out of this thing?" John tapped his boot against one of her tires. "When was the last time you got tires?"

Ann looked closely. "Oh, my God! That one's cracked!"

"Sure is. Be glad to help you out with that."

Ann tried to remember the last time she got new tires. A long time ago. "Thanks, but I can't right now. I need to get Emmett to the Manor House."

"Yeah. Frank Johnson mentioned that when he came in for an oil change. So, if you're related to Emmett, you must be related to the Johnsons too."

"They're my dad's cousins," Ann said. "Listen, I appreciate your help. But I think I should go before he changes his mind."

"You really shouldn't be drivin' on those tires," John said. "Anything could happen." He pointed to a huge red Silverado parked nearby. "My truck's right here."

Ann shook her head at the monstrosity. "He would need a ladder to get up in there," she said. "He's already in my car; I don't want to ask him to move again."

"Yeah, you're prob'ly right."

Ann pulled her keys out of her coat pocket. "I do have a question though. What about the money you gave him?"

"It's his. I'll write up an offer to purchase and he can sign it later."

"Maybe I should take him to the bank," Ann said nervously. "Where's the bank? Do you have more than one bank in town?"

John smiled at her. "I think you're right. You should take him to the Manor House before he changes his mind."

"Yes, good idea." She looked up and down the street. "Where is it?"

"Hey, relax. How 'bout this? I drive you and Emmett over there in your car, and you bring me back here after he gets settled. If a tire blows, at least you'll have some help. 'Sides, I never drove an antique Saab. Might be fun."

Ann looked at John a moment and considered her situation. He seemed nice enough, and a local businessman wasn't exactly just any guy off the street.

"Want to call the Johnsons first?" John asked. "They know

me." He held out his hand again. "But you don't. What'd you say your name was?"

Ann let him shake her hand again. "Ann. Ann Olson."

"Okay, Annie Oakley," he teased. "Let's go before the old guy falls asleep."

Ann gave John her car keys. "Sorry to keep you waiting," she told Emmett as she got in the back seat.

"No trouble," he drawled sleepily. "I'm in no hurry."

As they pulled away from the curb, Ann noticed Gordy glaring at them from his pickup parked across the street. Even if he was her dad's cousin, she didn't trust Gordy-with-the-withered-hand.

A block down, John turned right, drove about a mile, and pulled into a parking lot where he stopped under a long blue canopy. A sign on the modest building said "Manor House Senior Residency."

"I could have found this okay," Ann told him.

John caught her in the rearview mirror. "I know," he said through a grin.

A skinny middle-aged woman with short, spiky, pumpkin-colored hair and an orange skirt and sweater opened a wide glass door as John helped Emmett out of the car.

"Hi, John," she said happily. "Hello there, Emmett! So good to see you again!" Emmett walked past her while the woman kept talking to him. "Archie and Fred were glad to hear you were coming today. Gracie too." Then she turned to Ann. "Hi, I'm Lily Brentson, director of the Manor House."

"Nice to meet you. I'm Ann. But, how did you know he was coming?"

Lily looked at John adoringly. "John called from Melody's."

SEVEN

"We call this our common room," Lily told Ann as they walked with Emmett through a wide archway and into the big room. A Christmas tree with hundreds of twinkling lights stood in the center. Elderly men and women, some in wheelchairs and others with walkers, far outnumbered the younger visitors mingling about.

"Emmett, you ol' son of a gun!" a man with a cane yelled. "What took you so long?"

Despite his limp and cane, the man rushed to Emmett with astonishing speed and thumped on his back vigorously. Ann feared Emmett might topple over, but he anchored himself and seemed to enjoy the attention. The man glanced at Ann and then did a double take.

"Do I know you?" he asked.

"I don't think so," Ann said.

"Okay, Fred," Lily told him. "Why don't you find Emmett a seat?"

Fred gave Ann one more hard study before leading Emmett toward a man in a wheelchair.

"Don't forget to ask Emmett for the money I gave him," John told Lily quietly.

"So you're not buying the truck!" Ann said sharply.

John smiled at Ann, keeping his voice low. "I am buying the truck, but Lily will put the money in his account here, and we'll square up after the truck is sold. Don't look so worried. Lily's record is spotless. She took good care of my dad."

"Your dad was a dear," Lily said affectionately. "Just like you."

"Aw, shucks, ma'am," John joked. Moving closer to Ann, he

nodded in Emmett's direction. "See, I told you he had friends here."

"He does," Lily said. "Fred Noble's the one with the cane—the one who thought he knew you. He was in the Army with Emmett. The one in the wheelchair is Archie Torkelson. He's Emmett's cousin on his mother's side."

Ann nodded, but her mind was on the snapshot of Fred she had seen among Emmett's Army pictures. Perhaps Fred Noble's memory of her was real.

"Unfortunately, we'll be losing Archie soon," Lily continued. "His sister's moving him to her place in Minneapolis. But Emmett has other friends here."

Fred, who'd been staring at Ann, now squinted at her. Ann sidestepped slightly so John's body blocked Fred's line of vision.

"When John called, he said you're Emmett's cousin," Lily said.

"Actually, he's my dad's cousin."

"Where you from?"

"Milwaukee."

"You don't sound like you're from Milwaukee," John said. "They got a regular accent down there."

Ann couldn't help it. "You betcha," she teased, mimicking the phrase he'd used at the café.

When John smiled and Lily looked confused, it somehow pleased Ann that Lily didn't get the little joke.

Lily straightened up and cleared her throat. "So," she said to Ann. "Are you here to manage Emmett's affairs?"

"Oh no, not at all."

"May I ask what brings you to our fair little town then?"

"A sabbatical project."

As soon as the words were out, Ann wanted to take them back. Being an outsider was bad enough; she didn't want to also sound like a show-off. But Lily had already reacted.

"Sabbatical," Lily said, stretching out the word as she looked up at John. "You mean like college professors do? My, my."

Ann noticed John's sudden attention. "Yes. I teach college," she told Lily. "But Frank and Betty Johnson are the ones to talk to regarding Emmett's affairs. I'm really just here to visit."

"Of course," Lily said. "Sorry for all the questions. I just like to know friends and relatives of our residents. I'm sure Frank and Betty will be glad Emmett's back here for the winter. Looks like he lost weight since last year though."

Ann looked at Emmett. He'd removed his shabby jacket but not his hat. His trousers, secured with a piece of rope, covered bib overalls. His shirt was torn open at one elbow, revealing another shirt underneath.

John followed Ann's gaze. "He needs a bath."

"And some new clothes," Ann added.

"No, no, no," Lily said. "Old clothes. Emmett says clothes should be worn until they wear out. He hates showers too. Says they use too much water. I honestly don't know where he gets these ideas."

"Probably Henry David Thoreau," Ann mumbled, thinking of Emmett's bookshelf.

Lily leaned in. "Beg your pardon?"

Ann smiled politely. "I'll go back to his house and see what I can find."

"Find some underwear," Lily added discreetly. "He goes through those pretty fast. And don't worry if the clothes you find aren't clean. We wash and sanitize everything."

"His eyes don't look good," John said.

"They were infected last year too, but he'll have a complete physical," Lily assured Ann. "We'll get him some drops."

Ann sighed. "Anything else?"

"Let's see. Last year he brought a tape recorder with some classical music. Maybe you could find it."

"And his teeth," John added.

"I've never seen him with teeth," Lily said.

Someone called Lily's name and she headed toward the

direction of the voice. "Sorry. Busy day, John." She smiled too
politely at Ann. "Come back whenever you're in town, okay?"

After Lily was gone, John cocked his head toward Emmett.
"Wanna say goodbye?"

Ann gave John a hesitant nod and headed for the three men.
Emmett had taken his hat off. His white hair was short over his
ears and longer in back. In the bald spots on top, Ann saw scabs
and dirt.

"I have to go now," she told him. She almost hugged him
but stopped herself.

"Don't be a stranger," Emmett told her.

While John joked with the three men, Ann watched Emmett.
Didn't he realize he was the stranger? Surely, he knew what she
wanted from him. Feeling suddenly anxious about spending
actual father-daughter time with this strange little man, she spun
around and headed for the exit.

"You okay?" John asked when he caught up with her. When
Ann didn't answer, he added, "I know how you feel. When I
brought my dad here, his whole life fit in a little old suitcase."

Ann wiped a tear from her eye. "Emmett didn't bring a
suitcase."

"Still he's better off here than alone."

Outside, snowflakes dotted Ann's sleeve, reminding her it
was winter, she was far from home, and her tires were bad.

John seemed to read her mind. "I really can help you with
tires."

"I don't think I have a choice." She held her keys out to him.
"Would you mind driving again?"

"My pleasure."

As they pulled out of the parking lot, Ann felt she needed to
say a few things to John in defense of Emmett. "I appreciated
your help at the café," she began.

"Just bein' neighborly, darlin'," he replied with a self-satisfied
grin.

"But I didn't like the way you tempted him with the money. In fact, I think you scared him when you said he'd freeze if he stayed in his house. I think you came on kind of strong."

John's grin disappeared. "Didn't mean to offend. And it's happened before—old folks freezin' to death. I figured I'd lay it on the line like I used to with my dad. Old men still think like men, ya know. They want their own way. I just limited his options." He glanced at her briefly. "Always worked with my dad."

"What if he changes his mind about the truck?"

"He won't. We shook on it. For his generation, that's as good as signin' his name."

"But what about the money? Do you always carry that much cash around?" She started to apologize for sounding so demanding, but John didn't seem to mind.

"I told Frank Johnson I'd buy Emmett's truck before he went to the Manor House," he said. "And the money was actually for a guy who did some work out at my place. I always pay him cash, but when I saw Emmett, I figured I'd do the truck deal and go to the bank again later. That's all."

"I'm sorry," Ann said. "I didn't mean to suggest you're dishonest."

"It's okay, I know what they say about car dealers." He grinned and nodded at her. "You just don't know me as a person yet."

Yet? Ann wondered. *Does he expect me to be his next deal?*

As they passed Melody's Café, John slowed and pointed across the street. "Did you see a guy in a blue pickup over there when we came out of the café?"

"Yes. Why?"

"He's the one usually drives Emmett around. Course you're a lot prettier than Gordy-with-the-withered-hand."

"Why did you call him that?"

"Everyone does on account of his crippled hand. I don't

know who started it."

"I think my grandmother did," Ann said quietly.

"So Gordy's another cousin?"

"Yeah. Another cousin."

"Well, you know what they say," John drawled. "We can't pick our family."

Ann looked out the side window. Sure, Gordy was part of her dad's family, and she felt sorry for him. But he had a spooky way about him. She didn't trust him and she didn't want to think about him. She turned toward John and decided he didn't mean any harm.

"My car smells like Emmett's house," she said with a slight chuckle.

John was quick. "Ha! That's his best cologne! Old Wood Smoke—for all the times you wished you had a furnace."

His humor lightened Ann's mood. She knew he was trying to impress her and he was doing a good job of it, which is probably why she didn't notice the red and white sign for Maplewood Motors when he turned.

"It won't take long to change out your tires if we have the right size," he said when he stopped at the service shop entrance. "Ever notice your car sort of slippin' between gears?"

"Slipping?"

"I'm not a mechanic, but I got a feelin' your car's got another problem." He guided her inside, past cars on hoists and others with hoods open. John called to one of the mechanics. "Jerry! Get the tire specs on the Saab out there and call me, will ya?"

"Saab?" a voice called back.

"Yeah, Saab. It's the only one out there; you can't miss it!"

From the shop, they went through the customer waiting area, down a hall, and past several offices to a double door leading to a large showroom. There, John took a few papers from a receptionist who greeted Ann politely. A salesman with a young couple examining a new truck nodded to them. A phone echoed from somewhere, and John quickened his pace toward a large corner office, where he dropped into a leather swivel chair and picked up the receiver. The desk nameplate said "John Bennett—Owner." *No wonder he was the take-charge type,* Ann thought.

As John talked, hung up and dialed again, she stood in the doorway taking in his well-appointed workspace with a picture window view of Main Street. On one wall several framed photos showed a younger John standing next to different spotted horses under banners reading "World Champion Appaloosa Horse Show." Outstanding Dealership plaques and certificates proclaiming "John Bennett—Newland Business Citizen Award" hung on another wall.

A loud, raspy voice drew Ann's attention to an elderly man in a Green Bay Packer cap, sitting across the showroom near a coffeemaker and a box of donuts. Another man about the same age occupied the opposite chair. Strings dangled from the earflaps of his red-and-black plaid hat. Packer cap seemed to be in charge of the conversation.

"So I says to Gus, I says, 'Hey, Gus, ain't yer brother-in-law a little too old to be livin' off you? Is he touched in the head?'"

Earflaps nodded like a bobble head. "Yuh, yuh, yuh."

"No normal grown-up man lives offa his sister and her husband!"

"Yuh, yuh, yuh."

"I guess maybe Gus is the simpleton, huh? Ha! Ha!"

Ann stepped back inside John's office, muffling her laughter with both hands.

"Leftie and Stony," John whispered as he hung up the phone.

"Lefty and Stony?" Ann said through her giggle. "They're like cartoon characters!"

"Yuh, yuh, yuh," John teased. He picked keys off a pegboard next to his desk and motioned for Ann to follow him.

"Afternoon, boys," he called to the men. "How's it goin'?"

"Hey, John!" Packer cap yelled back. "You hear ol' Casey's retirin'?"

"You don't say? I thought he got a job over at Seed-N-Feed."

"Job? Hell, he's dumber 'n a sacka seed corn!"

John laughed then called to another man in a Maplewood Motors sweater. "Keep an eye on things, will ya, Brad? I won't be long."

Brad gave Ann a friendly nod and a thumbs-up.

"Where are we going?" she asked John as he held the door open for her.

"We don't have your size tires, and I figure you need somethin' to drive now, right?"

Light snow was falling, and Ann suddenly remembered her predicament. "You rent cars too?"

John stopped at a dark green SUV. "No. Pretty customers like you get a free loaner. I think you'll like this one."

"Little old lady took it back and forth to church?"

John unlocked the door and gave her a wink. "Yep. In Florida."

"It's big," Ann said, peering inside.

"It's a Chevy Blazer—not much bigger than your car. Ten years newer, though, and the tires are good. Give it a try."

Ann got behind the wheel while John went around to the passenger seat. He turned the key, adjusted the heat, and explained controls for the lights, wipers, four-wheel drive, tape player, and cruise control. "That's it," he said. "Let's go."

Ann tightened her grip on the wheel and eased forward. John's voice faded away as she silently scolded herself for this crazy trip up north in the winter. And now car trouble.

"So how 'bout it?" she thought she heard John say.

"How about what?"

"Supper with me tomorrow night."

"Oh, I, I don't think so. I won't be here very long, and it's already snowing."

"I know we just met, but look at all we've been through so far."

Ann's phone rang, startling her. "I bet that's Betty," she said, pulling over to the curb where she unbuckled her seat belt in order to get the phone out of her coat pocket.

"Thank goodness I got you!" Betty said. "Gordy told us Emmett wasn't home."

"But Gordy saw us at—ah, never mind," Ann told her. "I'm sorry, Betty. I should've called earlier. Emmett's at the Manor House."

"Really? Are you there now?"

"No, a couple of my tires are bad and . . . "

"Now listen," Betty told her. "You get yourself to Maplewood Motors on Main Street and talk to John Bennett. He's a nice honest guy. And when you see him, ask him if he still wants to buy Emmett's truck."

Ann thanked Betty, returned her phone to her pocket, and looked at John sheepishly. "Betty asked if you still want Emmett's truck."

"We could talk about that over supper too." At Ann's hesitation, John tried again. "My mom always said good food brings good talk."

"Don't get me wrong. I do appreciate the loaner and all your help, but I think I should get to Betty's before the storm hits."

John looked puzzled. "What storm?"

"The snow and winds and drifting you told Emmett about."

"Oh. These few flakes won't amount to much. Little white lie, I'm afraid." When Ann wrinkled her brow, he added. "Got the job done, didn't it?"

Ann had to admit she was glad to have Emmett out of his icebox of a house, but did that mean she owed John a date? He seemed pretty sure of himself, but she didn't wan to call him conceited or arrogant. She couldn't even remember the last time she'd gone out on a date. She pondered his invitation as he guided her around the block and back to the dealership where he gave her his business card.

"It's all here," he said. "Office, cell, and home. Call me anytime."

"We forgot about your truck at the café."

"No problem. I'll get it later."

John got out and snowflakes melted in the warmth he left on the leather seat. He closed the door and waved as she drove off. *Okay, he's a nice guy*, Ann thought. *A very nice, pleasantly mature, handsome man.* She continued thinking of him all the way to Emmett's driveway, where she stopped because of the tire tracks. Someone had driven in and out recently. *Gordy?*

EIGHT

Ann drove forward carefully, hoping she wouldn't find Gordy parked behind Emmett's house. He wasn't. But someone with big feet had recently left wet footprints on the porch steps. She looked around cautiously as she approached the door and listened a moment before swinging it open all the way. More wet footprints crossed the kitchen to a cup of still-warm convenience-store coffee sitting on the cookstove. *Gordy knows Emmett spends winters at the Manor House,* Ann reasoned. *He probably won't be back.* She came inside and closed the door, confident she could search Emmett's house in frosty peace.

Standing in the little kitchen, her eyes fixed on two doors she hadn't noticed on her earlier visit. One opened to dark and damp-smelling basement. The second opened to memories. This was Nana's old bedroom. Squares of blue paint marked places on the otherwise faded walls where pictures had once hung. Ann remembered a big bed with a colorful quilt to hide under when thunderstorms raged outside. Nana used to tell her not to be afraid because the sky would soon be as blue as the walls again. And little Annie always believed Nana because she always told the truth.

Ann welcomed the sudden memory flash, but today Nana's room looked spookier than a thunderstorm in the night. The old lace curtains were faded and brittle to the touch. Clouds of gray cobwebs swayed from the ceiling and bulging plastic trash bags covered most of the wood floor. Shredded food packages, empty cans, and Styrofoam containers showed through holes in some of the bags, and a sour smell hung over the whole mess. Ann was about to leave when she noticed a pile of clothing across the room near an old wardrobe. She needed clothes for Emmett.

She dragged a garbage bag out of her way and shrieked when a mouse scurried out of it. The creature ran along the baseboard to a small hole where it disappeared near skeletal remains of another mouse locked in a trap. Ann hurried to the kitchen for a broom, and then came back to the bedroom and whacked furiously at the garbage bags. When nothing else ran out, she kicked bags aside to make a clear path across the room. Then, turning its wooden latch, she slowly opened the wardrobe to the smell of mothballs. An ancient black suit coat hung limply from its hanger on a bent pole. A handkerchief drooped out of the breast pocket and a tiny gold cross was pinned to a lapel. Ann brushed it and another old suit jacket aside. Emmett didn't need funeral attire. Not yet anyway.

With the broom handle, she gingerly sifted through the clothes on the floor, unable to imagine anyone undressing in this freezing house. She found two acceptable pairs of pants, three long-sleeved shirts, and unopened packages of underwear and socks taped to a Christmas card from Frank and Betty. No pajamas. She piled the clothes at the kitchen door and went to look for the tape recorder Lily had mentioned.

In the living room, Ann put her finger on Emmett's wall thermometer and held it there a moment. The mercury rose ever so slightly but fell back to thirty-nine degrees when she took her finger away. Mice had gnawed on Betty's cookies and the Styrofoam box from the church lady. The barrel stove was stone cold. She sighed and shook her head. It was hard to think her father actually lived like this.

With no tape recorder in sight, Ann pushed aside the old curtain behind Emmett's rocker, opening the room to its full size. The windows in this half of the room were darkened by heavy shades. She yanked on one and it rattled to a dusty heap at her feet. Carefully, she removed the two other shades and turned to face an ancient recliner patched with duct tape and draped with a brownish, full-length wool coat. A dirty comforter and pillow were on the floor. Ann poked the coat with the broom before lifting it slowly. Heavier than she expected, it was also torn and filthy. A military insignia patch with the interlocking letters Y and D was attached to one sleeve. *Was this Emmett's Army overcoat?* She wondered. *Why would he keep the old moth-eaten thing? And why didn't he have a bed?*

She found Emmett's tape recorder on a stack of grocery bags near a window. Ann put it and his few cassettes in a bag, and then noticed a decent pair of corduroy slippers under a tall, stately piece of furniture. She slapped the dust off and added them to the bag then inspected the old piece more closely. No doubt the best thing Emmett owned, Ann guessed it to be over five feet high and four feet wide, divided into four sections, one on top of the other. The top section and two lower ones had knobs set in the bottom edge of their framed glass fronts, making it easy to see the mess of papers stuffed inside each one. The solid door of the second section had a keyhole but no knob. Ann took the car key from her pocket, thinking she could use it to pull the door open, but it appeared to be locked.

Gently, she pulled the knob of the top section and found that the framed glass was hinged on top in such a way that she could easily lift and slide it safely inside the unit and out of the way. Ann knew she was prying, but hoped to find a clue, maybe one little thing to make this trip worthwhile. *Besides,* she told herself, *if Emmett would die tomorrow, someone would have to go through his things anyway.* It was an easy choice.

She removed several copies of *The Old Farmer's Almanac* and put them aside along with old seed catalogs, newspaper clippings, and junk mail. When she grabbed a handful of junk mail, two pocket-sized spiral notebooks fell to the floor. She opened one and scanned page after page of carefully printed columns listing sales of eggs, milk, and strawberries. More pages listed payments for work Emmett must have done for others. "Rec. $1.50—J. Pratt fence work." "Rec. $2.00—B.T. roof repair." One entry dated October 1961 read, "Sold Cow, Old Ugly, to Jacobson—$15."

The other notebook contained fewer pages and was more worn. Ann opened it to the first page and stood closer to a window to read the faint penciled script.

> *Sunday, October 8, 1944. This morning I remembered our small Norwegian church back home and tried to think of familiar passages and musical liturgies. I thought of how the congregation blended in song while the pipe organ rolled out the accompaniment. I can still see the wooden pews and the thin red carpet in the aisle that led the faithful to the altar. Now the only red I see is blood, and I pray God has not forsaken us.*

The handwriting was definitely Emmett's because it matched his letter in her laptop. The words and phrases carried the same eloquence she had seen in letters he'd written to her dad. "Emmett liked words," her dad used to say. And here Emmett didn't sound like the heretic he pretended to be with Irene the church lady either. She wondered where he was in October of 1944. Intrigued, Ann turned the page.

> *May 3, 1945. A little snow mixed with rain. Mountains are golden in the late afternoon sun. Today, we crossed another border and the Yankee Division of the U.S. Army entered Austria.*

Austria! Could it be this easy? Ann read quickly, hoping for a reference to Anna Miller or any other mention of her mother.

> *No one knows what to make of the stories of Nazi labor camps. They don't tell us much. Still, in the midst*

of uncertainty and horror, I can't believe I first saw her in a garden, smiling and planting seeds. I am determined to stay alive. I now have someone to live for.

"Her who?" Ann asked aloud. She turned the page to see smudges and erasures. "My Dear," had been crossed out and replaced with "My Dearly Beloved." Ann read through the crossed out words and crowded, incomplete sentences—no doubt the draft of a letter.

You have completely disarmed me with——. Your loveliness has captured my heart. I hope you understand my feeble attempts to——. I find myself wordless in admiration of—

Ann read the page two more times, irritated with the blank spaces. *Why didn't he address her by name? Did he ever send this letter?* The next few pages didn't answer those questions, but rather listed things Emmett wanted to do when the war ended, including intricate plans and drawings for a storage shed, a chicken coop, and a vegetable plot.

Next, after one page labeled, "Things to remember," Ann found pages of detailed observations, each with their own headline.

Frugality of French, Belgians, and people of Luxembourg.
Picturesque mountains, valleys of fields and meadows.
Bombed church, priest saved large crucifix.
Rainy Thanksgiving Day near Givrycourt.
Christmas Eve at Eschdorf with prisoners.
Plane shot down, men parachute.
Flares light up the night like day.

Roaring guns.
Nightly patrol of enemy planes.
Refugees wandering, lost.

For each item, Emmett had also recorded what he was feeling at the time. Cold, tired, and scared were repeated often. She paged forward to the next dateline.

June 6, 1945. Prachatitz, Czechoslovakia. Warm and clear. I often think back to those days and nights in France—the pup tents useless against the snow and wind, the fear of mines, the longing for letters and news, the uncertainty, the dead. This Sunday morning I watched people walking behind a horse-drawn cart carrying a small coffin. Many cried and carried flowers. I try to console myself by thinking these days will never be relived.

July 19, 1945. Moved again. Now situated in south central Germany near Fulda in a large hay meadow recently cut of crop. Tent City. Weather warm and dry but I can't sleep. I dream about the bombing, the burp guns, the Nazis Tiger tanks, the white phosphorus shells, and the ear-splitting explosions.

August 7, 1945. Hammelburg, Germany. Yesterday we saw "Salome, Where She Danced," a fair picture made memorable by Technicolor scenes and Viennese music. We sat on the ground at an outdoor theater overlooking a wide valley.

"What happened to Austria?" Ann said aloud. "And who's we?"

She felt cold to the bone now, not only because of the frigid house but also for what Emmett's notebooks might reveal. She stuffed them in her jacket pocket and rechecked the junk mail and other papers she'd set aside. Satisfied there were no more notebooks to be found, she loaded his small television, rocker, clothes, and tape recorder in the back of the Blazer. Driving to the Manor House, she couldn't help checking her pocket now and then, wondering how to finally make Elise listen. How could she make her sister care about Emmett, about what had happened between him and their mother so many years ago?

The Manor House smelled of sauerkraut and aides were pushing folks in wheelchairs, probably to the dining room for supper. After the aide at the front desk got a maintenance man to unload Emmett's things, she drew up an itemized list of his belongings.

"Will you be joining Emmett for supper?" the aide asked as she handed Ann a pen to sign the list.

"Thanks, but I have to get going."

All Ann could think of was reading more of Emmett's notebooks before seeing him again. When she turned into the Johnsons' driveway, Mitch barked and ran alongside the Blazer all the way to the porch where Frank was holding the door open for her.

"Betty waited supper," he said. "She said you had car trouble."

"Yes, this is a loaner from Maplewood Motors while mine car's in the shop."

"Looks like a newer model. Good man that Bennett."

"Yes, I'm sorry I'm late," Ann said as she hung up her coat. "We dropped Emmett off, and then I had to go back to his place to get him some clothes."

Betty looked up from the kitchen counter. "We?"

Ann explained how she met John at the café, and how he gave Emmett money for his truck and persuaded him to go to the Manor House.

"I couldn't believe how cold it was in the house," Ann told

them. "But I'm sure you know."

"He won't take any help or advice from us," Betty said. She took her meatloaf out of the oven and looked at Ann. "Honestly, Annie. If he wasn't family, I don't think I'd bother with him just because he's so contrary."

Ann nodded, wondering what contrariness was in store for her. "You were right about the mess over there. The bedroom's full of trash."

Now Betty glared at Frank and raised her voice. "Gordy's supposed to take care of the trash!"

Frank sat at the table and shook open the newspaper. "Don't worry, Bett, I'll get after him again."

"I saw Gordy in his truck outside Melody's," Ann said. "I think he was watching us."

"He's nervous about you bein' here," Frank told her.

"Nervous about what?"

"He's got it in his mind that you're gonna buy Emmett's place," Betty said.

Ann couldn't believe what she was hearing. "What?"

"Yeah, well, Gordy's a damn fart in a whirlwind sometimes," Frank grumbled. "Gets all kinds of stupid notions. I'll keep him out of your way."

Ann took a chair across from Frank. "Thanks. You can also tell him I'm not buying Emmett's place. But I have to admit, I do like the tall glass cabinet thing in his living room."

"You mean Nana's old barrister," Betty said. "Emmett sold most of her antiques over the years, but for some reason, he hung on to the barrister."

"Prob'ly for the same idiotic reason he keeps that old barrel stove instead of gettin' a furnace," Frank scoffed.

Betty brought bowls of carrots and mashed potatoes to the table where the meatloaf already waited. "Aw, Frankie, let it be. He always said what was good for his folks was good enough for him."

Frank put his paper down and began filling his plate. "Well, he'd be dead now if John wasn't straight with him."

"Now there's a man who's had hard times," Betty declared as she settled in her chair. "John's mother died when he was pretty young and his wife died too. He doesn't have any family. Very sad."

"He seems so calm and happy," Ann offered.

"Well, everyone gets over hard times. So, what do you think of him?"

Ann hoped Betty wasn't the matchmaker type. "He seems nice. He was definitely helpful." She paused then added, "He asked me out."

Frank chuckled. "Ha! That was fast."

Ann gave him an uncertain nod.

"Oh, go ahead, Annie," Betty said. "Heaven knows you could do a lot worse than John."

Ann laughed. "I think I have!"

The wall phone rang and Betty jumped up to get it.

"Well, I don't know," Betty told the caller a minute later. "I need to go. Yes, okay. I'll see you in church." She sat down again and served herself a scoop of mashed potatoes. "Our gossipy neighbor says one of the unmarried girls at the bank is pregnant. I don't like the way she's calling the poor baby illegitimate just because there's no father."

Ann caught Betty's eye. "Every baby has a father."

"Yes, well, you know what I mean, dear."

Ann thought a moment. If she was going to get to the truth, she needed to ask questions of people who might actually know it. She put her fork down and took a deep breath.

"I feel I should tell you both something," she said. "I'm not really here because of a sabbatical project. I'm here to find out about my birth parents."

"I admit I had a feeling about that," Betty said.

"You did?"

Betty reached for the carrots. "Yes, dear. After all, you and your sister were born up here, and you lived at Emmett's for a while."

"Yes, I think I know why."

Frank stopped buttering his bread. Betty stared wide-eyed, waiting for Ann to say more.

When she couldn't think of a better way, Ann simply said, "My sister and I both have birth certificates showing that we were born up here and that our father is unknown." She paused a moment before adding, "I don't have any proof. But I came here to find out if Emmett is our father."

Betty closed her eyes and nodded ever so slightly.

"Did you know, Betty?" Ann asked.

"Well, I know your mother came over from Europe and lived at Emmett's. I saw her a few times, but I didn't really know her. Frankie and I had just gotten married and I guess I was busy setting up our place. Besides, Emmett never wanted any company. My mother used to invite them for holidays but they never came." She smiled at Ann. "I did see you and your sister a few times when you were little because Mother and I used to go over to get strawberries. You were both so cute." She lifted a forkful of mashed potatoes. "My mother said Emmett was depressed for years after your mother died."

"Come on, Betty!" Frank said dismissively. "Emmett can hardly look at a woman let alone marry one and have kids."

"So how do you explain why Annie's mother was over there?"

While Betty tried to jog Frank's memory, Ann went to the hall to get the notebooks from her jacket. She sat down, turned to the smudged "Dearly Beloved" page, and passed it to Frank.

"I'm sorry," Ann told them. "I didn't mean to snoop, but I did, and I found these notebooks in the barrister. Read this."

"Well, I'll be," Frank said after he'd read the page aloud.

"But Emmett never married," Betty reminded Ann. "Neither did Clayton."

"You don't need to be married to have kids," Frank said. He turned to Ann. "But if Emmett *did* marry your mother, why would he keep it secret all these years? Ha! *How* could he keep it secret all these years?"

Ann shrugged. "Good question. That's why I'd like to look around at Emmett's. I'd ask him for permission, but the truth is, I don't want him to say no." Tears came to her eyes. "I promise I'm not here to steal from him or cause trouble. I just want to know the truth."

Betty patted Ann's arm. "Of course you do, dear. You go right ahead. We trust you. If anyone comes by, tell them you're family, and you're helping us clean up the place."

Frank reached for the ketchup and clicked between his teeth. "And if you find any money, let us know."

Later, in the quiet of her bedroom, Ann moved the nightstand lamp closer to the bed, and read from the notebooks. The entries were not in chronological order and many dates were missing. She tried not to skim over them too fast, while watching for any mention of her mother's name.

March 10, 1945. In convoy, winding generally SE along forest of evergreens en route to the front. Cooler here than in the valleys and many patches of snow.

May 18, 1945. Vyssis Brod, Czechoslovakia, Bohemia. Three years, three months, and twelve days in the Army. Discharge points: 85 required, have 58. Made friends with a particularly bitter and disgruntled private. He spent years studying law and says the Army cheated him of his future. He always quoted literary classics to emphasize a point, yet constantly reminded me not to emphasize formal education over inherent good judgment. He got shot the day we came upon a nest of SS troops. Good man.

The last entry had no year after the date.

July 17. We took a walk and followed the sound of a piano. Found a GI alone in a house without a door, playing a lilting Strauss waltz, one of her favorites.

Her favorites, Ann said to herself. After she put the notebooks in her laptop case for safekeeping, she lay back feeling tired but unsettled, her mind crowded with words. *Illegitimate. A child not worthy of inheritance. Bastard. Unwanted child.* Even love child, the label she'd given herself, carried the same stigma, the same guilt.

Ann read through the notebooks again and when sleep didn't come, she went to the window and stared out at the night. After a few minutes, two deer stepped out of dark, crossed the driveway under the light on the barn's peak, and disappeared again into the shadows. When her feet got cold, she put on a pair of socks and curled under the covers, imagining a little girl chasing shadows of deer.

NINE

Half awake, Ann thought she heard a door close. She listened for a moment, then went to the bedroom window and saw Frank walking across the driveway, playfully throwing his arm out to a tail-wagging Mitch. As she watched him open and close the barn door, she wondered if he knew more about Emmett than he was willing to tell in front of Betty.

She dressed and went downstairs. In Betty's pantry, she quietly rummaged around until she found cocoa powder and sugar, and then mixed those with milk in a large measuring cup, microwaved it, and divided the finished hot chocolate between two insulated mugs. She put her jacket on and took the mugs out to the barn.

"Hey, hey, hey!" Frank said when he saw Ann. "What are you doin' up at this hour?"

Ann held up the mugs. "I thought if I brought you some hot chocolate, you might give me a little tour of Johnson's Magnificent Holstein Parlor."

Frank laughed and took a mug. "Thanks, this is mighty nice." A calico cat curled around his legs. "Be glad to show you around, but first we gotta get Kitty here her breakfast."

Despite the odor of manure, the barn interior was quite clean. Frank led Ann along lines of big black-and-white heads that poked through metal rails and munched on hay and grain from narrow troughs.

"How many cows do you have?" Ann asked.

"I'm down to thirty-five. My dad had sixty when I was a kid and we milked 'em all by hand. We worked in shifts back then. When I took over and installed the milkers, he said I was gettin' soft. He wouldn't approve of my smaller herd either, but I gotta think about callin' it quits one of these days."

Frank handed Ann his mug and went to the first cow. He gently hand pumped milk into a small bowl and set it down for the waiting cat.

"Gordy helps you, right?" Ann asked him.

"He comes twice a day to clean up. But I don't let him handle the milkers. Those things aren't cheap."

She followed Frank down the aisles, watching him clean udders, disinfect teats, and attach individual milkers. He moved among the cows surprisingly fast, checking dials and knobs, explaining how the cows go to the stanchions on their own as part of the twice-a-day routine, and how the individual milk collectors measure each animal's production. When they got to the end of the next row, a cow bobbed her head as if asking for attention. Her milk collector was nearly empty.

"That's Celeste," Frank said. "She likes bein' scratched."

Ann scratched gently behind the cow's ear and Celeste lowered her long lashes.

"I pet 'em now and then so they know I appreciate their efforts," Frank said, patting Celeste's rump. "But next week she'll be gone. She'll be good beef for some family."

"You mean butchered?"

"She's gettin' old. That's the way it goes." He released the milk collector from Celeste and set it aside.

Ann gave Celeste a final pat and followed Frank to the next row of cows, thinking of how to word her next question.

"Say, Frank," Ann began. "Yesterday at the Manor House Fred Noble acted like he knew me. And I'm wondering. I mean, you know why I'm here."

Frank turned to face her and shook his head confidently. "Not your man, Annie. Fred never had kids on account of he can't."

"Are you sure?"

"He told me himself. I don't think a man would admit that unless it was true."

Ann nodded. "Okay, what about Archie?"

"Torkelson? Loggin' accident snapped his spine when he was nineteen. Never married, no kids. The only good thing to ever happen to Archie was gettin' money from his uncle. Emmett and Clayton got some, too, because they're related to the Torkelsons on their mother's side." Frank downed the last of his cocoa and handed Ann his mug. "I better finish up here. Betty hates waitin' breakfast."

When Ann came back in the house, Betty turned from her griddle of sizzling bacon. "My goodness, Annie, what were you doing out there so early?"

Ann held up the mugs. "I took Frank some hot chocolate and he gave me the grand tour."

"Frankie's pretty proud of his cows." When Ann yawned, Betty asked, "You sleeping okay upstairs?"

"Yes, fine; I've just got a lot on my mind, I guess."

"Hmm. Too bad Nana's not here. She must have known your mother quite well since she lived over there at the same time."

"Yes," Ann agreed. "I often wish I could turn the clock back."

Later, when Ann walked out to the Blazer for another trip to Emmett's, Frank waved from the barn, motioning for her to wait.

"Say, Annie," he called as he came closer. "What do you think about sellin' Emmett's place?"

"He wants to sell?"

"Hell, no. But if he stays at the Manor House for good, he'll have to sell everything anyway."

"Does he have a power of attorney?"

"You mean a lawyer? We got a lawyer in town. Name's Studt."

"No, I mean someone to handle Emmett's affairs. You know, someone to make decisions for him. My brother is power of attorney for our mom."

"Then you should do it," Frank said.

"But I told you I don't have any proof Emmett's my father, Frank, and you know him much better than I do."

Frank took the toothpick he'd been chewing on out of his mouth and threw it on the ground. "Not anymore I don't. Emmett and me don't talk much anymore."

"Who helps him with banking or grocery shopping?"

"Gordy. Course Betty don't approve, but Emmett can do what he wants." Frank ran his gloved hand over his unshaven chin and cast a quizzical eye at Ann. "But I wanted to ask you—I mean, since you're up here to, you know, find the truth, why don't you keep an eye out for bank statements over there?"

"I don't have a right to take his personal property."

Frank raised his eyebrows. "Those notebooks are his property."

"You're right. I shouldn't have taken them without his permission even though you and Betty said it was okay."

"Well, if he's your father, I guess you got a right anyway."

"Even if he is my father, Emmett's property is his business unless he authorizes someone else to manage it for him."

Ann couldn't decide if the look on Frank's face meant he truly didn't understand or if he was pretending not to.

"Betty said we can just say you're cleanin' up his place," he told her. "Everyone knows he might as well live in a hole in the ground. And it seems to me you're not gonna find what you want without goin' through his stuff like you been doin'." He clicked through his teeth and gave her a sideways glance. "Right? So why can't you keep an eye out for a few things Betty and I might need someday?"

"You mean as his power of attorney?"

"No. As family. He is Betty's cousin, after all. And I know

she cares about him."

Ann sighed. She needed both Frank and Betty on her side in order to have any kind of access to Emmett's things. "Okay," she said. "I'll keep an eye out."

Out on the road, Ann thought less about power of attorney and more about being grateful she could cross Fred Noble and Archie Torkelson off as possible fathers.

The temperature inside Emmett's house was now the same as the temperature outside—thirty degrees. Ann dragged one of the chrome chairs to the barrister and searched the second glassed section, where she found small volumes of poetry— Whitman, Dickinson, Frost, Tennyson, Yeats. She remembered a poetry class she had taken in college only because she needed an elective, not because she liked poetry. But by the evidence in front of her, Emmett not only liked poetry, he studied it. Scraps of paper marked favorite pages, where verses and words were underlined and marginal notes referred to other pages or other books. She stacked them on the floor and got to her knees in order to open last glassed section, which was also completely packed with papers.

She leafed through gardening catalogs and handfuls of junk mail before coming to a large white envelope marked "Last Will and Testament of Albert Pederson" and an expandable folder held shut with a string. She put Abert's will in a paper bag for Frank, then took the string off the folder and opened it to dozens of old envelopes.

They were all addressed to Lena Pederson with Emmett's APO return address. Obviously, Emmett had been diligent about writing home while he was in the Army, and Ann understood why his mother would have kept them. But why would Emmett keep them? She took her gloves off and slid a thin sheet out of one of the envelopes.

Dec. 19, 1944. Somewhere in France
Dear Ma,
*It's Sunday and high time for me to get on the beam
and answer your swell letters mailed on the 26th, 28th,
and 30th of November. I got all of them yesterday. I also
received the fruitcake you sent and it sure was a welcome
treat. I am sending you a big hug and a pat for Bowsie. I
miss having that old dog follow me everywhere.*
*We were told Roosevelt's president again. He has
certainly been in a long time now, hasn't he? Have you
heard what camp Billy Sands is at now? Before I left he
told me he was going to marry one of the Brewster girls. I
sure hope he can stay in the States a long time yet.*
*Well, news is rationed, so I will close and get a line off
to Aunt Lizzie and Gracie. With loads of love and best
wishes. So long, Emmett*

Aunt Lizzie must be Granny Elizabeth, Ann thought. *But was
this the Gracie that Lily had mentioned?* She put the letter back in
its envelope and sifted through the other sections of the folder.
She could hardly believe her luck when she spotted three small
notebooks. She took them out and sat back in the chair to read.

*May 15, 1945. We were diverted back to
Czechoslovakia a few days ago to scare out any remaining
enemy. Thank God the last attack was called off. We
are now lodged in an abandoned house on the banks of
a river that furnishes power for a mill. It's good to have
regular food again, and I do my best with tedious tasks I
am given. We are all tired of this war. All we can do is
wait now for the official announcement about going home.*

Ann couldn't help notice how the writing in Emmett's folksy
everything-is-fine letter was so different from his more refined

notebooks. The next page jumped two months ahead.

> *August 14, 1945. Lambrechten, Austria. The sensational news of the atomic bomb brings sobering thoughts of its potential. It's hard to imagine the destruction, and we cannot undo what has been done. Anticipated surrender of Japan brings mingled joy and anxiety. I yearn for home, but won't mind extra duty now that my heart is full of love.*
>
> *Must write to Gracie, Karl and Mother.*

Ann wondered at what Emmett must have been going through by the way he mentioned "sensational news of the atomic bomb" and "a heart full of love" in the same paragraph. She put her gloves back on draped Emmett's Army coat over her cold shoulders before continuing.

> *August 21, 1945. Lambrechten. Joined a group of civilians and other GIs for a trip to Salzburg for a Mozart festival. The dome of the cathedral was destroyed, but most of the city's architecture remains intact. Power is still off in much of the city, so musicians read their music by light of individual candles. At the end of the program, they blew out their candles one by one to great applause by the audience. I couldn't help laughing when she saluted a lieutenant on our way out and said, "You bring my Yankee back to me, no?" I am lost in romance.*

> *August 24, 1945. Linz, Austria. Arrived yesterday. Now lodged in apartments near the Danube. More damage here and citizens suffer from lack of food. Large numbers of DPs are camped all around doing the best they can. We often go for long walks. It is odd to be talking about the end of the war here in Hitler's*

hometown. Uppermost in my mind is going home and whether I will be going alone.

"Geez, Emmett!" Ann said, pulling her hat down over her ears. "Names would be good here!"

Suddenly a voice yelled, "Anyone home?"

Ann jumped. Footsteps crossed the kitchen and John laughed when he saw her, causing Ann to toss Emmett's old coat aside and get to her feet.

"Oh, hi. I'm just cleaning up a bit," she explained.

"Betty said you might be here. Neat old barrister he's got there." John didn't seem bothered by the dirt and mess. He rapped on a wall. "Typical old farm house—no insulation. You shoulda made a fire. There's enough paper here, and I saw wood on the porch."

"Oh, no! We can't burn any of this!"

John snickered a bit. "Looks like a lot of junk to me. It was the same with my dad. The older he got, the more he didn't know what to keep or throw away."

Ann put the notebooks in her coat pocket. "We're at that point with my mom now."

"Your dad around?"

"No, he died in March."

"Too bad."

Ann picked up the paper bag and began retrieving the books from the floor.

"Allow me," John said, getting down on one knee. "Been a long time since I carried a girl's books."

Once they were outside, Ann thanked him but didn't know what to say next.

"I might have your tires tomorrow," John said as Ann got in the Blazer. "And my mechanic's workin' on the engine."

"I like the Blazer, by the way."

John handed her one of the books he was carrying. "So

you'll go out with me tonight?" He grinned and handed her another book. "We got a decent supper club up here." Another book. "They even got heat." Another book. "How 'bout six o'clock?" He gave her the last book.

Ann couldn't help smiling as she piled the books one by one on the seat beside her. "Okay. Six o'clock is fine."

John was pleased. "Great," he said, putting a forefinger to the brim of his hat. "See you then."

It'll just be a little neighborly thank-you-for-your-help supper, Ann thought as she drove back to the Manor House. *It's not really a date. So why am I thinking of it as a date?*

TEN

Lily Brentson was standing at the reception desk when Ann arrived.

"I didn't find any pajamas for Emmett," Ann told her.

"He doesn't need pajamas. He sleeps in his clothes. Habit I guess, and we don't argue with him. By the way, the other clothes you brought are all too big, I'm afraid. So now he needs everything except socks. I let him borrow a shirt from Archie."

Ann thanked her and started for the common room, but Lily stopped her. "Do you have a minute?"

"Sure."

Lily directed Ann to her office and invited her to sit down. "Betty called this morning and said you mentioned a power of attorney for Emmett? I can help get you set up for that."

Frank sure didn't waste any time telling Betty that he talked to me earlier, Ann thought. *And Betty passed it right along to Lily.* "No," Ann said. "I only mentioned it to Frank because he asked what I thought about selling Emmett's place. I believe they need a power of attorney or guardian status to do that."

"Right, Lily said, taking a manila folder out of her desk drawer. "We need HIPAA paperwork for him too. With our new licensing, we have more forms to fill out. Do you know about HIPAA?"

"It ensures privacy for medical records."

"Yes." Lily lowered her voice. "But just between you and me, he's been coming here every winter for fourteen years, and I've never seen him so frail, physically and mentally. He thinks he's fine, but he needs help, and he needs it now."

"Frank and Betty don't know where to start."

"I'm sure they're concerned and I sensed the hesitancy in Betty's voice when I asked if she wanted to be the main contact for him." Lily smiled pleasantly. "I'm glad to see another family member taking interest." She handed Ann a sheet of paper. "Understand this isn't standard procedure, but in Emmett's case, I think showing this to Frank and Betty would help them make a decision. It's the report from the nurse who examined Emmett yesterday."

Ann looked over the checked boxes and short handwritten notes: Suspect congestive heart failure. Osteoporosis seems worse than last year. Both eyes infected. Short-term memory should be checked. Possibly anemic. Malnourished. Blood pressure low. Seborrheic dermatitis on head. Infected navel.

Ann thought she'd misread. "Infected navel?"

"Well, the first thing we did was get him in the bathtub," Lily said. "The aide noticed his, ah, red belly button right away. Some skin peeled off the soles of his feet too."

Ann's eyebrows went up. "What?"

"Proper hygiene and good food will help. We see these things a lot, especially with folks who've been living alone. Aside from the health issues though, Emmett's actually one of our easier residents. He behaves and he always pays his bill. Which reminds me." Lily took another sheet out of the folder, made a quick note on it, and passed it to Ann. "This sheet details our residency fees."

"He pays $2,800 a month?" Ann asked, looking up from the paper. "What's included?"

"Everything—room, meals, laundry, janitorial, and administration services and fees. Outings are extra. The smaller number in the other column is his Social Security income. Unfortunately, our fees will go up when our nursing home status is approved." Lily sat back and took her glasses off. "Emmett doesn't have anyone else except Archie and Gordy. And I'm sure you realize neither one of them would be a suitable choice."

"For what?"

"Power of attorney or guardianship or whatever the family decides." When Ann didn't say anything, Lily added, "We don't have a health directive for him either—which he doesn't seem to understand. He hasn't signed the resident contract or the HIPAA form yet, and technically I can't admit him without those."

"I can't take him back home. His house is absolutely uninhabitable."

Lily closed her eyes and nodded. "I know, I know." Her voice got sweeter. "But the good news is the social worker seems to think he's ready to have someone help him out. And I think he really likes you."

Ann felt uncomfortable, wondering for a moment whether Emmett had talked to Lily or anyone else about the adoption. "He doesn't know me," she said.

"Really? I got the impression he knew you quite well. I heard him telling Fred Noble about you and your sister. Alice, is it?"

"You mean Elise? Emmett mentioned Elise?"

"Yes! I'm glad there's a history there."

After a short rap on the door, an aide stepped into Lily's office.

"Excuse me, Lily. It's Blanche again."

"Okay, I'm coming." Lily gave Ann two business cards. "Sorry, I have to go, but I'll be waiting to hear back from Frank and Betty—or you. Here's a card for Howard Studt, our local attorney. He helps most of our residents with their affairs. The other card is for the social worker. She's great at figuring these things out." She led Ann out the door and locked it before heading down the hallway. "Emmett was in the common room a while ago," Lily said over her shoulder. "Glad you stopped by. Show those sheets to Betty and let me know what the family decides."

Ann folded her jacket over the papers before going to the

common room, where an aide glanced up from her magazine then went right back to it. Ann saw Emmett in a recliner that had been set back as far as it could go. He was effectively trapped until someone came to retrieve him. A petite and prim elderly woman sat on the couch next to him, her gray hair arranged in a bun on top of her head, and her walker waiting nearby. As Ann got closer, she noticed that Emmett's clothes were about three sizes too big. He was also clean-shaven and pale—like an antique rag doll that had had its complexion viciously scrubbed off.

"Hi, Emmett," Ann said. "Remember me?"

He managed a weak grin. "Of course I do."

The woman put out her hand and piped up cheerily, "I'm Gracie."

Ann put her jacket and the papers on a chair and took Gracie's small, feathery-soft hand. *Was this the Gracie that Emmett had referred to in his writing?*

"Nice to meet you. I'm Emmett's cousin Ann."

"How delightful!" Gracie said sweetly. "Sit here next to me on the davenport."

Gracie's tiny voice complemented her tiny body. Ann chuckled. "My dad always said davenport instead of couch."

"Yes, well, I don't know why they have to go and change perfectly good words. Emmett and I talk about those things all the time. He was the best writer in grammar school." She smiled affectionately at Emmett. "He used to pull me in the coaster wagon too."

Emmett grinned shyly.

"That's a nice memory," Ann said.

"Yes. They all are." Gracie positioned her walker in front of her and moved forward as if to stand.

"You don't have to leave," Ann told her.

"Oh, I must. It's time to check on Blanche. She gets anxious, and I'm sure she's waiting for me."

Ann automatically reached out to help, but Gracie got to her feet on her own.

"I'll see you later, Emmett. You be good now." She whispered to Ann, "He's tired. You have a nice visit. He doesn't get much company."

Ann watched Emmett's eyes follow Gracie scooting her walker toward the hallway. "I can see why you like it here," she said. "It's warm and comfortable, and it's good to have friends to visit with."

He picked at a fingernail. "It's not home. Most folks I knew are gone now." He looked at Ann. "My brother Clayton killed himself."

Okay, Ann thought. *What is he thinking?* "Yes, I know," she replied.

"He strung a rope up in the barn." He tightened his lips across his toothless mouth.

For a moment, Ann thought he might cry. "I'm very sorry," she said. "I don't think anyone ever gets over losing a loved one."

"He was my kid brother! We both survived wars, but he had no respect for his own life! A man should have self-respect!"

Ann stiffened against his outburst, remembering her dad's final months—how he'd zero in on something and surprise them with an angry comment. Her dad's doctor had said, "Your dad knows his time is short, and his fear is coming out in anger." Perhaps it was the same with Emmett now.

"I'm very sorry about Clayton," Ann said. "With all due respect, some people aren't as strong as others."

Still frowning, Emmett softened his voice a bit. "Everyone comes home with remorse and regrets about war. I had bad dreams for years. You never forget battle. You never forget feeling guilty about surviving. Nothing prepares you for what war does to you."

"I believe you," Ann replied calmly. "My dad used to say the same thing."

"Karl was lucky, you know. He was in the guard first. He had more training than I did." Emmett shook his head. "Even so, war's a terrible thing. A stupid, terrible thing! There are times I can't believe I was there."

"Dad was in Italy."

"Yes, he fought at Monte Cassino. I was at the Battle of the Bulge."

Ann took advantage of the opening. "Would you mind telling me what it was like?"

He studied her face a moment as if trying to decide whether he wanted to reply. "People always ask about the war." Ann started to apologize, but Emmett kept talking. "I tell them it was noisy. I thought I would go deaf. Or crazy. Our clothes got stiff from the cold and sometimes our guns even froze up. There were so many wounded, and some of them froze to death before a medic got to them. Imagine. Of course they give you these awards," he snickered, indicating with a thumb and forefinger. "A little piece of shiny metal. A tiny piece of colored ribbon. Decorations they call them. You risk your life, and they trim you like a Christmas tree." Emmett turned his face toward the windows and wrung his hands. "We slept close together in the snow, listening to men crying in the darkness. We risked our lives every hour of every day, and they kept telling us to be proud. How could we be proud when we were watching our friends die right before our eyes?"

"It must be hard to think about that."

He continued as if he hadn't heard her. "I was infantry. Field rifleman. I was always a good shot. Squirrels, rabbits. But to kill another human being? That's unthinkable." Emmett shook his head. "Infantry's the worst position. They don't tell you that when you sign up. I think I walked clear across Luxembourg and Belgium."

He paused and looked around the room. *Austria*, Ann

thought. *Please talk about Austria.* "Did you see any other parts of Europe?" she asked.

His gaze settled on a window. "Of course. We got into parts of Germany and France, then Czechoslovakia and Austria." He waved his hand over his lap. "We were back and forth, back and forth at the whim of the generals."

"I hear Austria is lovely."

"It was," he barely said.

Ann tried to gauge his temperament. "I hope you got a break sometimes. Dad said he went to USO shows."

Emmett didn't seem to hear her. "Once my outfit was lodged in a big hotel in Linz right on the Danube River," he said toward the window. "Linz is in Austria. The Army simply took over the place. It was the common thing. There was a piano in the dining room, and one of the hotel workers could play. So sometimes we got a little songfest going." He rested his head against the back of the chair. "Let's see. There was Fredrick and Honelore. And Hans and Mitzie. She worked in the hotel. Everyone liked Mitzie. She sang like an angel."

His voice trailed off, his eyes closed, and his hands gradually relaxed in his lap. "Emmett? Emmett?" Ann said, watching his chest rise and fall steadily.

The aide with the magazine walked over with a blanket. "He's fine," she whispered. "He nods off a lot but he can nap here. We'll keep an eye on him."

"Wouldn't he be more comfortable in bed?"

"Actually, his bed is pretty much like this anyway." She drew a crooked line in the air with a finger before spreading the blanket across Emmett's legs.

Ann thanked her and put her jacket on, reluctant to leave Emmett, hoping no one would forget about him. He seemed comfortable, and Ann didn't know what to do to make him more comfortable, so she walked away.

Near the reception desk, she heard a voice say, "Well,

look who's here." She recognized Fred Noble but focused on buttoning her jacket, pretending she didn't hear him.

Fred spoke loudly, insistently. "I know why you're here. Emmett and me go way back. He doesn't have much left, you know."

A big man with a nametag that said "Bruno" came out from somewhere. "You want somethin', Fred?"

Fred ignored him in favor of giving Ann the once-over. "I know you lived up here when you were a kid. I suppose you came to see what you could get off Emmett now, huh?"

"It's none of your business," Ann told him.

Fred's eyes narrowed. "You're adopted. You're not real family."

Bruno was now between Fred and Ann. "Come on, Fred, let's go." To Ann, he said, "I apologize, ma'am. Sometimes Fred here forgets his manners."

Ann hurried out the door and across the parking lot to the Blazer, frustrated and confused by Fred's accusation. *Why does he care? And how does he know I'm adopted?*

She got behind the wheel and turned the key just as a car parked alongside her. Ann waited while two people took a huge poinsettia from their car. When they were out of the way, she put the Blazer in reverse but quickly shifted back to park when she saw Gordy's truck turn in. She ducked slightly, catching a glimpse of Fred Noble waving to Gordy from the Manor House entrance. Gordy glanced over the parking lot before he went inside, but he didn't see her. Ann realized Gordy didn't know she was driving the Blazer instead of her old Saab and felt relieved. *Just as well,* she thought as she drove off. *The longer he remains in the dark, the better.*

ELEVEN

When Ann got back to the Johnsons', she found Frank sitting at the kitchen table. Betty greeted her from behind the counter.

"Hi, Annie. John Bennett called right after you left. He said he'll be here at six, and call him if that's not okay. I bet he takes you to Giovanni's Supper Club. It's the nicest place around here."

"Is it a fancy place?" Ann asked, thinking of the skirt and sweater she'd brought along. It was her mom's rule. Always pack something a little dressy because you never know.

Betty brought a plate of cheese, sausage, and crackers to the table. "No fancy places around here. We're having a little snack. Want some?"

Ann joined them and put the paperwork from Lily on the table. "Lily asked me to give this to you. She said Emmett has to sign a medical release form and he needs an advocate to act on his behalf."

Betty reached for the papers.

"More nonsense," Frank grumbled. "The Manor House used to be a simple place for old folks. Since they remodeled, they're gettin' all legal and official."

"They have to follow the law, Frankie," Betty told him.

Ann decided to avoid the topic of power of attorney for now. "I kept an eye out like you said, Frank," she said. "And this is what I found so far." She emptied the paper bag out onto the table.

"How can Emmett be malnourished?" Betty said, frowning over Lily's note. "I send food over with Gordy all the time."

"I told you Gordy prob'ly eats it, Bett," Frank told her. "He's always lookin' for a free meal. Why do you think he eats here?"

"And look at how expensive it is over there!"

Frank put his glasses on and reached for Albert's will. "I tell ya, Bett, he's got money somewhere," he said.

"He inherited from their Uncle Oscar," Betty said. "You remember?"

"Course I remember. Emmett wound up with what was left of Clayton's share too." Frank looked at Ann.

Ann shrugged, "I don't know anything about that, Frank."

Betty turned her attention to the airmail envelopes spread across the table. "I don't see any letters from when Clayton was in Korea."

Frank scowled. "Emmett prob'ly threw 'em in the burn barrel same as Clayton's casket flag."

He unfolded Albert's will and Betty read over his shoulder.

"Look, Frankie. It says, 'If either Emmett or Clayton is married at the time of my death, his share of the estate shall be forfeited to the unmarried son. If both Emmett and Clayton are married at the time of my death, I bequeath my entire estate to Stewart Halvorson.'"

Frank slapped the table. "Ah-ha! That's Gordy's father! Now I know why Gordy thinks he's gettin' the farm! I bet he saw this. He's always snoopin' around."

Betty read on. "Any surviving wives or children of my sons, natural or adopted, are not included in any distributions." She looked at Ann. "What an awful thing to do."

"Natural or adopted," Ann repeated. "Sounds like he wanted to cover all bases."

"Why on earth would Albert do such a thing to his own sons?" Betty asked.

Frank scowled. "Because Albert was never more than a heartless S.O.B. That's why everyone avoided him as much as possible. Clayton survived Korea but he couldn't escape the war with his own father." He reached for one of the letters.

"The writing in his letters is a lot different from his notebooks," Ann told him.

"Good," Frank said. "I can do without the five-dollar words." He took a letter from the pile and read aloud. "Germany, March 26, 1945. Dearest Ma. Greetings and a big hug to you. I hope everyone is well. Thanks for your swell letters and for the newspaper clippings. I enjoyed those. I'm glad you got the laying hens, and the coop Clayton built sounds real nice. We moved again since I wrote last. We are camped on a high hill. I can't say where, but it's a good place for tents."

Frank peered over his glasses at Ann. "Mail was censored, you know. See the inspector mark on the envelope? Same as when me and Clayton were in Korea. We weren't allowed to say exactly where we were. They told us to write cheery letters. Ha! Bombs goin' off all over the place, and we're supposed to be cheery!"

Betty patted his arm. "Read some more, Frankie."

Frank pushed his glasses up on his nose and read from the letter. "'Have you heard from Karl? We hoped to get together to see some sights before we come home. It's hard to believe I joined up in February of '42. It seems like a generation ago. I'm still only a private, but I hope you know I'm doing my best. I will have a lot to tell you and Clayton when I get home. Time to go back to work. Love, Emmett.'" Frank folded the letter and put it back in the envelope. "Wonder if he told them anything when he got home. He never wanted to talk to me about bein' over there."

"He talked about the Battle of the Bulge today," Ann said. "He said he thought he'd go crazy."

Frank was astonished. "He told you that?"

Ann shrugged. "I guess he felt like talking."

"He's taken a liking to you," Betty said approvingly. She elbowed Frank.

Frank took his glasses off and cleared his throat as if wanting to avoid giving bad news. "Here's the thing, Annie," he said. "We talked it over, and under the circumstances, we think you should be the one to handle Emmett's affairs."

Ann shook her head. "I already told you, Frank. You folks can handle it."

"Truth is, Annie, we'd rather not," Betty confessed.

"And from what you told us," Frank added, "you're the logical choice."

Ann tried not to sound impatient. "And again, I said I don't have any proof of anything yet."

"But we'd feel so much better if you did it," Betty told her.

Frank fixed himself another cracker. "You said power of attorney wasn't complicated. I told you we got a lawyer up here if you need one. Howie Studt."

"It's not that, Frank. No matter who handles his affairs, Emmett has to agree. And why should he agree to have me handle his affairs when he hasn't seen me since I was a child? He doesn't know me. And I don't care about his money—if he has any."

"He's got it all right," Frank said. "And he opened up to you. I bet he'd tell you what he's got."

Ann pretended she hadn't heard his suggestion. "Lily mentioned the same attorney, and I'm sure he'd be willing to help."

Betty sighed with relief. "Oh, thank you, dear!"

"I didn't say I would do it, Betty!" Ann said.

Frank went for his jacket, and then turned to look at Ann. "Think about it, Annie. It makes sense for you to step in after all these years."

As Betty prepared supper, Ann took a bath. Frank's logic made no sense at all. He wanted to know about Emmett's money for some reason, yet he wanted to unload Emmett's care onto her. Suddenly, staying with Betty and Frank felt uncomfortable, but she had no other place to go. Newland didn't have any motels and was miles from the nearest one. She'd have to put up with them until she got what she had come for—or gave up.

After dressing in her wool tweed skirt, a scoop-necked black angora sweater, and knee-high black leather boots, Ann added her pearl earrings and stood back from the mirror, smoothing her skirt. It would have to do.

John arrived promptly at six, wearing jeans, leather jacket, cowboy hat, and boots—no different from what he had on at the café. Ann felt overdressed.

"Thanks for helping out with the ol' boy," Frank said, shaking John's hand. "I appreciate you takin' Emmett's truck too."

"No problem. I'm sure I can find a home for it," John replied, his eyes on Ann.

During Betty's third compliment of Ann's outfit, Ann put her coat on and John followed her outside.

"We'll leave the door open!" Betty called after them. "Have a nice time!"

"You do look awful nice," John said as Ann stepped up into his truck.

"Thanks. It's all I had that didn't smell like Old Wood Smoke cologne."

John laughed and he closed the door after her. As she watched him walk around to the driver's side, Ann took a deep breath and blew it out. *What will we talk about? Certainly we have nothing in common.*

"You know, you're not the professor type," John told her after he climbed in the truck and turned the key. "You're more the Doris Day type."

"Pardon?"

"You remember her. She was cute and funny, and she had great platinum blond hair."

"Mine is old lady white, I'm afraid."

"Well, I like it. Shows you're not hidin' anything. It even matches mine." He laughed at himself as he turned out of the driveway and onto the road. "What do you teach down there in the big city anyway?"

"Communication courses. Usually public speaking, interpersonal behavior, communication theory, and family dynamics."

"Public speakin'. You mean like givin' speeches?"

"Yes."

"I gave a few speeches. You know, town meetin's and stuff. What are those other ones?"

Ann gave him her standard definitions. "Interpersonal behavior is about how people use language and gestures, how they argue or persuade each other, and behave in groups. Family dynamics deals with closer relationships. The theory course basically explains topics in communication research."

John stared ahead. "No offense, but I'm surprised people actually study that stuff."

Ann felt a bit defensive. "What do you mean?"

John glanced at her. "Like I said, no offense. Just seems to me gettin' along is mostly common sense."

"In what way?"

"Well, like right now. If I see you gettin' upset, it would be a good idea for me to back off a bit. It's like I tell my salesmen. If they come on too strong, they'll scare the customer off. But if they can sorta lead the customer to do most of the talkin', chances are they can get their foot in the door and make a deal. Common sense, isn't it?"

Ann couldn't resist a grin. "Seems you've got it figured out."

John squared his shoulders. "Well, you know what they say, it's all about mutual gain." He glanced her way and grinned again. "I went to a few sales seminars."

She thought of the professor of economics she went out with once. He spent the entire evening lecturing her about his theory of production and consumption of goods. Boring. But John didn't seem like the lecturing type. This could turn into an enjoyable evening after all.

"Yesterday at the Manor House," John said, "you said something about a research project. What are you researchin'?"

"Officially, I've got a semester off to research how family stories affect family relationships." Ann caught John's puzzled look. "I'm researching stories about my family."

"Good for you. Family stories are the best. My mom used to say her best story was me."

"What do you mean?"

"Mom couldn't have kids, so they adopted me."

"I'm adopted too." Ann stopped short, surprised at how easily she shared that.

"I knew we'd have somethin' in common," John said, flashing her a grin. "So which family you researchin'? Your adopted family or the other one?"

His directness caught her off guard. "Um, both, I guess," she said.

"Goin' back so you can move forward, huh? I heard that in a sermon once."

Ann focused on the road in the headlights and hoped John wouldn't ask questions she didn't want to answer.

"There's Giovanni's," John said, pointing to a neon glow in the distance. "Best Italian food in the county."

TWELVE

Frank Sinatra's voice crooned from overhead speakers as the hostess led them to a table with red place mats and a candle stuck in a Chianti bottle. John helped Ann with her coat then took his jacket and hat off. Ann liked his full head of thick, white, curly hair, and his Irish fisherman sweater fit him perfectly. A young man wearing a long white apron brought them menus and lit the candle.

"What'cha got for specials tonight, RJ?" John asked, ignoring his menu.

"Beef ravioli and spinach lasagna, sir."

"Ravioli. Those little pillow things?"

"Right."

"Good, I'll have that."

RJ smiled at Ann. "Evenin', ma'am," he said, pen and pad ready.

Ann quickly decided on the spinach lasagna special.

"Bring us your nice red wine too," John told RJ.

"You must come here a lot," Ann said after RJ left. "You didn't even need the menu."

John made a silly cross-eyed face. "Dyslexia. I hate menus."

"Must have been tough in school," she said politely.

"Yeah. I dropped out. Got my GED in the Navy, but I wasn't a very good student."

"Well, from the looks of it, you're doing something right. I was a little surprised to see such a big business in such a small town."

"We have customers from surrounding towns too," John replied. "And a lot of repeat customers. In fact, this is our twenty-fifth year. The girls in the office and some of the guys' wives are already plannin' our anniversary celebration. Should be fun."

Ann liked the tone of reply. *He sounds grateful for his employees,* she thought. *Not arrogant about his success.*

RJ came back with a bottle of wine, filled their glasses, and left again.

"To you," John said, raising his glass.

Ann held up her glass. "To you—for getting Emmett to the Manor House and for lending me the Blazer. Thank you very much."

Ann closed her eyes and took a sip of the sweet red wine. When she looked up, she found John holding his glass, watching her. He gave her a nod before taking a drink.

"Mmm. Good," he said. "My dad made wine when I was a kid. He worked at the grocery store, and they let him have the overripe fruit. What we didn't eat went into the wine crock. I was the official taster." John grinned at the memory. "Still got the old crock, but the wine's long gone."

RJ brought their salads and a basket of garlic bread.

After a few bites of her salad, Ann decided to ask. "I hope you don't mind, but I'm curious. What do you know about your birth parents?"

"Nothin'," John replied, unwrapping a pat of butter. "All I know is my real mother's name was Dorothy. Dorothy Brown."

"You know her name?"

"Prob'ly not her real name," John said, spreading the butter on his bread. "See, before I was born, my folks lived in Chicago. Dorothy had a room across the hall and they got to be friends. She told my mom she didn't know what to do when I came along because she didn't have a husband and her parents threw her out." John unwrapped another pat of butter. "Then one day my mom saw Dorothy walkin' down the street with me and a bundle of stuff. Mom got suspicious, so she followed Dorothy to a park. She said Dorothy kissed me and put me down on a bench with the other stuff and walked away."

Ann gasped.

"Yeah, the idea of bein' a helpless little baby all alone on a park bench still gets to me sometimes. They'd call it abandonment these days." He spread the butter around. "Luckily, Mom grabbed me off the bench and brought me and Dorothy back to the apartment. And a few days later, Dorothy Brown disappeared from my life."

"They were able to adopt you that fast?"

"Well, not in the strictest sense of the word." When Ann cocked her head in curiosity, John explained. "See, Mom was always a little chubby. She said no one would have noticed if she was pregnant or not."

"You mean they passed you off as their own without going through the adoption process?"

"Well, Dorothy was gone. If they went to the authorities, they mighta taken me away. So they kept quiet."

"Did you ever hear from her?" Ann asked.

"Don't think she wanted to be heard from."

"What about you? Did you ever want to contact her?

"Never had a reason to. My folks were poor, but they were good people and they were good parents. They even moved up here so I could have fresh air and sunshine. Mom kept chickens and a big garden, and she could make soup out of anything, so we were never really hungry." He imitated a woman's voice. "My mom used to say, 'Johnny, go out and get me a big fat hen.'" He laughed. "I guess I was eight when I chopped my first head off!"

They were laughing together when RJ brought their dinners. When they were alone again, John continued in a more somber voice.

"My mom was a gem, but she died from cancer when I was fifteen. That's when my dad started drinkin' and I got a little wild. Got some sense pounded into me in the Navy, and when

I came home I started sellin' cars. Found out life's easier with money, so I just kept workin' at it." He lifted a forkful of ravioli. "I talk too much. Tell me about your research. How's it going so far?"

Ann focused on dicing up her lasagna, thinking of what to say, mulling over Elise's comment about dredging up family dirt. "I guess it's complicated," she finally said.

"Yep. Most good stories are."

His kind face softened her resistance. After all, she didn't have to tell him everything. "I was born up here," she said.

He took the bottle of wine and refilled their glasses. "Great beginning! Then what happened?"

Ann felt him watching her nervously rearrange the lasagna on her plate.

"Come on, Annie. It's your turn. Let's see if you can top my park bench story."

She shook her head. "I don't think so."

He put his fork down and reached for the Parmesan cheese shaker. "It's all history, you know. Can't change what's already happened or what our parents did or didn't do. It is what it is."

She sighed deeply. "I don't want to bore you."

"You're not borin' me at all. But you hooked me, so you have to reel me in."

Ann considered what to say. She couldn't help liking him, and he seemed trustworthy enough. Then she thought of Betty, who may have already blabbed all over town by now about Emmett being her father. Ann took a sip of wine and gave a little shrug.

"My sister Elise and I were adopted when we were five and three. Whenever I asked about the adoption, Mom always told me to ask Dad, and Dad said not to talk about it. The only thing he told us was that we were born up here and our mother was Anna Miller from Austria. She went back to Austria for some reason, and she died over there. The whole topic was hush-

hush, so I grew up thinking adopted wasn't a good thing."

John nodded thoughtfully. "What could be so bad about adopting two little girls?"

"That's what I want to know. And even if Anna Miller was her real name, can you imagine trying to find the right Anna Miller here or in Austria?"

"Like trying to find the right Dorothy Brown, I suppose."

"Exactly."

"What was your real father's name?"

"Unknown," she said.

"Hey, we have the same father!" When Ann didn't smile at his little joke, John apologized.

"It doesn't matter," Ann replied.

"But it does. Otherwise why would you come up to little ol' Newland in the wintertime on bald tires?"

Ann had to admit John was right. She took another sip of wine, feeling its warmth all the way down as she tried to think of how to answer.

"I should mind my own business," John said, stabbing another chunk of ravioli. "But I know one thing. You can't put a puzzle together until you take the pieces out of the box."

Ann rested her fork on her plate. Maybe it was the wine, or the wonderful way his white hair contrasted with his dark eyes, or maybe it was his commonsense approach. Whatever it was, she felt herself relaxing.

"Okay," she said. "Puzzle this out. Remember I told Lily about my dad and Emmett being cousins?"

"Right."

"Well, their grandmother, Nana, lived at Emmett's after the war, and Anna Miller supposedly helped Nana with housekeeping. But, as I figure it, she was pregnant with me when she left Austria."

"So your father's back in Austria someplace?"

"Possibly. Except that Emmett was also stationed in Austria."

John stared at her, a piece of ravioli dangling from his fork.

Ann gave him a slow nod, sighed, and sat back. "After Dad died, I found a letter from Emmett in the garden shed—as if my dad had hidden it out there. Emmett wrote about a picture he sent for my sister and me and said he'd like to see us again. Again. Well, I connected that letter with a picture I took from my Granny Elizabeth's old photo album showing Emmett in an Army uniform sitting under a tree all snuggly with a woman. You can't see her face, but you can see curly hair just like my sister's." Ann took another sip of wine. "I guess you can see where this is going."

"Yeah, quite a story. If Emmett's your father, it makes sense why your mother came over. Huh. I didn't know Emmett was married."

"Everyone in the family says he never married. Neither did his brother Clayton."

John finished her thought. "And we all know bein' married has nothing to do with havin' kids."

"Bingo. And Emmett's cousin—my dad—adopted us. Another mystery." Ann took long drink of ice water and silently reminded herself to go easy on the wine. She looked at him and lowered her voice. "I probably shouldn't have told you any of this."

"Don't worry about me, darlin'," he said. "I'm a secret keeper from way back." He winked at her as he loaded his fork. "And I wouldn't want to scare you off."

Ann stared at him; worried she'd said too much to a man she didn't even know.

John leaned forward. "Hey, I mean it. I deal with people's secrets all day long. Customer credit ratings, employee personal problems. You can trust me. 'Sides, why would I want to tell anyone your personal business?"

For some reason she couldn't explain, Ann did trust him. When he smiled at her, she smiled back. "Okay. Thank you."

"It's a good puzzle," John said. "Maybe there was an agreement to keep you girls in the family. Maybe they knew you woulda froze your little pigtails off if you stayed at Emmett's. And I'm sure you were a cutie too."

Ann chuckled. "How did you know I had pigtails?"

"You seem like the pigtail type." He poured more wine into each glass. "So why didn't you come up here before now?"

"Life got in the way, I guess—marriage, full-time job, kids."

"And?"

"And I was a good girl. I had his address on a little slip of paper in my drawer and every year I made a resolution to write to him, but I never did. I knew the adoption thing was a touchy subject with my parents, and as much as I wanted to know, I just couldn't go behind their backs. Then this year Dad died, my mom was diagnosed with dementia, I got my sabbatical, and I finally gave myself permission to come up here. I decided I wanted to know once and for all—even though my sister said I'm selfish and disrespectful." She took a sip of wine. "So here I am—selfish and disrespectful. And now that I've met Emmett, I'm a little nervous too."

"I don't believe you're selfish or disrespectful. What are you nervous about?"

"The truth, I guess." Ann dabbed her mouth with her napkin. "Mind if I ask your opinion on something?"

"Shoot."

"Betty and Frank want me to be Emmett's power of attorney."

"I'm POA for a few folks up here. Nothin' to it."

"I know, but I don't want people thinking I came up here to take over."

"Well, for one thing, since you're adopted, you're legal family. And it might help you get closer to the truth."

"I know."

"So, if your intentions are honorable, who cares what

people think? It's family business and it's plain to see Emmett needs help. Bein' his POA would be an advantage in the long run." John took his wallet out of his back pocket and then put a business card on the table in front of her.

"You're the third one to recommend Howard Studt," Ann said after reading the card.

John collected the remains of his salad on his fork. "He's my brother-in-law."

"Your brother-in-law?"

"Well, he was. My wife—Howie's sister—she died. Anyway, me and Howie have been friends since grade school. You'd like him."

Ann stared at the card, saying nothing.

"Problem?" John asked.

"I don't know. Ever since I can remember, Emmett was the family joke. The old hermit with no indoor plumbing, no phone, no appliances, no furnace. And now that I met him, I can add no teeth, shabby clothes, and mouse crap on his bread. It's embarrassing."

"Howie don't care about any of that. 'Sides, bein' poor's nothin' to be ashamed of. I survived."

"I'm sorry, John. I didn't mean that like it sounded."

John mopped his plate clean with a crust of bread. "No harm done. Just call Howie."

"I found notebooks."

"Notebooks?"

Ann took one of Emmett's notebooks out of her coat pocket and held it up as if it were a trophy. "He mentions Austria in one of these."

"Ah-ha!" John said. "The plot thickens. How 'bout a sample?"

Ann flipped the notebook open to a random page, angling it toward the light of the candle so she could read.

Even now, after all this horror, we will endure because of the love we share. In the end, only love matters, only love lives on. Love shall be our strength.

"Ol' Emmett wrote that, huh?" John said. "I'm impressed."

"Wow," Ann said. "I can't believe I picked this page. Did you notice how he says 'we' and 'our'?"

"We who?"

Ann put the notebook back in her pocket. "My question exactly. I think I have a right to pick his memory a bit. Don't you?"

John grimaced a bit. "I don't know, Annie. Callin' up old memories can be painful for some people, 'specially old folks."

"But I only want the parts about me."

"And those parts would include him and your mother, wouldn't they?" John gave a shrug. "Then again, since you prob'ly saved him from freezin' to death, I guess he owes you."

"You're the one who saved him from freezing. I just went along for the ride."

"I sure wouldn't want my daughter knowin' everything I done."

"Do you have a daughter?"

"No, but I used to wish I had kids. Too late now." He put his glass down. "You have kids?"

"Yes, two." Ann smiled. "Along with two grandsons and a granddaughter on the way."

"Wow. You don't look like a granny."

"I'll take that as a compliment," Ann teased.

John smiled at her. "Which is how I meant it." He threw back the last of his wine, laid his fork and knife across his plate, and winced as he shifted in his seat. "Did you have enough to eat?"

"Yes. It was wonderful, thank you."

"Good, because I have a suggestion. You're real easy to talk to, but this seat's hard on my old bones. Got thrown off a horse and broke my pelvis a few years ago. Sometimes it bothers. How 'bout we go to my place and talk? It's not far and I'd like to hear you read more, if you don't mind."

Guess I should have expected this, Ann thought.

John held up his right hand. "I promise—no funny business. I'll even introduce you to my new pup."

Ann hesitated. He seemed sincere, and he did promise there'd be no funny business. "What kind of pup?"

"Cute little chocolate Lab."

Ann looked at her watch. "I told Betty I'd be back by ten," she said, lying through her teeth.

John smiled again. "Whatever it takes, ma'am."

THIRTEEN

Over the next twenty minutes of dark country roads, Ann let John entertain her with more stories of his childhood while she silently questioned her agreement to join him at his house. She was about to suggest he take her back to Betty's when he turned down a wide driveway. All she could see in the headlights were thick trees and a rail fence running along both sides of John's truck.

Where the trees ended, the driveway expanded into a huge circle between a log house and a barn that didn't quite look like a barn. Soft light from inside the house spilled out onto a large wraparound porch. John parked under the barn's overhead light and walked around the truck to let Ann out.

"Home sweet home," he said. "Let's go get the baby."

Ann followed him to the barn, where she got a whiff of hay, leather, and a hint of brown sugar. When John flipped a light switch, she saw a clean, spacious interior.

"This is nothing like Frank's barn," she said. "Smells better too."

"I always liked carriage barns, but I like the old-fashioned gambrel too. So I combined those styles when I built this one."

"Oh," Ann said, not having a clue what a carriage barn or a gambrel looked like.

John led her past halters and bridles hanging neatly above three saddles on racks to a row of large stalls, where a whining noise was coming from. He slid the door to one stall open and a wiggling brown pup shot out, dancing around John's boots in unfettered glee.

"Annie, meet Little Miss Chip, the chocolate Lab."

Ann knelt to pet the rambunctious puppy and noticed another animal slowly emerging from between bales of hay, yellow eyes flashing. A one-eared, flat-faced, honey-colored cat came forward, holding its bent tail erect. Chip ran playfully toward it but at the last minute the cat flattened itself on the floor, causing the puppy to somersault clumsily. John scooped the puppy up before she could launch another attack.

"You're no match for ol' Rutabaga, Chip," he said, roughing the pup's floppy ear.

Ann watched the cat limp back to the hay bales. "Chocolate Chip I get," she said. "But Rutabaga?"

"Ha! Yeah, well, an ugly cat needs an ugly name."

"Poor thing."

"He was pretty chewed up when he wandered in here, but now he's got his own little kingdom. Even makes himself useful. The mice see his face and have little heart attacks right on the spot."

Ann chuckled at the thought of mice clutching their little chests and heaving over. "Emmett said you had horses," she said. "I saw pictures of them in your office."

"Those are pictures from my horse breedin' days. The horses I got now are just for pleasure. Hay burnin' lawn ornaments you could say. They're outside."

"Isn't it too cold?"

"They're outside animals. Fresh air's good for 'em. They got a wind shelter and automatic water. I bring 'em in when the weather gets bad. Come on. I'll show you."

Still holding Chip in one arm, John put his other arm around Ann's shoulders and guided her back outside, then directed her to follow the fence and look for a white rump.

"I can't see them," she said. "It's too dark."

"Guess you'll have to come back in the daytime." John pecked her on the cheek, causing Ann to step back in surprise. "Sorry," he said, taking his arm off her. "Couldn't help it."

"Okay," Ann said shyly.

John led her to the rustic front door of his house. It was trimmed in nickel-size metal studs and looked heavy, but when John pressed the latch, it swung open easily.

"You don't lock your house either?" she asked.

"Don't need to out here."

He put Chip down and she ran inside, barely gaining traction on the polished wood floor that gleamed beneath a beautiful stained glass ceiling fixture. Ann took Emmett's notebooks from her coat before John hung it on a wooden peg. While she removed her boots, he worked his off as well.

"Guess our moms had the same rule," he said.

The foyer divided the kitchen from the living room, but Ann's attention was drawn to the open stairway straight ahead and its bannister of gnarled and polished wood. A patchwork quilt hung on the wall where the stairs turned and disappeared. Soft jazz drifted overhead. She was glad it wasn't country, her least favorite. Trying not to gawk, she followed John to the kitchen, where knotty cabinets with leaded glass inserts faced an antique dining set nestled in a semicircle of windows. The tile countertops were bare except for a coffeemaker, a bowl of apples, and a napkin holder.

John pointed toward the far side of the kitchen. "I got two bathrooms down there in the guest rooms and one upstairs in the loft in case you need one." He opened the refrigerator. "Can I get you anything? Wine? Apple juice? I don't have beer or soda, but I make a mean cup of cowboy coffee."

"No, thanks, I'm okay." From what Ann could see, there wasn't much of anything in his refrigerator.

John gestured toward the living room. "We can sit over there by the light."

A floor lamp was just bright enough for Ann to make out the furnishings in the living room. A large Navajo print rug and coffee table filled the space between a dark leather couch and two matching chairs. On one wall hung a painting of Indians on horseback looking out over a valley. Below it stood a pair of cowboy boots full of dry flowers, and an antique crock, perhaps his dad's old wine crock. Embers glowed in a fireplace made of stones that reached all the way to the cathedral ceiling, which was framed in a box work of beams. Betty's mismatched furniture and scratched tabletops crowded with family photos were humble in comparison to John's polished floors and artwork—a kind of cowboy nobility, if there was such a thing.

Chip settled under the coffee table with a chew toy as John coaxed the embers back to flames and added another log. Ann sat on the couch.

It's all so perfect, she thought, *like a picture in a magazine. And what about the soft music and romantic fire? Had he planned on company tonight?*

John came to the couch and turned the light up a notch. "I got carried away when I built this place," he said. "It's too much house for one old guy. That's why I leave the lights and music on. Otherwise I feel like I'm comin' home to a big empty cave."

He sat down and casually positioned one arm along the back of the couch behind her shoulders. Ann was surprised only by the fact she didn't mind at all.

"Okay," he said. "Let's see what else the ol' boy has to say."

Ann selected a notebook and began reading.

> *Boarded ship August 26 and sailed for France August 27, Sunday, 1944. Flying fish and gulls. Seasickness. Ate standing up on the slippery stairway. Holds crowded with tiers of canvas cots 3, 4, 5 high. Many other ships with thousands of men on board. Landed on the beach September 8.*

"Does he say where?" John asked.

Ann turned the page. "Yes, here."

Impressions of Normandy. Walked up the long steel causeway leading to the beach where the invasion had been in full force ninety days previous. Installations still planted on the gray sand. The country seems lush and green after nearly two weeks on the water. Hiked over muddy roads with a monstrous pack, rifle, and overcoat to a temporary bivouac, and then more hiking. Showers every half hour. Small towns are all somewhat war torn but almost intact compared to Montbourg, which is almost a total ruin. Most people are friendly. Some women wear wooden shoes that clatter on the pavement. Nearly all the men wear Tam o'shanters.

"Tam o'shanters?" John asked.
"Like a beret, I think."

October 7, 1944. The roaring planes and exploding shells are with us all day and night. We live in dugouts like animals, barricaded with sandbags, earth, mud, logs, brush, whatever we can find as protection from fragments. Modern warfare is upon us with a force I could have never imagined.

December 1944. Somewhere in France. Screaming meemies, six-barreled guns, the terrible antitank 88s, and 120 mortars pass by constantly. Early this morning a German tank made a direct hit on a squadron. Many injured screamed for help but we couldn't get to them. A German soldier fell into our foxhole. The smell of his burning body will haunt my memory forever. Shall I be killed in the field or die of fear? I pray for courage to face this ungodly nightmare, but I fear God is not listening.

Ann closed her eyes. "My God."

"I wonder if he was at the Battle of the Bulge," John said. "My uncle was there. He told me it was a frozen hell."

"Emmett was there. He said he thought he'd go crazy. Now I know why." She turned the page. "There's no date on this one."

> *In the midst of this filth and hopelessness, somehow I must try to maintain my human dignity. I must keep my body strong and my mind clear. I am still young. I want a life as smooth as a gliding Strauss waltz. I will not have peace unless I can find the strength to forget this carnage and move on. I must discard it, for neither this place nor time is mine. I have plans. A better life is waiting for me.*

"At least he looked forward to the future," Ann added.

"Maybe writing took his mind off the war," John suggested. "You know, like using positive self talk to get motivated."

"And deal with what he was going through." She continued reading.

> *December 11, 1944. Metz, France. A break from battle. We are lodged in a vacant hotel with the constant roar of hundreds of planes. This uncertainty is nerve-wracking. The big local church nearby has been freed of mines and booby traps so people come to pray at all hours. I, too, pray for deliverance from this horror. I pray for the man with no feet and the crazy woman who pulled her hair out and the children with lifeless eyes. Sometimes I fear this hell will never end. I have seen too many people die, too many bodies frozen in grotesque shapes, beyond help but at least free of this earthly horror. I am cold and tired and so afraid. There are suicides all the time. Civilians and soldiers too. But I can't. I must survive. I must survive, and then I must forget.*

Ann fanned the pages of the notebook and shook her head. "When I talked to him, Emmett seemed angry that Clayton took his life, but here it sounds like he considered suicide himself. Can you imagine?"

"Unfortunately, I can," John replied solemnly.

Without another word John went to the foyer, little Chip loping after him. Ann couldn't see the front door from where she was sitting, but she could hear John open it and gently urge the puppy out. A few minutes later, she heard the door open again and John calling Chip in. When he came back to the living room, Ann sensed something was wrong.

FOURTEEN

"I suppose Betty told you about my wife," John said as he sat down.

"No," Ann lied, not wanting to admit Betty told her his wife had died—and not sure she wanted to hear more.

He leaned forward, elbows resting on knees, hands dangling. Chip came over and John gently scratched the pup's ears as he talked. "We dated in high school. I was head over heels about her. When I joined the Navy, she said she'd wait, but then she wrote and said she married another guy. Huh. I wanted to jump overboard. Joyce was the love of my life." He turned slightly toward Ann. "Still I kept hopin' we'd be together someday."

John sighed and went to the fireplace.

"When I got back from the Navy, most of my friends were married or gettin' married. I tried to date but no other girl seemed right." He poked at the logs. "Everyone knew Joyce's marriage wasn't workin' out, and sometimes she called me when she was at a bar and needed a ride home. I didn't mind except I hated seein' her like that." He moved the logs around, sending sparks up the chimney. "One night, she drove off the road. She didn't get hurt too bad, but the car was wrecked. I was sellin' cars so I found her another one easy enough. Then her husband suspected somethin' goin' on between us. When he started hittin' her, she left him."

John came back to the couch, sat back, and crossed one ankle over the other knee, the toe of his sock hanging loose.

"We got married as soon as we could after her divorce," he said. "She told me she couldn't have kids, so I figured we could adopt. I'm adopted. Why not? Well, she started cryin' and goin' on and on about how she couldn't take care of kids." He threw his hands up. "So I said, okay, no kids. She had nervous days sometimes, so I always treaded lightly." He paused briefly. "Later I found out she was gettin' pain pills from two doctors. She said she had back pain from the accident, but she was takin' pills for depression too." He inhaled deeply and breathed out the words. "You know what they say, hope dies last."

Ann started to tell him he didn't have to go on. The truth was she had heard enough, but he kept talking.

"One day I came home for lunch and found her passed out on the bed. I got her to the hospital as fast as I could but it was too late. She went into a coma and all they could do was put her on life support." He stopped for a moment and cleared his throat. "I promised her I'd never leave her. I told her there'd never be anyone else. I promised her anything if she'd just open her eyes. A week later, they said she was brain dead, and I should give my permission to pull the plug."

"Oh, John."

He glanced at Ann briefly. "I had her for six years and five months. Guess I went a little crazy after she died. Drank too much, drove like a maniac, spent too much time alone. Even broke my pelvis 'cause I forced my horse to jump a fence and I got thrown. Stupid. Howie put me straight. He said I was barn blind. You know, seein' only what I wanted to see when it came to Joyce. He was right, and if it wasn't for him, well, it was a long time ago. I guess talkin' about suicide stirred it all up again."

"I'm sorry I mentioned it."

"Not your fault. Funny, though. Bad stuff happens when we're kids, and we bounce back and forget most of it. But when you're an adult, the bad stuff sticks forever."

A log burned through and dropped into the ashes, startling Chip to her feet. John leaned over and lowered his hand to the floor, enticing Chip to come over for a reassuring ear scratch.

"I only dated a few ladies since Joyce," he said. "Nothin' serious. Usually they wore too much perfume or sparkled too much or needed too much attention."

Ann thought back to yesterday when she'd met John in the café. She'd been wearing jeans and a sweater and her pearl button earrings. She didn't use much makeup and didn't care for hairspray or perfume. It was another thing she liked about John. No smelly cologne—no artificial anything that she could detect so far. Had she really met him only yesterday?

John sat back again and took Ann's hand. "Now you— you're different."

"Yeah, I'm a plain Jane," Ann said, hoping he wouldn't detect her rapid pulse.

"You are just fine. So, here's the big question. Are you seein' anyone? 'Cause I know I'd like spendin' more time with you."

Ann felt suddenly cautious. "I won't be here very long, John."

"Hey, I promise! No buttin' in your business with Emmett. No more sob stories either and when you get tired of me, no hard feelin's."

A parental voice in her head said *no, you've had your share of dating disasters.* Then a calmer voice reassured her. *Don't be afraid, he's okay.* That was the voice she was listening to when he kissed her.

It was a good kiss. More of a you-are-special-and-I'm-attracted-to-you kiss than a let's-go-to-bed-now kiss. When he slowly backed away again, her body moved toward him as if pulled by a magnetic force. She straightened up quickly, feeling her cheeks blush.

"Don't worry," he said, tightening his hand over hers. "I admit I feel guilty because I couldn't help Joyce. But I'm okay. Just a regular guy."

Ann shifted her position, ready to lighten the conversation. "Regular guy, huh?" she said. "So explain how horses and cowboy boots with flowers in them fit with selling cars and Chicago jazz?"

John laughed. "It all started with Hopalong Cassidy and Roy Rogers."

"And Cisco and Pancho?"

"Yeah," he said, pleased at her recollection. "Except my first horse was a really big dog some neighbor gave us. His name was Ol' Blue because he had one blue eye and one brown eye. My mom got me some used cowboy boots and a cap gun from somewhere, and my dad found me a hat and made me a holster out of an old belt." John laughed at his story. "I made a pretty sorry-lookin' cowboy, but Ol' Blue and me had fun chasin' bad guys all day long. As for the car business—ha! I was damn sure I wasn't cut out to be a farmer."

Ann loved the way he laughed at himself, knew himself, and shared himself so openly. "And the jazz?" she asked.

"My dad always listened to jazz on the radio." He nodded toward the boots with flowers. "The flowers are for my mom. Anything else you want to know?"

"I don't think so."

"Good. Let's read some more."

He kissed her hand, released it, and propped his feet on the coffee table. Ann smiled. No one had ever kissed her hand. She went back to the notebook.

> *December 27, 1944. Received two letters from home today. Ma's letter said Billy Sands is somewhere in England and Claude Morgan is here in France. My writing feels erratic and my mind disconnected. All I can think of is going home.*

"No date on this one," Ann said.

> *Got a letter from Fred in the field hospital. Shrapnel got him in the groin the day we shared a foxhole. I was lucky to get a face full of dirt and ringing in my ears. After*

*a few short months, I can call myself a war-weary GI,
lucky to be alive. Wrote Ma. Censorship has loosened, but
I won't write about the horror and demoralization here.
Some things can't be written. I have no idea how long I
will be here. I must not be pessimistic.*

*We are living in a large civilian home near the
Moldau River. Another case of the Army taking over
some of the best civilian homes for troop quarters. People
here seem to take our intrusion as a matter of course,
and the ones temporarily evicted from their homes show
little resentment. One of the boys traded cigarettes for a
phonograph and records. The Strauss waltzes thrill me as
always. I hope long bitter battles will soon disappear from
my memory. Perhaps we have emerged from the Valley of
the Shadow into sanity and more peaceful ways.*

"Hey, when's your birthday?" John asked.

"What?"

He nudged her. "Come on. Frank already told me you're
fifty-three."

"Guess I'll have to talk to Frank. When is your birthday?"

"May 20th, 1944."

"Okay, mine is July 15th, 1946. Why?"

"Because that means your mother got pregnant in the fall
of 1945. Why not read stuff from around that time first?"

"Good idea," she said, reaching for a different notebook. "I
think 1945 is mentioned in this one."

When she sat back, John whispered in her ear, "Your hair
smells great, by the way."

"Thank you," Ann said softly. "Now listen."

*March 10, 1945. Germany. In convoy riding to
the front generally southeast through a deep forest of
evergreens and picture book scenery. I try to listen for*

birds, but they are outdone by the drone of planes and regular rumblings and blasts of artillery. Some people from the village ran toward the woods as we passed. I will never forget how four of our men beat an SS man almost to death, or the woman kneeling and crying over a child's body in the muddy street.

April 8, 1945. Suhl, Germany. There seems to be an abundance of food here. We see liberated French and Polish soldiers, and hundreds of laborers of a dozen nationalities but not the long lines of refugees we saw elsewhere. One little boy asked for chocolate but I had none.

Ann turned the page. "'July 19, 1945. A day in Czechoslovakia.' Wait," she said, skimming ahead several pages. "I thought this notebook was the one that mentioned Austria. He's skipping around."

"Maybe he grabbed whatever notebook was handy." John yawned. "Don't matter. Keep goin'."

From a vantage point by a wide-open window on the second floor of a Gasthaus here, I have an excellent view of the north end of town. Like an extended reel of a movie life goes on in this old world setting. The day is warm and clear and a brisk wind blows steadily, rustling the leaves of huge hardwoods outside the window. Even the observance of the Sabbath is not allowed to interfere with civilians harvesting the vital hay crop. Down the long tree-lined avenue comes load after load of the sweet-smelling hay. Wagons are drawn by a yoke of oxen that lumber along heavily as a driver uses a stick to keep them moving. Children ride on top of some of the hay wagons, laughing and enjoying their lofty perch.

August 1945. The prospect of months of occupation duty in Austria is not at all unpleasant. Despite our relative youth, I think we all feel ourselves to be old soldiers these days, close-knit in bonds of common experiences. Not brothers of kin but brothers of survival. We wear our Yankee Division patches and combat infantry badges with genuine pride, but talk always turns to home. Ma's letters take me back where I want to be. The USO helps.

September 15, 1945. Linz, Austria. One of the most memorable nights of my life was last night. Anna invited me to attend a little party to celebrate her birthday.

Ann paused. "Did you hear that? It says Anna. It's her birthday!" She repeated the date and continued.

She shares an apartment with two other young women. They had all decorated the main room with wildflowers. Anna said she baked the apple strudel just for me, and Fritz brought a huge bottle of a kind of thick wine made from apples. It proved to be quite sour but tasty. As we emptied the contents of the bottle, the party became less formal and a more noisy. Johann and Fritz had brought their guitar and violin, and I found out later it was all set up to find out if I could dance. Anna insisted and I could see no way out. Much to my surprise I was not a complete failure. The evening passed too quickly with more wine and singing. Anna and Gertrude sang "One Glass of Wine" in German and almost brought tears to my eyes. Gertrude and Fritz invited Anna and me to come with them on a day trip to the mountains. I know it would be wonderful, but I doubt if I will be able to go.

"I don't believe this," Ann said as she turned the page.

October 7, 1945. Vilseck, Germany. Perhaps it is the height of folly to make elaborate plans for the future, but at the same time it is well to have some concrete ideas. Based on the theory that we all live only once, I would like to do these things: Go to the Univ. of Wisconsin under the G.I. Bill of Rights to study agriculture. Study German and some journalism. Find a job and earn as much as possible for my ultimate ambition to return to Austria to study further, perhaps farm and write, and, of course, return to the love of my life.

"Wait. He goes from occupation duty to my mother's birthday party in Austria to Germany, and then back to the love of his life?" Ann flipped pages back and forth. "What happened in between?" She paused and listened to John's deep, steady breathing. His arm drooped heavily on her shoulders. "John?"

He gave her a little one-arm squeeze. "Sorry, honey. I guess I'm more tired than I thought. What time is it?"

Ann checked her watch. "Nine thirty. Why don't you take me back to Betty's?"

"How about I take you back at ten? I'm listenin'."

"Oh, yeah? Where was I?"

"UFO show."

Ann chuckled and turned another page. It was not dated and no location was noted.

We walked to the church just as the bell rang for nine p.m. With news of the end of war, the bell seemed to toll for peace. Nights of gladness, days of love, my soul revels in the image of her . . .

"Her what?" Ann turned the notebook closer to the light. "It's no use; he erased the last few lines." She turned the page.

We took a walk to the river just outside of town and found a place in the woods with more privacy. We climbed down the slope to the river. It was too cold and running too fast for a dip. But we took our shoes off and walked hand in hand along the bank toward the mill.

"Now we're gettin' somewhere," John said.

"But that's it, and again, no date, no names. Wait! Look at this! It's marked 'draft.'"

Dearest Darling, How can I explain my negligence! I have no reasonable excuse for my tardiness at writing except I am a sad sack! Truly I should have written days ago. I am not going to offer any weak-kneed excuses. Castigate me, my dear. Castigate me sorely before I err so again. I shall think of—

Ann scowled. "Castigate me! Geez, Emmett! The rest is erased. I wish this was in chronological order."

John whispered in her ear, "That's one thing I like about teachers. They make you do it over and over again until you get it right."

His whispering gave her goose bumps and his joke made her giggle. When he kissed her ear, Ann knew she was weakening. "Maybe you should take me home," she suggested.

"Your home's too far away."

When John leaned over to kiss her on the mouth, Ann was ready.

FIFTEEN

At five o'clock the next morning, Ann woke with John on her mind. He'd dropped her off at eleven thirty after what he called "some good old-fashioned neckin' on the couch." It was innocent enough, but John had to know she found him attractive. She wondered how many women he'd dated since his wife's death. He seemed generally content and confident, but was he a psychological wreck on the inside? He said he promised Joyce he'd never love anyone else, but was that a convenient excuse to play the field and avoid commitment? Then again, how could he love anyone else after pulling the plug on his beloved brain-dead wife? Ann was wondering whether she'd let her guard down too soon with John when she heard the kitchen door open and close.

Turning the quilt aside, she went to the window and looked down to see Frank walking across the driveway in the glow of the barn's overhead light. A cat marched regally ahead of him, ignoring playful swipes of Mitch's forepaw. Their daily routine had begun. She propped the pillows against the headboard, pulled the chain to the nightstand lamp, and settled back with a few of Emmett's letters.

December 27, 1944.
Somewhere in France
Dear Ma,
I hope this finds you fine and dandy. Just today I got your Christmas card. Thanks a heap. I get regular mail from Aunt Lizzie and Gracie too. I am always tickled to hear things are running smoothly at home.
All is well here and I am fine. I'm sure you know we

have tangled with the Heinies already. Where and how of course is not to be divulged. Rest assured, I am hale and hearty and right as rain.

Have you received any of the allotment checks yet? You should get $45 each month from now on. Use it. Don't save it for me, Ma. I don't need much money over here.

It's hard to believe it's been nearly three years since I left home. I am sorry I haven't written much lately. I shall try to improve. I think of you every day. I must close now but send loads of love.

Emmett

P.S. Inga wrote and said she heard Karl plans to get married as soon as he gets home. Did you hear that?

So there was Emmett, Ann thought, possibly fresh from battle but still hale and hearty, right as rain, sending money home, and grateful for regular mail from home. Some letters offered detailed descriptions of scenery. In others, he promised to keep safe and urged his mother not to worry—as if he was on vacation instead of slogging along some foreign muddy road with a rifle on his back. No mention of Anna and the postscript didn't make sense.

Ann couldn't remember when her dad got home after the war, but Karl and Ruth didn't get married until February in 1948. Emmett was simply wrong. The floor creaked outside her door, followed by each step's moaning as Betty descended to the kitchen. Ann scanned a few more letters, but when she heard dishes clattering she got dressed and went downstairs.

"Morning, Annie!" Betty said from the stove. "So? Did John take you to Giovanni's?"

"Yes," Ann replied on her way to the bathroom. "And you were right. He's a very nice man."

As she washed up, Ann heard a loud vehicle pass the bathroom window. Moments later it roared past again. When she got back to the kitchen, Frank was sitting at the table.

"Now Gordy's sayin' you took stuff from Emmett's house," he told Ann.

"Well, he's right. I took notebooks and letters and Albert's will. But how does he know?"

Frank waved his fork over his plate. "Don't matter. Don't put any stock in what he says either. I told him to stay clear of Emmett's or else."

The wall phone rang and Betty hurried to it. "No, no, dear," she said into the receiver. "Not too early at all. Yes, she's right here." She stretched the cord toward Ann. "It's your sister."

Elise didn't waste any time on pleasantries. "I'm glad you gave me this number because I couldn't get through on your cell. No need to worry anymore, but I just wanted to tell you Mom had some kind of stroke."

"Oh, my God!"

"She's okay now; the nurse is checking her blood pressure. I'm out in the hall."

"What happened?"

"She called 9-1-1 about one thirty this morning because she couldn't move her legs. At least she remembered Neal's number, and he got there in time to let the EMTs in."

"Was it definitely a stroke?"

"The doctor called it a peripheral vascular something."

"I'll come home right away."

"You might as well stay there. The worst is over."

Ann detected indignation in Elise's voice.

"Of course Karen and Neal couldn't take off work," Elise continued. "And you're there, so I didn't have any choice but to close the shop and come over here."

Right. I'm here and you're there, Ann thought. *That's why you're angry.* "Aren't they going to keep her for a few days?" she asked.

"I guess I'll find out when the doctor shows up," Elise said sharply. "And I thought you said you didn't tell Mom you were going up north."

"I didn't. Why?"

"Neal said that just before they took her to the hospital, she said you were asking questions about the adoption."

"I haven't said anything to Mom about the adoption for years; you know that."

"Actually I don't know that. I only know what you tell me."

The accusation in Elise's voice rang clear. Ann stepped around the corner into the hall, stretching the phone's cord after her, away from Betty and Frank's inquisitive ears. "Are you suggesting Mom had this stroke because of me?" Ann asked as quietly as she could. "Or are you telling me I lied to you?"

"All I'm saying is you went up north and Mom had a stroke. She's never had a stroke."

"Mom's seventy-five, Elise," Ann said calmly. "She's got diabetes, dementia, high blood pressure, and clogged arteries, and—"

Elise interrupted. "Which is why she doesn't need any more worry while you're off doing your own thing."

Ann leaned against the wall, tears coming to her eyes. "Can I talk to her?"

"The doctor's coming. I should go."

"Wait! Is she at St. Luke's?"

"Of course. I have to go. I'll talk to you later."

The line went dead. Ann sniffled and closed her eyes. Betty's mop and bucket in the corner smelled like pine cleaner, and Frank's barn jacket smelled a lot worse in the close confines of the hallway. She heard a chair scrape across the floor and Frank say something about his tractor. Ann brought the receiver back to the kitchen.

"Mom had some kind of stroke. My sister says she's okay. I suppose they'll run some tests before they send her home."

"I'm sure she'll be okay, dear," Betty replied. "They do all sorts of magic these days."

"Yep. It's rough to see our parents get old," Frank added.

Betty gave a light chuckle. "We're the old ones now, Frankie."

After breakfast Ann drove to the Manor House. She'd simply say goodbye to Emmett, then go back to Betty's for her things, and head home. She thought of her dad during his last days in the hospital. He made them all promise never to take Ruth to a nursing home, looking Ann in the eye until she promised out loud. She was the oldest, he said. It was up to her. But Karl couldn't have predicted how Ruth's increasing forgetfulness, mood swings, confusion, and occasional bursts of anger would make being with her so difficult. The diabetes would be bad enough without the dementia, Ruth's doctor had said. Ann knew it was time to talk to her brother and sisters again about the promise they'd all made.

When she saw the outline of the iron bridge ahead, she realized she'd absentmindedly headed for Emmett's instead of the Manor House. Not wanting to navigate a Y-turn on the narrow road, she drove on and turned down Emmett's driveway, knowing she'd have more room to turn around behind the house.

She slowly circled the span of gravel between his house and barn, taking in the panoramic view of the only home Emmett had ever known. Sure, the house was run-down, but the whole place was definitely peaceful in a melancholy sort of way. Suddenly, a rabbit hopped out from under the porch. Ann hit the brake and the animal hopped under the Blazer. Not wanting to run over the stupid little creature, Ann shifted into park, got out, and kneeled on the gravel to peer underneath. The rabbit was crouched against a tire, wisely frozen in place. She slapped the ground to get the animal moving but it wouldn't budge. Then Ann heard heard a loud muffler roaring up the driveway.

She had just enough time to stand up and clamber onto Emmett's porch before Gordy's truck reeled around the house. He slammed on the brakes, causing the snow blade mounted on front of his truck to rock awkwardly. He looked satisfied to have separated an obviously startled Ann from the Blazer.

"You got no business here!" he yelled out the truck window. "I know yer stealin' Emmett's stuff!"

"I'm not stealing his stuff!"

"You think you know everything! Well, I know about you and your sister."

"What do you know?"

"Ha!" he sneered. "Just because you sucked up to Bennett to get yerself a new car don't mean you can sucker everyone else! This place is gonna be mine when Emmett's gone! I'm the one been lookin' after him! Not yer fat-ass Betty!"

From her vantage point on the porch, Ann could see a crowbar, a rope, and a chainsaw in the bed of his truck. *A coincidence,* she thought. *I hope.*

Gordy jabbed a finger at her. "I know we ain't cousins neither! Yer adopted. Yer nobody!"

The Blazer's engine was still running and Ann took a step forward as if to make a run for it. That's when Gordy let the truck inch forward, looking viciously pleased when he heard the snow blade scrape the bottom step. Ann glued herself against Emmett's door. When Gordy's plow blade broke the flimsy railing, he swore and yanked the truck into reverse. The railing collapsed completely as he backed up.

"He don't have nothin' for you!" Gordy yelled. "You hear me? Nothin'!"

Ann shouted back, "I'm not stealing anything!"

"Yer lyin'!"

She took her cell phone out of her pocket, hoping Gordy didn't know she couldn't get a signal this far out.

"I'm calling Frank," Ann shouted over the noisy muffler.

"I think he'd like to know you're here." Gordy frowned as she pressed keys on her phone and acted through her little ruse. "Hello, Frank? I'm at Emmett's. Gordy's here and he said I'm taking things. Yes. Okay. Good." She held the phone away from her ear. "Frank said he's calling the police if you don't leave right now."

"Ha! Yer bluffin'! We ain't got no police around here!"

"I meant the sheriff. He's calling the sheriff."

Gordy glared at her. Ann stared back. She was afraid. Wasn't there an old movie about a one-armed guy who killed a woman? Maybe she could call his bluff. She mustered her courage and held the phone out. "You want to talk to him?"

"Bitch!" he barked. He yanked the truck into gear and hit the gas, sending gravel spitting from under his tires. "Bitch!" he shouted once more as he peeled down the driveway.

Ann ran to the Blazer, scrambled inside, slammed the door and locked it, finally scaring the rabbit out from underneath. Her heart pounded all the way to the Manor House, where her fear turned to anger at the sight of Gordy's truck parked in the lot.

She slapped the steering wheel in frustration as she drove past and circled back to Betty's. *Fine*, she grumbled to herself. *You just have your little adolescent hissy fit, Gordy-with-the-withered-hand. You're not getting in my way.*

SIXTEEN

Frank was coming from the barn when Ann got back. He waited for her at the porch steps, and Ann tried not to act as angry as she felt.

"Darn thing leaks," he said, holding up his thermos. "Lost most of my coffee on the barn floor. What's the matter? Was he crabby today?"

"I didn't see Emmett because I ran into Gordy. Or rather, he almost ran into me."

As they took off their boots in the hall, Ann told him what happened.

"He's a bully, Annie. Always was." Frank hung up his jacket and puffed himself up. "Kid needs a kick in the pants."

"Are you sure he's related to us?" Ann asked sarcastically.

"Who?" Betty called from the kitchen.

Frank explained, and while Betty apologized to Ann for Gordy's behavior, the phone rang.

"Sure, she's right here," Betty said to the caller. With raised eyebrows, she handed the phone to Ann and whispered, "It's Howie Studt."

"Hello, this is Ann Olson."

Frank and Betty took their usual places at the kitchen table, watching Ann expectantly.

"Hello," a deep voice said. "Howard Studt here. Is it Ann or Annie?"

"Anna, but you can call me Ann."

"Fine, you can call me Howie. Lily Brentson at the Manor House told me you'd be willing to serve as power of attorney for Emmett Pederson." He seemed hurried. "I have a simple POA draft I could show you. I understand you're his cousin?"

Ann sat at the table. "He's my dad's cousin." She shot a look at Frank and Betty. "In fact, we were just talking about power of attorney for Emmett."

Frank and Betty both looked down at the table.

"Good, good," Howie said. "Would nine tomorrow morning in my office be convenient?"

"Not really. My mom's in the hospital, and I need to get back to Milwaukee. Can we talk about it when I get back?"

"Have you checked the weather? We're supposed to get snow later. Not much maybe, but they're saying the roads will get slippery from here to Madison. You might want to wait a day."

Ann went to the window. Sure enough, flakes were already coming down.

"Supposed to be all clear in the morning," Howie said. "We could do the paperwork before you leave."

Ann talked over the receiver to relay the invitation to Frank and Betty. Betty nodded, but Frank didn't move. Ann confirmed and hung up.

Betty said, "I'm so glad you said yes."

"The meeting is for all of us," Ann told her.

"I thought you knew where we stood on this, Annie," Frank said.

"I wish you'd reconsider, Frank. If you're power of attorney, Gordy might get off my back and respect you a little more, too."

Frank crossed his arms, closed his eyes, and shook his head. "I'm not gettin' involved. Emmett burned the last bridge between us."

Betty went to the stove. "I'm sorry, Annie," she said, adjusting the flame under a pot. "Frank and I can't do this."

Ann felt herself getting impatient. "It's not difficult, Betty. All you have to do is make sure his bills are paid, or talk to the Manor House or a doctor now and then." She turned to Frank.

"It's really not a problem."

Frank rested his arms on the table. "Remember I told you about Emmett burnin' Clayton's casket flag?"

"Yes."

"Well, I didn't tell you everything."

"Frankie, don't," Betty said.

But Frank went on. "When Emmett found Clayton hangin' in the barn, he went for the sheriff. The sheriff and a deputy came out with the coroner. They took Clayton away a' course. But they took Emmett in for questionin' because Clayton had cuts on his face and arms, and Emmett's face was scraped up too."

"So they had a fight," Ann said.

"They never charged Emmett with anything," Betty said, "because they realized there was no way he could have gotten Clayton up there. He was a hefty man."

Ann didn't want to think about Emmett putting a noose around anyone's neck.

Frank spoke again, his face now quite flushed. "Clayton was ten years younger than Emmett. Strong as a bull, too, but he drank. He drank to forget Korea and their sorry-ass father and any other demon he had rattlin' around in his head. Him and Emmett argued a lot." His eyes narrowed. "Nothin' against you, Annie, but you gotta know Emmett and me have our differences, and I don't feel I owe him anything. He can get his own attorney. He can afford it."

"Excuse me, Frank, because I don't mean to seem ungrateful or anything. But why do you think Emmett has money?"

Betty shot Frank a glance. Frank curled his lip and studied Ann's face.

"I've been truthful with you folks," Ann added. "Is there something else I should know?"

Now Betty sat back as if Frank needed more room to explain, as if she knew what he was going to say.

"Me and Clayton had a deal," Frank began. "When Clayton got money from his uncle, we planned to be partners."

"Partners?"

"Yeah. At the time, our neighbor over here to the south was sellin' out, and Clayton wanted me to go in on the land with him so we could expand this place as partners. He wanted to get away from Emmett."

"It was a bad idea from the beginning," Betty told Ann.

Frank glared at her. "How do you know? It coulda worked out just fine!"

Betty's composure told Ann she'd been through this argument a hundred times.

"Clayton and me wrote up a deal," Frank told Ann. "We signed it. He agreed to invest five thousand dollars, and I was gonna put in the same."

"With what money, Frank?" Betty asked firmly.

"From the stupid insurance policy you insisted on gettin'. The only ones that ever benefit from those things are the insurance companies!"

"Insurance is for a rainy day, Frank!" Betty's face was getting red now. "Who do you think paid for your gallbladder operation?"

Frank slapped the table. "If we had more land, we coulda borrowed against it like everyone else does and had plenty for a new gallbladder and a new barn! And today we'd be doin' a damn sight better than we are!" He looked at Ann. "You wanna see the papers we signed?"

"No, Frank," Ann said calmly. "I believe you. But Clayton's gone now. I don't see how Emmett's responsible for a deal you made with Clayton."

"You don't know how we do things here," Frank said with a slight smirk. "Clayton signed money over to me. Emmett owes me that money."

Ann didn't know what to say. Frank's argument was full of

holes. She glanced toward the window. Snow was falling faster now and the furnace kicked in, breaking the silence in the room. Frank stood up.

"It's a fact. Clayton and me made a deal."

"Maybe you did," Ann told him. "But unless you have some legal document—even though I don't know what kind it would be—Emmett is Clayton's legal heir."

Frank threw up his hands and went to the hallway. "Put some coffee in my thermos, will ya, Bett? I'm going out to the barn."

"You said it leaks."

"Put it in one of those big mugs then!"

Angrily he pulled his boots on, grabbed the mug Betty offered, and swung out the door carrying his jacket.

Betty cleared her throat and closed the door. "I'm sorry, Annie. Frankie and Clayton were close. Frank always said Emmett worked Clayton too hard."

"Maybe Emmett thought work would help Clayton get over his demons," Ann said. "He seemed quite sad when he told me about Clayton's death."

Betty looked over her glasses at Ann. "Guilt has many faces."

"What do you mean?"

"I'm not saying Emmett caused Clayton's death, but I know Emmett had no patience for drunkenness. And Frank's right. Clayton and him did have a deal." She took a package of macaroni out of the cupboard. "I hope you don't mind chili for supper again. I promise I won't overdo the spices this time."

Ann sighed. "Sure," she said. Her mind felt heavy. *How many secrets does Emmett have?*

Since the snow had changed Ann's mind about going back home that afternoon, Betty recruited her to help bake for the church's Christmas cookie exchange. Soon Betty's continuous chatter and their combined fussing over pecan fingers, shortbread, date pinwheels, and chocolate drops took Ann's mind off both Gordy and Frank. But the cookies did make her think of her mom. While Betty put her baking supplies away in order to start supper, Ann went upstairs and dialed Ruth's hospital room.

"Hi, Mom! It's Ann. How are you feeling?"

"Oh, I'm fine. Everyone's been so nice."

Ann smiled; Ruth sounded well. "I'm glad, Mom. I was worried about you."

"I told you I'm fine. Wait a minute. Karen wants to say hello."

"Hi, Annie!" Karen said brightly.

"Hi. Aren't you usually at work at this time?"

"I only worked half a day because I was going to take Mom to her doctor appointment this afternoon. We don't have to do that now because he saw her today. They just released her."

"How is she?"

"Okay, I guess." Karen lowered her voice. "Annie, when will you be back? We need to get together and talk." Then a louder, "No. Mom! Wait! Wait for me!"

Ann pressed the receiver to her ear. "Karen?"

Karen spoke faster. "The doctor said if she doesn't get her blood sugar under control, the next stroke would be worse. One of her toes is infected because she cut her toenails again too. They gave her some antibiotics." It sounded as if Karen was talking and running at the same time. "Don't worry. Take your time coming home. Mom's fine and I took tomorrow off. I have to go, Annie. She's going down the hall."

"I'll be there tomorrow," Ann managed to say before they hung up.

Ann felt a catch in her throat. After diabetes struck Ruth at age seventy, the family scrambled to learn about the disease and help Ruth understand diet restrictions, neuropathy, and why she shouldn't cut her own toenails. But it was no use. At least she wasn't on insulin yet.

When Frank came in for supper, he seemed calmer. "I didn't mean to go off on you, Annie," he said as they sat at the table. "It's not your fault."

"It's okay, Frank. I think we can still be friends." She gave him a wink.

Frank nodded in return. "Snow let up," he said, settling over his bowl of chili. "They got a lot more down in Mauston, so it's good you waited. Supposed to be clear tomorrow. I called Emmett's neighbor to plow over there. Gordy don't do it unless Emmett's around."

"Gordy never showed up today, did he?" Betty asked him.

"Naw. He's prob'ly in town drinkin' beer and talkin' smart. I had just about enough of his whinin'. The one-armed whelp."

"Frank!" Betty scolded. "For heaven's sake."

"What? He scared the crap out of Annie! Just because he's crippled don't give him the right to be a jackass."

Betty waved her hand as if to clear the air, but Ann was pleased to think Frank was on her side again.

"By the way, Annie," Frank said. "Next time you're at Emmett's, you might wanna check upstairs."

"Why? What's up there?"

"A bedroom. I figured you might want to check it out before the place gets snowed in."

Ann nodded. Of course, Frank was right. How could she have forgotten her first bedroom?

By nine o'clock, Ann was upstairs with a cup of tea and a few of Betty's cookies. She got in bed, pulled the quilt up to her chest, and took the extension phone from the nightstand. She didn't want to tell either of her kids about Gordy, but she felt they should know about Ruth. During the separate calls,

Lisa and Mark both assured Ann that Ruth would be okay. Ann expected nothing less—she had thoughtful kids. As she hung up from the second call, she noticed John's card on the nightstand and realized she didn't know if her car was fixed. She hated to bother him at home, but he did say she could call anytime. She dialed his home number.

"Hi, it's Ann.," she said when John picked up.

"Oh, hi. Thanks for calling me back."

He sounded distracted, or at least not very friendly.

"I'm sorry," Ann said. "I didn't know you called."

"I left a message with Betty earlier."

Too businesslike, Ann thought.

"My mechanic thinks your transmission's goin' out," John told her. "Course he never saw a Saab before. But if he's right I'd say that between the tranny and the bald tires, it's a good thing your guardian angel pays attention.

He's irritated about something, Ann thought. "I need to go home," she said.

"When?"

"Tomorrow. My mom had a stroke."

"She okay?" he asked, sounding more obligated to be polite than genuinely concerned.

"Yes, as far as I know, but I want to make sure. It's a good time to go home anyway. I need to get ready for Christmas. But I need a car."

"Take the Blazer. You're comin' back after Christmas, right?"

"Yes."

"Okay, drive it until then. If you decide you don't want it, we'll work somethin' out."

"Thanks, John. I really appreciate your help."

Ann expected more words of comfort about her mom, but he didn't offer them. Instead, he said, "No problem," and hung up without saying goodbye, leaving Ann with the dial tone.

Maybe he had a bad day, Ann thought as she put the receiver back.

Or pressed the OFF button by mistake or lost his signal.

She listened to Frank's snoring, ready to grab the phone if John called back. When he didn't, she almost dialed him again then stopped, hearing the tone in his voice again, wondering if she had offended him somehow. No. She knew she didn't. She lay back and stared at the ceiling, feeling tired, wishing she had a glass of wine, wondering if John was prone to moodiness. Maybe he was too good to be true after all.

SEVENTEEN

By 8:55 the next morning, Ann was parked on Main Street, staring at gold lettering on the front door of an old mansion: Howard A. Studt, Attorney at Law. She went in and introduced herself to the woman behind the desk. Tall windows, lace curtains, wall sconces, potted ferns, and upholstered furniture echoed the charm of old parlors in years past—or at least the way she imagined them.

"Nice to meet you," the woman said. "I'm Howie's wife, Margie. He'll be right with you. Are you enjoying your visit so far?"

"Pardon?"

"John said you were here visiting. John Bennett? He referred you. He's Howie's best friend. He said to treat you special. Of course we treat everyone special. Especially John."

Margie probably knows about the dinner date too, Ann thought as she nodded politely. *Nothing like small-town gossip.*

An older couple came out of a hallway to the reception area, followed by a stocky man in a suit and tie. "Stop by if you want more copies," he said as they left.

"Howie, this is Annie," Margie said, sounding like a proud parent.

"Ah, yes," he said approvingly. "Good to meet you." He gestured toward the hallway. "My office is this way."

Ann guessed Howie's office must have been a dining room at one time since a built-in buffet cabinet served as a bookcase.

"Will Frank and Betty be coming?" Howie asked as he offered her a chair across from his desk.

Ann sat down. "No, they changed their minds at the last minute."

He sat back, pursed his lips, and nodded slowly.

"You're not surprised?" Ann asked.

"No. Lots of folks aren't comfortable with lawyers even when they need serious legal support. And I'm more than a little familiar with Emmett, the contrarian. Are you willing to act as POA on your own?"

"I think so, but what do you mean you're familiar with Emmett, the contrarian?"

Howie pointed to a portrait on the wall. "My dad handled the probate settlement for Emmett after Clayton died." He lowered his voice. "It's a small town; everyone knows about Emmett burning Clayton's coffin flag and getting arrested after Clayton died."

Ann shifted uncomfortably in her chair. *Maybe everyone knows Emmett,* she thought. *But what do they really know about Emmett?*

"My dad knew Emmett ever since grade school," Howie continued. "In fact, when I saw him in town a few weeks ago, he talked to me as if I was my dad. Considering Emmett's general bouts of confusion, I'd say time is of the essence, as they say."

"I know. He's old and frail, and I don't see how he can go home again." Ann hesitated a moment and then asked, "What would you recommend? I mean if he were, you know, your father."

Howie put a sheet of paper on the desk so she could follow along as he pointed out power of attorney, guardianship, and other options. "Given his age, I suggest the durable power of attorney encompassing financial and medical authority. I assume he has some savings or else he wouldn't be at the Manor House. Ultimately, of course, his property will have to be liquidated, and you'd want control of everything. Until he dies. Then his will takes over."

"He has a will?"

"Hmm. Good question." He went to the door and called Margie, who came immediately. "Do we have a will for Emmett Pederson?"

"I don't remember seeing one," Margie said. "Unless it's in the boxes we haven't sorted out yet."

"Thanks, honey." Howie closed the door again. "I have to apologize, Ann. I'm still going through Dad's old files." He sat down with an overweight sigh. "In the meantime, I'll check with the courthouse. If there's a will, we'll find it. Of course, you don't need a will to do the POA."

And without a POA, Emmett's left to do as he pleases whether it's good for him or not."

"Correct. I'm sure social services knows about him." He made finger quotes. "He's a vulnerable adult." He handed her two papers stapled together. "This is a simple, generic POA form. All you do is fill in the particulars, but it must be signed and witnessed before you can move any of his money around or sell any property for him and so on."

"What if he objects?"

"Usually after I explain how their assets are safe with a POA, folks go along with it." He opened his day planner. "Do you have a cell phone? I have an appointment at the Manor House later today. I could stop and talk to Emmett and call you later."

"I'd appreciate that."

Howie looked at her, pen in hand. "One thing I've learned about Emmett over the years is that he's a lot more cooperative if you treat him like the intelligent man he is and not like the illiterate old coot everyone thinks he is."

Ann smiled and nodded. "Yes, I agree." She gave him her cell and home numbers. "And if I change my mind later? Or if Frank and Betty change their minds?"

"I'll draft a new document."

"I have a feeling they won't change their minds."

"Me too," he said. "Do you have any questions?"

"One more question. Do you know anything about an agreement between Emmett's brother Clayton and Frank Johnson? Frank said he and Clayton agreed to a land purchase together. Frank told me they signed papers and he's entitled to some money."

Howie made finger quotes again. "People sign papers to sell vehicles or land all the time, and then when their friendly handshake deal goes south, they realize they don't have a leg to stand on. I never heard of any deal with Clayton and Frank, not that they didn't have some sort of deal. However, as the one and only legal heir, Emmett wound up with what was left of Clayton's estate, including any money that may have been supposedly promised toward a venture with Frank."

"Did you know Clayton?"

"Everyone knew Clayton. Well, I should say, everyone knew of Clayton."

"What was he like?"

"He drank and he gambled. Threw his life away if you ask me. I never saw two brothers so different." Howie twirled his pen around between his fingers. "Emmett saved Clayton's life once."

"He did?"

"Well, twice actually. Once when Clayton fell through the ice on Shepherd's Lake. And the second time when Clayton gassed himself in his camper trailer." Ann raised her eyebrows as Howie continued. "The only reason I know is because I had just gotten my driver's license, and I drove my mom out to Emmett's place because she baked a pie for his birthday. When we got there, we saw Emmett pulling Clayton out of the trailer. My mom told me to go to the neighbor's and call the doctor, but Emmett told me not to because Clayton was okay. Afterwards, my mom told me Clayton was drunk and didn't know the gas was on, but that night I heard my dad say Clayton knew exactly what he was doing."

"Maybe Clayton needed some psychiatric counseling," Ann said.

"Probably." Howie stood up as if to signal the end of their visit. "I suppose some people need that from time to time." He paused and rearranged a few folders on his desk. "But back then we only had one overworked family doctor up here—not like all the specialists you have down in the city. Even today with the clinic, people go to friends or family when they're troubled about something. And no one wants to talk about suicide, so if that's on your mind, you're pretty much on your own."

Ann left Howie's office thinking about the privileges power of attorney afforded her. She didn't want to take advantage of Emmett. She told herself she was helping him even though it was mostly for her own reasons.

As she drove past Maplewood Motors, she wondered if John was in a better mood than yesterday. Maybe it was a good idea to limit their relationship to strictly business. *After all,* Ann thought, *he obviously still has strong feelings for his deceased wife, and I didn't come up north for romance.*

Turning off Newland's Main Street, Ann found herself pleasantly distracted by the lovely scenes all around her on the narrow county road. With no other cars around, she slowed down and allowed herself to appreciate how the sun danced on trickles of melted snow running across the asphalt. Old barns, silos, and farmhouses she'd passed yesterday now looked like charming cutouts dusted in sparkling sugar. Even the old iron bridge looked strong and new against the clear blue winter sky. When she got to the middle of it, she stopped for a moment, and looked down at the frozen creek. In summers long past, it had been deep enough for boys like her dad and Emmett to drop in from branches of overhanging trees. But those days were gone and so was her dad. Only Emmett, her father, was left to answer her questions.

Once at Emmett's, she felt oddly energized. She stood

behind the house, looking out over the fields, breathing in the cold air, and congratulating herself. She'd found her father and, as a dutiful daughter, she would be his power of attorney. And today, his old house was going to give up some of its secrets. She could feel it.

EIGHTEEN

Ann checked Emmett's thermometer. Twenty-eight degrees—the same as the temperature outside. This time she just grinned and pulled her hat over her ears. Emmett was warm and safe now. She stepped into his living room and stared at the glass knob of the door behind the chrome dining set for a moment before shoving the table aside. When she pulled the door over the rags stuffed under it, a wave of cold air hit her. She stood there a moment, staring up the steep, bare staircase, and then took one squeaky step at a time until she came to another door at the top.

Pushing that door open sent a swirl of dust up to a beam of sunlight coming through one of the cracked windows. Old furniture crowded one corner of the room, perhaps strategically placed out of the sun's damaging rays—a dresser with curved drawers, a large steamer trunk with a domed lid, a treadle sewing machine, a brass headboard with painted porcelain knobs, a miniature table, a child's chair. Three tall, cut glass hurricane lamps, their wicks long dried out, stood regally along the back edge of the dresser. A large porcelain bowl held a matching pitcher. Despite their dusty coats, Depression glass bowls, plates, and vases in red, pink, green, yellow, and cobalt blue, many with with ruffled edges and etched designs, covered the rest of the dresser top.

As Ann stood back to take in the whole scene, she nudged a rocker and set it in motion. Had her mother rocked her to sleep in this chair? What words of comfort had her mother whispered? Why couldn't she see her mother's face? She ran a gloved hand over the top of the small table, remembering a little tea set and a doll in a blue spotted dress. If it was possible to feel affection for a room, she felt it now, along with a tinge of apprehension.

"The hell with Gordy," she said aloud. "This table and chair are mine, and I'm taking them."

She put the table by the door and turned her attention to two cardboard boxes with "DISHES" penciled on the flaps. The first was full of wads of brown paper protecting gorgeous cups, saucers, plates, and bowls, all edged in delicately painted rosebuds. The second box held matching serving bowls and platters, and tarnished but lovely silverware wrapped in soft cloths. It was all too fine for a poor farmer.

Ann repacked the boxes and turned to the trunk. About three feet wide and two feet high, it was trimmed with wood slats and leather handles and looked like something out of an old movie. She knelt before it, took the rusty nail out of the latch, and raised the lid. Wrapped in more brown paper was a white linen tablecloth and napkins, hand-embroidered with pink roses, each piece neatly folded as if waiting for a party. Next was a small calendar from 1946, the year she was born. Her birth date in July was marked with a heart.

Under a small blanket—pink on one side and blue on the other with white rabbits woven into the fabric—she found children's clothes. One T-shirt with a cowboy and pony had obviously been worn a lot. Did it really look familiar, or did she just want it to? Next she lifted out two identical dresses in different sizes with hand-stitched buttonholes and embroidered flowers on the collars, a sun hat, and a pair of children's red leather shoes with teardrop designs cut through the tops. Finally, two hand-knit scarves, one red with "AM" embroidered at one end, the other blue with "EM." She smoothed them across her lap—one for Annie Miller and one for Elise Miller.

Eagerly, she reached for the boxes on the bottom of the trunk. The shoebox contained dark blue pumps about her size. They were brand new, but Ann guessed the style to be 1940s. A flat white box held a full-length white satin slip and a pair of stockings with seams. Inside the largest box was a neatly folded dark blue skirt and matching jacket. Ann held the jacket up and admired the buttons studded in blue stones. The jacket had no label. A closer look at the buttonholes convinced her the suit was handmade. She sat back on her heels, fingering a button with one hand and the satin slip with the other. These things had to be her mother's.

A cold dampness settled on Ann's neck as she folded the suit back into its box. Suddenly she felt strange, unable to take a breath. A clammy feeling crept over her and her throat seemed to be closing up. She felt an urgent need to get outside to the fresh air. Half-stumbling down the stairs, she went out to the back porch and leaned against the house, feeling dizzy, perspiring and shivering at the same time. The pressure she felt in her chest scared her. Conscious of her rapid heart rate, Ann pulled the collar of her jacket open and tried to breathe deeply as her legs went numb.

I can't have a heart attack now. Please don't let me have a heart attack.

Then Ann felt arms around her, raising her up, supporting her. She barely felt her feet on the ground as John all but carried her across the driveway and lifted her into his truck.

"Are you dizzy?" he asked as he got behind the wheel.

Ann put her head in her hands. "Yeah," she panted. "What are you doing here?"

"I saw you go down Main Street and figured you came out here. I wanted to see you before you went home. Just be still and breathe, okay? Should I call 9-1-1?"

"No." Ann put her head back and took a deep breath. "I don't know what happened. My whole body wanted to collapse. I felt like I wasn't getting any oxygen. It was scary."

"You coulda froze out here."

"I coulda froze *in* there," Ann joked weakly.

"Do you feel any pressure in your chest?"

Ann took a deep breath. "I did, but it's better now. I don't know what a heart attack feels like."

"Anything else? Cold sweats, heart palpitations, shortness of breath, dizziness?"

"Yes. Yes, everything."

"Panic attack," John said with certainty.

"Panic attack?"

"Joyce used to get 'em. What were you doin' when it happened?"

"There's all this old stuff." Ann's voice faltered. She fanned her face with her hand and took another deep breath. "I'm sorry," she squeaked through tears. "I found clothes that must have been my mother's. And little girl dresses—mine and my sister's."

"Okay. Calm down. Let's get some soup and warm you up."

Ann nodded and tightened her coat around her. While John drove, he listened without comment as Ann's words tripped over each other in her excitement.

"From the pictures I've seen, Aunt Lena would have never fit into the suit, and between cooking on a woodstove and hauling water to do the wash, I can't imagine her having time to embroider napkins. Someone was saving those things for an occasion that never came. And I have a feeling Emmett knows who. After he admits he's my father, I'm going to demand to know why he didn't marry my mother and why he gave us up."

When they reached Melody's Café, John parked the truck and faced her. "Better now?"

"Yes. I'm sorry I rattled on and on."

She expected a hug, but he didn't even give her a smile. He got out of the truck and walked slightly ahead of her until he got to the door of the café. He held it open for her but looked away. Ann felt uneasy.

"What soup you got today, Lenore?" John asked when the waitress brought menus.

Without taking her eyes off Ann, Lenore replied, "Chili and tomato bisque."

"Two tomato with grilled cheese sandwiches and hot tea."
He looked at Ann. "Okay?"

Ann nodded, noticing how Lenore gave her one more odd
look before leaving.

"I must look like a wreck," Ann said.

"You're salvageable," John replied, unwrapping his
silverware.

Ann excused herself and headed for the ladies room, where
the mirror told her she did look a bit rough. She cleaned the
mascara smudged across her eyes and fluffed and finger combed
her hair. She took the lipstick she always kept in her jeans pocket
and applied some to her lips, then dotted her cheeks with it and
rubbed it in. After several deep breaths, she came back to the
booth and wrapped both hands around the mug of tea Lenore
had left.

"Feel better?" John asked.

Something's wrong, Ann thought. *He looks too serious.* "Yes,
thanks to you again," she said. "I admit I dreamed of this day.
But now after meeting Emmett, I feel rushed, as if I don't have
much time left."

"Yeah. My mom used to say that was a sign to start livin'
faster," he said solemnly.

After Lenore delivered their lunch, John put a chunk of
sandwich in his soup and sloshed it around with his spoon.
Despite his interest after rescuing her at Emmett's, he now
seemed withdrawn. Ann figured she'd spooked him with
her panic attack or whatever it was. She tried to engage him,
proving she was back to normal, but he offered little in return.
He looked tired and preoccupied. Ann decided to stop talking
and just finish her lunch.

When they left the café, John held his hat in place against
the wind but didn't offer her his arm. Ann closed her collar and
followed him. Suddenly, he turned around and pulled her into
the recessed entrance of a vacant store, grabbed her and kissed

her long and hard on the mouth.

"I love you, Annie," he said, his eyes tearing up. "I love you and I have to tell you something."

His grip on her upper arms was strong. "I think you just did," she said.

"I mean about Joyce. About me."

"You don't have to tell me anymore about that. I understand you still love her."

"She was in a coma, but I promised. I promised her I'd never love anyone else. I told God I didn't want anyone else. Now, I'm havin' a hard time. With you and me, I mean."

"We didn't do anything wrong. Just a few innocent kisses. And as soon as I get some information from Emmett, I'll be gone."

"Don't you see?" he said tenderly. "I don't want you to go."

"You know I need to go home," Ann said in her most practical voice. "I have a job and a house and a family in Milwaukee, and you have your home and your business here."

She looked at his face. She loved his rugged good looks and his cowboy hat. His helpful nature and his thoughtfulness. His humor and grammatical errors. He felt trustworthy and real. Everything about him felt so good—except this volcano of guilt or regret or whatever was erupting right now. She didn't want to find fault with him, but his fingers were digging into her arms.

"Could you let go, please? Your grip is pretty strong," Ann said as calmly as she could.

John released her and sighed, lowering his head until the brim of his hat touched her forehead. "I'm sorry," he whispered, rubbing her arms.

A gust of wind stirred a little pile of dry leaves at their feet as if to finally sweep away autumn debris and heavy thoughts.

"John. No hard feelings, remember? No hard feelings. We agreed."

"Yeah. Okay."

No, it's not okay, she wanted to say. *I love you too. I want to hold you. I want you to forget Joyce and love me.*

John looked toward the street and wiped his gloved hand across his face. "Yeah," he said. "Yeah, okay. I'm sorry." He patted her arms. "I hope I didn't hurt you. I'd never want to hurt you."

The drive back to Emmett's was quiet. Ann knew she'd fallen for John more completely than she could have ever imagined. She chewed on her lip and stared at the road ahead, almost feeling Joyce sitting between them. It was one thing to compete with a real live woman, but competing with a ghost was impossible.

Behind Emmett's house, John parked alongside the Blazer and reached for her hand. "Are you okay? I mean, you feel okay about bein' back here?"

Ann swung her door open and got out. "I'm fine," she said politely.

He followed her to the porch.

"You don't have to come inside, John. I only want to get a few things."

"I want to help you."

Ann shrugged in agreement and led him to the upstairs bedroom.

"Birdseye maple," John said of the old dresser. He opened the top drawer and lifted out a tin box. "Did you see this?"

Faded blue flowers twined around "Greetings to Mother" printed on the hinged lid with "Assorted Deluxe Chocolates" in smaller script. Inside was a folded paper that said "Happy Mother's Day from your Annie and Elise." Emmett had formed each letter perfectly.

Ann unfolded the paper and stared at a child's crayon drawing. A line of solid green ran along the bottom edge, and a ball of yellow filled one corner. Four figures stood side by side, each with a hollow circle for a head, two vertical lines for legs, and two horizontal lines for arms. Each head had two scribbles for eyes and a big crooked smile. The letters A-N-I-E in blue ran awkwardly along one edge of the paper.

Ann sniffed back tears. "See? This is what I mean."

John put his hand on her shoulder. "You okay?"

"My kids used to draw like this. Now my grandsons do."

He smiled tenderly. "Guess they take after you. Take it home and show them."

"I wish I could take all of it."

"I think you should take what's yours."

They took the small table, the rose bud linens, and clothing out to the Blazer. After he closed the hatch, John stepped closer to Ann. When she didn't move away, he wrapped his arms around her, rocking her slightly.

"I didn't mean to sound like I was brushin' you off on the phone last night." He kissed her lightly on the forehead and stepped back. "You are a special lady, Annie. I don't want to offend you or hurt you. And I hope you don't think I'm weird for still having feelings for my wife."

His wife, Ann thought. *Of course. In his mind, she's still his wife, and she might as well still be here. And what exactly does he mean by special lady?*

"I guess you have the right to love your deceased wife. I mean—I'm sorry, John. I shouldn't have put it that way."

"You're right. She is deceased."

"And I can't take her place," Ann said gently. "It doesn't work that way."

John looked at his boots. Ann wasn't sure what to say next. A chill swept over her—not from the cold but from the longing in her heart. She'd never rejected anyone as graciously as John was rejecting her right now. She started to reach for his sleeve but withdrew her hand and quickly dug in her pocket for her keys. She felt she should say something kind. Then again, she knew what it felt like to be pitied, and he probably had had his share of pity since his wife died. She needed to go now, to let him go.

"You're special, too, John. You really are," she said, twirling her key ring around her finger. "And I, ah, just remembered. Lily told me Emmett's clothes are all way too big. I'm sorry, but I really should go. I need to get him some clothes someplace so I can get back to Milwaukee before dark."

John opened the driver's door and Ann slid behind the wheel. "There's a Shopko at the end of town."

Ann turned the key. "Lily said he won't wear new clothes."

"Try the Salvation Army behind the grocery store on Main."

He closed the door, cutting off Ann's last words of thanks. She followed John's truck to town and tried not to think of spending the day with him, cuddled up in front of his fireplace— or in his bed. She told herself it was good he couldn't see her through the Blazer's tinted windows, couldn't read her mind. But another voice inside said, *No, it doesn't matter if he can read your mind. This is a man you can let in.*

NINETEEN

Ann checked out of the Salvation Army store with three pairs of gently worn pants, five flannel shirts, and John still on her mind. She couldn't help imagining a routine with him. She'd see him off to work in the morning, and in the evening they'd make love on the living room floor. *Stop it,* she told herself. *You're menopausal, you've never made love on the floor, and he's still in love with Joyce. End of story.*

At the Manor House, Ann gave the clothes to the front desk attendant and walked to the common room, where she stopped at the archway. A few residents were playing cards, others were watching an old movie on television, and a few were with visitors. Emmett was alone in the far corner, propped back in a recliner with a small blanket over his legs.

Ann wanted to appear glad to see him, but her mind was on the clothes and other things she'd found in his house. What else did he have stashed away in his old memories, and how much would he share? She imagined asking him the questions she needed to ask and falling apart in front of him. He might get angry or upset. They'd ask her to leave and take him to his room. She felt a headache coming. When Emmett looked in her direction, she willed herself toward him.

"Hi there, Emmett. How are you?"

"Oh, I can't complain." He chuckled lightly. "I suppose I'm old."

Ann slipped out of her coat and sat down. "I came to tell you I'm going back to Milwaukee tomorrow."

Emmett looked surprised. "You are?"

"I'm going home for Christmas."

"Yes, yes, of course. You'll want to be with your family."

The veins on the backs of his hands ran like blue cords under his frayed cuffs. He was so thin.

He yawned. "If my memory serves, you teach college, don't you?"

"Yes, that's right," Ann replied, as if he'd never asked her before.

Emmett nodded thoughtfully. "Education is so important. No one can take it away from you. Of course poor farm boys like me didn't get much schooling. But I was always a reader. People can learn quite a bit from reading. We didn't have a choice in the Army though," he added. "They didn't expect us to study. They just expected us to learn fast and not ask any questions. Karl did whatever the brass said. He made motor sergeant because he was good at taking orders. I had a hard time with being told what to do. I guess I was a rebel."

Ann noticed how Emmett remembered her dad's Army rank but not that she taught college. Perhaps Howie was right—the power of attorney designation would be just in time. Fortunately, it was the long-term memories she wanted.

"Rebel or not, Emmett, you seem like a pleasant person," she said kindly. "Gracie sure likes you. And I bet lots of other girls were fond of you over the years."

"Oh, I don't think so," he said shyly. "I never had much to offer."

"You had a farm," Ann replied. She wanted to sound interested in him, in his life, even though images of his upstairs bedroom now distracted her. "Farming is a wonderful livelihood, isn't it? Good clean living."

"But it's a hard life for a woman." He yawned again and brushed imaginary dirt off the blanket. "Karl had all the advantages. He lived in the city with all the modern conveniences. He had an education and a regular paying job. He was even a good dancer."

Ann thought she detected a bit of resentment or envy. Emmett rubbed his eyes as a young aide approached them.

"Hi," she said to Ann. "I'm Gail. He usually takes a nap about now."

More aides were escorting other residents from the common room. Ann checked her watch and promised herself not to visit at naptime. Her questions would have to wait. Gail took the blanket off Emmett's legs and jerked the recliner to the upright position. Ann reached out to help, but Emmett managed to slowly stand up by himself even though his fragile spine pitched him forward. He straightened himself as best as he could and cocked his head so he could see Ann's face.

"How tall are you?" he asked her.

"Five feet six."

"That can't be right. I'm five feet ten."

Gail laughed and pounced on his statement. "It's the osteoporosis, Emmett! It shrunk you all up!"

Ann flashed her a grimace and the aide lowered her head.

"I hope you have a pleasant Christmas, Emmett," Ann said affectionately. "I'll come see you when I get back."

"I expect I'll be here," he said. "Got no place else to go."

Gail offered him her arm as support, but Emmett brushed her away in favor of reaching for one chair after another until he got to the hallway, where he grabbed the rail that ran along the wall. Ann grinned as she watched him, wondering how much of his stamina was due to sheer stubbornness.

At the exit, Ann held the door for a man helping an elderly woman, who had her hair in a bun like Gracie.

Yes, Gracie, Ann thought. *She might remember one Anna Miller and two little girls. It's worth asking.*

Ann found Gracie alone in the dining room with a cup of coffee and a piece of cake. She smiled when she saw Ann. "Well, hello, dear! Annie, isn't it?"

"Yes, ma'am," Ann said, taking the chair next to Gracie.

"And you're Emmett's good friend Gracie."

The elderly woman's eyes crinkled with her smile. "That's right. We've been friends since grammar school. It's so nice you come to see him. He doesn't have much family left up here, you know. Would you like some cake? I only took a small taste, but it's got coconut in the frosting and I don't like coconut."

"No, thank you. But I would like to ask you something."

Gracie put her fork down and delicately wiped her mouth with her napkin. "Certainly, dear."

"My aunt told me a woman with two children lived at Emmett's years ago. By any chance do you remember them?"

Gracie didn't have to search her memory very long. "Oh, yes!" she said enthusiastically. "She spoke with an accent. Sometimes she did some sewing for my mother. She did lovely handiwork. You know, embroidery and fine stitching. She died rather young."

Ann was momentarily transfixed at the mention of her mother's handiwork. "Do you know why the woman came to live at Emmett's?"

Gracie nodded. "Emmett's grandmother lived out at his place. She needed help with the housework because she had arthritis so bad."

"But where did they all sleep?" Afraid of sounding critical, Ann added, "I mean, his house isn't very big."

"I'm sure it was all quite proper. Emmett's grandmother had a little cabin, and I imagine the housekeeper stayed out there." Gracie leaned closer. "She wasn't married, but she had two children," she added with a judgmental tsk-tsk.

It saddened Ann to think of the criticism her mother may have endured as an unmarried woman with children back in the '50s. That is, if she was unmarried.

"Some people think Emmett was the father," Ann said.

"Oh, no, dear," Gracie said dismissively. "That's a silly old rumor. Emmett never married."

"Is that why the children were put up for adoption after the woman died?"

"Well, old Mrs. Pederson couldn't possibly care for the poor little things. And of course it wouldn't be proper for Emmett and Clayton to raise them alone, being both bachelors. Besides, it was only the two of them to work the farm after their father left." Gracie sat back, remembering. "Albert Pederson was very demanding. I didn't really know how strict he was until Emmett took me to the Dairy Days Festival." She smiled sweetly. "My, my, we were so young. I was expecting him to propose, you know. But he told me he couldn't marry me or anyone else because he would lose his share of the farm if he got married. I never quite understood that." Gracie fingered the ring on her left hand and sighed. "Then Emmett went off to the war and I married Harold," she said in a dreamy tone. "He was a fine man, but Emmett was always special to me. Even if he was a poor farmer, he had more manners than most men around here." She paused and frowned. "Fiddlesticks," she finally said. "I can't remember her name. It seems to me it was such a simple name."

"Do you remember anything about the children?"

"My mother and I saw them a few times. We used to take things over there to be hemmed and whatnot. I never was any good with a needle and thread. My hobby was taking pictures." She held up a crooked finger. "I'll ask my son where my picture albums are! Maybe I have some of Emmett's place."

Ann brightened at the possibility. "Oh, Gracie, I would love to see them."

"I'll make sure you get whatever I have, dear."

Ann gave Gracie a little hug, wished her a lovely Christmas, and promised to visit again. She walked to the front lobby feeling lucky, wondering if it would be appropriate to seek out Gracie's son. Just as Ann reached the door, a man called her name.

"I just saw Emmett," Howie Studt said, hurrying toward her.

Ann felt a twinge of alarm. "What's wrong? He was fine a little while ago."

"And he still is. He signed the paperwork. I think he likes the idea of you as his POA."

"He does?"

"Yes. I also checked with Frank and Betty one more time to be sure. They haven't changed their minds. And as far as I can tell, Emmett is quite capable of making his own decisions, so I'm comfortable he understood the POA arrangement. In fact, I didn't mention you by name at all. I simply asked him who he wanted to help with his affairs, and he said Anna. That's you, right?"

And my mother, Ann thought.

"Lily already notarized for him," Howie went on. "She went back to her office, and if you have a minute, we could step over there and get you signed and notarized right now too."

In Lily's office, Ann signed across from Emmett's Edwardian signature, and Lily crimped the paper with her notary public embosser and signed her name. The process was simple and official. Ann now had legal control of Emmett's life—whatever was left of it.

TWENTY

Driving back to Milwaukee, Ann tried not to think about John's deceased wife. Rather, she focused on her kids and her grandsons, which led to thoughts of Christmas, which brought thoughts of her dad, who'd be absent this Christmas and all Christmases from now on, and then finally her mom's slow but obvious decline, and how everyone disagreed about how to help her.

At home, Ann found her mail on the kitchen table along with a note from Lisa to come for dinner the next day. After calling her daughter to confirm, Ann ate a simple supper of scrambled eggs, poured herself a glass of wine, and went upstairs for a soak in the tub. With her head resting on her bath pillow, and her feet propped on the opposite edge of the tub, she closed her eyes. She tried to see her mother, a young, unmarried pregnant woman traveling across the ocean alone, possibly knowing only a few words of English. Ann hoped her mother had more than just promises from Emmett. But if he loved Anna, as his notebooks indicated, how could he let their little girls go? Was he protecting his own reputation? Or did he want his daughters to have more than he did? Maybe Anna wrote Emmett when she was sick in Austria and told him to send little Annie and Elise to the city. Maybe she knew she was dying, and it was her idea.

Ann sank down until water covered her ears. She bent her knees and drew them up to her chest. Closing her eyes, she wrapped her arms around her legs and listened to the steady *dumpa, dumpa, dumpa* of her heart. It had taken her a long time to accumulate enough courage to go to Newland. How could she know she'd leave pieces of her heart there with Emmett and John? She sat up and frowned at her little stubborn bulge of tummy fat, wondering what John would think of her naked body. He had wrinkles and a little belly too. But men could get away with being less than perfect—just as when they father children and leave no betraying evidence behind.

She slept fitfully that night, dreaming she was a little girl on a ship with her dad. The ship kept going in circles while Karl kept repeating, "Some things you'll have to be satisfied not knowing."

When Ann arrived at Lisa's house the next afternoon, she was glad to see Mark's car already in the driveway. Her son and daughter were good people, and she was proud of them. They had both encouraged her search for her birth parents, even though Ann knew they really didn't understand what was driving her search. Sometimes she wasn't sure herself. There wasn't much she could tell them for certain yet—and she wasn't sure she should tell them about John at all.

Five-year-old Justin hugged her when she came in while Robby, nearly three, jumped up and down, shouting, "Dramma's here! Mommy! Dramma's here!"

Ann knelt in front of the younger boy. "Can you say Grr-amma?" she asked him.

"Rrr—Dramma!" he said, laughing.

Ann kissed his sweet little face. She loved being a Dramma.

Mark stooped to hug Ann. "What's with the Blazer, Mom?"

Lisa and Mark were both taller than Ann; they took after their father in that regard. She didn't regret divorcing him or telling him to go back to his rich so-called friends he preferred over his own family, but she did regret not leaving him sooner. Emmett had also chosen to remove himself from his children, and now Ann wondered whether either man had regrets about that.

"What about the Blazer, Mom?" Mark asked again.

"Oh. Well, the short version of the Saab story is that you

were right—I need a new car."

Seeing Mark's eyes, brown like hers, made Ann think of Emmett's blue ones. That meant the grandmother of her children—her mother—must have had brown eyes.

Her son-in-law, Gary, asked, "Did you sell your car?"

"No, but it might be dead," Ann replied. "Maybe you guys could look over the Blazer. I like the way it drives, but I don't have a clue about the engine or anything."

Mark and Gary looked at each other and laughed.

"What makes you think we know about engines, Mom?" Mark asked.

Lisa redirected her boys to the living room and came forward to greet her mom. Lisa was only three months pregnant, but she was already in the habit of patting her tummy.

"So what's the long story behind the car swap?" Lisa asked.

Ann explained how John had helped her get Emmett to the Manor House and loaned her the Blazer. She told them about meeting Frank, Betty, and Gordy. She omitted the parts about her scary encounter with Gordy, her panic attack, Emmett's mouse-infested house, John's beautiful home, his deceased wife, and the power of attorney decision. She also realized she was now the one keeping secrets.

"So what's the old guy like?" Lisa asked. "Is he a weird old hermit like everyone always said?"

"He is old. And frail," Ann replied. "And he's lived in the same old house all his life. Some of what my dad told me about Emmett being a loner seems to be true."

"And John?" Lisa teased in a singsong voice. "Are you going to see him again?"

"Well, it's kind of hard to avoid him. Newland's a small town."

"You know what I mean, Mom."

"We went out for lunch. Grampa's cousins said he was a nice guy, so I figured I could at least have dinner and thank him."

"I thought you said lunch."

Ann felt herself blushing. "We had dinner together too."

Mark and Lisa exchanged glances.

"Just be careful," Mark said.

"I appreciate your concern, but he seems like a nice man," Ann told him. "Emmett, too, actually," she added, hoping to turn the conversation away from John. She could have said she admired Emmett, but she wasn't sure yet.

"So Emmett's our biological grandfather?" Mark asked. "Your real father?"

Ann nodded. "So far, the evidence points in his direction."

"Do you know why he sent you and Aunt Elise away?" Lisa said.

"Not yet."

Justin looked up from his line of Matchbox cars. "Where are you going, Gramma?" he asked.

"I'm not going anyplace, honey," Ann answered.

"Are you coming to our house at Christmas? You came last year."

"Do you remember last Christmas?"

"Yes," Justin said, pointing to his racecar set on the floor. "You brought that for me."

"You're right," Ann said, surprised he remembered which toy she'd given him out of the many he had received.

Ann watched little Robby line up his cars. At three, he might have an emotional memory of last Christmas, but he wasn't quite old enough to express those memories in words. Elise was Robby's age when they lost their mother. *I would have been like Justin,* Ann thought. *Better able to connect the adults' conversation to my five-year-old understanding. But how long did a five-year-old kid's memories last? Are they replaced by more recent ones? Or are they tucked far back in a corner of my brain someplace, waiting to be revived? Why can't I call up the memories I want?*

Around the dinner table later, Ann felt grateful for the way her family teased and laughed so comfortably together. When Mark left soon after the boys went to bed, Gary retired to his computer, leaving Ann and Lisa at the kitchen table with their tea.

"So tell me more about the car dealer guy," Lisa said. "Do you like him?"

"Yes, I do. But he's there and I'm here."

"You could still see him once in a while."

"I don't know, honey."

"What color are his eyes?"

"Brown."

Lisa laughed.

"What's so funny?" Ann asked.

"You're in love with him, aren't you?"

"Because I know the color of his eyes?"

"Because I can see it on your face, Mom." She leaned forward and lowered her voice. "Do you remember when I met Gary?"

"I remember you made your mind up about him pretty fast. You were still with what's-his-name."

"Right. And when I met Gary I knew he was the guy I dreamed about when I was sleeping with what's-his-name."

"But I'm not sleeping with a what's-his-name," Ann said.

"You know what I mean. And I also hope you know Mark and I wouldn't mind if you dated again. Or even if you married again." Lisa swirled the last of her tea around in her cup. "If he was a nice guy, that is. I hate seeing you alone."

"I'm not alone. I have you and Mark and the kids. Mark and Nyla will be married this summer and I know they want kids. I'll be happily surrounded!"

Now I'm acting like my mom, Ann thought. *Putting up a front so as not to worry my kids.*

"You remember Gary's uncle?" Lisa asked. "The lawyer?

You met him at our wedding. He's divorced now and I bet you'd like him."

"I don't remember, Lisa. And I know you mean well, but please don't embarrass me by setting us up."

"Okay, but don't sell yourself short either." Lisa gave her an impish grin. "You're young enough to have another go at it, Mom."

Later that evening, when Ann turned down her street, she noticed her house was the only one without Christmas lights or a tree sparkling in a window. Even though Christmas was her favorite holiday, she'd skipped her decorations this year because of going up north. Now she suddenly felt gloomy, as if she'd shunned Christmas in favor of chasing after the elusive memories of an old man she didn't even know. Was she ready for another go at it as Lisa suggested?

She saw her answering machine blinking when she opened her door.

"Sorry I missed you," John's voice said. "Howie told me you got the power of attorney all squared away. I'm callin' to ask if you want a padlock on Emmett's door. Sometimes kids up here use empty houses for parties. I figure you don't want Gordy gettin' in either. The other thing I was wonderin' is if you want to sell the camper trailer Emmett's got over at his place. He might need the money. Give me a call if you want. Have a good night."

She pressed the message button and listened again to his rich, deep voice once more before pressing the delete button and going up to her bedroom. She couldn't talk to John now. No, not couldn't; she didn't want to talk to him now. She didn't want to think about Joyce. She didn't want to admit how much she missed John, either. She'd call him tomorrow when she might feel more like a practical power of attorney and less like a puddle of emotions.

TWENTY-ONE

As Ann made her morning coffee, the phone rang. She hesitated, thinking of what to say if it was John calling again. But her sister Karen's voice greeted her when she answered.

"Hi, Annie. How was up north?"

"Pretty good. Are you at work?"

Karen let out a sigh. "I'm on my break, but I need to ask you a favor real quick."

"Sure."

"Mom called me last night all anxious about Christmas. She said she needs to go shopping, but she's finished. I wrapped everything a week ago. She just got out of the hospital." Karen's voice began to falter.

"Karen?"

Karen sniffled. "She insists she's watching her diet, but she's got snacks stashed all over the place."

"She doesn't understand," Ann said sympathetically.

"I know. The other thing is, I let her drive when we went to the store yesterday just to see how she does. It was awful. It was like she forgot how to drive! She was all over the road!"

Ann put her elbow on the table and rested her head in her hand. "I think the four of us need to have a serious talk."

"I know, but Neal said Mom's not ready to move into assisted living."

"It's Neal who's not ready!" Ann said sharply. "I'm sorry. I don't mean to lose my patience, but it's impossible for the four of us to give her the kind of help she needs."

"I know, Annie. Yesterday she was really upset with me."

"She never gets upset with you."

"Well, yesterday she did. I told her very firmly to keep her pill container on the counter and she got mad. She said it makes her kitchen look like a drugstore."

Ann understood. No one ever bought Ruth anything for the house without checking her ever-changing color and décor scheme. "Okay," she said. "I'm doing a little shopping this morning, but I'll stop by this afternoon and see what I can do."

"Thank you so much, Annie. I owe you one."

"Don't be silly. We're all in this together."

Ann hung up. She knew her sisters and brother didn't want to talk about the inevitable. None of them ever said anything about the assisted living brochures Ann had given them over a month ago. And she knew they wouldn't be able to rely on their dad's "if it's not broken, don't fix it" rule much longer.

The mall parking lot was crowded and so were the stores. Christmas music streamed from everywhere while a small train full of little kids tooted its way around a track. Ann caught whiffs of peppermint and chocolate as she hurried around shoppers and kiosks. She wasn't a browser like Ruth, wandering among the stores, comparing bargains. Ann preferred to get in, get what she wanted, and get out. After she bought her last gift, she called her mom to say she was on her way.

"Neal's coming for supper," Ruth told her. "I made a coffee cake, but I think I need a few things from the store."

"I'm leaving right now, Mom. I'll take you to the store. Wait for me, okay?"

Ann snapped her phone shut, gathered up her parcels, and headed for the exit.

When Ruth didn't answer her door, Ann used her duplicate key to let herself in. Her mom's coffee cake was on the counter. The oven was on, too, but Ruth was gone. Ann turned off the oven and walked out to the garage. Empty house and no car.

Bad sign. Ann went back inside; she had no choice but to wait. She peeked in her mom's bedroom and saw dozens of wrapped Christmas gifts stacked in a corner. In years past, Ruth marked each one with initials or a name, but these gifts weren't marked. Ann looked under the bed, Ruth's favorite hiding place. Sure enough, more gifts. She purposely arranged a few gifts to stick out from under the bed skirt then sat at the kitchen table to watch for her mom. When Ruth arrived, Ann went out to meet her.

Ruth was too heavy for her five-foot-two frame, and today she'd shoved her plump little feet into cheap flats. "Hi, Annie," she said. "What are you doing here?"

"It's gift wrapping day, Mom."

"Oh, I already did that."

Ann let that go and grabbed the grocery bags. "Gee, Mom, aren't your feet cold? You have those nice walking shoes that the doctor ordered."

"Those old-fashioned things?"

Ann let that go too. No sense arguing about wearing sensible orthopedic shoes if they aren't stylish enough for Ruth. In the kitchen, they unpacked a gallon of milk, two pounds of baked ham, a pound of potato salad, coleslaw, chips, donuts, and cookies. By the looks of Ruth's pantry and refrigerator, one would think she was still feeding a family of six. Ann checked the freezer and found a bag of oranges; last week it was frozen lettuce. Ann casually put the oranges on the counter; a reminder would only embarrass her mom—or cause her to get defensive.

"Anyone else coming for supper besides Neal?"

"I don't know," Ruth said, surprised. "Did he say he was coming over?"

"I think he is."

"Good thing I made a cake then."

Ann offered to take her mom's coat to the hall closet as an excuse to get closer to the bedroom. "Are those gifts under your bed?" she casually asked.

"What?" Ruth came to her bedroom. "They must be Karen's."

Another constant frustration was trying to figure out if Ruth was lying in order to hide what she'd forgotten or whether she'd truly forgotten. While Ruth curiously examined the boxes Ann retrieved from under the bed, Ann brought her a few of the wrapped gifts so Ruth could see there was no way to determine who they were for.

"Let me see," Ruth said, inspecting the gifts. "I always mark them."

Ann slid a finger under the tape on one box. "We can check."

"Don't open it!"

"But we have to know who it's for. I'll be careful." She slid the box out of the wrapping and handed it to her mom.

Ruth held up a pink sweater and read Karen's name from the tag left inside the box.

"Karen will like that," Ann said, taking another box from the pile. "How about if we take all the gifts to the kitchen table? We can sort them out and decide which ones you want to keep. You saved all the receipts, right?"

"Of course! I always save the receipts!" Ruth declared as she wobbled off to the kitchen.

Over the next hour, they matched gifts to the receipts Ruth had miraculously found. But soon Ruth got tired and went to the living room to watch television. Working alone, Ann filled a shopping bag with duplicate gifts to be returned, including the turtleneck with her name on it. All her life, she hated turtlenecks. She shoved the bag under the table when Ruth came back to the kitchen and hovered over the coffee cake.

"Neal will be here for supper shortly," Ann reminded her.

Ruth said nothing as she cut the whole cake in a crisscross pattern and removed one piece to a small plate. Next, she took the day's mail from the counter and put it in the drawer with cooking utensils, moved her medication dispenser from the counter to another drawer, and removed the mail from the drawer and put it back on the counter. The senseless rearranging made Ann nervous. When the phone rang, she jumped to get it.

"Oh hi, Annie," Neal said. "I didn't know you were there."

"Yes," Ann chirped. "We wrapped gifts."

"Good. Karen was upset about the gift thing. I'll see you in about twenty minutes. Jason and I are bringing a pizza."

"Well . . ."

"Mom forgot, didn't she?"

"Oh, sure!" Ann told him sweetly. "Mom's got potato salad and ham and rolls. Here, I'll let you talk to her."

Ruth took the receiver. "I wish you would have called earlier, Neal. I would have gone to the store."

As Ann watched Ruth talk on the phone, she wondered what else she and her siblings could do to help their mom. They had a system of sorts in place, but it wasn't enough.

Ann took Ruth to her foot doctor and general practitioner appointments. Because her flexible work schedule and solitary lifestyle afforded more free time than the others, Ann did some house cleaning and stopped by for lunch or supper a few times a week. She filled Ruth's weekly pill organizer and checked the blood sugar levels recorded by Ruth's glucose meter. Missed readings had increased lately because Ruth kept forgetting to test herself.

Elise owned a small gift shop, which was closed on Sundays. So after church each week, she planned out the next week of diabetic meals and took Ruth for groceries. Their weekly excursions didn't stop Ruth from taking solo trips to the grocery store, however. Not long ago, Elise discovered a stash of illegal snacks, but rather than argue with Ruth, Elise simply threw it all out when Ruth wasn't looking, and Ruth replaced it all on her next forbidden trip to the grocery store. Elise seemed to think she had their mom's diet under control, but Ann knew better.

Karen had a full-time job as a pediatric nurse and a grandchild she often babysat for. She helped Ruth shower, did her laundry and some light housekeeping, and took her to the salon. Unfortunately for Karen, Ruth seemed to want Karen to do everything for her lately. Sometimes Ann felt slighted when Ruth preferred Karen's help. Other times Ann wondered why she should be surprised that Ruth preferred her own daughter.

Neal worked in public relations for the city. He and his wife both spent most weekends at their kids' school concerts and sport tournaments. As Ruth's power of attorney, he handled her finances and was supposed to talk to Ruth about selling her car, but he kept putting it off. He made excuses for Ruth's erratic behavior, naively insisting she'd get over Karl being gone and be her old self again. Karl's death hit Neal the hardest because he never accepted his dad's cancer in the first place. Ann saw the same denial keeping Neal from acknowledging his mother's increasing dependence on him.

Even though the siblings felt lucky to be able to divide the duties four ways, there was often an overlap, a chore done twice, or one missed, or a miscommunication here and there. Ann felt they were in a holding pattern—still adjusting to their dad's death while trying to navigate the maze of Ruth's needs.

Ann helped Ruth set out leftover stew, ham, rolls, potato salad, coleslaw just as Neal came in with Jason, his thirteen-year-old son, who carried the pizza. Neal made a point of sampling everything on the table while talking about simple topics that Ruth could contribute to. When it was time to leave, he slipped a plain envelope into Ann's hand.

"I found this in a kitchen drawer the other day when I was looking for mail," Neal said. "It's pretty cool. I thought you might like it. I made copies for Elise and Karen too."

At home, Ann opened the envelope and read her dad's

handwriting.

> *Hi Hon,*
>
> *I needed more than an anniversary card to tell you how much I love you and to thank you for these thirty-five years. Thanks is such a little word for all you've done to keep our family close. You helped me when I felt unsure and trusted me when I didn't deserve it. I don't have to tell you what I mean. You always know. You forgave my faults and kept loving me, and your faithfulness has been my strength.*
>
> *I know it was a little hard for you when the girls joined us. But it worked out okay, and I give you all the credit. We have a lovely home because of you. You treated all the kids the same, you taught them to be one family and to love and respect each other. I could write a book, but it would still end with "thanks." I am a lucky man. I love you, darling wife of mine. I love you very much.*

Karl had signed it "your loving and grateful husband." He never missed Ruth's birthday or an anniversary, holiday, or any excuse for candy, flowers, or a little surprise gift. He used to joke how he might be sentimental and old, but he wasn't foolish enough to forget who was really in charge.

The only part of the letter Ann disagreed with was "treated all the kids the same." Ann remembered Ruth often yelling at her for the same things Karen and Neal easily got away with. Ruth, not Karl, was the disciplinarian.

TWENTY-TWO

On Christmas morning, Ann was buttering her toast when the phone rang. She expected to hear Lisa or one of her sisters calling to remind her to bring something for the family dinner later. She answered with an enthusiastic "Merry Christmas! This is Santa Claus!"

"Merry Christmas, sweet face."

John's voice caught her by surprise—especially the sweet face part. "Oh. Merry Christmas to you too."

"I hope I'm not too early."

"No, not at all. I thought you were one of the kids."

"I guess I am a kid sometimes."

Ann detected sadness in his voice.

"I bet you have plans to be with your family today."

"Yes, I'm going to Lisa's to open gifts, and then we'll go to my mom and dad's. I mean my mom's. There's always too much food and it's a little noisy sometimes, but we always have fun. I mean, I hope so, because this is our first Christmas without Dad. I'm spending the night with my mom."

You're talking too fast, she told herself. *Saying too much. You sound nervous.*

"Yeah," John said with a sigh. "Christmas was good when I was a kid. I remember one year I got a little bag of cowboys and Indians. It might've only cost a quarter, but I was happy. My birthday was the only other time I got a gift. These days parents buy kids stuff all the time." He paused a long moment. "Did you get my message about the padlock at Emmett's?"

"Yes, I did. I meant to call you back. A padlock's a good idea. I'll tell Frank."

"I don't mind swingin' by and puttin' it on. It only takes a minute."

She wanted to tell him no; it wasn't necessary, too much trouble. But John seemed talkative. Was he trying to make up for—for what? Being in love with his deceased wife?

"I'd appreciate it if it's not too much trouble."

"No trouble at all."

Ann absentmindedly cut her toast into little pieces. "Thank you. So what do you have planned for Christmas Day?"

"Well, the weather's decent. I might take a little horse ride."

"The weather's not bad here either. Not too cold."

"Yeah. I was also wonderin' about the Blazer. You know when you're comin' back?"

"After New Year's. It depends on the weather."

John probably wants to get his business calendar in order, she thought. *That's okay. It's better this way.*

"Yeah, I guess so," John said. "Otherwise, I go to the auto auction in Milwaukee every other week or so. If you don't want it, I could arrange for you to drop it off there. Or if you want to keep it, I can send you the title."

"Any news on my car?"

"Well, it's not worth much as it is. Not sure what it would cost to fix. You might have to get it hauled to a dealer down there. I'll ask around, but folks up here tend to want domestic cars."

"Okay, I understand." Ann heard a clattering noise as if John was putting dishes in the sink.

"Well, have a good Christmas, Annie. Good talkin' to you."

Ann wished him Merry Christmas again and hung up, pushing her mangled toast aside before going upstairs to get ready for Christmas with her family.

At Lisa's, even in the midst of her grandsons' excited squeals as they tore their gifts open, Ann silently scolded herself for not sending John a Christmas card with a thank-you note about the Blazer.

"Mom? You with us?" Lisa asked as she handed Ann a gift.

"Sure, honey. Sorry. Brain drift. Wow, thank you. What a pretty wrapping!"

"You're sad about Grampa not being around this year, aren't you?"

"Yes. I guess I am."

Lisa gave her mother a one-arm hug. "Well, I bet Grampa's right here."

That afternoon family members crowded into the old south-side Milwaukee bungalow that they all knew so well: one bedroom down, two bedrooms up—one with a view of Lake Michigan—a kitchen with a pantry, a dining room with a plate rail and built-in buffet and china cabinet, and a living room full of family pictures. Ann and her sisters had helped Ruth set up the tree and decorate the living and dining rooms with greenery, strings of lights, and fake velvety poinsettias. The nativity set always went on the buffet along with a few Christmas angels from Ruth's ever-growing collection. The colorful little ice-skaters arranged on a mirror at the other end of the buffet were Ann's favorite. When she was a kid, she imagined she was the one with the red skirt and crooked smile who skated expertly on one foot.

When Elise arrived with her husband and son, she immediately signaled Ann to follow her to Ruth's bedroom, where she closed the door behind them. "Did you ever find anything about, you know, medical stuff?" Elise asked.

"Medical stuff? You mean about our birth parents? Why? What's the matter?"

"I have to go for a biopsy on Monday. They saw something suspicious on my mammogram, and my doctor said she'd get me in right away. So now I'm scared."

Ann was momentarily stunned but gathered her thoughts

quickly. "Hey, don't worry. Those things are usually fibrous tissue or calcifications or something. They show up on mammograms, but it'll be okay. You'll see."

Elise stepped away from Ann and went to the dresser for a tissue. "No one knows except Dave and Kyle," she said, carefully dabbing a tissue around her eye makeup. "I think Dave's nervous, but he never wants to talk about my female problems. And Kyle didn't say it, but I can tell he's afraid. No kid wants his mother to have—" She stopped and looked in the mirror to adjust her sweater. "Maybe our mother had lumps."

The comment surprised Ann. After all, Elise wasn't one to casually mention their birth mother. But this was different. This was about specific medical history—important and relevant information Ann hadn't considered yet. And even if she had pertinent information, what good would it do now? A wave of fear swept through Ann, but she knew that if she faltered Elise would crumble.

"I'm sure you have nothing to worry about," Ann said confidently. "You take good care of yourself, and thank goodness your doctor checks out every little thing."

Elise dug in her purse and brought out a blister pack of pills.

"What are those?" Ann asked.

Elise pressed out one of the tablets. "The doctor said these would help my nerves. I'll be fine. We better get out there. Mom will want to open gifts." She popped the pill in her mouth and swallowed it. "I'm good. Come on. Let's have Christmas."

In years past, Ruth oohed and aahed over each gift. Now Karen sat next to a quiet Ruth, keeping her focused, telling her which person to thank for which gift. Ruth seemed lost in her own thoughts, real or imagined. Neal sat in their dad's favorite chair and sipped coffee, watching others open their gifts while he set his aside for later just as Karl used to do.

Whenever the atmosphere got a little solemn, someone would remind the others to be happy because that's what their Dad would have wanted. Ann kept an eye on Elise, who gradually relaxed and seemed to thoroughly enjoy the day's celebration. And more than once, Ann imagined how Christmas Day was long ago for a poor little boy up north named Johnny, who was happy with his little cowboys and Indians.

After dinner, dessert, and the ritual division of leftovers, adults and children bundled up in coats and boots, wishing each other Merry Christmas one more time before heading home.

"Hope you don't mind if I spend the night, Mom," Ann reminded Ruth when they were alone.

"No, of course not, honey. You can stay as long as you want."

Ann put water on for tea and then joined Ruth, who was sitting at the dining room table, sifting through a stack of Christmas cards.

"We didn't get many cards this year," she said. "Postage is too high. Did you see this one from Dad's cousin Betty? You'd think she'd stop inviting us up there. We're never going."

Even though she lived alone now, Ruth always said "we" out of habit.

"But you went up there a few times, didn't you?" Ann asked.

Ruth took a cookie from the Santa plate on the table. "Not really. Nana's funeral was the last time. Emmett and your father got into an argument, though, so we didn't even stay for dinner."

Ann had never heard that story. "Really? What did they argue about?" she asked, trying to sound nonchalant.

"I don't know. Emmett could be a bitter person, but he's gone now too."

"Actually, he's not."

The teapot whistled and Ann got up to bring cups and tea bags to the table.

"Emmett died a long time ago," Ruth insisted.

Ann agreed. It was no use to keep correcting her.

Ruth dunked her tea bag up and down in her cup. "He was a hermit, you know. He wouldn't have been so poor if he had a regular a job. Dad and I had some hard times too but we kept working."

"You sure did," Ann said tenderly. "I remember Dad got laid off when I was in high school."

"He was out of work for five months," Ruth said, arranging her Christmas cards by size. "I don't know what we would have done without my father's help."

"I thought Grampa Meyer and Dad didn't get along very well."

Ruth patted the Christmas cards together. Ann hoped her mom was frowning over the mismatched sizes of the cards rather than the comment about Grampa Meyer.

"My father didn't want me to marry Dad," Ruth said plainly.

Ann had never heard this either, but if she seemed shocked, Ruth might not go on. "I guess I don't remember," she said calmly.

"I'm sure I told you we changed our wedding date a few times. My father thought Dad was putting me off, but your dad and I just had to work out a few things." Ruth took another cookie and smiled. "And I knew he was worth waiting for." Then she frowned again. "Course my folks really didn't like it when we adopted you girls. But it all worked out."

Ann was stunned. Where was this coming from after all the years of Ruth's "go ask your father"?

"I'm sure it was hard to take in someone else's children," Ann suggested.

Ruth playfully shook her finger at Ann. "Yes, especially when you wouldn't go to bed!"

"Me?"

"Yes, you. You wouldn't go to bed unless I sat next to you until you fell asleep."

"Wow. You never told me. I—I don't remember."

"Old Nana used to lie down on the bed with you until you fell asleep. She spoiled you. Elise went to sleep just fine, but I guess you were afraid of the dark."

"Maybe I was afraid of being alone," Ann said.

"Don't be silly. You weren't alone. Elise was in the same room and we were always nearby. You didn't want to go to school either."

"I didn't?"

"No." Ruth snickered a bit. "For two weeks, I took you to school and waited in the classroom until you settled down. I walked back after school, too, so I was there when you got out."

"I'm sorry. I don't remember," Ann said sheepishly. *Of course,* she thought. *I wasn't afraid of being alone. I was afraid of losing another mommy.*

"You got over it," Ruth said through a yawn. "Kids get over things." She took a sip of tea and set the cup aside. "I guess I'm more tired than I thought. You can stay up and watch TV if you want. It won't bother me."

There would be no more questions tonight, but Ann hoped the door on the adoption topic was finally cracked open. Then again, Ruth could slam it again anytime. Or forget. The one thing she couldn't do was say, "Go ask your father."

Ann got up and put her arms around Ruth. "Good night, Mom. I'll lock the door and get the lights. Thank you for taking care of me. And thank you for always making our Christmas so special."

It took Ann a moment to realize Ruth wasn't hugging back; she was crying softly. Ann held her mom closer, not sure what to do or say.

Ruth's voice cracked. "It's hard sometimes. It's so hard."

"I know," Ann whispered, wondering whether Ruth was referring to her health or being alone in the house or Karl's death or what.

"I miss your father. No one knows how much I miss him."

"Oh, I know. I know," Ann soothed, feeling a tear coming and patting her mom's back. "We all miss Daddy."

"We did our best for all of you," Ruth said, repeating Karl's standard line.

"Of course, Mom. You were wonderful parents."

"I love you, honey," Ruth said as she hugged Ann back.

Now Ann got emotional. Ruth had never told her "I love you" first. Ann felt surprised and comforted at the same time. It was a good feeling.

"I love you, too, Mom," Ann said, holding Ruth tenderly. "We all love you so much."

Ruth stepped back. "I'm okay. It's just because of Christmas." She wiped her eyes and turned away. "I put clean sheets on the bed upstairs."

Ann watched Ruth shuffle to her bedroom and close the door. Everyone knew Karen changed the sheets these days.

Ann sat on the couch and stared at the Christmas tree. Ruth wasn't one to demonstrate her affection the way Karl used to do. His arms were always open. He hugged and tickled and hugged again. Ruth always held back, and she held back with all of them, even with Karen and Neal, even on birthdays. "Here's your present," she'd say as if she were an attendant at the movies saying, "Here's your ticket." Then she'd say, "Now open it carefully so I can use the paper again." Ann smiled at the thought. But one thing for sure, Ann had always admired her mom for accepting whatever life dished out. She was practical and thrifty, efficient and persevering. There was always food on the table even if it was just another casserole. Their clothes were always clean and mended. And every Christmas, even in lean years, they all got what they wanted from Santa.

But how was Ruth now? Was she afraid of being alone? Did she ever reach across the bed for Karl or dream about him—or see his ghost? And what was it that Karl and Ruth had to *work out* before they could get married? Was Ruth referring to the adoption? It was something Ann had never considered. Maybe her parents had more than second thoughts about adopting her and her sister. She didn't want to think about it.

Ann switched off the tree lights, checked the doors, and went upstairs to the bedroom she used to share with her sisters. She got in bed and imagined her dad and Emmett arguing at Nana's funeral. A siren wailed in the distance. A dog barked and a car drove by. Ann thought of Betty's house—so silent at night except for Frank's snoring and the scratching above the ceiling fan. No doubt the mice were busy at Emmett's too.

TWENTY-THREE

Ann slept surprisingly well and woke up at 7:30, much later than usual. She went downstairs as quietly as she could, stepping along the outer edges of each step and completely avoiding the third step from the bottom. All the kids had learned how to avoid the squeaky sections, especially on those date nights when they got home too late. Her mom usually slept until at least eight thirty, but from the kitchen window Ann could see her mom's garage door standing wide open. Since she could also see the bumper of her mom's car, she figured something must have simply triggered the door during the night. She got the extra remote from the drawer and aimed it out the back door to close the garage. By the time Ann settled with coffee and the morning paper, Ruth was rustling about in her bedroom.

"Morning, Mom," Ann called. "Need help with anything?"

"Is that you, Annie? I'll be right there."

When Ruth finally came to the kitchen, she was wearing dressy pants, a matching stylish sweater, and jewelry.

"Wow, you're all dressed up."

"I have an appointment with the foot doctor."

"Um, I don't think so. Let's check your calendar."

Ann directed Ruth to her new 2000 calendar on the wall. The doctor's appointment was noted in red on January thirteenth. Embarrassed but convinced, Ruth sat at the table with her coffee and thumbed through holiday sale fliers. As Ann was talking Ruth into two soft-boiled eggs for breakfast instead of leftover cheesecake, the phone rang. Ann answered.

"How did it go?" Karen wanted to know. "Did Mom make it through the night?"

"Um, maybe. I didn't hear a thing."

Karen picked up on the clue. "Was the garage door open?"

"Yes. How did you know?"

"I'm so glad you were there, Annie. Neal saw the garage door open on his way to work last week, and Mom told him Dad left it open. I think she gets up at night thinking she's going somewhere. I can't help wonder what she does when no one's around."

"Who is it?" Ruth wanted to know as she held out her hand for the phone.

"It's Karen," Ann replied brightly, handing her mom the receiver.

Ruth asked Karen what she wanted for supper, and Ann imagined Karen trying to explain why she wasn't coming for supper.

"I'm saving the cranberry bread for Dad," Ruth told Karen.

Ann squeezed her eyes shut and bit her lip. It was already one of those days.

"We need eggs," Ruth said after she hung up.

Ann showed Ruth the full carton of eggs in the refrigerator, and Ruth quietly went back to her newspaper.

Ann stretched her visit over lunch. She never mentioned the previous evening's emotional conversation or the open garage door. When Ruth settled in front of her afternoon television soaps, Ann put a note on the counter about the plate of ready-to-heat leftovers she'd left in the refrigerator for Ruth's lunch. Instructions were already posted on the door of the microwave for how to reheat a plate of food. As always, Ann felt reluctant to leave Ruth alone, wished she lived next door, wished she didn't have to sneak leftover cheesecake outside to the trash.

Ann's phone was ringing as she unlocked her door.

"How did it go with Mom last night?" Elise wanted to know.

"She said she was sad about Dad," Ann replied.

"I know. She told me too."

"Did she ever tell you about how Gramma and Grampa Meyer didn't like it that Mom and Dad adopted us?"

"No. And why are you bothering her with all that?"

"I wasn't. We were talking and she just told me."

Ann heard Elise take a deep breath before speaking. "Leave it be, Annie. Will you? Especially now at Christmas."

"Okay."

"Well, I'm calling because I forgot to tell you my surgery will be at ten o'clock on the twenty-ninth at St. Luke's. I'd rather wait until after the first, but my doctor's going on vacation and Dave said it would be better to get it on our insurance for this year."

Elise paused and Ann imagined her sister thinking the same thing she was: St. Luke's was where their dad had taken his last breath.

"Okay," Ann said as calmly as she could. "I'll be there. No problem."

When Elise spoke again, the words came out without punctuation, the way they did when she was nervous or upset.

"They said they would scan the tissue right away, and let me know if there are concerns," Elise said. "Concerns. Nice and vague. I took another one of those pills the doctor gave me but I think I'm feeling better about this anyway. My friend Julie has fibrous lumps and she said they never find anything to worry about. I told Mom and she wants to be there so we'll pick her up on the way. Karen has to work but she doesn't need to be there. You don't either, actually."

Ann worked her jacket and boots off and took the phone to the living room. "I'm sure everything will be okay," she said.

Elise sighed heavily. "I also want to ask you something."

"Sure. What?"

"Did you tell Neal we should put Mom in a nursing home? I hate the way that sounds. Like you're boarding your dog.

Anyway, I talked to him this morning and he sounded upset."

"I didn't say anything to Neal about a nursing home. What's going on?"

"Neal told me you might have other thoughts about Mom because of the other stuff."

"What other stuff? What other thoughts?"

"You know. Because of going up north."

"I don't get it."

Elise took a deep breath and spoke slowly. "I don't know how to tell you this, but Neal wants to talk to Karen about Mom."

"Well, that's good. We should talk about Mom."

"No. I mean I don't think Neal wants us involved. Just Karen and him."

"Without you and me? As if we aren't family?"

"You know Neal had a hard time with Christmas, Annie."

"Yeah. So did everyone." Ann let herself drop onto the couch. "Geez, Elise, it's not our fault we're adopted."

"I know. We were lucky to wind up with Mom and Dad," Elise said. She paused a moment. "I suspect we didn't have a good life up north."

"Why not?"

"They've got stories on the news all the time about kids in rural areas who don't even have basic needs. And we all know what Dad thought of that old place. Did you see it?"

Ann smiled as she thought of Emmett's notebooks and other things she found in his house. She wanted to share everything with Elise but also wanted Elise to have an appreciation for Emmett himself.

"Well, Nana's little log cabin is still there and the old outhouse. Like Dad always said, Emmett's poor. The house is run-down, but I actually remembered it. The house doesn't have any indoor plumbing, and it was cold because he doesn't put much wood in the barrel stove. He's afraid of chimney fires."

Ann paused. *Say something positive about him,* she thought. "He's eighty-four, Elise. He's frail and bent over from osteoporosis, but his mind is still sharp. In fact, I took him for lunch because he didn't have any food in the house. Then I took him to an assisted living place in town where he usually spends the winter. We've had some nice visits." Ann thought she heard the phone click off. "Elise? Are you there?"

"Are you listening to yourself?" Elise scoffed. "Outhouse? Wood heat and no food? Dad was right! He *is* crazy!"

"Poor doesn't mean crazy," Ann replied. But why did she think Elise would excuse what she herself couldn't? "He said he was waiting for me," she added tenderly.

"How sweet," Elise said sarcastically.

"Come on. We can't change our history and we didn't choose our parents. No matter what I find out, we—both of us—are part of our parents and their history too."

Ann recognized John's voice ringing in her words. *We can't do anything about what's already happened,* he had said over his ravioli. *Or whatever our parents did.*

Elise cleared her throat. "Pardon me, but I won't be a victim, Annie."

"A victim? Why would you think of yourself as a victim?"

"Are you kidding? How can you live in a house with no plumbing? The place must be filthy."

"We lived there years ago when our mother and Nana were there," Ann said as patiently as she could. "Betty said Nana was a fussy housekeeper."

"How can you be a fussy housekeeper when you don't have running water?"

"People managed years ago. They got water from the creek."

"The creek?" Elise snickered. "You have got to be kidding!"

I should have seen that coming, Ann thought. "Well, the outdoor pump broke," she said softly.

Elise laughed, and Ann wondered what her sister would say

about Emmett's infected navel, his crusty scalp, and the rope he used to hold up his pants.

"I don't believe it," Elise said. "What about Dad's other cousins? Are they normal?"

Gordy's threatening behavior crossed Ann's mind and she dismissed it immediately. "They're very nice people," she told Elise instead. "Dairy farmers. Down to earth. Just like Dad always said."

"Yeah, fine. So how can you remember so far back anyway?"

"Do you remember when Karen rolled off the bed and broke her collar bone?"

"Of course. She was just a baby."

"And you were five years old at the time."

"That's different."

"Why? It was a few months after my fifth birthday when we were adopted, and I remember some things. Like the tire swing we had and wildflowers in the grass and Nana's molasses cookies."

"Maybe you made it all up because you needed some childhood memories."

"I don't think so," Ann said. "No one ever told me about Emmett's house and I remembered Nana's bedroom."

"How do you know it was a couple months after your birthday when we were adopted?"

"Granny Elizabeth told me one time. Well, I mean I heard her tell someone."

"She always told me we were too little to understand."

"We weren't always too little."

"So when are you going to ask him the big question?"

"When I go back."

Elise was quiet a moment, then asked, "What if we had the same mother but different fathers?"

"What?"

"It's possible, isn't it? Look at us. Your eyes are brown and mine are green. My hair is curly, yours is straight. You're bigger on top and I'm taller."

"But Elise, kids are different even when they have the same parents."

Elise continued her own line of reasoning. "But if I'm right, it wouldn't say much for our mother, would it? If she slept around, I mean. You said so yourself, Annie. We don't know. And who would dare tell us if it was true? And if you remember the house, why don't you remember her? I should think you'd remember her better than a house."

It was a good point, and Ann noticed Elise was back to saying "her" again.

"I can't explain it," Ann said. "Psychological block maybe. Or all the years of being told not to talk about it. Maybe I've got leftover trauma from losing our mother."

"What if she didn't die?"

"Why would Dad tell me she died of leukemia if it wasn't true?"

"I don't know," Elise said. "How would you feel if Dad told us she simply abandoned us?"

"I'd still want to know."

"Do you still have the picture you took from Granny Elizabeth's scrapbook?"

"What picture?"

Elise snickered playfully. "Come on, Annie. I know you have it. The one with Dad and Emmett and a woman. I saw it in your underwear drawer one time."

"Why were you looking in my underwear drawer?"

"Because Mom got you those undies with days of the week. Remember? Sometimes I wore a pair to school."

"Ha! No wonder I had days missing!" Ann laughed with her sister, but then asked more seriously, "Why didn't you tell me you knew about the picture?"

"I don't know. A feeling, I guess. And the curly hair. Because if she's the one, then Dad knew she was with Emmett. And if he did know, why didn't he just tell us Emmett was our father?" Elise groaned. "I think this medication is giving me a splitting headache. Now I need some aspirin."

"Okay," Ann said. She knew her sister was finished talking, finished thinking.

"Don't get me wrong. I guess if you find anything major, you know, like health records, you can pass that along."

Ann could hear the old resistance in her sister's voice. *Anything major? Isn't identifying our parents major enough? And "pass that along" doesn't sound like "tell me everything you find out."*

"What if I find more pictures?" Ann asked.

"I guess I'd be curious about those." Elise yawned. "These pills make me tired. I'll talk to you later."

Ann hung up and stared out the window, her mind racing with worry. The sky was overcast; maybe snow was on the way. She covered her face with her hands, trying not to think about Elise going through surgery, chemotherapy, and months of recuperation. If their mother did have lumps, it didn't matter because they'd never know. More than anything else, Ann wanted her sister to be okay.

She wandered to another window and saw John's Blazer parked in her driveway. She imagined crying on his shoulder and his reassuring words. But she might not be going back to Newland for a long time and John should know. She composed herself and dialed his office number. Then she realized it was Sunday. Surely John wouldn't be in his office, and she could get away with leaving a message. But John answered on the first ring.

"Bennett here."

"Oh, hi," Ann said nervously. "I was going to leave a message. Why are you in your office on a Sunday, especially right after Christmas?"

"Just checkin' the books. Not much else to do. What's goin' on?"

Ann sat down at the table and told him about Elise and Ruth, using them as logical reasons for her delay in mailing him the title for her Saab, trying to sound calm and friendly but not needy.

"Sorry about your sister," John said. "And I know it's tough to have a parent with dementia. When my dad started wanderin' off and messin' his pants, I knew I couldn't care for him anymore."

Ann shook her head at the thought of her mom messing her pants.

"At least there's more places for old folks down there," John added. "I mean—"

"It's okay. And you're right, there are more places down here."

"Did you, ah, get a call from the Manor House?" he asked.

"Oh, God. Now what?"

"Don't worry," John said calmly. "Emmett's got a respiratory infection, but he's on antibiotics. He's okay. In fact, he looked real good on Christmas Day. He was eatin' cookies with his buddies."

John didn't sound as gloomy as he had the day before. But the news about Emmett disturbed Ann. He was fragile and he was four hours away. "You saw him?" was all she could manage.

"Yeah. Lily invited me to the family Christmas dinner over there. They do a nice job."

So he's seeing Lily, Ann thought. *No wonder he sounds so cheery.*

"I'm sorry; I need to go," she said. "I'm going to my daughter's." She frowned at her lie and added quickly, "Thanks for telling me about Emmett. I'll call the Manor House. I just wanted to let you know about the title."

"When you comin' up again?"

"I don't know yet."

"When you do know, will you give me a call?"

Ann couldn't help giving him a rather curt "Sure." She added a quick goodbye, putting her own meaning on his words: *Let me know when you're coming, so I can be sure I'm not with Lily.*

Ann hung up and put her elbows on the table, resting her head in her hands, thinking of Elise, her mom, Emmett, John, and Christmas without her dad, watching her tears leave spots on the place mat.

TWENTY-FOUR

On surgery day, Ann came to the hospital with a big bouquet for Elise. She found Ruth and Elise's son, Kyle, sitting in the waiting room.

"Well, hi, Annie," Ruth said, surprised. "What are you doing here?"

"I came to see Elise, Mom." Ann stooped to give her mom a hug. "Just like you."

"It's all over," Kyle told her. "Dad's in the recovery room with Mom."

While they made small talk, a woman in clean surgical scrubs approached and introduced herself as Dr. O'Hearn.

"Elise is fine," she said. "Everything went very well and the sample's clean. We don't have anything to worry about, but we always want to be sure because sometimes these things run in the family."

"Not in my family!" Ruth blurted out.

"Oh, of course," Dr. O'Hearn said. "I'm sorry. Elise told me she was adopted."

Ann caught the stunned look on Kyle's face. Ann had told her kids years ago about being adopted, making them promise not to tell anyone out of respect for Gramma Ruth and Grampa Karl. Apparently, they'd kept their promise to not tell their cousin Kyle. And, true to her own promise, Elise never told her son either.

Shortly after the doctor left, a nurse wheeled Elise toward the waiting room, her husband following behind singing, "Here she is! Miss America!"

After Ruth and Ann hugged Elise, Kyle came forward, gave his mother a quick hug, and then stepped away. "Glad you're okay,

Mom," he said, heading for the elevator. "I, ah, want to get my car washed. I'll see you guys at home, okay?"

"What's the rush?" Dave called after his son.

Elise took Dave's hand. "Let him go, honey. He was scared. I'm sure he'd rather not talk about it."

Ann gave Elise one more hug and whispered in her ear. "Everything's okay, sweetie. No more fears. I love you so much."

"Me too," Elise replied warmly.

Ann was walking to the parking structure, feeling grateful and relieved, when her cell phone rang.

"Hi, Annie, it's Karen. Are you still at the hospital?"

"I'm just leaving. The biopsy was clean. Thank God, there's no problem."

"Oh, I'm so glad!" Karen said. "And Elise is okay?"

"Yes, yes. Just a small incision," Ann said. "She'll be fine. She's on her way home."

"Okay, I'll call her later. Listen, I'm on my break right now and can't talk long, but I wanted to know what you thought about us getting together to talk about Mom."

"Oh." Ann hesitated, recalling her conversation with Elise the day before. "It's okay, Karen. Go ahead. I understand if you and Neal want to handle it."

"You mean you don't want to come?"

Ann stopped to listen. "What do you mean?"

"To talk about it."

"Elise said you and Neal were going to decide about Mom."

"What? No. No, I told him I'm not making any decisions without you and Elise. He's a little confused, I guess."

"About what?"

"It's nothing really. You know what a perfectionist he is. I think it all started when he took Mom to get her will updated, and he couldn't find some papers he was looking for."

"Adoption papers. There aren't any adoption papers."

"He never said anything about that," Karen said. "He just asked if we could all get together Monday night at his house."

"Okay, I'll come. I don't know about Elise, though."

"She's got a few days to rest," Karen said. "I'm sure she'll be fine by Monday. Neal said Pam and the kids are going to a movie so the four of us can talk. Would six thirty be okay with you?"

Ann agreed and said goodbye. She drove home thinking of her own mortality, wondering how long she had before she'd need help from her kids—or some anonymous caregivers. Karl had died at eighty. Ruth was now seventy-five. In twenty-two years, she'd be seventy-five herself. The last twenty-two years had flown by. *Time to start living faster. Wasn't that the way John had put it?*

Ann was settled in front of the television with a salad when the phone rang.

"You're not going to believe it, Annie," Elise told her.

The excitement in Elise's voice made Ann wonder if her sister was on a medication high.

"Kyle told me what the doctor said about me being adopted," Elise began. "We actually talked about it, Annie! I told him. I told him everything. Well, at least everything I know."

Ann felt her whole body perk up as her sister went on.

"At first, he was angry because I never told him. He asked so many questions, and he really caught me by surprise. He was disappointed I didn't have any answers. Here I can hardly say birth parents, and he's calling those people his grandparents."

Those people, Ann said in her head. But Elise sounded different, more willing, perhaps, and Ann wanted her to keep talking. "Kyle's right, you know. We might even have relatives in Austria."

"I suppose Lisa and Mark know?"

"Since grade school," Ann replied. "I wanted them to hear it from me before Aunt Inga scared them to death with some fantastic story. I also told them not to say anything because I didn't want to hurt Mom and Dad's feelings."

"Honestly, Annie, sometimes I feel like I don't even know you."

"Yeah, well, sometimes I wonder if I know myself."

Elise chuckled. "I told Kyle about the garbage and the mice in Emmett's house and everything, and he just laughed. He couldn't believe you went in there."

"Emmett was living in there. I didn't have much choice."

"So, you'll go wherever the search for the truth takes you, huh? Spooky old houses or deep, dark shadows."

"There are shadows because there is light," Ann mused.

"Right. You sound like an obsessed treasure hunter or something. I wouldn't be surprised if you went to Austria to snoop around."

"It crossed my mind," Ann said seriously. "But I'd have to know if Anna Miller was her real name."

"Yeah." Elise paused. "So do you still think our real parents were spies?"

"What? When did I say that?"

"When I was about twelve."

"So I was fourteen. Why would you believe anything I said at fourteen?"

"Because I believed everything you told me. You were my big sister, and I trusted you."

"I'm glad you trusted me, but I'm sorry I said such a dumb thing."

"Well, for years the spy thing actually made sense to me," Elise said. "I even used to imagine that our unknown father didn't want to be discovered because he was famous or a criminal on the run. I probably saw too many old movies where the woman won't divulge the identity of the father for some reason like that. Of course, then the woman ends up with more trouble."

Elise's voice trailed off and Ann thought about how Elise was speaking out instead of keeping things inside like she usually did—a habit Ann blamed for Elise's frequent headaches. *Unlike me*, Ann thought, *spitting out questions and opinions like watermelon seeds.*

"Well, whatever. I just wanted to tell you about Kyle," Elise continued. "But the other thing is, Karen called me about getting together to talk about Mom, so I guess we're in on that after all. Maybe Neal's finally ready to sell Mom's car."

Ann followed her sister's abrupt change of topic. "Mom shouldn't be driving."

"I know, I know. But let's give Neal a chance to tell us what he's got on his mind. I don't want him to think we're talking behind his back."

"We're not talking about him behind his back. We're talking behind Mom's back."

"You know what I mean."

"Yes. You want me to keep my mouth shut."

"I just think we should give Neal time to adjust to the idea."

"Adjust to the idea that Mom can't live alone anymore?"

"Annie, I'm sure he values your opinion."

"Sure. Okay. I'll sit back and listen politely." She silently filled in what Elise wasn't saying: *We aren't Ruth's daughters and we have no say in what choices are made about her care.* Had it finally come to that? Was it time to acknowledge the "real children" of Karl and Ruth?

Elise offered a sweet "It'll be okay, sis" and said goodbye. Ann hung up, feeling every bit the crying child on the picnic bench again, watching her parents walk away from her.

TWENTY-FIVE

With his sisters sitting around his kitchen table sharing New Year's resolutions, Neal brought brownies and coffee and joked about the Y2K millennium crisis that never happened. Ann could tell her brother was nervous.

"Might as well talk about what we don't want to talk about," Neal said when he finally sat down. "You already know I think Mom should live as independently as she can for as long as she can."

"We all want that too, Neal," Elise said. "But Mom's health and safety come first, don't you think?"

Ann raised her eyebrows at her sister. Apparently, Elise had decided to speak up for a change.

"To tell you the truth, Steve and I talked about Mom moving in with us," Karen offered. "But all our bedrooms are upstairs. What if she fell down the steps? I can't quit my job to be with her all day. And if she tried to find the grocery store in my neighborhood, she'd get lost for sure."

"I got her using her credit card for groceries now," Neal said with triumph in his voice.

"I wish you hadn't done that." Elise said. "I take her for groceries every week, and I'm very careful about what she buys. When she goes alone, all she buys is junk food."

"She likes to have snacks for when the kids come over," Neal replied.

"She eats too much of it herself, but that's not even the point. Every week I make a list, but once we get to the store, all she wants to do is walk up and down the aisles to see what they have on sale. For her, it's an outing."

"What about Meals on Wheels?" Neal suggested.

"We'd have to be sure they do diabetic meals," Karen reminded him.

Elise shook her head. "She's such a fussy eater."

Ann pictured frozen food in a Styrofoam box on Emmett's table.

"What about a visiting nurse or some other social service program?" Neal asked.

"A gal at work got a visiting nurse for her dad," Karen said. "They don't do meals but they do check blood sugar levels. If we can't get Mom to watch what she eats, she could have another stroke."

"I got there minutes after she called me," Neal said defensively.

Ann touched his arm. "Of course you did. All Karen is saying is that next time it could be worse."

Elise shot Ann one of those now-you-did-it looks. Ann ignored her.

"Look at us, Neal," Ann told her brother tenderly. "We can't help Mom. Not because we don't want to, but because we aren't able to. For one thing, we're too emotionally attached. It's hard telling her what to do. And what if we do something wrong? I think deep inside we all know Mom's not really living independently as long as we are all helping her."

"I don't want to rush into anything," Neal said as he left the table.

"We're not rushing," Ann said after him. "We're talking."

When Neal came back, he dropped two assisted living brochures on the table and sat down heavily. "Is this what you want to talk about?" he asked Ann.

Karen picked up a brochure. "This is the one Annie gave me. They have a shuttle for the grocery store and the mall." She skimmed the brochure. "Here's a whole calendar of stuff going on too. It would be so nice if Mom had some ladies her own age to talk to. Did you see this, Neal? They have a dietitian!"

Elise picked up another brochure. "I think they all have dietitians."

"Those places are expensive," Neal said.

"Mom's got her Social Security benefits, pension, investments," Ann told him. "And she'd have money from the sale of the house. I think she's got enough assets to provide for her care."

Neal looked Ann in the eye. "So now you want to sell the house?"

"It'll have to be sold someday."

"No offense, Annie. But as I recall you didn't want to be Mom's power of attorney, but now it seems you want to make all the decisions."

"No, Neal," Karen said. "You know why Mom wanted you to be power of attorney."

Neal looked a bit sheepish. "Because I'm her only son?"

Ann noticed her brother's neck getting red the same way their dad's neck reddened when he was getting angry.

"Okay. Fine. And I want her to make her own decisions," Neal stated.

Elise started to say something, but Ann interrupted and faced her brother.

"You saw some of her decision-making the other night. Christmas gifts she didn't even know she had, unopened mail stuffed in kitchen drawers, oranges in the freezer, and driving around alone. And I saw you turn the thermostat down like you always do because she cranks it up to eighty whenever she feels a draft."

"Those are all little things we can manage," Neal said calmly.

"But it only takes one little thing to go wrong, Neal," Ann said, shaking a finger. "One forgotten pot on the stove. One little fall on the ice because she insists on wearing those stupid little flats. Next time it might be worse than just a speeding ticket." Ann stopped, took a deep breath, and rubbed the back of her neck. "I'm sorry. I didn't mean to go off."

Karen looked alarmed. "Mom got a ticket? For what?"

"Inattentive driving," Elise said. "And speeding."

"Why didn't anyone tell me?"

Neal apologized to Karen and lowered his head. "The doctor also told me she's anemic."

"I hope that doesn't mean another prescription," Elise said. She counted off on her fingers. "She already takes pills for her heart, blood pressure, arthritis, cholesterol, and dementia, plus the vitamins and acidophilus I got her. And the B12 shot she gets once a month."

"And if she falls and breaks a hip, she'll need more than medication," Ann added.

Karen struggled to speak. "You mean a nursing home?"

Neal shook his head. "Dad would never accept that."

"Dad's not here," Ann said gently.

Neal spoke again, this time with utter concern on his face. "The doctor's also worried about her kidneys."

Elise put a hand to her mouth, stunned. Karen wiped her eyes with a napkin.

"Which doctor?" Ann asked him.

"Her GP. He said something about her protein levels."

Ann sighed deeply. "I'll call him."

"There's something I haven't told anyone either," Karen sputtered. "When I went to Mom's last week, I found her up on the kitchen counter! She said she was looking for her pills. I about had a heart attack! I showed her where her pills were—right there in her daily pill organizer. Then she yelled at me for moving it!" Karen sniffled and wiped her nose. "She says she takes her pills, but she gets mixed up about which are the morning ones or the afternoon or the nighttime ones. I don't even think she knows what day it is half the time. I thought she would get better. I wanted her to get better so bad, but she won't, will she?" Her voice cracked with emotion. "She's getting worse."

As Ann watched Neal pick at crumbs on his plate and Karen search her purse for a tissue, she thought about the resemblances she'd often seen between Karen and Ruth and between Neal and Karl.

Karen was the image of her mother in so many ways. Her hair was fine like Ruth's and she had the same little crease in her earlobes. She was also prediabetic now, an unfortunate trait inherited from Ruth. As for Neal, he wasn't quite as tall as his father, but he had Karl's wide thumbs and square jaw. He was safety conscious in the same overprotective way and sometimes laughed a bit through his nose just as Karl used to do.

Over the years, Ann had dismissed comparisons between herself and Karl or Ruth. Ruth's sister used to say Ann cooked just like Ruth, but of course there was no comparison between Ann's use of fresh ingredients and Ruth's reliance on canned cream of mushroom soup. Ruth herself used to say Ann was stubborn like Karl, but then she told Neal the same thing. Elise, on the other hand, seemed to go out of her way to do things the way Ruth did—except for eating so many carbs. Elise *wanted* to show she was like Ruth, and sometimes it was so painfully obvious.

Ann finished her coffee and stared at the empty cup, thinking of a mug she had once seen. It was printed with "I've finally become my mother!" and Ann had realized the words had no meaning for her. It was the same when she heard people say, "I'm just like my dad." She wanted to say that and know she was right. She rubbed the back of her neck. It felt sore between her shoulder blades again.

Karen spoke up. "I think we should visit a couple of these places, Neal."

He put his elbows on the table and massaged his temples.

"Maybe we could check other places too," Karen suggested.

"At least see the facilities."

"How could we ever talk to Mom about moving?" Elise asked.

Neal looked at Ann. "I know you wanted me to talk to Mom about selling the car."

Ann nodded. "Did you?"

"Not exactly. But a guy at work said families could have the DMV send a letter to an elderly family member to come in for a routine driving test. He said his dad didn't pass the test and his license was revoked." He looked at each of his sisters. "I know Mom wouldn't pass a driving test."

"Then why bother?" Karen wanted to know.

"Because," Elise said, "Mom wouldn't be able to blame us for taking the car away."

Karen gave Neal's arm a gentle slap. "Deal! If you do the DMV thing, we'll start looking at assisted living places."

"I'll talk to her doctor and see if he's got any suggestions," Elise offered. "You know, based on her physical needs and diet and everything."

"As long as it's not a nursing home," Neal insisted.

"I don't think Mom needs a nursing home at this time, Neal," Ann said kindly.

Later when Neal hugged each of his sisters goodbye, Ann noticed tears in his eyes.

"Remember when I fell off the pier at Pine Lake?" Neal asked her.

"Of course. You were only six and you couldn't swim."

"You jumped in after me. You saved my life."

"Ha! And I couldn't swim either!" Ann touched Neal's face. "You were my little brother and I loved you. It was an easy choice."

"You always took care of me. Whenever Mom wasn't around, I wasn't afraid because you were there. I should have told you that a long time ago."

Ann was touched by his memory and his appreciation. As she hugged her brother, she whispered, "Mom will be okay. We'll take care of her."

TWENTY-SIX

Over the next couple of days, Ann's nervous energy took over. She cleaned her mom's house from top to bottom, returned her mom's extra gifts to the mall, bought gifts for Frank and Betty, and spent time with her grandsons. The daytime outings helped occupy her mind, but her solitary evenings felt restless. She tried to write something for the sabbatical project she was supposed to be working on but couldn't concentrate on it. She reread all of Emmett's notebooks and became frustrated again with missing pages. She couldn't even get lost in the book she'd received for Christmas because it was a romance novel, and her mind kept picturing John in place of the featured heartthrob.

The day Ann cleaned out her bedroom closet, she imagined growing up on Emmett's poor farm. She probably wouldn't have had an excess of clothes or shoes. Maybe she would have married a farmer—or John, the cowboy car dealer. She hadn't heard from him since Christmas—not even a Happy New Year call. But she couldn't help thinking of him every day, and the more she thought of him the more she realized her loneliness. She used to say living alone was different from being lonely. Living alone meant doing as she pleased, going where she wanted, making her own decisions. But over the past few years, lonely had overwhelmingly displaced living alone.

When the power of attorney paperwork came in the mail, Ann called the Manor House for an update on Emmett. Lily sounded perky—annoyingly perky. She said Emmett was feeling much better and aren't antibiotics amazing? She asked Ann about the weather in Milwaukee and when she was coming back to Newland. Ann welcomed the update on Emmett but couldn't help picturing Lily and John together.

She hung up and went to the window, scolding herself for feeling like a jealous teenager. It was another cloudy day, but there was no snow in Milwaukee's forecast for the remainder of the week. Without another thought, she dialed Betty.

"Happy New Year!" Ann said when Betty picked up the phone. "Want some company from Milwaukee?"

Early the next morning, Ann packed the Blazer and headed for I-94. The next several hours flew by, and with '60s music in the CD player, her mind was more on John than Emmett. When she reached Newland's snow-lined Main Street, she followed Howie's directions to the bank, parked in the lot, and took the POA paperwork inside. A friendly receptionist made a brief phone call and soon a middle-aged, chubby woman with a stern brow, a purple sequined sweater, and glasses hanging from a purple beaded lanyard walked over to Ann and introduced herself as Mrs. Chambers. She smelled like grape Kool-Aid. Ann followed her to a small office where a nameplate on the desk read "Mrs. Chambers—Vice President Accounts." No first name. Ann couldn't remember calling anyone Mrs. since high school.

"Attorney Studt said to call if you had any questions," Ann said after she explained the reason for her visit.

Mrs. Chambers sniffed over the POA document. "May I see some identification please?"

After Ann produced her driver's license, Mrs. Chambers pecked numbers into her computer and took a sheet from her printer. "This is Mr. Pederson's current balance."

Ann stared at the paper. "Are you sure?"

Mrs. Chambers raised her chin and adjusted her glasses. "Absolutely. Is there a problem?"

Ann tried to hide her shock. Emmett Pederson had just over thirty thousand dollars in his savings account. "He doesn't even have indoor plumbing," Ann said under her breath.

"I beg your pardon?"

"Ah, nothing. Can you also please give me a printout of his checking account activity over the last three months? We can't find his checkbook and he doesn't remember where it is. The family also thinks it would be a good idea to cancel his old accounts and open new ones just for safety's sake."

"Mr. Pederson does not have a checking account with our bank." Mrs. Chambers frowned suspiciously. "I expected to see Frank and Betty Johnson on Emmett's account someday. Or Gordy Halvorson. He always brings Emmett to the bank."

Ann offered her best conciliatory smile and cleared her throat. "Yes I know, but they asked me to help. I forgot he doesn't have a checking account."

Mrs. Chambers waited. Perhaps she was used to being told more. When Ann didn't elaborate, fingers tapped the keyboard again. The last strike caused the printer to spit out two sheets of paper. Mrs. Chambers slid them across her desk.

"This first sheet shows the last three month's activity on his Gold Club account. And this form needs to be filled out and signed the same way you signed the POA document. I assume you want automatic monthly transfers of funds to the Manor House?"

"Oh. So you already know he's there?"

"He's been going there for years," Mrs. Chambers said as if Ann's question was completely stupid. "Everyone knows that." She removed her glasses and let them fall to the safety of her lanyard as she headed for the door.

Alone in the office, Ann filled out the form, and then looked over Emmett's banking history that showed a weekly withdrawal of fifty dollars, perhaps payment for Gordy's so-called help. She took a pen and paper from a plastic holder on the desk and scribbled out a few numbers. A note in her packet from Howie indicated the new rate for full-time residency at the Manor House. Emmett's private room would now cost him $3,500 a month. Without counting his measly Social Security income, the money he had in the bank might cover nine months at the Manor House before his house and property would have to be sold.

Ann folded the scrap of paper and put it in her pocket as Mrs. Chambers came back with a new account number and a folder describing the bank's many convenient services. Ann thanked her briefly and walked outside to snow falling in loose clumps. Chicken feathers her dad used to say—the kind of snow that never amounted to anything.

She got in the Blazer, turned the key, and switched on the wipers, thinking about her next stop—Maplewood Motors. She had no idea what her old car was worth or what kind of deal John would offer on the Blazer. She trusted him, but regretted not doing her homework. Mostly, she hoped she wouldn't embarrass herself by appearing too eager to see him, or too upset if he admitted that he was now dating someone else.

TWENTY-SEVEN

When Ann arrived at Maplewood Motors, she noticed John looking out the showroom window but avoided his eyes. She parked a few rows away and searched her laptop case for her checkbook and the title for her old car. *Remember, no hard feelings,* she said to herself. A minute later, someone rapped gently on the Blazer's window, and Ann turned to see John, his leather jacket open and hat in hand.

She opened the door. "Hi. I was just coming in."

"May I please take you to lunch?"

He looked great, even happy. Happy and handsome. She'd missed him too much.

"Thanks, but I told Betty I'd be there for lunch."

She sensed John knew she was lying, but it looked as if he didn't care.

"Please, Annie. I have to talk to you."

"I decided to buy the Blazer," she said with a smile.

"Good," he replied, his brow slightly creased. "Okay, so can we go for a little drive?"

Ann gave a noncommittal shrug and maneuvered herself over the console to the passenger seat, ready for John to point out more features of the Blazer.

"It's good to see you again," he said as he got behind the wheel and steered out of the lot. "Betty told me you were coming back today. I was watching for you."

No hard feelings, Ann reminded herself. *But he was watching for me.*

"Got somethin' for you," John said, handing her a small envelope. "I put the padlock on Emmett's door."

Ann spilled two small keys into her hand, one newly cut and

one old, rather ornate and worn. "Thank you."

After a few blocks, John turned off Main Street and pulled up to a large metal storage building. "Come on," he said as he got out.

"What?"

When John didn't answer, Ann followed him to an overhead door, which he unlocked and hoisted over their heads. Taking Ann's hand, he guided her inside, where beautiful old wagons, buckboards, and carriages were lined up in rows. Ann caught whiffs of leather and mothballs.

"These are for the annual Dairy Days parade," John said. He lifted a canvas sheet off a topless white carriage with red velvet seats. A narrower, bench-like seat was mounted on the front, obviously for the carriage driver. "It's called a visa vee carriage. Sounds like a credit card but it means face-to-face. Funny name for a buggy. Don't get excited though; that's the only French I know. Sorry for the mothball smell. Helps keep the mice away."

"I don't understand. Why are we here?"

John took a deep breath and exhaled slowly. "It's just a place to talk, Annie. I didn't want to talk in my office, and I figured I wouldn't get you out to my place. I need to tell you a few things. I been doin' a lot of thinkin' since you left."

"Me too, John, and there's no need to explain."

"Yes, there is a need. I want to explain. Please. Can you give me a few minutes?"

He offered his hand to help her step up into the carriage, and when she slid across the seat, he swung up next to her, causing the carriage to rock gently.

"After you left," John began, "Howie and me went out for a few beers."

So he cried in his beer over me, Ann thought. *No,* she told herself. *Be fair. Give him a chance.*

"You remember I told you Howie and me were friends since we were kids?"

Ann nodded.

"Yeah, well, after my mom died, I was over at Howie's a lot. Mrs. Studt always made me stay for supper and take a plate of food back for my dad. Course Joyce was Howie's sister, so I saw her a lot, and Mr. and Mrs. Studt didn't object when we started datin'."

At the mention of Joyce's name, Ann silently hoped this wouldn't take too long.

"See, I knew Joyce was takin' diet pills in high school. Howie used to tell me she had mental problems, not diet problems, but I always figured he was jokin'. I never asked Mrs. Studt about Joyce's mental state because I didn't want to upset her. I guess I didn't want to upset myself either. But when we went out for a beer, Howie said his mom wasn't doin' too good, so I went to see her over Christmas and we got to talkin'." John stopped and cleared his throat. "She told me Joyce had a troubled mind and a sad heart. She said Joyce used to hear voices—like angels or ghosts, and she used to read the Bible and twist it all into doom and gloom." He paused a moment. "Remember I told you Joyce had herself fixed so she couldn't have kids?"

Ann nodded again.

"Well, Mrs. Studt told me Joyce got pregnant right after she married her first husband." John shook his head sadly. "She got the baby aborted because she believed the child was conceived in original sin or some nonsense. Mrs. Studt said it all boiled down to Joyce bein' afraid of livin'. Can you imagine? Afraid of livin'. If I didn't trust Howie and his mom, I wouldn't believe none of it."

He sat back, sniffled, and wiped a gloved hand under his nose. Ann saw pain on his face.

"Howie also told me it was his parents who actually made the final decision to take Joyce off life support. All these years, I blamed myself because they said I had to give permission. I know I went along with it, but I forgot about her parents tellin' me it was the right thing to do. And when I was talkin' to Mrs. Studt, I remembered other things."

John paused a moment, eyes squinting as his memories spilled out.

"I could never get Joyce to laugh. You know? Just laugh! She took everything so seriously. No matter what I did or said, she never seemed happy. I came home for lunch every day just to lift her spirits a little bit." He frowned now, his voice edging toward anger. "I knew she had pills for back pain. But when one of her friends told me Joyce had other pills, I started watchin' her more closely. Her behavior was so different day to day. I suspected she was addicted, but I never told anyone. Whenever anyone asked me how she was, I always said fine. I wanted her to be fine."

Now Ann shifted in the seat, feeling cold from sitting in the windswept building as well as from what John was telling her. He took another deep breath and sat still for a long minute.

"You know," he finally said, "people say we shouldn't live in the past. But we all live in the past all the time. All of our past experiences help get us through the present. Know what I mean?"

Ann nodded at his wisdom.

"You might think it's weird," John continued. "But on Christmas Day after I talked to you, I got this funny urge to go to the cemetery. And once I was standin' over her grave, I knew I could finally let her go. Holdin' on to her memory like I been doin' hasn't done me any good. I finally get it." He paused as if wanting to be sure she heard what he said next. "I want to be happy with you if you'll have me, Annie."

Ann let him take her hand, wanting to believe every word he said.

"Little Gracie also told me she knew you were a good person," John said.

"Gracie? Gracie who?"

"Gracie," John repeated. "You know. The lady at the Manor House. Gracie Studt. Howie and Joyce's mom."

Ann's eyes widened. "With the walker and little bun on top of her head? That Gracie?"

John nodded.

"I know her! I mean I talked to her."

"I know. She told me."

"She remembered my mother. She was going to look for pictures of my sister and me at Emmett's. She said Emmett used to pull her in the coaster wagon when they were kids."

John touched her cheek affectionately. "She told me too. But you'll have to ask Howie about the pictures. Gracie died in her sleep yesterday."

"Oh, no!" Ann said, feeling tears coming.

"I'm telling you all this because I don't want to lose you," he said. "I feel like I loved you all my life. I can't let you go, Annie. I don't want to let you go."

Ann wiped her eyes, letting his words sink in. One thing she knew—right or wrong, wise or foolish, she was in love with him. But she had to ask. "I thought you were seeing someone else. Maybe Lily."

"Lily?"

"Well, you said you were at the Manor House for Christmas."

"I went with Howie to see Gracie. Lily was there, but she's always there. I met her new boyfriend too, in case you're interested." He gave her a wink.

Ann felt her cheeks blush.

"I also been thinkin' about what you said about me bein' up here and you down in Milwaukee," John added. "And the way I figure it, if we want to be together, I know we can figure out a way for it to work."

He leaned forward to kiss her, causing the carriage to tip slightly and give out a long and painful groan. Their kiss broke into separate grins before he moved back to balance the carriage.

"Can you ever love an old fool?" he asked.

This time Ann moved over and put her arms around his neck. "No. But I can love you."

They kissed again, and a blast of wind rattled harnesses and antique jingle bells hanging on the opposite wall.

"We better go before someone wonders why these buggies are open to the weather," John said. He stepped out of the carriage and held his hands out for her. "I don't have a coaster wagon, but I promise to take you for a ride in my carriage someday."

Ann stepped down and into his arms. "I'd like that very much."

Snow blew across the sidewalk and gathered in little drifts in front of Melody's Café. John held the door for Ann and said hello here and there as they walked hand in hand to a booth. Ann wanted to tell everyone she was in love with John and he with her. Perhaps the whole town probably already knew.

After they settled in their booth, Ann removed the older key from the envelope John had given her. "You didn't tell me what this other key is for."

"Emmett's barrister."

"Oh my God! Where did you find it?"

"My mom had a locked cabinet for things she didn't want me gettin' into. She always kept the key on top of the cabinet and that's where I found Emmett's. I didn't open the barrister though. I figured you should do the honors."

"Thank you. Now I can't wait to get back to his place."

"And I hope you don't mind, but I did take a look inside Emmett's old camper trailer. It's a real mess inside. All kinds of books and magazines everywhere and piles of old clothes on the bed. The floor's rotten by the door, but if that was fixed and it was all cleaned up, it could make a neat little shelter for a deer hunter." He ticked off the features. "I'm guessin' it's a

'70s model. Propane heat. There's a little bedroom area, and the built-in table and benches fold down if you need another bed. The refrigerator's full of papers."

"There's a refrigerator?"

"Yeah, a small one. Typical for those campers."

Ann shook her head in disbelief. "But no refrigerator in the house!"

"I don't think the little stove and sink were ever used either."

"Stove and sink," Ann muttered. "Amazing."

After the waitress took their order for soup and sandwiches, John rested his arms on the table and looked Ann in the eyes.

"Emmett was in a good mood when I saw him over Christmas. But he's old and weak, Annie. I don't mean to tell you what to do, but if I were you, I'd get to the point with him pretty quick. You don't know how much time he's got. And if you want to know the rest of your story, I think you should be straight up with him."

"Straight up?"

"Yeah. Like the way you were with me on that first day."

"What do you mean?"

John chuckled. "As I recall, you interrogated me real good— tellin' me I was rude to Emmett and askin' me about the money I gave him for his truck. Remember?"

"I'm sorry. I just didn't want him getting upset. He's the only one who knows the truth about my adoption."

"That's why you gotta ask for what you want. Ask him flat out if he's your father."

"And if he gets mad and shuts me out? Then what? I don't know what to say. I don't know how to start."

"What did you do when you were a kid and other kids took your toys?"

"I shared."

"What about at work? How do you ask for a raise?"

"I wait for my yearly review."

John smiled and shook his head at her. "You know, if I was always polite like you, we wouldn't be sittin' here together."

"You're polite enough, John. And I know I've been procrastinating. But I just met him. I'm trying to understand him."

Ann stopped talking while the waitress arranged their lunches on the table. When they were alone again, John crushed a cracker over his soup.

"Emmett's a man from another time," he told her. "They talk less and say more and do what needs to be done. They expect the same from others. I have a feelin' he'd tell you if you just ask."

"I don't know," Ann said with a sigh. "Maybe straight up is a guy thing." She leaned across her plate and lowered her voice. "I know I wouldn't have gotten away with saying he'd freeze his nuts off if he didn't get out of his freezing house."

John laughed. "Okay, you got a point there. But next time you're at the Manor House, just watch how those lady aides deal with some of those crotchety old boys. They don't let 'em get away with bein' stubborn. They don't take no for an answer either."

Ann tasted her soup, and then put her spoon down. "What if he says yes? What if he says he is my father?"

"Either he is or he isn't, honey. Seems to me you don't have a choice either way."

Ann shoved a piece of lettuce back into her sandwich. "He's not at all what I expected. I found out he's got money too." She whispered the amount across the table.

"It's like a lot of old folks up here. They live like paupers but when they die, you find out their kids inherited all kinds of money. Like old Mrs. Dawson. She goes around shiverin' in a coat you can practically see through, but last week she came in with her son to buy him a truck. I tried to talk 'em into a good used truck, but her son kept insistin' he needs a new one, so she gave in." He frowned. "Makes me sick when I see stuff like that."

"Emmett doesn't have kids," Ann mused. "At least he didn't until I showed up."

"It don't matter now. Whatever money he's got will all go to the Manor House or wherever he winds up unless he dies before his assets are all gone. And if he's your father—if you can prove he's your father—you and your sister would get whatever's left anyway."

"Unless he's willed it to someone else. Like Gordy."

John positioned his sandwich for a bite. "Does he have a will?"

"I don't know. Howie's looking for one. But I didn't come up here hoping to inherit anything. I just came up here to find my father, and all I want is for Emmett to tell me the truth. I don't think my sister would care about an inheritance either."

"You never know, honey. Some people sing a different tune when money's involved."

TWENTY-EIGHT

Ann entered the Manor House behind a group of people carrying helium balloons and a cake. When it was her turn to sign the guest registry, she asked the aide behind the counter, "Someone's birthday?"

"No, one of our residents had a stroke," the aide replied. "His family came to cheer him up."

Ann followed the balloons to the common room, where the balloon people had gathered around a man in a wheelchair. She recognized Fred Noble right away and knew he'd never harass her or anyone else ever again.

She saw Emmett on the other side of the room near a window, dwarfed by the oversized recliner he was sitting in. He had a blanket draped over his legs and wore the same tired-looking expression Ann remembered from her dad's congestive heart failure.

"Hi, Emmett," Ann said cheerfully as she approached.

"Hello there," he said as if he wasn't sure who she was.

Please don't let his brain leave him yet, Ann thought as she took her jacket off and sat in the chair next to him. "I heard you were sick. But it looks like you're feeling better now."

"I can't complain," he muttered. "I suppose I'm old."

She grinned at the same little quip he'd made when she visited him before Christmas.

"You're Karl's daughter," he said.

"That's right," Ann replied with relief. "And I have a question about your camper trailer. I have a friend who's looking for one." She hoped he wouldn't ask who wanted the camper because she'd have to make something up fast.

Emmett picked at a button on his flannel shirt. "Huh. Yeah, I used to call it my pad. When Clayton's rowdy friends came over to play cards, I went out to my pad for some peace and quiet."

"If you aren't using it anymore, maybe you could make some money off of it," Ann said.

"Seems to me I paid four thousand for it. Still good as new," he said confidently. "Your friend can come out and look at it if he wants." Emmett stopped and thought a moment. "You teach college, don't you?"

She wasn't entirely surprised at another repeat question. How long would it be before his memory evaporated entirely?

"Yes, I do."

"Gracie went all the way through high school," he said. "Clayton too. Course I only got up to the ninth grade. But I read more than the others."

Ann nodded politely, wondering if he knew about Gracie, not wanting to tell him she had died. "Well, I'm sure you learned a lot from being in the Army," she said, hoping he didn't recognize the same prompt she'd used weeks ago.

He gazed at the window. While Ann tried to think of another innocent-sounding prompt, Emmett looked back at her.

"You want to know about the war, don't you?" he asked plainly. "Everyone always asks about the war."

"Well, I . . . "

He continued more loudly than Ann expected.

"War is a charade. It's a charade of carnage. Nothing more. I saw things no human being should see." He studied her face a moment. "There's no sense to war. Do you understand? It's the child of stupid politics and greed. One side always wants what the other side has. Thousands of innocent people on both sides get slaughtered and maimed just because they're in the way of someone else's point of view. It's a centuries-old failure of humanity."

Ann expected him to ask her to leave him alone. But when she said, "I agree with you," he continued in a softer voice.

"They told us we were patriotic, but no one thinks about patriotism when they're in combat. When you're in the thick of it, all you want to do is survive. Even now, after all these years, I still can't believe I was there."

He coughed several times, wincing and wheezing, trying to catch his breath. Ann got the attention of an aide who smiled and nodded as if to say, "He's okay." A minute later, Emmett continued in slow, measured sentences.

"Karl was a motor sergeant. I never got past private. Never wanted to."

"I bet you were glad to get home again."

"It was one of the happiest days of my life." He pinched his nose with two fingers and wiped them on the blanket. "We didn't have fancy things, but my mother made a good home for my brother and me. She always wanted the best for us."

"I'm sure she did," Ann said respectfully. "And I bet she knew you'd have a pretty girl someday."

"I didn't have much to offer."

But you didn't dismiss the thought of a woman in your life, Ann wanted to say, wishing they could talk about what he wrote in his notebooks, wishing she could read his mind.

"Karl was the lady's man," he added. "Good dancer. He came up on leave when I was in Austria during the occupation. Some of the local folks showed us around."

He coughed again and closed his eyes, his breaths short but steady. A moment later he began snoring and an aide came toward Ann.

"Excuse me," she said. "I'm Patty. He eats better if he has a nap before supper." She touched Emmett's shoulder. "Emmett? Emmett? How 'bout gettin' a little nap in before supper?"

Patty carefully raised the back of the recliner.

"One of the other aides let him nap here," Ann told her. "He seems comfortable."

"We're not supposed to do that." Patty instructed Emmett

to take her arm and when he did, she helped him to his feet and waited while he steadied himself.

Ann gently patted his shoulder. "I'll see you tomorrow, okay?"

"Sure," he said weakly. "You can tell your friend to come out and see the camper."

Patty walked alongside him, but she didn't offer her arm. Ann had noticed that the aides were all different. Some were friendly, others not so much. Some seemed happy to help the residents, and others acted like they didn't want to be bothered. It seemed to Ann that Emmett would have been okay in the recliner, but he didn't have a choice. She wondered whether she should ask about what choices he did have and how she could be sure he got what he preferred. She also regretted talking about Emmett as if he hadn't been right there—like Irene the church lady had done. She didn't want his feelings to be ignored, his opinions to be cast aside. She left, feeling she had let Emmett down. She should have said something. One thing for sure, being straight up would have to wait for another day.

She pulled her gloves out of her pocket and the folded envelope from John fell onto the floor. With the little keys in her hand, she walked to the exit. The innocent clumps of snow from a short time ago had turned into a translucent curtain of white. She dialed her cell phone and told Betty she wanted to make a quick stop at Emmett's house.

"You might want to save that for another day, Annie," Betty said. "It's getting windy, and the snow's supposed to pick up."

"I won't stay long. Don't worry. I'll keep an eye on it."

"Well, you be sure and call us if you have trouble."

A small drift had already accumulated across Emmett's driveway, but Ann drove over it easily. She parked and sat in the Blazer a moment, watching the wiper blade trying to keep up with the snowflakes, thinking she should head back to Betty's.

But then she noticed the barn door standing wide open. *It must have blown open in the wind.* She turned off the ignition and walked to the barn. Tentatively, she stepped inside, taking in smells of old wood and earth.

The ceiling was low, but the dirt-streaked windows on the far wall provided enough light as well as a view across Emmett's acreage to the hardwoods in the distance, now only dark outlines against the falling snow. Beneath the windows, a rough-hewn workbench held an assortment of ancient hand tools along with old coffee cans full of nails, nuts, and bolts. A long, rusty saw and aged garden implements hung below swallows' nests plastered between the rafters. She followed the workbench to a doorway, where she had to duck her head in order to enter another room of the barn. Thanks to her tour of Frank's barn, she recognized milking stanchions, cobbled together as these were with mismatched boards. The same carpenter must have made the two humble stalls along the opposite wall.

As she turned back toward the door, Ann noticed a rope coiled up on a small bench. Momentarily spooked at the thought of Emmett's brother swinging from a rafter above her, she hurried back to the Blazer. That's when Emmett's camper, partially hidden behind bushes alongside the barn, caught her eye. Surely, it would take just a minute to check it out.

She opened the camper door and stepped carefully over the rotted flooring John had warned her about. Clothing and bedding was scattered everywhere; it was like someone's messy miniature apartment. She opened cupboards and drawers one by one, finding nothing but a few dishes, utensils, and lots of mouse poop. The refrigerator was another story. It was stacked with old papers as if Emmett used it as a safe.

One thing that caught Ann's eye right away was a flash of gold. She picked it up—a plaster cast about the size of her hand depicted a ship inside a life preserver. The words "Cunard White Star Line, Queen Mary" were printed on the life preserver, and underneath it was a newsletter with the heading: "Rollin' Home—On Board H.M.S. Queen Mary, Monday 26 November 1945." News items included an article about a crime wave in New York, scores from recent pro football games, examples of how food prices back home had gone up—a dozen eggs had gone up from thirty-six cents to fifty-five—and numerous other reminders of how things had changed back home. The main purpose of the newsletter seemed to focus on updating returning soldiers on life back home in the States, as if they could just slip back into their former lives and forget about tanks and bombs and the dead friends they had to leave behind.

Under the newsletter were issues of both *Stars and Stripes* and *The Grapevine*, a newsletter of the 26th Infantry Division. One issue featured a picture of Ava Gardner in a two-piece swimsuit and the caption "Why We Fight." One *Stars and Stripes* headline announced, "Resistance Ends in Northern Reich." Another headline proclaimed "WAR ENDS" in large white letters on a red background. When Ann reached for a stack of *Newland News* issues from the '40s and '50s, the wind howled and branches from nearby bushes whipped the camper relentlessly.

She put a few of the newspapers in a paper bag for Frank and Betty, and when she saw a shoebox sealed with duct tape in the back of the refrigerator, she decided to take that too. On the way out, she spotted a green metal box under the camper's built-in table. Too enticing, she grabbed it as well.

Snow now filled the footprints she'd made just minutes earlier. The wind blew the snow horizontally, but when she saw a pickup drive by, Ann decided the roads must still be okay. She quickly put the bag and metal box in the Blazer, went to the porch, and opened the padlock on Emmett's frozen shell of a house.

Facing the barrister, Ann put the little key from John into the keyhole. The hinged front fell open toward her, creating a writing surface. Eagerly, she pulled the chain on the lone bulb hanging from the ceiling, sending it and its cobweb cocoon swinging eerily.

Unlike the three glass-fronted sections she had cleaned out on previous visits, the interior of this desk-like section was surprisingly tidy. Built-in shelves separated four small drawers along the top of the compartment from two slightly larger drawers below. The shelves held neat stacks of stationery, envelopes, and outdated stamps. Every drawer had something in it: old coins, a pocket watch complete with a fob and chain, skeleton keys, fountain pen tips, and one tiny toy soldier holding a rifle. When she saw a small leather notebook, she eagerly opened it only to have pressed flowers fall out from between the blank pages.

Ann put the smaller items in an envelope and turned her attention to a stack of small black-and-white photos, all curled with age. Some showed GIs marching in long lines or eating out of cans. Others showed ruined buildings and ragged refugees pushing two-wheeled carts. One showed men sitting on a roadside with American soldiers standing guard over them. Emmett had written "German prisoners of war" on the back. She pulled out another envelope to put the photos in and four pocket-sized notebooks fell out in front of her.

The next blast of wind rattled the windows. *Just a few more minutes,* Ann told herself. She moved closer to the window for better light and opened the thinnest notebook.

> *Sunday, May 1, 1949. A fine spring morning begins my favorite month. As the situation now stands, the outlook for the crop year is good. The oats are coming up already, and the grass is greener each day. Today I'll be hauling more manure and splitting more wood for Torkelsons. As of this date, they owe me $20 for work completed thus far.*

> *Friday, May 6, 1949. Pastures are green, trees leafing*

out. Orioles are back. Worked out at Schultz's. Dynamited stumps and piled logs. He paid me $3. Tomorrow I'll take the team back to Carlson's and finish plowing.

The next page was divided into columns, showing money received for other work: $5 for disking a field, 60 cents an hour for sawing wood, $3.60 for an afternoon of dynamiting stumps. The last page was different.

Thursday, May 12, 1949. Warm and fair day. Stayed home. Anna minded the baby while she worked a patch for beans. I planted early potatoes. Nana spent the day washing clothes.

Anna! And the baby in May of 1949 would certainly have been Elise, born the year before! Eagerly, Ann picked up the next notebook—a larger red one with the spiral spine at the top instead of along the side. Here, the pages were numbered. She flipped ahead until she saw a 1945 date.

August 29, 1945. Linz. It was my pleasure to visit Mitzie at her home last night for the most enjoyable evening I have spent since I arrived here. It would have been so easy to take advantage. But I shan't tarnish the love of my life. The souvenir edelweiss she gave me to remember her by was not necessary. I will have her with me always.

Ann shook her head. It sounded as if this Mitzie was the love of his life rather than Anna. Was Emmett suggesting he hadn't been intimate with Mitzie? Or Anna? Which one wouldn't he tarnish? She turned the page.

September 5, 1945. Linz. Up to this point I have

gladly avoided affairs of the heart. But sweet and winsome Mitzie has caused me emotional upheaval. I can hardly be separated from those beautiful eyes that have seen so much of war and trouble. She is a survivor. She could get by anywhere. We are quite natural together. She completely disarms me with her warmth and in moments of serious gravity, when she is recalling her life, she is sad but so lovely in her storytelling. I am captivated and cannot resist my desire to be with her.

At the apartment yesterday, Johann played guitar and Mitzie asked me to sing. The only song I could remember was "My Bonnie Lies Over the Ocean." She laughed and encouraged me by singing "My Yankee Lies Over the Ocean." I'm sure everyone knows how smitten I am with her.

Ann didn't like what she was reading. Emmett was clearly in love on September 5, 1945, in Linz, Austria—but not with her mother. She couldn't read fast enough.

September 10. Linz. Karl arrived today with another Wisconsin fellow. I invited them to join Mitzie and me and a few other friends to visit the famed Berchtesgaden— Hitler's mountainous retreat. We traveled by train and enjoyed a luncheon in the dining car. We proceeded by truck and finally climbed a steep pathway to the Eagle's nest. From there the peaks rose on two sides and the great cliffs yawned above the valley two miles straight below— an awe-inspiring view. I paid for our train tickets and lunch, but it was Karl who received Mitzie's attention. I hate to admit he, like mostly anyone else, has more to offer her than me. The thought of Austria as her home is both satisfying and heartbreaking.

September 21, 1945. Linz. The past few days have been rainy and fall is in the air. I am feeling an overwhelming depression and it's not because of the weather. Remnants of war are ever present and all the anxiety of the world is written on the faces of the people. Mitzie fears winter since Linz suffers from too little of everything. My heart aches to make her happy in every way. But will she accept me?

September 23. Linz. Yesterday Mitzie and I walked to a civilian theater near her place. It was raining and we shared her umbrella. Upon arriving at the theater almost soaking wet, we learned to our chagrin that we needed reservations. Without those, we had no choice but to walk back, arm in arm. The evening proved to be delightful despite the weather. We shall be together. It is only a matter of time.

September 24. Linz. The news of our imminent departure from Linz came officially today. It was somewhat of a bitter pill for me in view of all the gay times I have enjoyed here. Tonight she was sad, and I wondered for whom. If we are separated by circumstance of war or heart, I dread the thought of living without her.

October 7, 1945. Vilseck, Germany. My heart and head are heavy with grief at no word from my beloved. Perhaps it is the height of folly to make elaborate plans for the future, and still I anguish over how to proceed. There is no life without Mitzie. I must win her back. Pa won't like me working off the farm, and he'll never understand how the sweet events of the past few months have replaced the agony of these past few years—nay, the agony of my life. My love has profoundly altered my philosophy of life. I cannot sleep for want of her. Daytime hours and wretched chores do not dissuade me from desiring her. I can hardly compose myself at times. My whole being suffers knowing Karl has won her over. I will never be happy without her.

Ann skimmed the next few pages quickly, listening to the wind, hoping to see another mention of her dad with Mitzie or Emmett with Anna. She was really cold now, but page twenty-six grabbed her attention.

October 10, 1945. Vilseck, Germany. Viewed in retrospect, the events of the past few months have had a profound effect on my philosophy of life in general. I must set aside a few days for the sole purpose of deciding on a course of action. I must be practical and not depend on any chance bit of luck or a golden happenstance of opportunity because there probably won't be any. I must depend on myself and my own character and apply all the knowledge I have gained in my years of hardship and loneliness. I must decide my fate with dignity.

October 12. Vilseck, Germany. Today we are scheduled to leave for France on another leg of our trip home. We are told it will be a long ride—some of it in 40x8 foot boxcars. Others are in good spirits about finally leaving Europe, but I feel lost. Psychologically and emotionally, I wonder how I shall endure the pain. While we wait for orders to embark for the States, we spend hours attending shows at the Red Cross club. One show, "Her Highness and the Bellboy," made me wonder if Mitzie could ever love a farm boy like me. Mother has been so ill, and were it not for the additional pain it would cause her, I would desert now and return to Austria where my heart lies. I am not the same person I was four short years ago—flotsam with no real anchorage. I feel more like 50 than 30. I yearn for peace in the heart after these months of turmoil and horrid dreams. I yearn for a letter from my love. Only she can sustain me.

Ann turned the page.

October 30. Le Havre, France. I am chafing under the monotony of the unexpected delay here. Tortured by an increasing restlessness and lack of news from home or my love, it is becoming increasingly difficult to find any interesting ways of passing time. It is nearly a month since we left the division and Linz, and still we have no assurance of an early return to the States and civilian life. Army entertainment and the Red Cross provide scant consolation. My dreams are still tortured by the memory of Mitzie's sweet, piquant face. I could leave here and go back to her. But no. Our best chance is in the States.

Then a line dividing the page and the word "DRAFT."

Nov. 9, 1945. Le Havre, France.
Dearly Beloved,
The written word is so woefully inadequate at expressing a love like ours. Words elude me like a will-o'-the-wisp, taunting me in my helplessness. But even so, I am certain you will understand if I am unable to convey to you in writing my affection and longing for you in these few humble phrases. How I miss you, my dearest love. Your letter was like a reassuring caress, a touch of your hand on paper to strengthen me.

Nov. 10, 1945. Today we have been notified that we are to sail for England tomorrow, there to board a ship for the States.

Ann wondered who "Dearly Beloved" was and what had happened to Anna. With the next blast of wind, the kitchen door flew open.

"Annie?" John's voice shouted. "Come on, honey! We gotta get out of here now!"

TWENTY-NINE

Ann shoved the notebooks and the envelopes with Emmett's things in her pockets and followed John outside. When she started for the Blazer, he grabbed her arm.

"We'll get it tomorrow," he shouted over the wind as he led her along the side of the house. He helped her over the two-foot drift blocking Emmett's driveway and led her to the road where a Maplewood Motors plow truck waited, warning lights flashing and engine running.

"This is awful!" Ann said, once they were both inside. "Stupid me for not paying attention!"

"Don't worry. I been out in worse than this."

"How did you know I was here?"

John shifted into drive and eased forward. "I was sendin' everyone home when Betty called. She was afraid you had an accident. And when I saw the light on in Emmett's house, I knew you were here." He glanced in her direction. "Hope you don't mind, but my place is closer."

"Okay," Ann said, trying to see the road through gusts of blinding white.

When they finally reached his driveway, John lowered the plow and easily carved a path to his house. "Go inside," he told her. "I need to get the horses in."

Ann called Betty, told her she was fine and confirmed that John had a guest room. When she looked out the window, Ann saw John holding onto his hat and Chip as he took long strides toward the house. She met him at the door.

"All secure," he said, putting Chip on the floor. "Everyone's safe and warm. Including us."

"Thanks to you again," Ann said. "I called Betty."

"Did you tell her you're spending the night here?"

"I told her you had a guest room."

"Yep, I do."

He removed his boots and said something about the weather forecast, but Ann was distracted by Chip sniffing around a familiar-looking trunk and two cardboard boxes in the living room.

John followed her gaze. "I, ah, forgot to tell you about those. I brought 'em over here after I put the lock on Emmett's place. Hope you don't mind."

Ann gave him a quick peck on the cheek. "You're amazing."

While John added logs to the fire, Ann opened the first box marked "Christmas" and unwrapped plaster figures of Mary, Joseph, the baby Jesus, camels, kings, and shepherds.

"My grandmother had a set like this," she said, arranging the figures on the coffee table.

John joined her on the couch. "My mom too. I think it was required."

The second Christmas box was full of little bundles of newspaper. They unwrapped each one carefully until the coffee table was covered in antique glass ornaments in glistening colors and different shapes—orbs, bells, teardrops, teapots, fruit and nut shapes, Santa heads, pinecones, delicate musical instruments, and animals of all kinds. In a final nest of newspaper, Ann found handmade ornaments made of fabric—animals, flowers, and birds trimmed with buttons, beads, feathers, and embroidery.

"These are precious," Ann said. She unwrapped the last bundle and held up little sleds made of thin wood slats. Someone had painted *Elise* on one and *Anna* on the other. "Look. One for me and one for my sister."

"Someone loved you," John patted her thigh. "That's a good thing, you know."

"I'm okay. No more panic attacks."

"Atta girl."

"But I do have something else to show you." Ann got the notebooks from her jacket pocket and pointed out references to her dad and Mitzie. "My mom and dad were engaged. Dad was cheating."

"It's not unusual for a guy to be stuck on two women at the same time," John said. "Especially guys in war. Maybe your dad missed your mom. Maybe he needed—you know—"

Ann frowned. "You mean my dad couldn't help himself?"

John shrugged.

Ann rolled her eyes. "And what about Emmett? He told me he never had much to offer a woman. He said my dad was better looking and a better dancer. Imagine the blow to his self-esteem when his cousin Karl steals his girlfriend."

"Okay, but Anna was the one who came to Newland, honey, not Mitzie. Maybe Emmett realized he liked Anna better. It's Anna's name on your birth certificate, right?"

Ann gazed at the crackling fire. "Yes. And even if I don't like the idea of my dad having an affair, I'm still stuck with why Karl and Ruth adopted Emmett's daughters. It just seems so strange." She nodded and turned to John slowly as an answer came to her. "Wait a second. Maybe Nana had something to do with it."

John raised his eyebrows. "There you go. I bet she didn't want to lose track of her two little great-granddaughters. And since Emmett wasn't married, and considerin' his living conditions, he might have seen the sense in givin' you and your sister up. Maybe in the end they all figured you'd at least still be in the family."

"Yeah," Ann said sarcastically. "And that fixed everything."

A strong blast of wind whistled around the house and Chip jerked awake. She cocked her head and listened for a moment, then stretched and pawed John's pants leg.

"Chip's hungry," John said. "Are you hungry?"

"I am actually."

"Good, because I made a batch of my mom's spaghetti sauce yesterday, and it's darn good even if I do say so myself. Even got some brownies and ice cream left."

John fed Chip and adjusted the flame under his pot of spaghetti sauce while Ann filled another one with water for pasta. He opened a bottle of red wine as she set the table. They ate and talked, and it seemed to Ann the only thing missing was the Frank Sinatra music.

After mopping up the last of his ice cream with a chunk of brownie, John went to the living room, threw a couple of logs on the fire, and disappeared around the corner. Moments later, Ann heard Elvis Presley's voice and saw John step out to the center of the living room, arms outstretched. "May I have this dance?"

Ann went to him. "Thought you were a jazz man."

"I am except for the King," he said, giving her a quick twirl. "And a few other moldy oldies."

They danced through dozens of songs from the '50s and '60s and Ann relaxed, pleasantly surprised at how well she matched John's sure steps. Maybe it was the wine, but every time they danced past the front window, Ann found the growing drifts on the driveway more beautiful and the howling wind more romantic. Finally, Ann couldn't help a satisfied yawn.

"Gettin' tired?" he asked.

"No, not really," Ann replied, feeling suddenly nervous about sleeping arrangements.

John took her hand. "This way, my lady. I'll show you your accommodations."

He led her across the kitchen and down the hallway to a bedroom with an adjacent bath. Her bed for the night had a headboard of twisted, polished saplings and a beautiful quilted spread. Built-in cabinets lined one wall of the spacious bathroom, and a huge jet tub filled one corner.

"You're welcome to whatever's here," John said, opening cabinets and drawers near the sink. "Towels are in here, and a hair dryer and a brush. There's even a new toothbrush, toothpaste, and some makeup."

"Makeup?"

"Yeah. Howie's cousins stayed with me when his son got married last summer. They forgot all this stuff." He opened a drawer and handed her a large, neatly folded T-shirt with an American flag on the front. "They forgot this too. Guaranteed to bring patriotic dreams. It's even clean."

"Thanks. It's perfect."

"You're perfect," John said.

Here it comes, Ann thought. *He'll put his arms around me and waltz me right over to the bed.*

"Well, it's still early," he said, clearing his throat. "You like Scrabble?"

"The game?"

"Yeah. Howie's son taught me how to play a while back. Ha! And with your education and my dyslexia, I figure we're evenly matched! 'Sides, I have the official dictionary and more wine!"

Ann tossed the patriotic dreams shirt on the bed. "You're on!"

John scored high points with hulk, pink, and vex—words he'd memorized as point getters. Ann fought back with voice, haze, and fluid. When she protested his Q-A-T for a double on the Q, John grinned and handed her the dictionary.

"Okay, no more Mrs. Nice Guy," Ann teased.

Halfway through the second bottle of wine, Ann won by seventeen points, insisting she'd worked hard for every one. John toasted her victory and drained his glass before getting up to let a reluctant Chip outside. Ann was cleaning up the Scrabble tiles when John came up behind her and kissed her neck. She turned and he kissed her again on the mouth. The kiss was wonderful, but Ann couldn't help stiffen when she felt his hand brush the bare skin of her lower back. She also noticed a slight buzz from the wine and eased away slightly, smoothing her sweater down.

"I'm really tired," Ann said with a nervous chuckle. "I'm sure I'll be asleep as soon as my head hits the pillow."

John gave her a quick nod. "Right. Yeah, okay. I'll put Chip upstairs in my bathroom for tonight. She might whine a little bit, but she'll settle down."

They said goodnight and Ann went down the hall to the guest room. John wanted her. She could feel it. But it was too soon. Wasn't it? She undressed and then slipped the flag T-shirt over her head, wondering how long it would be before she couldn't resist sleeping with him. When the music from the living room stopped, she heard him call Chip upstairs. Ann got in bed and pulled the weighty quilt over her. Gradually, Chip's whining subsided, but Ann's mind roared on like a freight train. It happened every time she had more than one glass of wine. She didn't think she was drunk, but then she'd never been drunk—something people never believed when she told them. One thing for sure—no, she wasn't sure—how much wine did she have tonight?

She curled up and John's story about Joyce floated in her head along with Emmett's voice saying, "I didn't have much to offer," and "Karl was the lady's man." So just when did Karl stop being a lady's man? The wind howled. Ann rolled over and hugged the pillow. Soon her mind was running wild with images of her most willing and immediate surrender to John's loving embrace. When she heard the gentle tap on the bedroom door, she didn't hesitate to say, "Come in."

THIRTY

Half asleep with eyes closed, Ann pulled the quilt around her, but no matter how she tried to cover them, her feet stuck out. She curled up, listening to the rumble of an engine outside. *Must be a snowplow or something,* she thought. But it didn't sound like plows she usually heard on her street. This one passed the house several times, getting louder, fading away, louder, fading. She rolled onto her side, realizing she felt uncommonly good this morning. Rested. *What was the word? Rapturous. Right. Good word.* But something felt different.

She opened her eyes and sat up. The bed—not her bed—was a mess, one corner of the fitted sheet pulled off. Her patriotic dreams nightshirt was on the floor along with socks that weren't hers. She stretched to pick up the shirt and quickly slipped it over her head and fell back on the bed, recalling the night before. John had come in just as she was falling asleep. He got in bed with her and said he loved her. She'd wanted him as much as he wanted her, and what followed next was indeed rapturous.

Ann gathered her clothes and quickly washed and dressed. She dabbed on some mascara from the bathroom cabinet while listening for sounds of John in the house. Where was he? All she could see out the window was a white field and snowy evergreens. *And why didn't I wake up when he got out of bed? I must have been zonked out.* She hoped she hadn't snored.

In the kitchen, Ann found a pot of fresh coffee and two mugs waiting on the counter. She filled a mug as John passed the window on a big orange tractor. Holding Chip on his lap, he plowed the last snowdrift aside. When he turned around and saw Ann in the window, he waved Chip's forepaw. Ann waved back, giggling at the cap with earflaps that had replaced John's cowboy hat. A smile crept across her face as images of the night before replayed in her mind. In every way, John felt so right.

She walked from one window to another, admiring the layout of John's place. Evergreens edged the driveway all the way to the road. A split rail fence enclosed a wide space around the barn, where John's horses stood around a feeder, sharing hay. Sun flashed off the copper weathervane atop the barn, and eager chickadees flitted around a feeder near the porch. Ann sipped her coffee and felt her whole body warm with contentment. *I could get very used to this,* she thought as he came inside.

"Mornin'!" John said, taking his hat off and putting Chip on the floor.

"Good morning," Ann said with a grin. "Nice hat."

John laughed and hung the hat on a peg. "You weren't supposed to see this. Sleep okay?"

Ann felt herself blush. "I did. Eventually."

"I hope you're not sorry. Because if you are . . ."

Ann stood on her toes and kissed him. "I don't know what you're talking about."

"I'm glad you stayed last night," he said as he put his arms around her.

"As I recall, I didn't have much choice."

"I guess the good Lord works in mysterious ways after all." He hooked an arm over her shoulders and led her to the kitchen. "Plowing snow on a beautiful morning with a pretty girl watchin' from the window is about as good as it gets." He poured himself a cup of coffee. "Got me thinkin'."

"Thinking?"

He took a cast-iron frying pan from a bottom cupboard. "I'm starvin'. You hungry?"

"You were thinking about eating?"

"Yeah, for one thing."

He adjusted the flame under the pan and went to the

refrigerator for bacon and eggs. Ann waited, but he didn't elaborate.

"It's seven thirty," Ann said. "When do you have to be at work?"

"I called and said I'd be late," John said, slicing open the bacon. "Brad'll take over until I get there. They'll manage."

"I suppose they'll talk about us."

"I suppose so." He arranged the bacon in the pan with a fork. "You know, out there on the tractor, I was thinkin' we fit together pretty good. And I'm wonderin' if you could be satisfied with an old wannabe cowboy who's learned from his mistakes."

He didn't ask it as a question, and Ann wasn't sure how to answer.

He glanced at her. "You're worried Joyce will get between us."

"The first cut is the deepest," Ann told him as gently as she could. "Isn't that what they say?"

"She was part of me for a long time, Annie," he said in a matter-of-fact tone. "I can't change that. But I told you I'm ready to move on. And I know I want you in my life."

"But I live in Milwaukee and you live here."

John moved a few slices of bacon around in the pan, then put the fork down and said, "That's just geography." He took her in his arms and buried his face in her hair, sighing deeply. "I'm nothin' special. You know that. But I am good on my word. I'm sayin' I love you, Annie. And I want to love you for a long, long time."

Ann leaned into him. "I love you too," she said. And she knew she meant it.

They took their time over breakfast, laughing together when Chip licked her empty plate across the floor.

"She never leaves a crumb behind," John said.

"That reminds me," Ann said. "The Blazer's still at Emmett's with my clothes and stuff."

John took their dishes to the sink. "You worry too much. I have a big truck with a plow, remember?" When he came back to the table, he took her hand. "Come on. You haven't seen my bedroom upstairs yet."

The Johnsons' kitchen smelled of onions.

"I'm so glad John picked you up last night," Betty said over a pile of potato peelings. "That storm was awful. I'm making soup for lunch, but I could make you breakfast if you're hungry."

Ann put her bags near the stairway, thinking about how she and John had created their own storm. "Thanks, Betty. But I had a little something at John's."

Frank winked over his newspaper. "A little something, huh?"

Ann hoped they weren't wondering about her grin as she brought a shopping bag to the table. "I brought you each a little Christmas and thank-you gift," she said.

Betty tore the paper of a crystal vase. "Oh, you shouldn't have! But it's lovely. It'll certainly dress up our old living room!"

"Just what I need!" Frank said of his gift. "Look at that, Bett. A stainless steel, shatterproof thermos. Thanks a million, Annie."

"I'm sorry I didn't get you anything, dear," Betty said.

"Letting me stay here is a perfect gift, Betty."

Betty held up her forefinger. "Oh, and before I forget!" She took an envelope from the windowsill. "It's from Grace Studt. I didn't know you knew her."

"I met her at the Manor House," Ann said, tearing the envelope open. "She's a friend of Emmett's. I mean she was. She died yesterday."

"Oh, my," Betty replied. "A letter from the dead."

When Ann opened the card, she didn't see anything except the black-and-white photo of herself and Elise in matching plaid dresses. Ann guessed they were about five and three years old. They were holding hands and looked a little scared. Another photo showed them standing in front of the same bush between Karl and Ruth, both looking uncertain at best. Another showed a much younger Granny Elizabeth and Grampa Olaf standing behind an unsmiling Ruth, who sat in an Adirondack chair with both little Annie and Elise on her lap.

"I never saw these," Ann said, passing a photo to Betty. "But I'm sure they were taken in Granny Elizabeth's backyard. I'd know that chair anywhere. How did Gracie get these?"

The last picture showed Ann and Elise in different outfits sitting in front of a cake and a stack of plates. On the back, someone had written, "Official celebration." The processing date printed in the border of the photo was November 1951. Ann opened Gracie's card again and read aloud.

"These pictures were taken by my mother when she went to Milwaukee to visit her family. My mother was a good friend of your Grandmother Elizabeth and Emmett's mother, Lena. I think Mother took these pictures for Emmett. It looks like a happy day for you and your sister. I hope you have a blessed Christmas. Love, Gracie."

"I guess that answers your question," Betty said.

Frank picked up a photo. "You don't look too happy in this picture, Annie."

"You noticed that, too, huh, Frank?" She picked up one of the photos. "One time Dad told me I was a serious child," she said softly.

"You were very lucky to have such nice parents," Betty told her.

Ann nodded. *Except for not answering my questions*, she thought. She put the photos inside Gracie's card and set it aside. "I have more things from Emmett's."

Ann brought the shoebox to the table, cut through the duct tape, and lifted the lid. Right on top was an Army cap. She handed it to Frank.

"It's his garrison cap," he said. "Just like new."

Frank put the cap on the table, smoothing it out as if it were a holy relic, while Ann removed military ribbons, pins, patches, a dog tag, and Emmett's discharge paper from the box. Frank reached for the paper.

"Northern France," he said. "Battle of the Bulge." He sat back, thinking. "You know, for a while after Clayton and I got back from Korea, the three of us would go out for a beer once in a while. Course Emmett never wanted to talk about the war, and pretty soon he didn't come with us anymore. Too many memories, I guess. But we all had memories."

Betty patted Frank's hand. "At least you got on with your life."

"It wasn't easy," he said, picking up a pin with a rifle on it. "See this? It's a combat infantry badge. It means you actually faced the enemy. I got one too. One guy told me they gave CIBs to the lower ranks in order to boost morale." Frank examined the pin with his weatherworn hands, wincing as if gunfire echoed in his head. "The only thing that boosted my morale was when I heard we were going home."

"Emmett said soldiers risk their lives in battle only to get decorated with ribbons like a Christmas tree," Ann said. "After what I read in his diary, I think I understand what he meant."

"The real award's on the inside," Frank told her. "Every soldier knows these decorations are for the pride of servin' your country. For doin' the best you can do." His lips quivered a bit. "But I guess Emmett's got a point. These little bits don't make up for the agony."

Ann emptied the paper bag next. Pushing the *Stars and Stripes* issues aside, Betty reached for one of the old copies of *Newland News*. "Look," she said. "It's Lena's obituary."

"Emmett's mother," Ann said. "She died right after the war, right?"

"Yeah," Frank said. "Lena died and Albert took off. Hell,

if Nana hadn't stepped in, her precious little Albert woulda lost the farm. She stopped him from sellin' the place because she knew Emmett and Clayton woulda been left high and dry."

"Emmett and Clayton both inherited money from Lena's brother, though," Betty said.

"Sure," Frank said. "That's how they bought new trucks and campers. I tried to tell them to save some of the money."

"He saved some," Ann told him.

Betty and Frank's expectant looks reminded Ann that as POA she was supposed to be protecting Emmett's privacy.

"How much does he have?" Frank asked.

"He's got enough to cover the Manor House for a while. Then he'll have to sell the farm."

"He can't possibly go home again," Betty said. "We saw him at Christmas. He's so thin."

"He won't like sellin' the farm," Frank declared. "Not one bit. Can't imagine anyone wantin' it, though. Gordy always said he wanted it, but Torkelson's family offered him room and board *plus* fifty bucks a week to watch Archie when they're at work." He looked at Ann and clicked through his teeth. "I 'pect Gordy's gone for good. I can just see him livin' the high life in Minneapolis." Frank had been eyeing the green metal box from Emmett's, and now he pointed to it. "What's in the tackle box?"

"Is that what that is?" Ann asked. "It's locked."

"Yeah, I noticed. You got a key?"

"Nope."

Frank moved the box closer and fingered the padlock. "I can break it open if you want."

Betty crisscrossed her sweater over her ample bosom. "Maybe we shouldn't. I mean it's Emmett's personal property."

Ann considered Betty's comment. If there was money in the box, Frank might insist on taking some of it to cover the deal he had had with Clayton. She braced herself.

"If there's money or valuables in there," Ann told them,

"I'll have to call Howie Studt and tell him. He might want me to get a safe deposit box at the bank."

Betty looked at Frank. "She's right, Frankie. We don't want any trouble."

The kitchen clock loudly ticked off seconds as Frank considered Ann's words.

"Okay," Frank said. "So you want that lock off or not?"

"Off," Ann replied.

Frank went to the basement for a hammer and chisel while Betty scurried to arrange the box on a thick towel in order to protect her tabletop. The padlock fell away with one solid blow, and Frank slid the box over to Ann triumphantly. When she raised the now-dented lid, a small black-and-white photo of a uniformed Emmett, his arm around an attractive woman with dark curly hair, looked back at her. On the back Emmett had written *"Anna and me—September 2, 1945."*

Betty squinted at the photo. "I never dreamed he had a sweetheart."

"Not just a sweetheart," Ann said quietly. "The mother of his children."

The picture was similar to the one Ann had found in her grandmother's album years ago. Her mother was wearing the same spotted dress; her curly hair fell the same way on her shoulders. But this time, Emmett and Anna were standing closer to the camera and out of the shadow. Her mother's face was perfectly clear, and she could see Emmett's fingertips showing from behind her mother's waist.

Ann held on to the first photo while she picked up the second, also labeled September 2, 1945. This one showed Karl and Anna standing alongside a row of flowers. Karl was beaming his familiar smile, hands at his sides. Anna clutched a purse in one hand and what looked like binoculars in the other, but she also seemed to be leaning away from Karl slightly.

A picture of little Annie and Elise on their stomachs on a

pile of dirt was next. Ribbons tied to Annie's pigtails brushed against the small shovel she held, and she was grinning mischievously. Elise's curls stuck out beneath a white scarf, her eyes squinting in the sun. On the back, Emmett had written, "Annie and Elise, July 15, 1950, Nana's garden." It had been taken on Ann's fourth birthday. Betty mentioned how cute Ann and her sister were, but Ann was half-listening.

She wondered about her mother's posture in the second photo. *Maybe this was when Karl had come to Austria on leave. Maybe Anna had just met Karl and wasn't comfortable getting too close to the unfamiliar American GI with the broad smile.* Ann felt tears in her throat. *You would have liked my dad, Mother.*

She put the photos down and lifted out two pocket-sized spiral notebooks but set them aside in favor of a portrait folder. The studio photo inside, carefully highlighted in pastel colors, took her breath away. On the back, Emmett had written, "Anna, March 1946." Ann stared at the picture. Her mother had brown hair, brown eyes, and lips colored in faint pink. She wore a small cross on a chain around her neck and pearl earrings. Shoulder-length curls framed her oval face, a few strands drooping onto her forehead. Ann couldn't take her eyes off her mother's face.

"Look, she has brown eyes," Ann said softly. "And brown hair like I had at one time. She even liked pearl earrings like I do. And judging by the date, she's pregnant with me."

"How about that," Frank said, leaning to get a glimpse. "She sure looks like you."

"All these years," Betty said. "All these years and no one knew."

Ann sighed. "Well, someone knew."

"Who?" Frank asked.

"Emmett and my parents. And Nana had to know. Maybe Granny Elizabeth too."

Ann told Frank and Betty about the notebooks she'd found in the locked section of the barrister and gave them the briefest summary of Mitzie and Karl, and Emmett and Anna.

"At least my dad was telling me the truth when he said he met my mother at a USO show. He just didn't tell me that he was also there with another girl."

"Does your mom know about that?" Betty asked.

Ann ignored the judgment in Betty's voice and didn't answer; she didn't know the answer.

"Clayton had a girl in Korea," Frank said plainly.

Betty was alarmed. "He did?"

"Yeah, pretty little thing. A lotta guys had girls." He held up his hand as if pledging an oath. "I didn't, Bett. Just so you know. That's the God's honest truth."

While Betty drilled Frank about infidelity, Ann picked a red velvet pouch out of the box. Inside, rolled in a wad of cotton, were the gold cross necklace and pearl earrings pictured on her mother's portrait. She could almost feel her blood pressure spike.

"Oh, my God," she whispered, her hands trembling as she arranged the jewelry on the table.

"They're the old screw-on kind," Betty said, admiring the earrings. "Look how pink the pearls are."

Ann showed Frank the empty tackle box. "No money, Frank," she said as she opened one of the small spiral notebooks. "But look, this is dated 1951. That's the year I was adopted." She read aloud.

> *June 1951. Set aside a few days for the sole purpose of deciding on a course of action. Be pragmatic and determined in your solitude. Adolescence is long over. Time for courage of convictions to rise above fears and emotions. And just as there is no substitute for hard work, honesty and patience have their own rewards.*

Frank frowned. "What does all that mean?"

"Sounds like he was trying to work something out in his mind," Betty suggested.

"Mumbo jumbo if you ask me," Frank scowled.

Time for courage, Ann repeated to herself. *Maybe mother had died by June of 1951.*

On the next page, Emmett had written a poem. Ann read aloud again.

> *So many starlit nights I have looked to the heavens,*
> *Meditating on the inexplicable mystery of it all,*
> *Profoundly moved by infinite reaches of space,*
> *Rejoicing in the dark enigma that sages and savants*
> *cannot resolve.*

"Listen," she said eagerly. "Here's another one."

> *What matters if I stand alone?*
> *I wait with joy the coming year;*
> *My heart shall reap where it has sown*
> *And garner up its fruit of tears.*
>
> *The stars come nightly to the sky,*
> *The tidal wave unto the sea;*
> *Nor time nor space, nor deep nor high,*
> *Can keep my own away from me.*

Frank stood up and coughed. "I think he went overboard on the fancy writin'," he said, going to the hall for his jacket. "I gotta get back to the barn."

Betty left the table before Ann could start reading again. "I need to finish my soup," she said. "I'm sure you'd rather read the rest of those by yourself anyway."

Ann turned page after page of more poems. *My father,* she thought. *A poor man, an uneducated man. A man who appreciated literature. A man who had kept a beautiful diary while trying to survive the horrors of war. A man who wrote poetry. A man with a tender heart who needs to tell me the rest of the story about my beautiful mother.*

As she put the old newspaper issues back in the paper bag, an eight-by-ten, plain brown envelope fell out from between them. Ann slid a knife along the sealed edge and peered inside at airmail envelopes.

"More poetry?" Betty asked as she peeled a carrot.

"Just some airmail envelopes. I'll save them for later."

"That man sure is a pack rat," Betty mumbled to her soup pot.

Ann put a rubber band around the pictures from Gracie and slipped them into her jacket pocket. "Be with me, Mother," she whispered. "We are so close now."

THIRTY-ONE

When she got to the Manor House, Ann didn't see Emmett in the common room. Fearing the worst, she flagged down an aide.

"He didn't want to come to the dining room to eat like usual," the aide said. "But I'll bring him a tray as soon as I can. He's in 236."

Emmett's room was small but clean. A machine with tubing and a mouthpiece waited on a cart. His television was on, but no sound was coming from it. His hospital bed with safety rails on both sides probably felt like a recliner. He was lying on top of the bedspread, propped with pillows, and facing the window on the opposite wall. Ann took a deep breath. She had enough evidence, and now she felt she had enough courage. She closed the door to just a crack and went to his bedside. The Christmas card she'd sent him was on the nightstand along with one from Frank and Betty. She picked up another card and read the handwriting inside. "With fondest affection and love, Gracie." Ann wondered if he knew Gracie had passed away. When she put the cards back on the table, he turned toward her.

"Hi, Emmett," Ann said brightly. "How are you today?"

Emmett smacked his lips and blinked a few times. At first he seemed disappointed, as if he was expecting someone else. "Oh. Well, I can't complain."

"I was surprised you weren't in the common room."

He rubbed his eyes. "Huh. I should be. People die in bed." He almost smiled, but then frowned as if he'd misspoken. "Gracie died," he added solemnly.

"Oh, I'm very sorry," Ann said, as if this was news. "She was a very nice person."

"Yes. She was a good friend. She had a good life." His hand trembled as he pointed a finger at Ann. "You're Karl's daughter."

"Yes. Mind if I sit down and visit awhile?"

"Of course not."

Ann moved a chair closer and slipped out of her jacket, telling herself to get to the point before she lost her nerve. She felt her voice shaking when she said, "I'm hoping you can help me understand something about my own life."

He seemed interested but didn't say anything. Ann glanced away for a moment to gather courage and construct her question. "I believe you knew my mother, didn't you?"

"That I did. That I did."

Go easy, Ann told herself. *One little step at a time.* "I'd be very grateful if you would tell me about her. I was so young when she died."

"Yes, you were. You and your sister were both very young when she died. She was very young when she died too. She was only thirty-one. Too young."

Ann felt encouraged by his willingness to talk. "I, ah, have a few old pictures. Maybe you could tell me about them." Ann held out the picture of herself and Elise standing in front of a bush, wondering if he'd question where the photos came from. "This is my sister Elise," Ann said, pointing. She glanced at him briefly, expecting to see a sign of recognition. "And this is me."

Emmett took the photo and held it closer to his face. "Hm-mm."

Disappointed at his casual response, she gave him another photo, and again he brought it close to his face.

"Do you wear glasses, Emmett?"

"Oh, I guess I have some somewhere. But I manage without."

She handed him another photo.

"That's Aunt Elizabeth and Uncle Olaf," he said. "And Karl."

Ann offered him the pastel portrait of Anna.

"Yes, yes," he barely said.

She watched his mouth tighten over his toothless gums and felt her own jaw clench over her pressing need to get him to talk without making him angry. She handed him the photo she'd found long ago at her grandmother's. "Here's one with you and my dad and—is this my mother with you? I can't tell because of the shadow on her face." Her voice cracked. "Could you please tell me about her?"

Emmett took the photo, looked at it for a moment, and put it on the bed. "She worked at a hotel in Linz."

Ann waited a minute, but he didn't offer any more. She handed him pictures from Gracie and his tackle box one at a time, watching his face as she pointed out details and named names. He spent a long minute staring at the photo of Anna and Karl standing together. Then he straightened all the photos out and gave them back to Ann. He did not seem perplexed, confused, angry, or anxious.

"And she came here after the war?" Ann asked.

"Yes. There were special ships for war brides because GIs married girls over there."

Ann could hardly get the next question out. "So she was a war bride?"

Emmett started to speak but stopped, his neck and face reddening. Ann was about to say she had a right to know about her own parents, but he slammed his fist on the bedcovers and caused Ann to jump.

"I had nothing!" he blurted out. "No money, no property of my own. Where and how would we live? All I knew was farming. He was never a farmer. The land provided but he never helped us. He was spiteful. He wanted us to fail."

"Who?"

Emmett glared at her. "My father, of course."

Ann's brow wrinkled at the thought of having a spiteful,

angry man as her grandfather instead of Karl's dad, Olaf, a kind-faced man who told silly riddles. When Emmett wiped his nose with his hand, she took the box of Kleenex from the nightstand and put it on the bed within his reach.

"So after Anna got here," she said, "you didn't marry because of your father?"

Emmett took a tissue, dabbed his eyes, and wadded the tissue into a tight ball. Ann knew she'd opened a wound. But it was also her wound. All she could do was watch him stare at the bedspread until he spoke again.

"My father said I would lose my inheritance if I got married," he finally said. "He told Clayton the same thing. We had forty acres all told, and Clayton and I knew it would be split between us some day. Twenty acres isn't very much, but it's enough for a decent living."

"But do you think your father would have really disinherited you if you married?"

Emmett looked at her and squinted slightly. "My brother and I grew up in absolute fear of our father, and we learned early never to put anything past him." He paused and sighed. "I guess I made the farm sound rather grand when I told Anna about it. But she was so intent on coming; I couldn't tell her about my father's threats. When she got here, he said she was taking advantage. Every now and then he'd pull out his will, but Nana said we should do our best to put up with him because he did odd jobs around town and we needed the money." His voice grew quiet. "After Anna died, Nana told my father to get out. That's when we found out that our farm was part of her and old Pa's original homestead. So you see, our father's will was as crooked as the lawyer he got to write it. Nana owned our farm all along." He pointed his finger at Ann. "No one knows that."

"I won't tell anyone." He nodded at her promise and Ann asked, "So Anna spoke English?"

"She was smart. She knew English from working at the

hotel. She always worked hard, always had a kind word for everyone. Whenever I felt down, she gave me hope."

Ann thought a moment about her next question. She wanted to sound understanding rather than accusatory because she wanted answers not an argument. "After Anna died," she finally said with as much respect as she could muster, "why didn't you let my sister and me stay with you?"

Her question didn't seem to faze him. "Nana took care of you until Karl came to get you. Just like she wanted."

"Nana?"

"No, your mother."

"I don't understand. Why didn't we stay on the farm with you after our mother died?"

Emmett answered as if admonishing a child. "What would an old bachelor like me do with two little ones?"

Ann eyed him cautiously a moment. "I know this might be hard for you to talk about. But I want you to know that as hard as it is for you to tell me, that's how hard it is for me not to know."

His brow wrinkled in uncertainty.

"Do you understand?" Ann asked. "I don't know how else to say this." She felt her words catch in her throat. "I mean, you—you're our father, Emmett. Why did you give my sister and me up?"

He bolted to attention. "Where did you get such a preposterous notion? Your father is your father!"

Now Ann glared at him. "Yes, you're right, my father is my father! But he's 'unknown' on my birth certificate. I don't know his identity, Emmett. But I am sure you do!"

"Of course I do!" Emmett pointed to the photos on the bed. "He's right there! There's your father!"

"What?" Ann stretched to see. He was pointing to the picture of Karl and Anna standing together. "What are you talking about?"

"I lost my Anna to Karl! He stole her heart! He took her away from me!" Emmett picked up the color portrait of Anna and shook it in Ann's direction. "I sent those pictures to him after she died. He didn't even thank me! I took care of her. I kept her safe right up until the end. Cared for his daughters, too, until he finally claimed them. He never even thanked me for any of it!"

He's confused, she thought. *Or had there been duplicates or other pictures?* "Wait, Emmett, wait! I know about my dad and Mitzie. I'm asking about Anna."

"It was a pet name."

"I don't understand."

He threw the portrait on the bed and raised his voice as if she hadn't heard the first time. "A pet name. A nickname."

Ann felt a wave of dizziness, as if all the air had been sucked out of the room. "Are you saying Mitzie and Anna were the same person?" she asked breathlessly.

"Of course," he said, as if there was no other possible answer to her silly question.

Ann sat back and stared at him, her face contorted in disbelief. "What?" she half-whispered. "You must be mistaken."

"I am not mistaken."

Ann's mouth felt dry, her face hot. *He's old,* she told herself. *The adoption happened almost fifty years ago. All the years of hiding the truth have changed reality for him. But why would he lie?*

"You have a sister too. Ellie."

"Elise," Ann said, feeling shaky now. Karl had always called her sister Ellie. "My dad—I mean Karl—didn't tell us much," she stammered. "He said our mother died in Austria. But he never told us. He never told us he was our father."

Emmett's fist hit the bed. "He promised! He promised Nana he would tell you and your sister everything! He gave his word!"

Ann folded her arms across her chest and squeezed her eyes shut, trying to control the short, desperate breaths between her tears. She didn't want to admit Emmett's story made sense. It was the last explanation she could have imagined, but it accounted for all the years of secrecy. It explained Ruth insisting she ask Karl about the adoption. It explained Karl avoiding her questions. During the war, her dad had a lover, and his lover was her mother. It was all so simple, so incredibly simple. Ann opened her eyes, and Emmett's voice seemed miles away.

"She loved Karl," he said, shaking his head, his voice calm and sad. "She would never have wanted him to keep the truth from you. She would have never wanted that."

Ann leaned toward him. "Will you help me, Emmett? Please. Tell me the rest. You're the only one left who knows."

He closed his eyes and hung his head.

"You're the only person on earth who knows," Ann repeated. "You're the only one who knows. You're the last one. I don't have any memories of my mother. I don't know what happened between Anna and you and Karl, but I want to know." Her voice squeaked like a little girl begging to be listened to. "I think I have the right to know. And you're my last hope." She paused and added softly, "Just like Anna was your hope."

He blinked a long blink and the minute that passed felt like an hour to Ann.

"It doesn't seem so long ago," he finally said. "Ever since we were kids, your father was more like a brother to me than my own brother. We were closer in age. We understood each other. We agreed on so many things. We even joined up about the same time. He shipped off to Italy, and I went to France. Such misery." He shook his head but then brightened a bit. "I met Anna when my outfit went to Linz. She was beautiful. She sang like an angel."

It seemed his words were guiding Ann across a raging river, one stepping-stone at a time. But then he stopped.

"Please don't stop," Ann said. "Please."

He sighed. "She had a younger brother, Frederick, and a

sister Helena. Her mother was named Anna too."

Ann wiped her eyes, feeling a little numb. "Helena is my middle name," she said.

"Yes, I know. Her father was Joseph. Joseph Muller."

Ann thought she heard wrong. "My birth certificate says Miller. M-I-L-L-E-R."

"No," Emmett told her gently. "It's with a U, not an I."

How many other mistakes are part of this story? My story? Ann wondered. "Where did they live?" she asked. "What did Anna's father do? Was he a farmer?"

"No, he was a jeweler," Emmett said. "And rather well-known before the war, as Anna used to say. He made those earrings and the necklace in the picture there. He made jewelry for all of them before he sent them back to Austria."

"What do you mean?"

"Anna's father was a Jew. He was involved in the resistance. One time Anna told me she didn't even know if Muller was his real name. She said he moved the family to Lidice in Czechoslovakia when he realized Hitler was gaining power. Lidice was predominantly Catholic and Anna's mother was Catholic. They thought they would be safe there." He faced the window, paused a moment, and then seemed to sink further into the pillows. "But Hitler's barbarians finally came to Lidice. They murdered Anna's father and all the other men. Even the boys. Thank God, Anna and the others were back in Austria with her uncle by then."

Ann tried to imagine her mother's family separating in desperation, perhaps knowing they'd never see each other again. She reached for one of the Christmas cards and the pencil on the nightstand and scribbled a few notes, wishing she'd been taping their conversation, hoping that Emmett would keep talking and that she could keep listening.

Emmett turned back to face her. "Do you know about the USO?"

"They entertained the troops."

Emmett nodded. "Once Karl and I got leave at the same time, and he came to Austria for a show. I introduced him to Anna. Karl was a sergeant. Of course he was handsome and taller than me—a good dancer. I was just a private, a poor farm boy with no education. I saw the way they acted together. Later I found out she was writing to him. I knew what was happening, and there was nothing I could do, so I stepped back." He gestured as if to push away an invisible something. "That's what a gentleman does. He steps back. He steps back."

"But you loved her."

"Yes. I loved her. I always loved her." His voice grew quiet. "I still love her."

He turned to the window again, and Ann wished she could see inside his head, read his mind for just five minutes. He seemed to be breathing faster. She didn't want him to become exhausted from talking, but she didn't want him to stop either.

"Karl and I had a falling out at Nana's funeral," he said. "Of course, Anna was gone by then. Karl blamed me for not providing a proper home." He coughed a few times and wiped his nose with a Kleenex. "When your mother died, Nana wrote to Karl and demanded him to come and get you and your sister. I know because I helped her write the letter. When he finally came to get you, I heard him promise Nana that he'd tell you girls everything when you were old enough to understand. The next time I saw him was at Nana's funeral. That was 1964. I asked him if he gave you the pictures I sent and he said he was handling things his own way. I reminded him of his promise to Nana and he got angry. He said it was none of my business." Emmett frowned and his hand slowly curled into a fist. "I don't remember who struck first. But I do remember I punched him in the nose, and he knocked me up against a tree. Then he went back to Milwaukee." His fist relaxed and he shook his head. "We didn't write anymore."

Ann couldn't picture her passive dad threatening anyone, let alone shoving Emmett against a tree.

"I knew Anna loved him," Emmett said. "And I knew she wanted you to be with your father. All I could do was hope he would tell you about her."

"Dad gave us our birth certificates," Ann said. "He said our mother died in Austria of leukemia. Nothing else, Emmett, except that we lived at your place until the adoption. That's all he told us."

"He promised!" Emmett said angrily. "A decent man keeps his word!"

Ann dropped her head and clenched her hands together so tightly she felt her fingernails cut into her palms. Now Emmett's irregular breathing seemed to echo "decent man, decent man, decent man." It was a long minute before he spoke again.

"We were out of our minds with gladness when the war ended. His voice was soft now, as if he was just waking from a dream. "I wanted to marry Anna and take her back with me. But GIs weren't permitted to marry German or Austrian women. I had to leave her behind, but I told her I'd get her here somehow. I sent her money whenever I could."

"So how did Anna get on the war bride ship if she wasn't married?"

"I wrote to the chaplain of my old outfit and told him she was Czechoslovakian and that she was having a baby. I sent him the money and he took care of the rest. Of course, I didn't know I was telling him the truth about the baby."

"Where was my dad—where was Karl at that time?"

Emmett took a cautious deep breath as if trying not to cough. "Karl mustered out the end of January, about six weeks after me." He closed his eyes. "Anna admitted being with him."

Ann looked again at the photo of Karl and Anna standing alongside some flowers. Mitzie wasn't missing from Emmett's pictures after all. As Ann tried to get her next question out, an aide came through the door with a tray.

"Here's your dinner, Emmett." She turned to Ann. "Sorry it took so long. I got sidetracked."

THIRTY-TWO

"I'm not hungry," Emmett told the young aide.

She put his tray on the table and positioned it over his bed. "Well, try to eat something, okay? My goodness, Mr. Pederson, you have to eat. I'll lose my job if you starve to death."

He chuckled weakly and coughed. "You're good to this worthless old man."

"You're not worthless."

"But I am old."

"That you are. You're as old as you should be at your age." Laughing at her own joke, the aide took the cover off his plate and cut up the roast beef. When she helped Emmett sit up, she felt around under the pillows and showed Ann the pills she'd retrieved. "It doesn't do any good to stuff your pills under your pillow, Mr. Pederson."

When he didn't look at her or answer, she shook her head and left, taking the pills with her.

Emmett stood his fork up in his mashed potatoes. "These come out of a box," he told Ann. "We grew real potatoes. Pontiacs. Real beans too. These are rubber."

The gravy on Emmett's plate looked gray. "Try the meat," Ann suggested.

He stabbed a piece of meat with his fork and smelled it. "No," he said, putting the fork down.

Ann took the roll from his plate, buttered it, and handed it to him. "Here. I know home cooking is better, but you can hardly ruin a roll."

She watched him break off a chunk of the roll and put it in his mouth and gum it slowly. Together his skeletal body and ill-fitting clothes barely made for a wrinkled lump on the bed. She had to get him to eat.

"Shall I ask them to bring you something else?" Ann asked. "Maybe some soup?" He shook his head. She leaned toward him and whispered, "How about some ice cream?"

Emmett perked up a bit, a grin brightening his face. "Now that sounds pretty darn good."

Ann patted his shoulder. "I'll be right back."

In the dining room, Ann asked for a scoop of chocolate ice cream. The woman gave it to her in a plastic mug. "Easier for them to hold," she said.

On her way back to Emmett's room, Ann spotted the aide who'd brought Emmett's tray; her nametag said "Gina."

"What were those pills for that Emmett hid under his pillow?" Ann asked her.

"Heart and blood pressure," Gina replied. "I think the other one is for his breathing."

"Don't you have to watch him take his pills?"

"Sometimes I do. I'll bring him some applesauce later with the pills all crushed up in there. He likes applesauce."

"Should I talk to him about not hiding his pills?"

Gina lowered her voice. "Well, I'm not officially a nurse yet, but I'd say no." She gestured toward the ice cream Ann was holding. "I think he should have what he wants. He made it this far."

Back in Emmett's room, Ann found him with his head slumped forward, the fork on the bed. She rushed to his side. "Emmett! Are you okay?"

His voice was coarse. "Leave me be."

Ann sighed with relief. "I brought you some ice cream." He raised his head and slowly opened his eyes. "Look," she said. "Ice cream. Chocolate."

"Well, well, I declare," he said. He took the mug from Ann, and, with a shaky hand, managed to get a small chunk of ice cream on the spoon. After another bite, he said, "We made ice cream on Independence Day. Strawberry. We always grew strawberries."

Ann sat down, pleased to see him eating. "I bet it was wonderful."

"Better than store-bought," he assured her. After another spoonful, he gazed at Ann affectionately. "You had long hair when you were little. So pretty in the sunshine. Anna braided it. And after she was gone, I braided it."

Ann smiled. "You did?"

"I sure did. I did everything I could to make us a real family," he said. "And I thought she was happy until—well, Karl came up a few times. He said he came up to see Nana, but I knew what was going on."

"And then my sister came along," Ann interjected.

"Yes."

She hesitated a moment before asking her next question. "Did he love her? Did my father love my mother? Did Karl love Anna?"

Emmett sighed. "I didn't want to believe it for a long time. But it's only fair to say he did."

"Do you think he wanted to marry her?"

He dropped his spoon in his mug and rested it on his chest as he talked. "There was a situation with Aunt Elizabeth and Uncle Olaf. They were strict Lutherans. Just like my own folks."

When he paused, Ann filled in the rest. "And Anna had a Catholic mother and a Jewish father and two children."

"Yes. They let prejudice get in the way of their sensibilities," he said with a frown. "They seemed to forget Karl's responsibility regarding his children. Anna was a decent person. They both made a mistake, but she also let Karl take the easy way out. She made no demands on him. Why, she never even told him about the second child."

"You mean she didn't tell him when my sister was born?"

Emmett shook his head slowly.

"Why not?"

"Because he was married by that time and she didn't want any trouble."

"Trouble? But Dad already knew about me, didn't he?"

"You don't understand. Your mother was scared."

"Of what?"

His voice was sad. "She didn't know anything about this country. She had bad dreams. She was afraid someone would take you children away from her. During the war over there children disappeared all the time. Some were put in orphanages because their parents were gone or couldn't feed them. Some were kidnapped or sent away. And so many died in the death camps."

Ann glanced toward the window. It was frosted over, making it impossible to see outside. Maybe her brain was frosted over too, making it impossible to take everything in. She imagined what it would be like to fear for her children or grandchildren. Her head began to throb.

"We managed," Emmett said. "Clayton and I worked odd jobs here and there when we had to. Anna made a garden. We all worked. Then one day, Anna got a letter from her sister. Her mother was very ill, and the news made Anna terribly homesick and depressed." He hesitated, his voice almost drifting away. "She had headaches, and she was so tired all the time. Nana made her eat spinach every day for the iron." His lip trembled. "But it didn't help. All she wanted was to see her mother, so I borrowed money for her ticket." He turned toward the window again. "By the time she got to her sister's, she was real sick. It was leukemia, cancer of the blood. I was a hopeless wreck when I found out. I couldn't do anything, and she was so far away." He sighed and faced Ann. "Thank goodness for Nana.

She wrote to Karl right away and demanded that he do the right thing."

Ann wiped tears from her eyes. So she and Elise were bastard children after all and as such, they had gone from being the family secret to being the family embarrassment. *It wasn't our fault,* she told herself. *We were just children. It wasn't our fault.*

"One day, the minister came over with some other people," he continued. "They wanted to take you and your sister away."

"What happened?"

He took a deep breath, which brought on relentless coughing. Ann waited on alert as she watched him work it out.

"I told them a cousin was coming to get you. I didn't tell them about Karl and Anna, of course. But when Karl finally got here, Nana gave him quite a tongue-lashing. I heard everything. She told him she would not allow her family to be shamed by her great-granddaughters going to an orphanage. She said he'd go to hell if he refused to acknowledge his own children." He paused and cautiously took another deep breath. "Nana was a good woman, a formidable woman. Ol' Pa was a good man, but Nana was the one who kept everyone in line. She ruled the roost."

"So Nana was responsible for my sister and me going to Milwaukee," Ann hung her head. "To save the family from shame."

"You mustn't think of it as shame," he said. "Little children have no reason for shame. You had a father, and children should be with their rightful parents. It was the right thing to do."

Ann thought of Karl helping her with her arithmetic, teaching her to ride a two-wheeler. He was a good father. How could he be a good father and still keep the truth from them all those years? "I wish my father would have told me," she said.

Emmett handed his mug to Ann. His ice cream had melted into a chocolate soup.

"They say love is for fools," he said. "I guess we were all

foolish. Karl and Anna and me. All foolish."

"I don't think love is foolish," Ann said tenderly. "I also want you to know I would be proud if you were my father."

A tear ran down one cheek. He reached for her hand and she took it. "No, no, no." he said. "The way it was is the way I told you."

Ann wiped her eyes with her free hand. She wondered how long it had been since he'd reached out for anyone. He patted Ann's hand before folding his old fingers together across his chest. Ann hoped her mother had had feelings for Emmett, at least as a devoted friend. For a fraction of a second, Ann wondered whether Emmett and her mother could have also been lovers, but she dismissed the thought. They would have had the opportunity during the years they were together on his farm, but Ann felt Emmett truly meant what he said about "stepping aside." As broken-hearted as he must have been, Ann believed he had honored Anna's choosing Karl.

"I am so grateful to you, Emmett. I want you to know I'll never forget what you did for me. I know my mother was lucky to have you, and my sister and I were lucky to have you too."

He blinked slowly. "I didn't do much," he said. With a shaky hand he wiped his eyes again and cleared his throat. "There are things upstairs at the house. Anna's mother's dishes and a few other things she brought with her. You take what you want. It's all yours now. After she died, I realized Anna was saving those things for herself and Karl. I don't know why I kept them."

He closed his eyes and Ann watched his chest go up and down. For a moment, she was back in the hospital with her family, watching her dad's chest go up and down as he slept, wondering when his breathing would finally stop. *My dad. My father. One and the same.* She could feel the words pressing against her lungs.

"I have known my father all along," she heard herself say. *"I knew him. All this time, I knew him."*

Emmett's eyelids fluttered a bit, and Ann wondered whether she'd spoken out loud. She didn't think so. She tried to imagine the Emmett her mother knew. He didn't have Karl's height and broad shoulders or the handsome face and ready humor. A younger Emmett may have seemed geeky with his careful attention to language and his serious manners. His ears stuck out. Nothing about him was especially notable except for those penetrating, icy blue, expressive eyes, and his determination to be an educated gentleman in spite of his poverty.

She leaned over and kissed him on the cheek. "Can I get you anything else?"

"There's an attorney in town," he said without opening his eyes. "Studt's his name. I'd like to see him."

"Sure. I'll tell him," Ann said. "And I'll come and see you again real soon, okay?"

Ann sat with him until he began to snore, then she quietly took her jacket and walked to the doorway, where she stopped and looked back at the man she'd long believed to be her father. At one time, his home had been her home, and he cared for her, her sister, and her mother. If he faded away by morning, he'd go without burdens. He'd kept his promises and released a treasury of his own memories. It had been hard to listen to what he told her, but she loved him for every word. She knew she'd always love him.

THIRTY-THREE

Wet snow was coating the parking lot and Ann's cell phone was vibrating in her pocket when she got in the Blazer—probably John wondering about lunch. She needed to see him.

"Hi Ann, Howie Studt here," he said when she answered. "I'm calling because I found some documents you might find interesting. It's a little complicated, to tell you the truth."

"I know; it's been one of those days."

"Pardon?"

"Oh, nothing." Ann sat back to listen. "What did you find?"

"Well, I have two sets of certificates of birth for you and another child, Elise."

"My sister," she said, pressing the phone to her ear, not sure she'd heard right. "Did you say you have two sets of birth certificates?"

"Ah, actually three counting the hospital notices I found, but they're different."

"Different? How?"

"The hospital notices and one set of county certificates show your mother as Anna Miller and your father as unknown. But the more recent county certificates show your mother as—pardon me if I mispronounce this. It looks like A-n-n-e-l-i-e-s-e. Anna-leece? Muller. M-u-l-l-e-r. Born in Linz, Austria. Her father's name is Josef—J-o-s-e-f Muller, born in Mi-ko-luv, Mor-a-vi-a, and her mother, Anna, is from Linz, Austria."

"Anneliese," Ann repeated softly.

"Yes."

Ann was stunned. Anneliese. Not Anna. Not Mitzie. Anneliese. "Anna and Elise," she whispered. "Anna and Elise. She named us after herself.*"*

"I'm sorry? I didn't catch that."

"It doesn't matter. I'm listening."

"Okay. Well, the certificates from 1951 show your father's name as Karl Olson of Milwaukee. I have adoption papers, but they don't seem complete. I have letters too."

"What?" Ann blurted out. "Are you sure? Are you looking at the adoption paper or the birth certificates?"

"I'm looking at birth certificates," Howie replied politely. "You can stop by today if you want. I have to leave shortly, but Margie can show you everything."

Ann's throat felt thick. She tried to swallow.

"Are you okay?" Howie asked.

"Yes, yes, I'm fine. I'm coming right over."

So, there was no doubt. Emmett had told the truth. Ann pressed the off button on her phone and rested her forehead on the steering wheel.

"How could you, Daddy?" Ann sputtered. "How could you not tell us?"

Tears flooded out. When she finally looked up, the windshield was foggy and a man was approaching her.

"I wanted to take you for lunch, but you didn't answer your cell," John said when he opened the car door.

"Oh, John. I was with Emmett. And then Howie called. Everything Emmett said was true." She began to cry.

"Scoot over, honey."

John moved the seat back and got behind the wheel, then hugged her as best as he could over the console. Ann's troubled thoughts tumbles out: ". . .hit me like a ton of bricks," "How could he do this?" ". . . never wanted to talk about it."

"It's okay," John soothed, giving her his handkerchief. "Just sit back and take a deep breath. Go slow. I'm listenin'."

Ann told him what she'd learned from Emmett and Howie. Whenever she stumbled over the words, he gently urged her to continue, and when she stopped he squeezed her hand.

"Sounds like it all sort of piled up on you. But, hey, it's better to have the truth, isn't it? It's what you wanted."

Ann didn't answer.

"At least you got your questions answered."

"Howie has adoption papers at his office."

"You want me to go with you?"

Ann wiped her eyes and nodded.

"Howie had to go out," Margie said, leading them around boxes to a corner table in Howie's office. "I apologize for this mess. We knew Howie's dad kept lots of paperwork, but we never realized he had documents here that should have been taken to the courthouse. If there was a fire—oh, God, don't even think about it! He wasn't negligent. But he always said the law shouldn't get in the way of people's lives." She took a manila folder from Howie's desk and gave it to Ann. "This is from Emmett Pederson's file."

"Oh, my God," was all Ann could say when she saw the adoption certificate. The simple form was dated October 26, 1951, and showed Karl and Ruth Olson as the adoptive parents. But there were no signatures on the document. "Can I have this?"

"Oh, I'm sorry. I need to take it to the courthouse for filing."

"But it's not even signed," Ann replied weakly. "Can I have a copy?"

"You can get a copy from the courthouse," Margie told her kindly. "It's ten dollars."

John looked at Margie and winked. "How about savin' her a few bucks, Margie girl?"

Margie shook her finger at him. "You're just like Howie and his dad," she joked. "No respect for protocol." She took the paper from Ann and pointed to the large white envelope also in the folder. "Howie said whatever is in there is yours. None of it has to be part of the public record. I'll be right back."

Ann emptied the white envelope onto the table. The first sheet was a carbon copy of a letter typed on old stationery of Harold R. Studt, Attorney at Law. Ann read aloud.

> *August 19, 1951*
> *Dear Mr. Olson,*
> *In reference to your inquiry regarding the status of the two minor girls, Anna and Elise Muller, now residing with your grandmother, Mrs. Ingeborg Pederson, I offer the following information.*
> *Wisconsin has several Catholic orphanage asylums . . .*

Ann gasped at the words and swallowed hard, giving herself a moment to take in what she was reading.

> *. . . Catholic orphanage asylums including at least one in Milwaukee. Some of these are authorized to handle adoptions; others work through agencies. A Catholic orphanage would no doubt also require the rite of Catholic baptism. In addition, a public search for relatives is often required before adoption is authorized. Sometimes siblings are separated, however, finding good homes for them is the prime concern. They are lovely little girls and I imagine many adoptive parents would find them quite desirable.*
> *Orphanages also require birth certificates. Your cousin, Mr. Emmett Pederson, has told me he has copies. Once all documents are secured and the girls are properly registered with an orphanage or adoption agency, your petition for adoption can be considered.*
> *Yours truly,*
> *Harold R. Studt*
> *Attorney at Law*
> *cc: Mr. Emmett Pederson*

Words spun in Ann's head. *Orphanage asylums. Parents would find them desirable. Public search. Catholic baptism required. Siblings separated. Petition. Registered.* She didn't like the harsh formality of the letter, as if she and her sister were simply cute little figurines in an estate sale. Then again, these were powerful words, persuasive words. What did Howie's dad know? What was his intention with this letter?

She picked up another letter and read her dad's handwriting aloud slowly.

> *Dear Attorney Studt,*
> *Thank you for returning my telephone call. You said it had to be in writing and I hope you don't mind if this is handwritten. This letter is to formally acknowledge that the two little girls in my grandmother's care at my cousin Emmett Pederson's home are my natural daughters.*

A sound came out of Ann—something between a gasp and a squeak. John touched her arm, and she sighed and kept reading.

> *Emmett is willing to vouch for me in this matter. The only other witness I can provide is my grandmother, Mrs. Ingeborg Pederson. I am hoping the testimony of these honorable family members will be sufficient proof of my relationship to Anna and Elise. I would like to move both girls to my home in Milwaukee. I am grateful for your confidence in this matter and thank you for your generous offer to help. However, under the circumstances, I wonder if there is any reason to pursue a formal adoption.*
> *I would appreciate it if you would call and tell me how we should proceed.*
> *Cordially,*
> *Karl Olson*

"My dad sounds like an attorney," Ann said. "This doesn't sound like him at all."

John sat back and nodded respectfully. The next letter, dated August 4, 1951, was typed. Ann read aloud again.

> *Dear Attorney Studt,*
> *I am having someone write this for me because my English is not so good. My grandson is Karl Olson. I talked to him about his little girls, Anna and Elise. Their mother was Anna Muller. She came here from Austria. Karl said he would marry her but he didn't. I told Karl to do the right thing for his little girls. Anna also sent him a letter before she went to Austria to see her mother. She died in Austria. Anna was a good person. I want my great-granddaughters to be with their father. I need your help.*
> *Yours truly,*
> *Mrs. Ingeborg Pederson*

"That's Nana," Ann said, passing the letter to John. "My dad's and Emmett's grandmother."

"And your great-grandmother."

Ann smiled slightly as she opened the last letter, dated October 1, 1951, also written by Karl.

> *Dear Attorney Studt,*
> *Thank you for meeting with me last week. My wife and I will be happy to meet with you in your office on Friday, October 26, as you requested. I appreciate your willingness to keep the conditions of our meeting confidential.*
> *Cordially,*
> *Karl Olson*

"Confidential," Ann said without looking up. "Confidential.

A family secret is born."

"It was Nana," Ann began when they got back in the Blazer. "She must have pressed my dad—my father—to do the right thing. And my mom—Ruth—she must have known, and she never, ever said anything. Nana made it all happen."

"Never underestimate the power of a little old lady," John said.

"Yes, but my mom and Granny Elizabeth protected him. How could they go along with this whole adoption story—this lie?"

"Maybe they wanted everything to look more, you know—"

"Legitimate," Ann said.

John pulled away from the curb. "Things were different back then, honey."

"Not when it comes to doing the right thing, John. My dad must have hoped this day would never come. They must have all hoped no one would ever find this stuff way up north in little ol' Newland."

Ann stared out the window and clutched the documents from Howie's office, thinking of the pictures from Gracie that showed Karl and Ruth and two little girls—two innocent objects of a big secret. Her thoughts raced. *Karl and Ruth loved each other. It was obvious by the way they spoke to each other, helped each other, respected each other's feelings. But did Dad tell Mom everything? Or had he led her to believe they were adopting two poor little girls in need of a home rather than his own daughters? Or if Mom knew about Dad's affair, she must have loved him enough to protect his secret all these years.*

John reached for her hand. "You okay?"

"On Dad's last night in the hospital, they brought another bed to his room so my mom could stay overnight," Ann said. "We were told he wouldn't last the night, and it was hard to leave Mom there. I no sooner got home than the nurse called and told me to come back. When I got there, the tubes were all out of him, and he was under the covers like he was asleep. Mom was looking out the window and crying. I put my arms around her and she just cried and cried and cried." Ann stopped, her heart in her throat. "Mom kept telling me she loved him. I remember her tone of voice—as if she thought I didn't believe her. I told her we all knew they loved each other because they made us all so happy together. I meant what I said and I still believe it. But now I feel so bad for Mom. I wonder how often she thought about Dad together with Anna. How often did she cry over his lies?"

"Maybe it didn't matter as time went by," John said simply.

"Well, the adoption part of it always mattered to me," Ann insisted. "Why couldn't he have made a deathbed confession to my sister and me? Or Mom could have told us the truth after he died. She wouldn't have had to tell my brother or my other sister. Elise and I would have kept quiet if she wanted us to. We were good kids; we would never do anything to hurt Mom or Dad. It would have all been so much easier with the truth."

John glanced her way. "Would it?"

Ann sighed and shook her head. "I don't know. All my life I tried to be truthful. With my kids. On my job. And now I find out my childhood is rooted in lies. And how am I going to tell Elise that our dad didn't even know about her until after our mother died? Can you imagine how she'll feel? How am I going to tell her our adoption was invented as a way to shut us up?"

John winced. "Maybe you don't have to tell her those parts."

Ann shot him a hopeless look. "Then I'm the one lying!"

They drove the rest of the way back to the Manor House in silence. There, John parked alongside his truck and faced her. "Life goes along on its own terms," he said gently. "Someone's always gettin' hurt or left out. But then things get better and we go on. Isn't that right?"

Ann sighed and stared out the window. "I don't know. I feel like I have to start my life all over."

THIRTY-FOUR

Back at Betty's, Ann headed straight for the stairs.

"Are you okay, dear?" Betty asked.

"No. I have a terrible headache. I'm going to lie down for a little while."

"Do you want some aspirin?"

"I have some upstairs," Ann said, going up the steps.

"I put Emmett's tackle box and his other stuff up in your room."

Ann thanked her.

"I'm making fried chicken for supper," Betty called after her. "I'm sure you'll feel better by then."

Ann offered another thanks, went to her bedroom, closed the door, and stretched out on the bed. With her arm over her eyes, she tried to breathe deeply and relax, even though her head was buzzing with questions.

When she opened her eyes again, the room was dark and smelled of fried chicken. Her headache was gone. She switched on the nightstand lamp and saw Emmett's tackle box on the floor. The old bed frame squeaked as she reached for it. She took out her mother's jewelry, fastened the gold cross around her neck, and then tuned the contents of the brown envelope she had put aside earlier out onto the bed. Smaller envelopes were rubber banded together. The one on top had a Linz return address and a faint 1945 postmark. Ann took a thin paper out of the envelope.

> *Meine liebe Emmett,*
> *I am so sad at the hurt I gave you. I want you to be happy. I think about you and your beautiful farm. I know*

I am different now with Karl. My heart is sad when I think about you. If you forgive me I am grateful. Liebe liebe Anna

So there it was. Her mother had chosen Karl over Emmett, and at this time a little Annie was on the way. She sat back against the headboard, running her finger over the precise penmanship of her mother's simple confession. Next, she picked up a postcard with a picture of Milwaukee's skyline. It was dated February 19, 1946, five months before Ann was born. She easily recognized her dad's handwriting.

> *Dear Emmett,*
> *I got the assistant manager job with A&P. Ruth's old man got me in. He likes me now! Ruth's a good girl. We plan to take the big step next summer. I think we can make it work. Mom and Dad say hello.*
> *Till next time, buddy. Karl*

Ann read the date again and shook her head, thinking of what Ruth told her about Karl putting their marriage off several times. "Oh, Daddy, you must have known about me by this time," she whispered.

The next two small envelopes were addressed to Miss Anna Muller in care of Emmett's home address.

> *November 16, 1947*
> *My darling Anna,*
> *Mother showed me the letter from Nana with news of your illness. Influenza can be very serious. I am grateful to Emmett for taking you to the doctor and I worry about you. It has been very cold here and I am sure it is even colder up north. Please be sure to keep warm, my dear little Mitzie.*

*I will write again very soon and will try to come and
see you very soon. Please do not be sad. Please know I
love you.*
Love, Karl

She stared at her dad's words. *My darling Anna. Worry about
you. Keep warm. Dear little Mitzie. Do not be sad. I love you. Love, Karl.*
The letter sounded so sincere. She wanted her dad to be sincere.
She didn't want to think he had taken advantage of Anna—or
that Anna had simply lost herself to his charm. Ann put her
head back.

There's no way to know why they did what they did, she thought.
*And it's only fair to say "they" because my parents were both responsible;
they both fell in love. Emmett said they loved each other, and for my own
own peace of mind, I have to believe it.*

She read the date on the letter again. It stated Elise was born
June 7, 1948, so Anna's flu in November was no doubt morning
sickness. And, by the address on the envelope, Karl had also
known Anna's proper last name.

She thought back to the day she saw her mother's name
on her birth certificate as Anna Miller. Karl never mentioned
the spelling error or that Anna was a shortened version of
Anneliese. Had he hoped it would never matter the same way
he hoped his daughters would be satisfied with not knowing the
rest of their story?

The next letter, dated August 2, 1948, was also written by
her dad, married to Ruth now for five months.

My dearest Anna,
*Please forgive me, darling, for not writing sooner. All
I can do is send you a little money now and then to help
you. Everything will work out, dearest. Remember, do not
write me. If you need to get a message to me, tell Emmett
and he will help. Love, Karl*

300 • Laurel Bragstad

Now Ann clenched her teeth in anger, stopping just short of tearing the letter to shreds. *You abandoned her! What the hell did you mean by "Everything will work out"? You married someone else. How was it supposed to work out?*

She threw the letter aside and reached for and airmail envelope addressed by Emmett to Anna in Austria. Inside was a letter Anna no doubt had carried with her on her voyage to the States.

> *My dearest,*
> *I received your lovely letter today. I was so happy to see it in the mailbox. Of course I read it very carefully and I understand. I want you to think about something. I am willing to re-enlist. Now with the end of the war, there is reconstruction everywhere. After we are married, I could sign up for Army reconstruction work over there, and you'd be close to your mother. I respect your desire to be near her, my love.*
> *If you do not like the idea of Army life, I ask you to reconsider coming here. My brother and I have 40 acres. You can ask Frederick to explain how it compares to farms there. I will inherit half the farm and have enough tillable acreage to support a family and enough space for two houses, so your mother could have her own place. I know she would be happy here, and she would be most welcome. We would have to work, but we will have to work no matter which path we choose. If you come here, we would command our lives together. The farm would provide an endless supply of fruits, vegetables, and meat, and a good, clean living for children we might have someday.*
> *I cannot tell you how I miss you, my dear little Fraulein. I urge you to make a decision quickly. Remember, dear heart, you have a home with me. I wait for you. I long*

*for you. I love you forever. Please remember that and
remember me.*

Ann winced at the sound of Emmett's desperation, how he
made the farm sound so appealing. She imagined her mother
standing on the deck of a ship bound for the United States,
clinging to this letter, wondering about a place called Newland,
and making promises to the child she carried—the child Emmett
didn't know about yet. The next envelope contained a few single
notebook pages, including an entry Ann never expected to see.

*July 15, 1946, 7 a.m. A little girl, Anna Helena,
born healthy and pink. My dearest Anna, a beautiful
mother. I shall do all I can to care for them.*

Clearly, even in the wake of Anna giving birth to another
man's child, Emmett's feelings for her hadn't changed. It was
impossible to imagine what he must have been thinking on that
day, not knowing the scene would repeat itself with the birth
of Elise two years later. Ann set this page aside, then quickly
arranged the others in chronological order.

*October 30, 1945. Le Havre, France, Camp Herbert
Tareyton. Chafing under the monotony of the prolonged
stay here and increasing restlessness and loneliness caused
by the absence of mail and any news of home. It is nearly
a month now since we left the division and Linz and
still we have no assurance of an early return to civilian
life. Army life has become particularly odious to me since
my stay in Austria and the idyllic existence of those
comparatively happy days. My dreams are still tortured
by the memory of Anna's sweet, piquant face and the
closeness we shared. How I miss her—it is so hard to
forget. I do not want to forget.*

November 12, 1945. Camp Tidworth, England. We arrived here yesterday evening after a 12-hour boat ride across the channel, and then a two-hour train ride from Southampton. Boarded our skip, the Marshal Jaffre, around 4:30 on the 10th and spent the night on the ship. Became seasick almost immediately, perhaps because I hadn't eaten for nearly a full day. When we disembarked, Red Cross girls were waiting with coffee and doughnuts. I managed to keep something down. Our temporary barracks is Tidworth House, an imposing mansion on 26,000 acres. Alas, more space between my beloved and me.

November 21, 1945. On board the Queen Mary. The QM is lavish and luxurious, especially the dining room with huge Egyptian motifs. I wander around the decks whenever I can, unable to sleep or eat, almost unable to write a few notes. My heart is miserable. Perhaps it was not wise to lose my heart as I did so profoundly, but I did no wrong. If I am to be criticized for loving with my whole being, I shall feel no regret.

November 28, 1945. Yesterday was indeed a day to remember. Long before daylight I was on deck to see if there was yet any sign of land. In the first light of day, there stretched a path from the ship's wake to the horizon where the first flush of light was on the water—a most beautiful sight. Everyone was on deck and a deafening cheer rose at first sight of the Statue of Liberty. I hate to say it seems like a year since I left Anna and those happy days, the music and wine, and the comfort of her arms. But soon I shall be a civilian once again, and I shall have the freedom to bring Anna to me.

Ann felt herself ache for Emmett's hopefulness and faith he had for the future he longed for.

> *December 24, 1945. Home. Spent the past few days getting reacquainted with my old haunts. Went to town with Clayton to pick up some civilian clothes and treated myself to a hamburger in town. Got myself a new pen, ink, and decent writing paper. Nana is planning a big Christmas celebration. Aunt Elizabeth wrote to say Karl might not make it home for Christmas. Ma has not improved, but she was delighted when I got the film developed and showed her pictures of Anna. Wrote another letter to my beloved this evening. I know she is conflicted. If she comes here, she leaves everything she has ever known. I must seriously consider how I could do the same for her.*

The next page jumped ahead to March 9, 1946.

> *Today we joined the others at Severson's sugar bush acres. I helped build the arch where the pan was placed to catch the sap as it cooked down. It was easy enough to assemble the simple fireplace with flat sandstones and clay for mortar and a stovepipe for the chimney. We tapped the trees and hung the pails under the dripping spiles, then carried the sap to the cooking pan. Anna liked to inhale the steam when we cooked down the sap. She had never collected sap before and it warmed my heart to see her having such a good time. As the evaporating process settled the golden liquid, Anna skillfully used a basswood paddle to skim thick foam off the top. I stayed long after Anna had gone up back to the house, and remained watchful that the sap didn't overcook as it reached the syrup stage.*

March 16, 1946. The spring breakup of ice on the creek is a spectacle I have always enjoyed, not only for the power it unleashes but also for the promise of lilacs. This week we watched as thick ice cakes broke away, screeching as they crashed like giant rafts against each other. Sometimes great chunks become lodged temporarily, causing others to grind to a halt, creating huge ice dams and backing water far into the woods. Would that I had such power.

Next, a gap of almost a full year.

July 19, 1947. Picked raspberries yesterday and Anna sold them in pint portions at the roadside stand in a matter of minutes this morning while little Anna toddled around in the daisies. The garden indicates a good crop of potatoes developing. Nana watched the baby this afternoon while the rest of us went to town for the annual dairy festival. The weather and countryside at this time combine to make our little part of the world a veritable paradise. Life is indeed a wonderful gift.

August 25, 1947. The harsh sun beats down relentlessly and while it is cooler than yesterday, the drought has been severe. The garden would perish without Anna's laborious watering. She tirelessly drives the tractor and wagon back and forth to fill cans with water from the creek to use in the house, the washhouse, and the garden. She and Nana have made plans for canning vegetables and making jam. As for Clayton and myself, threshing is now underway and we expect a decent crop.

Finally received my terminal leave pay. I will use the $142 for the dresser I promised Anna and for the insurance policy I have been planning. At $39 a year, I *hope it is a good investment.*

Farming is a hard life for a woman, Emmett had said. And here was Anna, making maple syrup, hauling water from the creek to save the garden, and canning vegetables. Those images faded when she turned the page and saw her dad's name.

October 27, 1947. Karl was up this weekend. He spent the nights over at Billy's place, but was here most of the daytime. He boasted about being promoted at the grocery store. Even though I envy his stable income, I saw a disagreeable haughtiness about him. Anna was glad to see him, but I was glad when he left.

Ann never heard anyone complain about her dad's company or describe him as a haughty man. He could be stubborn sometimes, but mostly she thought of her dad as a kind and thoughtful man. Had he come up north to see Anna and meet his little daughter? Was he trying to make a decision whether to marry Ruth or Anna? Or had he come to tell Anna goodbye?

December 1, 1947. Anna is finally back to her old self after what appears to have been a rather long bout with the flu. I've been working out at Larson's for several weeks now, but there's nothing left to do. I'll talk to old man Dexter tomorrow and see if he knows of any work. Sold another cow to Jorgenson, which means we'll have only four head to feed over the winter. The money from Jorgenson will allow a small Christmas for little Anna and enough to finish the roof on the porch just in time for winter. What's left will be spent only as absolutely needed.

Again, my mother with the flu, Ann thought. *How did she break the news to Emmett about a second baby on the way?* The next page propelled Ann to a page Emmett had dated March 1948.

> *Three years have elapsed since those delightful weeks in Austria filled with love and promises. But now I wonder if it would have been better had those weeks never happened. The news of Anna's condition and her admitted love for Karl still stabs at my heart. I often walk alone in the woods, my mind drifting back to those days in Linz. Even now as the love of my life has not remained faithful to our dream, I love her with all my heart. It's hard for me to think our being together was only my dream. Since Ma's funeral, Father's accusations and threats are relentless, and he has announced the conditions of his will with triumph. This final blow from him is insurmountable. I have nothing without Anna but I would have nothing with her. It is with great sorrow I concede to Anna's love for Karl. I simply don't know what else to do.*

The next page was dated a full year and a half later.

> *August 14, 1949. Little Annie always wants to help. I have to watch her carefully as she is so excited around the animals. When she gets underfoot I keep her busy. She likes to feed the chickens and find eggs. Nana keeps the baby close to her, but Annie is not to be confined. I made her a wagon and little shovel and she takes them everywhere. Baby Elise does not mimic her sister's boldness. Rather, she is cautious, less beguiled with mysteries of nature, and more careful in her manner. Both children are delightful, as curious and playful as any young creature. On many days, they can entertain themselves for a long time with a bucket of water and a few tin cups. We laugh at their antics especially when Anna bathes them outside in the large washtub. I must admit I was unsure at first, but as*

each of them has gotten older, I am happy they are with us. I am also happy they come to me occasionally when they need something or want to play. In every way I try to be a good father to them. Every night before she goes out to her cabin, Nana goes to their bed and gives them one last kiss goodnight.

It pleased Ann to think of herself and her sister playing with dolls and wandering around in the sunshine. It all sounded so innocent and happy. Then a two-year jump.

May 2, 1951. Dressed for her trip, she looked like the princess she was. I know she's trying to be brave and I can only guess at her bitter grief. Her eyes look tired even though she tells me she's feeling better. I see pain on her face. She knows this will be the last time she sees her mother. Nana and I took her to the train with the children. I regret with all my heart she must go all the way to New York and travel by ship from there alone. My Anna is so brave, but I have cried every night, as do the children. Nana manages to console little Elise, but Annie will not be comforted. She has trouble sleeping. Somehow, deep inside I fear the worst.

October 1951. How else can I feel except as a father to them? As Karl and Ruth shower them with toys and kind words, these are Anna's children. I pray they have not forgotten her voice already. I haven't and never will. Today I know in every way except for the will of God, these two children will be mine in my heart forever. I release them reluctantly.

Ann shut her eyes against her tears, picturing Karl and Ruth ushering two little girls into a car. Did she and her sister cry as they left the only home they ever knew? Did Emmett kiss them goodbye? Was he sad? Was he even there when they left? And when Anna got on that ship, did she wonder whether she'd see her two little girls again?

She imagined Emmett trying to return to the quiet life he had before Anna, before his days included two small children, before becoming the subject of gossip by his Milwaukee cousins, who all had bathrooms and furnaces and were all properly married before they had children.

Ann wiped her eyes and was putting the letters and notebook pages back in the envelope when she noticed two papers stuck to the bottom. She gently worked out a piece of onionskin stationery and a single notebook page. The onionskin was folded over a small photo showing five people standing in a garden, all of them smiling. On the back of the picture someone had written, "Familie—Mama, Papa, Frederick, Helena, Anneliese—Linz, Juli 1932." The thin airmail paper was dated June 12, 1951.

> Dear Emmett,
> My sister sends her love. The doctor says there is nothing he can do. She wishes you find care for the children. She said you will do the right thing. This familie photo is for Anna's children. I regret I can not write more now. Helena

The single notebook page was dated May 19, 1963. Emmett had squeezed his thoughts onto both sides.

> It has been twelve years since my Anna left. I pray for the power to turn back the clock to when we were together, to relive our dreams and romantic desires. But alas, I am finally left with nothing but memories of those happy days in Austria, the music and wine, the long walks along the

river. Anna, sweet and lovely, feminine and courageous. I shall always remember the optimism she arrived with, the undying hope with which she met each new day, the devotion and joy with which she nurtured her children. I must somehow live with the truth I can no longer deny. As my heart constantly burned for her, her heart burned for him. I realize it is easy to imagine a halo around the head of the ones we have loved, but even with the objectivity of time to contemplate, she is still all I want. She was and still is my one and only love. When Anna died, my dreams died, my heart died. I am pathetic.

No, Emmett, Ann thought. *You are not pathetic.*

She buried her face in the pillows and once again, for all she'd learned, for all she still didn't know or couldn't understand, she let herself cry.

THIRTY-FIVE

In the morning, Ann felt the burden of truth squarely on her shoulders. She knew her story was protected by Howie's professional ethics. She also trusted John. She believed he loved her and felt sure that even if she never saw him again, he would respect her privacy and that of Emmett. And what of Frank and Betty? She smiled at the thought of them asking Emmett about fathering two little girls. He'd call them liars—or worse—and they'd leave him alone with his supposed craziness. Then again, why did it matter what anyone thought?

It was a long time ago, Ann reasoned. *My parents made mistakes. It's not my responsibility to justify their actions with the rest of the world. Is it?*

She put the last of Emmett's notebook pages, letters, and everything Howie had given her about her fake adoption in her laptop case and went down to the kitchen. Frank and Betty were at the table with bowls of oatmeal. Betty uttered a half-sincere good morning.

"I suppose the stuff I left in your room yesterday was just more flowery writing," Betty added as Ann joined them at the table.

"Pretty much," Ann replied without looking up. "Poems mostly."

Frank gave a sideways nod toward the laptop case. "What's in the little suitcase?"

"I brought on the first day, remember? My laptop's in there and some notes for my project."

Ann wasn't comfortable with the lie, but she was comfortable about protecting her own privacy. And until she got back home, Emmett's letters and notebooks would remain in her laptop case and never leave her sight.

"Yeah, I suppose you have stuff to do since you're power of attorney now," Frank said. "I suppose you know more about Emmett than anyone." He drained his coffee cup, grabbed his jacket, and went outside.

Ann didn't like the sarcasm in Frank's voice. She looked at Betty. "Is he upset with me?"

"He's upset about the money."

"What money?"

"That Emmett took money from Clayton." Betty nervously folded her paper napkin into a smaller square. "You know. The money they inherited from their uncle. Someone at the café told Frank that Emmett swindled all that money for himself."

It had to happen, Ann thought. *They're suspicious. They don't trust me anymore.* "I don't think we should depend on something Frank heard at the café," she said, nonchalantly dropping a few raisins in her oatmeal. "Whatever Clayton had when he died would have gone to Emmett as his next of kin, including whatever money Clayton may have had at the time. It's the law, Betty. It was the same when your folks died and will be the same when your children inherit from you."

Betty unfolded her napkin again and chewed her lip, not looking up.

"I meant what I said when I came up here, Betty," Ann continued. "All I want is the truth about my parents. But if Frank thinks I'm doing something wrong when it comes to Emmett's affairs, we can simply put your names on the power of attorney paperwork."

"No, no, no," Betty said quickly. "Don't change anything."

"Do you want me to talk to Frank?"

Betty shook her head. "Never mind. I'll talk to him. I guess what you said about Clayton's money makes sense." She forced a smile. "And at least you found a few things to share with your sister, so your trip wasn't a complete disaster."

The phone rang and Betty hurried to get it.

"Yes, she's here," she said, stretching the cord toward Ann. "Oh, okay. Yes, I'll tell her."

"What?" Ann asked as Betty replaced the receiver.

"That was Lily at the Manor House. She said Emmett was dehydrated, so he's in the hospital for fluids or something."

Ann took one more bite of her oatmeal and went for her boots.

"It didn't sound very serious, dear," Betty called after her.

"Where's the hospital?" Ann said, grabbing her laptop case and digging in her coat pocket for her keys.

"About eight miles down from the Manor House."

Ann stopped at the Manor House to pick up Emmett's old tape recorder and Strauss tapes. At the hospital, she was directed to a dimly lit room, where she found him under the covers with an IV taped to his left arm. Oxygen prongs led from his nostrils to a tank alongside the bed, and his eyes were closed. But his tightly furrowed brow and set jaw told Ann he wasn't sleeping. She hadn't noticed his eyelids before—like bluish-pink onionskin. His plaid flannel shirt had been replaced by a droopy washed-out hospital gown that barely covered his protruding collarbones and the transparent skin of his arms. If he evaporated before her eyes right now, Ann wouldn't be surprised.

She put the tape recorder on the nightstand, plugged it in, and hit the play button. His eyes fluttered open.

"Hey, there, Emmett," she whispered. "It's me, Annie."

He blinked and studied her, trying to remember.

"It's Annie," she said again. "Anna's daughter. Remember?"

He smiled weakly. "Sure I do," he said. "Sit a spell."

Ann moved a chair closer. "How are you feeling?"

"Ah. The Blue Danube. Johann Strauss."

"Do you like it?"

"It's my favorite," he wheezed. "Some people wouldn't listen to Strauss during the war because he was Austrian like Hitler." Emmett closed his eyes. "Isn't that ridiculous? Strauss was born years before Hitler and his barbarians."

His chin quivered as the music stirred his memories. When the song ended, Ann pressed the pause button. "I can play it again if you like."

"Maybe later," he replied, wiping a tear away with a shaky hand.

"Are you able to breathe better with a little oxygen?"

"Oh, I guess I'm plumb wore out." He looked at her. "You're Anna's daughter."

"Yes, I am."

"And, if memory serves, you teach college."

"Right again."

"She used to call you her little chickadee."

Ann had gotten used to Emmett's mind suddenly taking another course, but this statement was too sweet to ignore. "Little chickadee?" she asked.

"She said chickadees are strong. Surely you've noticed them. They stay over winter. They don't fly south like other birds. They find a way to make it through the tough times. They're little survivors. Why, I don't believe I've ever seen a dead one."

Ann smiled at him. "I haven't either."

He raised a finger and shook it in her direction. "And you have a sister."

"Yes. Elise."

"Yes. Anna and Elise. Anneliese was Anna's real name. It's a pretty name, isn't it? She was your mother. And Nana is your great-grandmother. You're entitled to some inheritance."

"You've already given me my mother's dishes," Ann said, thinking of other things she'd also taken from his house.

"You take whatever you want from the house. I know I won't be going back." He paused a moment as if to let the reality of his statement sink in. "Take something for your sister too, but I'd like you to have Nana's old barrister. You're the oldest, and I believe it's what Nana would want.

He began to cough, a little at first, then more, and suddenly he seemed quite distressed by the force and persistence of it. Ann pushed the nurse's button.

"Let's see what's going on here, Mr. Pederson," the nurse said as she hurried into the room.

The hefty woman talked in soothing tones while she helped him sit up, urging him to spit in a plastic bowl. She checked the oxygen apparatus, rearranged his pillows, and eased him back against them. His face was red, eyes shut tight, mouth firm.

"He's fine now, aren't you Mr. Pederson?" the nurse asked. "I think he's okay for now," she told Ann.

Ann sat down again after the nurse left, watching Emmett breathe. She touched his arm. "I worry about you."

"No need," he wheezed.

When he drifted off to sleep, Ann slipped away to the nurse's station.

"Is there anything I can do for him?" she asked the nurse who'd come to Emmett's room. "I'm Ann Olson. I'm his power of attorney. Is there anything I need to know or do?"

"I don't think so," the nurse said as she paged through Emmett's chart.

"Is he taking his pills? He used to hide them under his pillow."

"We crush 'em up in his ice cream," the nurse said with a knowing grin. "Let's see. Nothing unusual at this time. The congested heart failure accounts for the excess fluid in his lungs and the coughing. I see you're the only contact listed. We've got a DNR on him, but don't worry, we do expect him to recover enough to go back to the Manor House."

"DNR," Ann repeated. "Do not resuscitate. Whose idea was that?"

"His."

"Oh." Ann felt helpless.

Back in Emmett's room, she found him slumped to one side. His mouth was hanging open and he was snoring softly. She covered him, watched him a minute, and then left him to the care of the nurses.

Over the next four days, Ann tried to keep her visits with Emmett upbeat and encouraging, and each evening John comforted and resuscitated her with food, wine, and love. When Emmett returned to the Manor House, he had a new breathing contraption and pills he'd probably hide under his pillow. Gradually, his spirit improved along with his appetite, and Ann came to see him every day. Emmett never asked about the little tape recorder she positioned on the nightstand in his room or near him in the common room. He never complained when she repeated questions he'd already answered. He talked and Ann never tired of listening.

One day she admitted being curious about why his house didn't have a furnace.

"There was no need. We all knew how to cook with wood and heat with wood, and we had an abundance of it."

"But you said you were afraid of chimney fires. Wouldn't a furnace have been safer?"

"They cost a lot of money, and we didn't have a lot of money. Farming doesn't pay a regular wage, you know, but we still had bills like everyone else. Fortunately we had our health, because we had no insurance of any kind."

His comment led Ann to wonder about the money Emmett and his brother had inherited, but she didn't have to ask.

"Clayton and I inherited some money from my mother's brother," he told her. "My Uncle Oscar. He never had any children, and we were told he made money as a traveling salesman. But everyone knew Oscar was a gambler. He left us a considerable sum, but it came too late." He took a deep breath, which made him cough slightly. "By that time, Anna was gone, and you and your sister were gone. And after Nana died and Clayton took his life, I inherited the farm, including Clayton's share. All told, I guess you could say I became a rich man. But I was alone." He looked down, folding and unfolding his hands several times. "Money isn't everything. My memories are worth more." He looked up at Ann and smiled slightly. "So, I managed fine without a furnace."

"What memories, Emmett?" Ann asked softly.

His old blue eyes seemed to twinkle, as if a beautiful scene was playing out on the wall behind her. When he started talking again, he seemed to be in a trance. He said Anna's favorite color was yellow, and he got books from the library to help her learn English. She could sew better than Nana; she dug up wildflowers from the woods and transplanted them around the house; she liked chocolate and Nana's molasses cookies. He said a bee stung Elise when she was just a baby, and Ann fell off the fence into the cow pasture. They thought her arm was broken but it wasn't. He said Anna insisted that he put a hook high up on the outhouse door so the girls couldn't open it by themselves.

He didn't talk about hardship or being poor, about hauling water from the creek for the animals, the garden, and bathing, or how they managed to stay warm in the winter with just a small wood burning stove. Ann wondered but didn't ask where they got water when the creek was frozen. She hoped the farm provided enough to eat and that life wasn't mostly hardship. As Emmett talked, Ann could see images, hear voices and laughter, taste Nana's molasses cookies. Emmett told her she might remember if she tried very hard, and Ann so wanted to remember—to go back for just a day.

That evening, John took her to Giovanni's, and Ann wondered aloud how she would ever forgive her dad.

"No one's perfect, honey," John said.

"But John, my mom—and my mother—they both trusted him. He betrayed their trust."

John sighed and broke off another chunk of garlic bread. "Did I ever tell you my dad had an affair?"

Ann shook her head.

"Mom was in the hospital and I was about fourteen," he said. "I was old enough to know that what my dad did was wrong and that my mom didn't deserve it."

"Did you forgive him?" Ann asked gently.

"I was mad at him for a long time. Years later I figured he must have lost his mind to grief and anger over my mom's illness." He paused a moment. "I loved my dad, but I couldn't forgive him for what he done."

"My dad didn't act out of grief or anger," Ann mused.

"I guess not," John said soberly. "But love can make us do crazy things too. I been there."

"So my dad, Karl, and Father Unknown are one and the same because of love? How am I going to explain that to my family? And that Dad lied to us?"

"I'd go for the truth," John told her. "It's a better story than you could make up. And you can't argue with the truth."

Much later, Ann curled up under Betty's quilt and listened to Frank snore. The idea of people living their own lives and making their own mistakes wasn't as simple as John made it sound. Or was it? *No*, she thought. *Dad was wrong and his mistakes—with whatever explanation we could imagine him offering if he were still here—will cause repercussions. The actions of parents do affect the lives of their children. And like it or not, truth lays bare what is or was; but it can't fix everything.*

On her final day in Newland, Ann stopped at the Manor House. They had Emmett in a wheelchair because the oxygen tank he depended on was too heavy for him to carry. She stood in the doorway of the common room and watched him a moment. If she hadn't come up north, he'd still be her dad's crazy cousin. Poor Emmett with his shabby clothes, his memories and Strauss tapes, and his wonderful, wonderful notebooks. Only a month ago, she didn't know him. Now she wanted to turn the clock back just to have more time with him.

He gave a little wave as Ann approached, and she was glad to see some color in his cheeks. She opened the small bottle of orange juice that had been left on the end table and offered it to him. He sipped carefully while they watched some of the aides dismantle the Christmas tree.

"You'll be ahead of the storm if you leave today," he said. "Time to hunker down and let winter take its turn."

The radio had reported clear skies, but Emmett was definitely a man who knew all about hunkering down for the winter. And this winter he'd be more alone than ever. Betty said she might stop by now and then, but Ann doubted either Betty or Frank would pay a visit. John said he'd come and talk to Emmett about the old days. He probably would.

After a few more remarks about the weather, Emmett got quiet—as if he'd run out of things to say or didn't have any words left in him. A chipper farewell didn't seem appropriate but neither did a somber one. So when he dozed off, Ann simply left. Somehow she knew he wouldn't mind, but this time, leaving him felt too final.

When she reached the highway, Ann turned the radio off. There was enough noise in her head—enough stories, notebook pages, and letters to sort out—and more than enough missing information.

She would never know her mother the way she had wanted to all her life. But at least now she knew her mother's proper name. She also finally knew something about her mother's family and that her mother had loved her two little girls. She had precious photos and stories, things her mother had touched and worn, and words she wrote. Even the word "mother" was now finally real. All thanks to Emmett, the old man who had kept his love for Anna alive in his heart all these years.

Ann touched her mother's gold cross, now around her own neck, and glanced at the pastel portrait of her mother on the passenger seat. What was behind this calm-looking face? Did she think she could win the man she loved by getting pregnant? Or was her love for Karl so strong that she'd risk coming to America alone and a second pregnancy even when she must have known he wasn't going to keep his word?

And what of Karl? Ann didn't want to think of her dad, her father, as a man who'd vow his love to a woman and then walk away when a baby came. How could the sensible, safe, and trustworthy father she knew be related to the man who played so carelessly with the lives of Anna, Ruth, and his children? Did he ever think about the two little girls he'd rejected when he was helping those same little girls with their homework? How could he say he loved them and was proud of them but keep the truth from them? Did he suffer under the weight of his secret?

And then there was Emmett—the one her family wrote off as a crazy fool, the one she suspected all these years as her irresponsible father unknown. Was Karl's promise the only thing that kept him quiet all these years? Or did he feel obligated to protect the memory—and actions—of his beloved Anna?

Their lives interconnected and Ann knew it was unfair to judge them. But by the time she got home, she felt crushed under the evidence she had brought with her and the responsibility it gave her.

THIRTY-SIX

After unpacking the Blazer, Ann poured herself a glass of wine and waited until she knew Elise would be home from her New-to-You Boutique. Ann had once shared the irony with Elise—the owner of a resale shop is adopted just as the clothes she sold would be. Elise didn't like the joke.

She recalled a summer day at the beach when she and Elise were teens and acquiring a tan was their prime concern. Stretched alongside her sister on the blanket, Ann had simply said she hoped to find out about their real parents some day. There was no malice behind her statement; she was sharing a thought, not making a threat. But Elise grabbed her things and ran most of the way home, throwing angry words over her shoulder to Ann: ungrateful, selfish, cruel, stupid, and creep, followed by, "You don't love Mom and Dad. You shouldn't even be in our family!"

Over the rest of that summer, Elise gave Karen all her attention—letting Karen borrow things Ann wasn't allowed to touch, fixing Karen's hair, polishing her nails. Elise also went out of her way to spend more time with her friends—even the ones she didn't like very much—anything to avoid Ann. Elise eventually came around, but not until she was sure Ann had had the worst summer of her life.

Years later, when they were both in their forties, Elise admitted seeing a therapist. At first, Ann didn't understand. Elise's husband was kind and attentive, her son was a good kid, she had lots of good friends, and it seemed Elise had always been closer to Ruth and Karl. But after months of gentle probing, Elise admitted her difficulty in dealing with the unacceptable unknowns of their adoption. Many times Ann suggested they find answers together and Elise always refused. Back to the therapist she went.

Ann took a slug of wine and dialed.

"I have a lot to tell you," she said when Elise answered, "but I'd rather not tell you over the phone. I know it's last-minute, but can you come over?"

Elise sounded hesitant. "Not really. I mean not now. Kyle and I need to get a few things for his dorm room before he goes back." She paused and cleared her throat, sounding unsure. "Is this information for Karen and Neal too?"

"Yes, but I thought you and I could talk first."

"I'd rather talk about whatever it is with all of us," Elise said. "Let them pick a day."

It would do no good to disagree, so Ann said okay and hung up. To her surprise, both Karen and Neal were willing to come over the next evening. She called Elise back and announced that her condition had been met.

Ann readied her coffee table with cookies, a box of Kleenex, Emmett's notebooks, letters, photos, and Anna's jewelry. Karen and Neal were dumbfounded, angry, and sad as Ann revealed what she had learned. Elise sat silently, staring at the coffee table, her arms folded across her chest.

"This means you're our half sisters," Neal said.

Karen looked at him with tears in her eyes, shaking her head. "I don't like the sound of that."

Ann squeezed Karen's arm. "You're my sweet little sister, silly. Nothing's changed."

"Last week Mom told me they were getting the girls up north," Karen said with a sniffle. "I knew what she meant, so I just let it go. But when she said Dad had an affair with a woman named Mitzie, I thought she was getting her soaps mixed up with reality. She wasn't, was she? She just kept it inside all these years."

"Mom always did what Dad wanted," Ann said. "We all

know that."

"I'm sorry, Karen," Neal said. "But right now I can't help thinking about when you and Steve had to get married. Dad was so angry. How could he, knowing what he did?"

Karen took another Kleenex. "Steve's a good man. It just took Dad a while to see it."

Neal leaned forward and put his elbows on his knees, holding his head in one hand. Ann noticed his hair was going white from front to back. Just as Karl's had done—and her own.

"Remember when Pam and I were having trouble?" he asked. "When I told Dad, he drummed it into my head about how it was the man's job to keep the family together." Neal squeezed a thumb and forefinger across his eyes and two tears fell onto the carpet. "Mostly he said I had to think about my kids. How could he forget what he did?"

Elise finally spoke up. "So why did all this happen?"

"It's a love story," Ann replied. "A love triangle, I guess."

A few quiet minutes passed before Elise replied. "I always knew there was something." The others looked at her with curious anticipation until she pointed to the color portrait of Anna. "I have the same picture."

All eyes focused on Elise.

"It was a long time ago," she said. "Dad told me Emmett sent it. I was supposed to show it to you, but I didn't want to."

Ann fell back against the couch. "What did you do with it?"

"It's in a box somewhere."

"In a box somewhere?" Now Ann's voice cracked. "You knew all along what she looked like and you didn't tell me? Why not?"

"I didn't want anything to spoil what we had."

"But you suspected something? All these years?"

"I didn't want to," Elise pouted. "You were always asking questions, and I saw how angry Dad got, and Mom clearly didn't want to deal with it." She hung her head, her voice barely audible. "I got mad at you, so I hid it. But then I found the other pictures."

"Other pictures?" Ann asked, unable to mask her parental tone. "Elise, look at me. What other pictures?"

Elise raised her head and sniffled over the words. "Granny Elizabeth had pictures of us when we were little. I found them in her buffet cabinet where she kept the good silverware. Then one time when we were over there, I was going to show you, but they were gone."

Ann stared at her sister in disbelief.

"Some were pictures of her—our mother."

"Geez, Elise! What happened to them?"

Elise shrugged. For an instant, Ann thought about telling Elise how Karl didn't even know about her birth. But no, that would be childish. They weren't children anymore, and Elise didn't deserve that. Elise, too, had suffered enough.

"Maybe Granny Elizabeth got rid of them," Karen suggested. "Emmett must have sent them. Or maybe Nana. Or maybe the mother of that Gracie you said you met."

"Whoever sent them probably thought Granny Elizabeth would give them to Elise and me," Ann said. "Maybe Dad got rid of them."

Karen sighed. "I remember one Mother's Day when Dad told me all Mom wanted was for us to be a happy family. At the time I thought it was kind of odd. We were always a happy family. But I bet Mom worried about all this coming out someday."

"Which explains why she never answered my questions," Ann said.

"It's a catch-22," Neal concluded with a touch of sarcasm. "The truth would have jeopardized our happy family just as hiding the truth protected our happy family. At least in Dad's eyes." He grinned at Ann. "One thing for sure, having the same father explains why you were always so stubborn."

Ann smiled at her brother.

"Annie," Elise said. "You're not going to bother Mom about this now, are you?"

"I have to admit I wish I knew what Mom knows. But I won't ask her."

"Promise?"

Ann nodded. "Promise."

When her kids came over later in the week, Ann tried her best to justify Karl's passion, Anna's dilemma, and Emmett's promise not to expose Karl. She described Ruth as a devoted wife. Granny Elizabeth, she explained, was overprotective of her son, and Grampa Olaf's opinion of his son's affair would always be a mystery since he wasn't mentioned in any of the letters. She tried to sound convincing when she said forgiving the past was the only thing she could do to heal the hurt in her own heart and mind. Ann concluded by saying they'd all have to be satisfied not knowing the whole story. She shouldn't have been surprised at her children's reactions.

"There's no excuse, Mom!" Lisa said, throwing the adoption paper back onto Ann's coffee table. "It seems to me Grampa was quite willing to forget he had two little girls!"

"I don't think he forgot about us," Ann said. "And I imagine he couldn't forget our mother either since he had to look at Elise and me all the time."

"What gets me," Mark said, "is all his preaching to us kids about being responsible. I respected him, and all along he was a hypocrite."

"Please, Mark," Ann told her son. "I admit my father made a big mistake, but he was a good father—to all of us. And he loved my mother. I believe he loved her just as I know he loved Gramma and all of us kids."

"But he had you and Elise before he had children with Gramma. And I can't believe the prejudice part—I can't believe I have grandparents and great-grandparents who couldn't deal with religious differences."

"There was prejudice then just like now," was all Ann could say. But inside she was proud of her son's disappointment.

Lisa sat back and crossed her legs. "Seems to me, besides little old Nana poking Grampa in the ass to do the right thing, Emmett's the hero in all this."

"I'm grateful to him," Ann told her daughter. "But I also know no parent is perfect. I know I'm not."

THRITY-SEVEN

John stayed at Ann's whenever he came down for the Milwaukee auto auction, and sometimes she went back with him. She stayed at John's whenever she was up north now not only because they wanted to be together but because Frank and Betty's persistent questions about Emmett's money and welfare had become what Ann called insincere and what John called baloney.

Some of Ann's visits with Emmett were short due to his energy level, but whenever he saw her he was eager to talk. He never mentioned the notebooks and neither did Ann, but she got the feeling he knew she had found them by the way he anticipated her questions or said, "I think you know about that." Emmett also didn't talk about the war unless Anna was part of the story, and his references to Karl began sounding more and more like the kind and thoughtful man Ann had known as her dad. For everything Emmett shared with her, Ann still wished for one pure and vivid memory of her mother—a glimpse of her face, a touch of her hand, one word spoken in her mother's voice. After all, she had known her father. Was it too much to ask to remember her mother? That was the question no one could answer.

As soon as winter thawed into spring, Ann took her camera out to Emmett's place. She wanted to remember the inside of the house, the barn, and the woods and creek behind his property. She even got a shot of the outhouse with the hook high on the door.

In May, Ann brought John to Ruth's birthday celebration. She knew he'd slip into her family's favor just as easily as he'd slipped into his boots that morning. More importantly, her kids found it easy to say "Mom and John" and her grandsons had no trouble calling him Grampa John, which pleased both Ann and John very much.

Ruth's birthday party also marked the celebration of her move to an assisted living complex called Orchard Hills. It took almost a week to sort keepsakes from junk in what Ruth and Karl had accumulated over fifty years. The new apartment couldn't accommodate the trinkets, plants, and collectibles Ruth had all over the house. Ruth was disappointed there was no orchard or hills at Orchard Hills either. On moving day, Ann and her sisters were in the nearly empty house with Ruth, talking about all they good times they'd had there when Ruth started to cry. While Karen calmed her mother, Ann walked through the rooms for one last inspection. When she looked in Ruth's bedroom closet, she almost didn't see the cardboard box way in the back. About the size of a toaster and the same color as the closet floor, it was easy to miss. Ann called her sisters.

"Hey, they forgot something!"

"Let me see," Ruth said, hurrying to her old bedroom.

"We'll take it back to your new place, Mom," Elise told her.

"No!" she said when she saw the box. "I need to open it now."

Karen found a step stool, and Ruth sat down and unfolded the box flaps.

"It's all in here," Ruth said.

"All what, Mom?" Ann asked her.

"Things for you kids."

Ruth lifted out drawings and worksheets from their grade-school days, and Karen and Elise knelt on the floor and chuckled over their childish artwork and handwriting. Ann stood above them, anxiously waiting for Ruth to get to the rubber-banded bundles she could see in the box. Finally, Ruth took the first one out and gave it to Karen.

"These are my old report cards!" Karen said. "Holy cow, Mom, I didn't know you kept these. My immunization record is in here, too, and my Girl Scout patches!"

"Of course. I keep everything," Ruth said in her matter-of-fact way.

While Karen reminisced about her fourth-grade teacher, Ruth gave her another bundle. "This is Neal's," she said. "Don't lose it. His football pictures are in there."

Next, Ruth handed Elise and Ann their bundles. Ann's was thicker and when she took the rubber band off, old photos fluttered to the floor. She stood over them for a moment, staring. There was a photo of her mother outside on a blanket with infant Elise, another showed Anna feeding chickens with toddler Annie, and another was of Emmett showing the girls a kitten. Ann slid down the wall and sat on the floor next to Elise, who was also staring at the pictures on the floor.

"Those are the ones," Elise whispered to Ann.

"Mom, where did you get these?" Ann asked.

"Oh, Dad brought them over from Granny Elizabeth's one time," Ruth said. "He said to save them for you girls. There are pictures of your mother in there. And Emmett, too, of course."

Ann picked up the photos. "I wish I had seen these a long time ago."

Elise nudged Ann, but the reminder not to ask Ruth any questions wasn't necessary because Ruth spoke up.

"I guess I forgot about them," she said. "But I know Dad used to look at them sometimes." Her lips quivered a bit as she pointed to one of the photos. "Her name was Mitzie. I guess it's a foreign name or something."

Now Elise perked up. "He told you her name?"

"He told me all about her."

Ann's head fell back against the wall with a thud. Karen touched Ann's arm, mouthing the words, "Ask her."

When Elise didn't protest, Ann asked as politely as she could. "Mom, what did Dad tell you about Mitzie?"

"He said she was your mother and he met her overseas."

She paused and lowered her head, twisting the wedding ring on her finger. When she looked up again, she had tears in her eyes. "One time I thought he wanted to marry her instead of me."

Karen touched her mother's hand. "But he married you, Mom. He loved you."

Ruth took a tissue from the pocket of her jacket and smiled sweetly. "I know, honey. I loved him too."

Karen gave Ann an encouraging nod, and Elise gave Ann a nod of her own.

"Why would he marry Mitzie?" Ann asked.

"Because of you."

"Me?"

"Well, you and Elise. He is your father, after all. And she's your mother."

Elise let the breath go that she had been holding. "How long have you known, Mom?"

Ruth shot her a defensive glance. "I always knew. Dad and I don't have any secrets between us," she said as if Karl were still around.

"Why didn't you tell us?"

"It wasn't my place to tell you." She sounded irritated but also sad, as if she'd been left out and didn't like it. "I wasn't involved. Besides, he already explained everything to you when he got these pictures from your grandmother."

Elise flashed a puzzled glance at Ann, who was mulling over what to say to keep Ruth from getting angry or distracted. Memories of Granny Elizabeth, Aunt Inga, and Ruth sitting over coffee and cake, whispering about "the girls up north," came back to Ann clearly—right down to seeing her little-girl self wedged between the wall and the china cabinet where these precious photos may have been hidden. *No more tears,* she told herself. *If we start crying, Mom might stop talking.*

"When Dad gave us our birth certificates, he told us our mother died in Austria," Ann said calmly. "Granny Elizabeth gave me a picture of her once."

Elise and Karen knew Ann had taken the photo from their grandmother's scrapbook—but they didn't flinch at the little white lie.

Ruth thought a moment. "The one with Emmett and Dad in their uniforms? I remember seeing it someplace."

In my underwear drawer, Ann said to herself, *where I thought no one would ever look.*

"Your mother was in the picture too," Ruth said. "I guess she had a different name but I don't remember."

"It says Anna on our birth certificates," Ann told her.

Ruth nodded absently. "Yes, but it was something else. Your father said she lived on a farm in the old country. That's why she wanted to stay up north on the farm with Emmett. He was a grouchy old hermit. He didn't have any education. He didn't even have a toilet."

Her name was Anneliese and she was from Linz, Austria, Ann wanted to say. *Linz is a big city. And Emmett was not a grouchy hermit.*

"Dad told you where she was from, Mom?" Elise asked carefully.

"Of course. How else would I know?"

Ruth picked up the packet Karen had set aside for Neal. She removed the rubber band from his high school football photos and thumbed through them, showing no sign of recognition or interest. Then she replaced the rubber band and set the photos aside again. She was becoming distracted.

Karen spoke. "The thing I don't understand, Mom," she said casually, "is why Mitzie would stay up north with Emmett if she had children with Dad."

Her knuckles already white, Elise seemed to freeze completely now, her eyes glued to the opposite wall. Ann held her breath. This question, the one Ann was working toward, the biggest question of all, was—she hoped—far less threatening coming from Karen, Ruth's own daughter.

"I guess there were concerns," Ruth said simply.

"Concerns?"

Ruth looked at Karen as if she should know better. "Well, for one thing, she had two children out of wedlock."

Ann saw Karen purse her lips and lower her eyes. The sisters had been all together the day their very angry dad told a pregnant and yet unmarried Karen that doing what she had done was like spitting in God's face.

What about you, Dad? Ann wanted to scream. But again she held her tongue.

"The other thing," Ruth added, "was that she was Catholic."

Karl and Ruth often pointed out people with ashes on their foreheads on Ash Wednesday, kids in their school uniforms, and nuns in stiff habits, and how fish fry Fridays in Milwaukee's restaurants started because Catholics wouldn't eat meat on Fridays. Ruth always used to say, "Someone should tell them fish is meat."

"Do you know if both of her parents were Catholic?" Elise asked.

The directness of Elise's question surprised Ann.

"Of course. Why would they be different?"

When Ruth glanced the other way for a moment, Elise caught Ann's eye and shook her head as if to say, "Don't even go there." Ann nodded. To tell Ruth that Anna's father was a Jew would invite more criticism. Besides, how would Ann explain how she knew?

Ruth adjusted her position on the step stool and waved a finger between Ann and Elise. "Of course, we got you two girls baptized in our Lutheran church right away. I made you matching dresses," she added proudly. "They were white eyelet."

Ann proceeded with caution. "You know what, Mom? I'm not even sure how adoption happens. Did you and Dad have to go up north to do that or what?"

"We sure did. Dad sent a letter to a lawyer up there. Then

he wrote to Emmett and told him what would be best for you girls." She stopped and frowned slightly. "Emmett didn't like the idea at first, but Dad's grandmother Nana got Emmett to do the right thing."

There's that phrase again, Ann thought. *Do the right thing. All Emmett ever wanted—besides Anna's love—was for Karl to do the right thing.*

"But Mom," Karen said. "If Dad is Ann and Elise's father, why was the adoption necessary?"

Ann silently applauded the second question she'd been itching to ask.

Ruth shrugged. "Don't ask me. Dad said we had to do it the way they do it up there. At least there was a lawyer so everything would be legal." Her brow creased. "Of course Emmett didn't come to the lawyer's office because Nana told him to stay away for good."

Ann lowered her eyes. *The way they do it up there? Nana told Emmett to stay away? Lies!* When she looked up a moment later, Ruth was taking stiff folders from the bottom of the box.

"These are for you two," Ruth said, passing them to Ann and Elise.

The studio portraits looked freshly printed. One was of Ann, perhaps a year old, her dark blond hair smoothed over to one side where a small bow had been fastened. The second was of Elise, grinning like the Cheshire cat under a halo of yellow-white curls. The third photo was dated December 1950 in what Ann now recognized as her mother's handwriting. In this one, the little sisters sat close together, Elise's hand in Ann's lap, both unaware their mother would soon be gone forever.

Her dad's words echoed in her head, the words he always said when she had trouble with math. *Keep trying. The answer is in there. All you have to do is keep working until you find it.*

Ann let her head drop. *You knew all along I'd get it,* she silently told her dad's spirit. *But if you would have just confessed, we could have avoided all the tears and grief. If you had confessed right from the start, I would have known you were really proud of me as your daughter.*

Elise tapped Ann's leg and passed her a snapshot. In it, a very young Annie stood in a field among stacks of grain. She wore a straw hat and her little outfit was dirty. She wasn't smiling.

THIRTY-EIGHT

On a beautiful morning in late June, Betty called Ann. "Emmett passed away peacefully in his sleep," she said reverently. "Clayton's buried next to Aunt Lena, but there's a plot for Emmett next to Uncle Albert. Of course, we'll have to order a headstone."

Ann was half listening, thinking back two weeks to the last time she saw Emmett. "I suppose I'm old," he'd told her after a bout with pneumonia. The poor people's friend, her dad had always called it. She felt tears in her eyes. Of course, she knew he'd die someday. Emmett himself talked about it, but not as a final reward, not as peace, not as anything a preacher might say to a crowd of mourners. Rather he told her, "Thoreau said we should try not to have too many regrets. And I say that if we're lucky, we learn a few things along the way." Ann could still see him closing his eyes and smiling as if submitting to what he knew was coming.

"I don't know what we'll do about a service," Betty said, drawing Ann back to the present. "He never went to church, but our pastor might be willing to say a few words. We'd have to bring his coffin to the church, though. It's the only way our pastor will do a funeral."

Months earlier Emmett told Ann he'd prearranged his funeral years earlier and paid for everything in advance, including his headstone and a simple bouquet of flowers.

"Emmett told me he didn't want a minister reading over his remains," Ann told Betty. "He said he just wanted his family and friends to come and say goodbye."

"I could ask our pastor to come just in case."

In case of what? Ann wanted to ask. Instead, she said, "I think we should honor Emmett's wishes." She left out the part about Emmett's wish to be cremated before being laid to rest with the other members of his family. "You can check with the funeral director up there if you want, Betty. It's all arranged."

Betty scoffed. "Fine. But I bet he didn't plan on spending eternity right next to Uncle Albert."

"I suppose not," Ann said, rolling her eyes. "And I hope you don't mind, but as his power of attorney I've already written his obituary. I'll email it to the funeral home."

Ann had already started Emmett's obituary, but her power of attorney status had nothing to do with it. Rather, she wanted people to know about his battle ribbons and the farm he loved. She wanted the words to be just right. She'd mentioned Clayton, who preceded Emmett in death, but left out any mention of Anna or children. If anyone was bold enough to ask, Ann was prepared to lie and say she'd written it the way Emmett wanted it written.

"Very well," Betty said. "I'll watch for the notice in the paper," adding that she and Frank would come to the service "because no one else will be there."

"Mind if I go with you?" Elise asked when Ann called her with the news. "I guess I'd like to see his old place. Do you mind?"

Of course, Ann was delighted.

On the day of his funeral, Ann placed a framed photo of a much younger Emmett in his Army uniform next to his urn. Over strains of Strauss's music, Betty told the funeral director that cremation was disgusting, and then tried not to act surprised when John and Howie showed up, along with some of the regulars from Melody's Café, and Lily and an aide from the Manor House. Even Frank was impressed when members of the local VFW post marched in with guns on their shoulders and stood in a respectable formation along the back wall. Gordy was a no-show, and no one missed him.

Once everyone was seated, Ann went to the podium. She said she was glad to know Emmett, her dad's cousin. She talked about Emmett growing up poor and reading every book in the library. She said the family in Milwaukee admired his self-sufficiency and simple lifestyle, even though she knew that was a stretch. She read a few entries she'd copied from his notebooks—a few lines about his Yankee Division, his description of the creek in the springtime with its thick ice cakes breaking away, screeching and crashing like giant rafts against each other, and the one about tapping maple trees for syrup. She left out the part about her mother using a basswood paddle to skim the foam off the top. She ended with one of his poems.

> *Evening falls around me,*
> *A mourning dove calls far away,*
> *I retreat to the comfort of shadows*
> *To wait the dawn of another day.*

A few people from the café offered brief condolences but didn't ask any questions about Ann's relationship to Emmett. No doubt what Ann overheard Betty tell her friend on the phone had gotten around. A certain cousin from Milwaukee, Betty had said, was too embarrassed to admit Emmett was her father and wasn't that all the pity. Ann knew Emmett would have approved her decision not to offer Betty any clarifying details. The people who needed to know the truth knew it, and that was enough.

Before they left the cemetery, Betty pointed out Nana's grave and complained about the wild violets that covered it every spring despite her every effort to eradicate them. Ann smiled to herself and silently vowed to transplant a few onto Emmett's grave as a testimony to his tenacious spirit—and to drive Betty nuts.

After lunch at Melody's, Ann drove Elise out to Emmett's.

When they came to the ironwork bridge, Elise demanded that Ann stop.

"You're not going across that thing, are you?" Elise asked.

"It's the only way to get there." Ann gave her sister a wry smile. "It's okay. Pretend we're kids and you trust your big sister. Take a look down at the creek Dad used to swim in."

Elise cautiously stretched to peer at the creek below. "It's full of rocks. Give me a nice clean pool any day,"

"John knows an Amish family that wants to buy the place," Ann said when she turned into Emmett's driveway. "It would be perfect for them because the man and his sons are carpenters. But since my power of attorney died with Emmett, the court will have to handle the sale. Frank and Betty will probably get the money. Or Gordy. They're his only next of kin."

Emmett's old house looked like it had grown out of the surrounding tall grass and colorful splashes of wildflowers. And despite Ann's excited description of heavy-laden raspberry bushes she'd found by the barn, Elise only groaned at the sight.

"We lived here? Oh, Annie, it's awful!"

Ann parked alongside a dumpster standing between the house and barn where Elise caught sight of the outhouse. "Don't' tell me we had to use that!"

"Not us. Emmett said little kids used a pot inside the house. He said the Amish still do that."

"You mean a chamber pot?"

"I guess something like that."

Elise shook her head and followed Ann to the porch, half of which had collapsed under a heavy spring snow. Sky blue morning glories wound their way through the wreckage and trailed up toward the second story broken window.

"The porch is still intact over here by the door," Ann said brightly as she removed the padlock. "John and I pretty much emptied the house, but we still have the barn to clean out." She swung the kitchen door open. "And I'm going to vacuum in here before the real estate agent looks at it."

Elise tightened her stylish sweater around her, ducking at the sight of cobwebs trailing from the ceiling. "Look at his stove!" Elise squealed. "It must be a hundred years old!"

"Yeah, isn't it great? Just imagine Nana and our mother cooking on it."

Elise only peeked in the living room. "This place is freaky," was all she said before hurrying back toward the door.

"Wait!" Ann called. "You have to see the upstairs. Our old bedroom is up there."

"I've seen enough. I don't see how anyone could live in this place. You don't need a vacuum cleaner; you need a torch!"

Ann joined her sister outside. "Emmett lived a simple life. He was happy here."

"How can anyone be happy here? Normal people have plumbing, Annie." A chickadee called loudly. Elise looked up and squinted toward the sunny treetops, then frowned at the house again. "I'm glad we didn't grow up here. Can we go now?"

"Only after you see the inside of our great-grandmother's little cabin. She wasn't crazy either, by the way."

While Ann marched through the tall grass, pointing out blooms in the woodsy shadows and the iris she was going to dig up and take home, Elise sighed in protest. "I don't know what your fascination is with this place," she said, stepping warily, her arms outstretched as if she were on a tightrope.

Nana's lilacs had finished blooming and now a hydrangea was showing off white balls of flowers near the cabin door. Ann cautioned Elise about a loose hinge as she pushed the door open.

"It stinks in here," Elise said, stepping onto the spongy floorboards of the one-room cabin.

Ann crossed the room to a rough-hewn ladder leaning against a wall. The bottom rung gave way when she tried to step up.

"Geez! Watch it!" Elise cautioned.

"Her bedroom was up there in the loft, but I only got a peek at it a week ago."

"I believe you. Let's go."

On their way out, Elise chuckled at the old skeleton key Ann found on a windowsill. "Perfect. Now you've got a key for your skeleton closet." She broke a few branches off the hydrangea bush and breathed in the flowers. "Granny Elizabeth had a bush like this, remember? She called it a snowball bush."

"I remember." Ann added wild daisies to Elise's bouquet. "What's your earliest memory?"

"Ha! I know you tried to put a sucker stick in my ear."

"I did?"

"I don't really remember that. Mom told me." She paused, and then asked, "So what's your earliest memory? I mean your own memory, not something someone else told you."

Ann thought a moment. "I remember sitting on Mom's lap with a blanket around me. It was pink on one side and blue on the other side and it had white rabbits on it. I remember her rocking me."

"How old do you think you were?"

Ann shrugged. "I don't know. Small enough to still sit on her lap, I guess."

"Remember those walking dolls we got one Christmas? Mom made matching dresses for them so we wouldn't argue who had the best."

Ann was half-listening, distracted by the pink and blue blanket memory. If the blanket was the same one she'd found at Emmett's, she must have been sitting on her mother Anna's lap, not Ruth's.

"I remember something else," Elise said as they walked across Emmett's overgrown yard. "I hated being adopted." She caught Ann's surprised look. "Well, it's true. And I know I never asked you this, but did you ever get the feeling Mom treated us differently? Not Dad, but Mom. Did you ever notice?"

"Yes, but I thought it was just me."

"It wasn't just you," Elise said. "I remember Mom yelling at me for doing something, and then Karen or Neal would do the same thing and not get yelled at. One time she forced me to sit at the table until I had eaten all my green beans. I thought I was going to throw up. But Karen could leave broccoli on her plate, and Neal didn't have to eat spaghetti sauce. He could get away with just butter on his noodles." She paused. "I still hate green beans."

"I used to pretend I was like Cinderella or Snow White," Ann said. "They were always so good, but no matter what they did, their stepmothers didn't like them. Of course, back then, I didn't know Ruth was actually our stepmother."

Elise kicked at a dandelion. "I never liked the word stepmother—probably because of poor old Cinderella and Snow White. And I'm not saying Mom wasn't a good mother because she was. She shouldn't have treated us differently, that's all."

"We weren't her children," Ann said. "And that must have been hard. But she loved Dad, and we all know she would do anything for him. I guess that included taking in you and me."

Elise didn't look convinced. "That sounds a little too simple."

"Do you have a better explanation?"

Elise shook her head.

Ann picked the head off a daisy and pulled the petals off one by one. "I remember one time when I was about ten, and I went to a friend's house without telling Mom. She was real mad when I came home. I told her she was yelling at me just because I was adopted. Then I saw this look on her face and I knew I'd struck a chord." Ann shrugged and threw the flower away. "Maybe that's when Mom started sending me to Dad with my questions. I think I really hurt her feelings."

"Mom and Dad were the only parents I knew or wanted to know," Elise said sadly.

"Is that why you never asked about the adoption?"

"I never asked because I was happy with the way things were." A tear ran down her cheek. "I guess I'm glad you did what you did." She tried to smile in spite of her tears. "I didn't have any choice anyway because you did what you did, and now I have to live with it."

"Me too."

Elise wiped her eyes. "I still have a problem accepting the love affair thing even though I'm glad to have the truth for Kyle. And I am glad you waited until after Dad was gone too."

"Unfortunately, his passing made it easier. I can't imagine how he would have explained himself."

"Cancer was punishment enough. I would have hated to see him tortured further because of mistakes he made a long time ago." Elise flashed one of her cautionary smiles. "And I would've never spoken to you again either."

"I loved Dad, Elise. You know that. I never wanted to hurt him. I wanted to know the rest of the story, that's all. I just never dreamed it would end like this."

"And now that we all know why he couldn't tell us, maybe we can get on with our lives."

Ann agreed, but inside she wished their dad were here to answer her remaining why questions.

Their next stop was Howie's office. Right after Emmett died, Howie had called Ann to say he would read the will right after the funeral since she'd be in town. He also asked for Elise's last name, and both sisters expected to hear they'd been granted their mother's things, even though Ann had already taken them from Emmett's house.

Frank and Betty were waiting in chairs across from Howie's desk, looking as if they expected a windfall. Gordy had been notified but didn't come. Howie began by explaining how conditions of the will could be satisfied only after debts had been paid; such as the $4,000 Emmett owed in back taxes. When everyone stated agreement, he read aloud.

"I bequeath three thousand dollars to my cousin Betty Johnson and three thousand dollars to my cousin Gordon Halvorson."

Betty puffed up a bit and Ann gave her an approving smile. Frank grumbled, saying it wasn't enough for all Betty's work, complaining how Gordy would fritter the money away foolishly because he never did a lick of work in his life. Betty told him to hush.

Frank and Betty were still sore at Ann for not telling them how much money Emmett actually had in the bank. Ann hadn't shared the notebook John found when he cleaned out Emmett's camper either, the one showing thousands of dollars Emmett had sent to Anna's sister in Austria, money he had inherited from his Uncle Oscar. "My inheritance shall be better spent by Anna's loved ones, who suffered and lost so much," Emmett had written.

Ann tried to do the math in her head. After subtracting Emmett's back taxes, his final Manor House bill, outstanding medical bills not covered by Medicare, and the cost of selling the farm, Betty and Gordy, as Emmett's only heirs, might inherit even more. She refocused her attention as Howie began reading again.

"Further," Howie said, "I bequeath the rest of my money, my real property in its entirety, with all furnishings and appointments, personal effects and memorabilia, farm equipment, camper trailer, vehicles, tools, untilled acreage, and wooded acreage beyond the creek to Ann Olson and Elise Garrett, daughters of Anneliese Muller, my dearest and everlasting love."

The news came as a shock to everyone except Howie. Elise didn't move. Ann swallowed hard.

"That's crazy!" Frank told Howie. "Are you sure?"

"Emmett dictated his will to my dad back in 1953," Howie told him. "A few months ago, he asked to see it, and the only updates he requested were to add Ann's and Elise's last names."

Ann thought back to when Howie said Emmett wanted to put their full names in his will in order to account for distribution of their mother's belongings. It had all sounded reasonable at the time.

"The social worker, Julie Lawson, witnessed the changes," Howie continued. "And we will both vouch for Emmett appearing fully cognizant at the time. I do not doubt the integrity of his intentions."

Elise stared at the floor. Betty reminded Frank that their kids weren't farmers and that Emmett's place was run-down beyond repair. Ann covered her mouth with her hand and held back the tears she felt coming. Crazy Emmett had found a way to leave everything to Anna by way of her children. "In every way except for the will of God," Emmett had written, "these two children will be mine in my heart forever. I release them to Karl reluctantly." It was another precious notebook page Ann planned to show Elise when they got back home.

"He sold off those hardwoods on the other side of the creek years ago," Frank reminded Howie gruffly. "He told me he needed the money."

"I can assure you the deed to his property still includes the wooded acreage across the creek," Howie replied. "He never sold any of it."

Frank looked Howie in the eye. "Those hardwoods are worth a lot."

"I have no idea," Howie said calmly shaking his head.

After Howie finished the proceedings, Frank left the office without a word of goodbye.

"He'll be all right," Betty told Ann. "He's grumpy because Gordy was included. But I must say, we can use the money." She looked over her glasses at Ann. "I'm sure you know it'll cost a fortune to fix the old place up enough to sell. Frank said a septic system alone would cost upwards of five thousand dollars, not counting the indoor plumbing. I can't imagine what a furnace or insulation will cost, let alone a proper kitchen and bathroom. But," she concluded, rolling her eyes and adjusting her glasses, "it was Emmett's decision to leave it to you and your sister, and so it will be."

Ann tried to ignore the hint of callousness in Betty's voice. It didn't matter. She didn't know Frank and Betty before she came up north, and soon she'd say goodbye to them until it was time for a Christmas card. By that time, perhaps the Amish family John knew would be all moved into Emmett's house.

That night, while Elise slept in the guest room, Ann and John curled up together in the loft bedroom. He bunched up his pillow and pulled her closer to him.

"I wanted to wait until after the funeral to tell you that they accepted my offer on the dealership down in Cedarburg today," he said. "And I found a buyer for this place and maybe one for your house."

"Oh, John, that's wonderful! Does that mean we can get the house we looked at in Cedarburg too? The one with the neat old barn and the pond?"

"Yep."

"I love that house! I know it'll be a longer drive for me to get to work, but it's closer to the kids, and it's perfect for us!"

"I already talked to Brad about managin' the store up here." John said as he nuzzled her neck. "But I'll drive up to check on things now and then."

"As long as you don't work yourself to death with two dealerships. I want to have many, many years with you."

"That's the plan."

She played with a curl behind his ear. "What do you think

about having our wedding ceremony and reception in our new home?"

He kissed her. "As usual, my darlin' soon-to-be Mrs. Bennett, I was thinkin' the same thing."

Acknowledgments and Thanks

I am very grateful to a number of people who helped me as I worked this story out of my head and onto paper.

First, I offer my most genuine thanks to the elderly WW2 veteran who inspired my "Emmett" in these pages. I feel lucky that we share family roots and for his diaries that I acquired after his death. To this farmer-philosopher who never married, who cherished the old ways and his privacy, and had a sweetheart in WW2 Austria, I echo his kind "Thanks a million" with my own.

Sincere appreciation also goes to Jeri Smith, whose friendship, eye for detail, and humor helped me focus, cut, embellish, and go on. Many thanks to readers Sheila Manhoff, Chris Braden, and Bonnie Blachly, and to other friends and colleagues who encouraged my efforts with generous advice and positive thinking. I thank the writers and authors around the tables at Red Oak Writing in Milwaukee for their patient reading, helpful marginal notes, and supportive comments. I am also grateful for the attentive work and skill of editor Dulcie Shoener. If I corrupted her fine work in last minute changes, I apologize to Dulcie and my readers. More thanks go to Shannon Ishizaki and the good folks at Orange Hat Publishing, whose expertise and fine finishing touches enabled the production of the book in your hand.

To my daughter for her earnest and unwavering, "You can do this, Mom," and to my son who helped me capture the cover photo and consistently cheered me on: I thank the universe for you every day I love you more than I can say. And finally, enduring love and gratitude to my sister Jeanine, who not only read many drafts and listened to my dreams but whose heart understands the story behind this story better than anyone.

Most of what Laurel Bragstad writes these days is for classes she teaches at Alverno College in Milwaukee, Wisconsin, and for her interpersonal communication course, which was published and distributed online by Cengage Learning. She has had a few academic articles and short, fun pieces published. Then once upon a time, in the midst of job, family, and a generally busy life, the story seed in her head began to grow into a cozy (family secrets) mystery.

A graduate of Alverno College and Marquette University, Laurel's roots are in Wisconsin, where she teaches, writes, reads, gardens, sews, and loves being with her family. *In the Comfort of Shadows* is her debut novel. Her second novel is in progress.

CPSIA information can be obtained at www.ICGtesting.com
Printed in the USA
LVOW08s0808140414

381549LV00002B/19/P